The Star That Always Stays

BY ANNA ROSE JOHNSON

HOLIDAY HOUSE • NEW YORK

The heavens declare the glory of God;
and the firmament sheweth His handiwork.

PSALM 19

Lone island of the saltless sea!
How wide, how sweet, how fresh and free
How all transporting—is the view
Of rocks and skies and waters blue
Uniting, as a song's sweet strains
To tell, here nature only reigns.

**JANE JOHNSTON SCHOOLCRAFT,
ALSO CALLED BAMEWAWAGEZHIKAQUAY**

Copyright © 2022 by Anna Rose Johnson

All Rights Reserved

HOLIDAY HOUSE is registered in the U.S. Patent and Trademark Office.

Printed and bound in April 2022 at Maple Press, York, PA, USA.

www.holidayhouse.com

First Edition

1 3 5 7 9 10 8 6 4 2

Library of Congress Cataloging-in-Publication Data

Names: Johnson, Anna Rose, author.

Title: The star that always stays / by Anna Rose Johnson.

Description: First edition. | New York : Holiday House, [2022] | Audience: Ages 8-12.
Audience: Grades 4-6. | Summary: When fourteen-year-old Norvia moves from Beaver
Island to Boyne City in 1914, she has to contend with a new school, a first crush, and
a blended family, but she also must keep secret her parents' divorce and her Ojibwe
heritage. Includes author's note.

Identifiers: LCCN 2021053824 | ISBN 9780823450404 (hardcover)

Subjects: CYAC: Stepfamilies—Fiction. | Family life—Michigan—Fiction. | Books
and reading—Fiction. | Ojibwa Indians—Fiction. | Indians of North America—
Fiction. | Christian life—Fiction. | Michigan—History—20th century—Fiction.
LCGFT: Novels.

Classification: LCC PZ7.1.J5915 St 2022 | DDC [Fic]—dc23

LC record available at https://lccn.loc.gov/2021053824

THIS BOOK IS DEDICATED TO MOM AND DAD AND GRANNY,
AND IN LOVING MEMORY OF NONEE AND PA

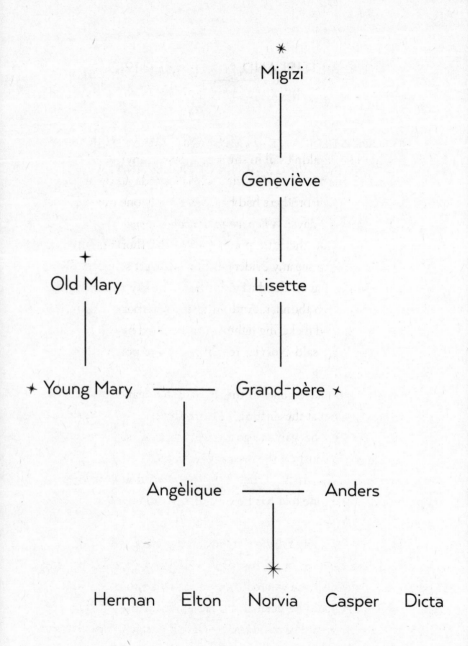

BEAVER ISLAND, *NOVEMBER 1910*
MKADEWZI | BLACK

"Pa promised he wouldn't sail in shipwreck season anymore."

The wind swallowed up Norvia Nelson's words, and she wasn't even sure if her older brothers had heard her. Only one question had circled the house for days: *When would Pa come home?*

Norvia ran from the little porch toward the shoreline of Lake Michigan, hoping to see any evidence of the stalwart schooner *Rouse Simmons* manifesting on the dusky horizon. The sky rumbled overhead, glowering with thunder. And the island's harbor—a collection of wooden docks and flickering lights—was battered by waves below.

"Nothing yet," said Norvia, returning to the porch where her brothers were waiting.

"He shouldn't have gone on this trip." Elton leaned against the doorway, gazing out at the shifting, gloomy waters.

"I say, the more he wants to go away, the better," said Herman—but he glanced nervously at the tossing waves, too.

Elton folded his arms. "I just don't understand why he'd break a promise like that. He *told* Ma he wouldn't go out on a late run ever again."

"He promised a lot of things," Herman shot back.

"And he's kept most of his promises," said Norvia, turning away from them. All she wanted was for her father to come home— then everything could be normal. He would stride in—smiling, she hoped—and Ma would be so relieved to have him safely back that she wouldn't be angry anymore. Perhaps Pa would even bring them gifts from the mainland—a necklace for her, something special for Ma—and they'd all laugh and sit around the hearth watching the flames of the fire unravel and snap and sparkle. . . .

"Let's go in," said Herman.

He was right. The wind was cold and the waterline empty. Norvia lingered just a few minutes more, then followed the boys inside.

Casper—the youngest of her three brothers—stood by the front window, pressing his face against the rain-spattered glass. "Suppose they've been wrecked off one of the Fox Islands. Suppose they have to send a search crew after 'em?"

"Don't say that!" said Norvia.

"Aww, Norv," said Casper. "It'd be exciting."

She looked through the pane too, straining her eyes, willing Pa to sail home to them.

"The waters around Beaver Island are kind to their sons," said Grand-père, who had come to look out the window with them. "He'll come home all right."

Grand-père is right, Norvia told herself, but uncertainty coiled around her heart. The house was quiet without her father.

Ma was in the kitchen, and the Marys—the children's beloved grandmother and great-grandmother—were helping her. Like Grand-père, the Marys had always lived in the cozy white cottage with them, and they were revered in the family. They were both French Indian ladies—dark-skinned, blue-eyed, and motherly. Pa was the first one to call them "the Marys," and while the Marys pretended they didn't like being addressed that way, the children could tell they did.

Waves crashing in the gathering storm disturbed the silence of the house. Dicta, Norvia's younger sister, let out a little cry—she hated storms, even when Grand-père tried to tell her it was "the sound of the thunderbird."

Perhaps if we start talking, she'll be distracted from the noise,

Norvia thought. She sat down by the hearth beside Grand-père, who had claimed his favorite rocking chair.

"Tell me about your great-grandmother," said Norvia, warming her hands before the fire. "The one who looked like me." She had heard these tales before, but each time they painted lush, elaborate scenes of bygone days in her mind. And now, they would keep Dicta's mind—and her own—off the storm.

Grand-père smiled at the faces of his daughter's listening children. The boys had joined them around the fire, and Dicta weaseled her way into Grand-père's lap (she was the only one small enough to still accomplish this feat). "My great-grandmother," he began, a remembering look on his face, "was born by the Red River over a hundred years ago—somewhere in Minnesota or Canada, I believe."

His eyes shone from the glow of the firelight. He gestured with his hands—the hands that had once been blackened with frostbite. That was another story he had told them.... He and his brother fell through broken ice into Lake Michigan one winter while transporting the mail to Beaver Island. Both Grand-père and Uncle Olivier had lived to tell the tale—even though everyone had given them up for lost.

Will they give the Rouse Simmons *up for lost?* Norvia wondered, the thought chilling her all over again.

But Grand-père's voice penetrated her thoughts, soothing her immediately. "Her name was Migizi, which means 'bald eagle' in Anishinaabemowin. Aren't those birds magnificent?"

Norvia nodded eagerly. "They're so big and beautiful—"

"The ship's back! I've spotted it!" Casper yelled, his face bright with excitement. "The *Rouse Simmons* is gonna dock and we can see Pa!"

Although she wanted to keep listening to Grand-père, Norvia scrambled up from the floor. As she ran to put on her hat and coat and dart out the door, she thought of how her grandparents had always provided such comfort for them—teaching them the ways of the past and the tales of their forefathers; dishing up food whenever Pa's gambling habits had left them penniless; giving them a sense of stability whenever seas grew rough.

But she could not wait to rush into her father's arms. Reunions with him were always sweet, and she'd had this one planned ever since he sailed off to deliver tanbark to Milwaukee: she would tell him all the little tidbits of news from his absence (like the McCauleys' new baby and the Republican rally); she would pass along an amusing joke that would make him laugh; and, most important, she would somehow make sure that he and Ma were happy together.

Norvia and her siblings waited at the bottom of the path leading to the house, watching the harbor and the docking ship for what felt like hours. Despite her patched sails and peeling paint, the aged *Rouse Simmons* was still a beauty of a vessel.

At last Pa came walking up the hill, tired but triumphant. Norvia ran to him and hugged him, delighting in all his familiarity, in that same old scent of tobacco. He kissed the top of her head and murmured, "*Min dotter,* have I not missed you?"

Then he swung Dicta onto his shoulders, tousled Casper's hair, and clapped Herman's and Elton's backs. "You all look well and good," he said.

"Papa, I learned to write my *full name!*" Dicta squealed.

"My smart little girl."

"Pa, what took you so long?" asked Casper breathlessly.

"Storms slowed us down," said Pa, dismissing the subject. "Too many winds from the Manitou Islands ... Where is your mother?"

"Inside," said Herman flatly. His tone added: *Not out here waiting, that's for sure.*

They walked back to the house with a strange, slow expectancy. Norvia suddenly felt wobbly, as if she had been the one aboard a ship instead of her father.

Grand-père opened the door for them. "Well? And how did it go?" he asked, smiling at the sight of his son-in-law.

"It went as well as one might expect," replied Pa.

Ma joined them in the entryway, dark eyes flashing with both relief and anguish. And Norvia understood that Pa's return would not be enough to overcome the torment he had put his wife through once again.

"Come say hello to Pa," said Norvia, reaching out to take her mother's hand. "The ship made it through the storms!"

"I'm glad," said Ma tersely, wiping away a tear. "Anders, I need to speak with you."

Norvia made one last, desperate effort. She hated to do it—she hated making herself the center of attention—but it was necessary. She sprang toward the fireplace and pulled up two empty chairs alongside Grand-père's rocker. "Come sit down, Pa! There's so much I want to tell you. You can listen too, Ma!"

Pa glanced at her—sighed a little—and then gave Norvia a pat as he followed Ma into the kitchen.

Norvia stood still, listening. It seemed no one dared to breathe.

Then the conversation began—and Norvia could hear the tension in their voices, as if they were already nearing an explosion.

"We discussed this, Angie. I had to sail with them," Pa was insisting. "It paid good money that I couldn't afford to pass up!"

"You saw what terrible weather was brewing!" said Ma. "You could have waited in Milwaukee!"

"Then I wouldn't have been paid at all," Pa shot back.

Norvia turned back to look at Grand-père. He had returned to his rocking chair, and now Young Mary and Old Mary joined him by the fire. She wanted their voices to drown out the argument in the kitchen.

"Grand-père, keep telling us about Migizi, please," she said anxiously.

Young Mary smiled at Grand-père. "Didn't you say her hair was supposed to be the thickest and most beautiful in the family?"

"That was the story my mother told me," Grand-père agreed. "I would say her hair was probably a good deal like Norvia's."

Norvia felt herself smile—this was her favorite piece of the family lore, and the reason why she often wore her hair long and loose.

Ma's broken sobs interrupted: "It's as if you don't care about us!"

Grand-père's voice resumed, even more rhythmic and comforting than before. "Sometimes Migizi was called Isabelle...which was her French name."

Norvia sat beside him and hugged her knees; the other children joined them.

"She knew all the stars by heart. She could name them all; knew all the great collections of stars. Migizi would look up into the night sky and point out all the animals that comprised the constellations— the fisher and the panther and the loon. Do you remember which one is the maang...the loon?"

Norvia did remember. She thought of the many times she had gone for walks after dark with Grand-père and her brothers, when the world felt immense and distant and the heavens raised a lofty roof of sparkles. "Yes," said Norvia, envisioning the loon's shape in the night sky. "I remember."

"Migizi's mother was a highly respected woman in the Reindeer Clan," said Grand-père. "As the story goes, one of Migizi's grandparents was a Dakota. In those days the Ojibwe and Dakota tribes did not always get along...."

Yes, this was much more relaxing.... This felt normal, even if she felt guilty for enjoying these tales that her father often scorned. A warm strength always grew inside her as she listened to the tales of her dark-haired ancestress.

"There are those who did not think much of Migizi because of the Dakota in her blood," Grand-père admitted, reaching out to stroke their cat, who lay asleep on the wood floor. "Other people, children especially, can be so cruel. But she would only smile when she heard their taunts, because she knew they would come to respect her, as long as she held her head up high."

"And she was your mother's grandmother," offered Norvia, who loved hearing about the exact lineage.

"Yes. My mother was Elizabeth—Lisette, of course, but in Anishinaabemowin, her real name meant *She gathers stories*," Grand-père recounted. "*Her* mother was Geneviève, and Migizi was Geneviève's mother."

Pa's voice cracked through the house, so loud that the kitchen couldn't possibly contain it. "Do you want me to just give up? Give up trying to get us a better life?"

"You aren't trying to do that!" Ma screamed. "You're just trying to get back to the way you used to live!"

But now it was almost as if none of them could even hear the wild conversation bursting from the next room. There was only the story. "Migizi's brother—or half brother—was one of the best interpreters in the country," continued Grand-père. "He knew Anishinaabemowin—which is the Ojibwe language—along with English and French and Cree and many other languages."

Ma's voice sounded even shriller this time. "There's *nothing* you can do to change it!"

"If Migizi wasn't part French like her daughters, then why was she called Isabelle sometimes and Migizi at other times?" Norvia asked, in another effort to prolong this conversation.

Her grandfather paused a moment, considering. "Migizi was her true Ojibwe name. When she was a little girl, her mother remarried, and Migizi had a new French voyageur for a stepfather. Somewhere along the way she received a French name and was given her stepfather's surname."

"You mean he made her *change her name*?" Norvia was shocked.

Grand-père chuckled. "Something like that, I suppose. Perhaps she was glad of the change. Who can say?"

But Norvia knew she would not have liked having her name changed by a perfect stranger. "He didn't want her to be an Indian?" she asked, suspecting the truth.

"I don't know, *chère*. I think it was simply the way it was done in those days."

"The old days," echoed Young Mary. Once again she smiled at Grand-père—a smile that made Norvia feel safe.

Pa spoke again—louder than ever.

"I know you're right! *You don't have to say it again!* There's nothing I can do about it. I know I'll never be able to do anything to change my life!" The kitchen door slammed open and Pa emerged, his face an alarming mixture of defeat and anger. He stared at Grand-père and Norvia.

"You're not filling my child's head with your old nonsense again, are you?" Pa demanded.

"Just the stories of their family, of their heritage," said Grand-père simply. "I don't think it's nonsense."

"Is it not bad enough that they have Indian blood—now they must learn all about it?" Pa's voice shook—and then he stormed out the front door.

Norvia trembled. Her mind kept replaying Pa's words, over and over again. *There's nothing I can do about it.... Do you want me to just give up?... Is it not bad enough that they have Indian blood?*

"I don't want you to get into trouble, *chère*," murmured Grand-père. "I will stop my rambling."

Over the next few years, Norvia would come to remember her grandfather's words, to hear them at scattered intervals during the tempests of her parents' lives. She would remember his tales of quarreling tribes and of the stepfather who changed Migizi's name. But mostly she remembered her father's face and the way it made her feel.

FOUR YEARS LATER

BOYNE CITY, MICHIGAN, 1914

CHAPTER ONE
BROKEN REVERIE

I'm standing before the castle-like structure of Boyne City High School, staring at its gleaming windows, my heart filling with the anticipation of beginning the journey into higher education. I'm wearing a lovely sailor-suit dress—brand-new—and my best chum, Helen Haney, is standing alongside me, laughing at something witty that my beau, a very Dashing Young Man, has just said—

"How can you marry him when you've only known him a month?" Elton's voice shattered the blissful silence—and Norvia's scribbled daydream. Her fountain pen fell to the floor with a startling clatter. "You just met him!"

A shaky feeling enveloped Norvia as she hurried down the staircase of this meager, unsatisfying house, which was so unlike their old comforting home on Beaver Island. When she reached Elton and Ma—they were on the back laundry porch—she halted in the doorway, rooted to the spot as her brother and mother stared at each other. Dicta and Casper sidled toward the porch, too, expressions of curiosity and concern on their faces.

"It's been more than a month," Ma said calmly. "I know exactly what I am doing, and I would appreciate it if you stayed out of this."

"Stayed out of this!" Elton repeated, his eyes widening. "I can't stay out of this! You're my mother!"

Norvia was caught between a thunderous applause in her heart for Elton's words and a sinking sympathy for her mother. But most of all, she felt that same rising despair, tempered with a pinch of anger. It was happening again—of course. Her world, spinning out of control.

The happy world of her daydreams would never come to fruition if other people kept dictating her life.

She looked out, beyond the back porch; beyond their out-of-the-way road lined with gently waving trees, where the occasional buggy rattled by. "I think...," Norvia began, trying to voice her true thoughts. *I think it's a terrible idea.* The words begged to come out, but then what was the use? Nothing she had said or done had kept Ma and Pa together.

"Do you even know what Mr. Ward does for a living?" asked Elton.

"He goes courting," said Dicta, playing with the oversize sash on her dress.

"He's a blacksmith," said Ma. Her eyes, which had been threatening to water moments ago, now looked dark and cold. "He's in excellent financial condition, but that's not the point. The point is that we're getting married because we have found mutual compatibility and... and real love."

Norvia felt as if wheels were churning in her head. *So what was the love you shared with Pa?* she demanded inside. False love? Pretend love? Insignificant love?

"His financial condition is beside the point?" Elton's voice sliced through the humid stillness of the summer air. "It's a perfectly legitimate concern to have about a complete stranger. Ma, he could be any kind of man. We don't know him. *You don't know him.*"

"He might be a convict," Dicta chirped as she bent down to scoop up Peggy, their black-and-white cat, into her arms. "Or a schoolteacher."

"Or another gambler," muttered Casper. He eyed Norvia reproachfully, trying to force her to agree with them.

Norvia took a deep breath and offered faintly, "Maybe...if you just waited a little longer...before you get officially engaged..." She avoided Ma's gaze.

"We're planning to be married on August twenty-fourth," said Ma, her face set.

Two weeks away.

Now the wheels had detached from Norvia's brain and were just rotating idly.

Two weeks. Two.

She leaned her hot cheek against a porch window, reveling in the feel of the cool glass. In the window's reflection, she could see a look of happy determination on her mother's face. Why, though? Why was marrying this Mr. Ward so important? Norvia hadn't even met this future stepfather, and dread tightened her stomach when she envisioned being introduced not only to him, but to his family as well. Her *stepfamily.*

Casper looked at his mother with a glint of hurt in his eyes. "Does this mean we'll have to move away again? I don't want to leave. And we don't need a new father, 'cause we've got one already."

"This isn't about getting a new father for you children," said Ma. "It's about—"

"Getting a new husband for you," finished Elton.

A stalemate. Everyone looked at one another, but mostly they looked at Ma. The moment stretched, and Ma's eyes dampened again.

"I'm sorry," Elton finally said.

Norvia was surprised by the ring of sincerity in his voice. Why wasn't he still angry? For her part, she still felt the same heated fear as before.

"Ma," Elton continued, "I'm sorry I was so harsh. But please— *please*—think this over before you plunge ahead."

"I'm not plunging ahead," said Ma, now serene. "I've given this a great deal of thought. So has Virg—Mr. Ward."

She had started to say *Virgil.* She had actually called this mere acquaintance by his first name. And she was planning to *marry* him!

"He's a wonderful person," Ma continued, her voice softening.

"He's kind, thoughtful, and considerate." A strange new glimmer in Ma's expression caught Norvia off guard. "He's a good, Christian man who values education and women's rights."

"You're positive?" Elton asked, very serious. "Please, Ma. If he becomes your husband, he'll control everything. Our money, our property . . . Are you *certain* we can trust him?"

"Yes. I don't have any doubts about his character." Ma paused before resuming her speech. "Mr. Ward and his family are coming for supper tomorrow night. His son, Vernon; his daughter, Marguerite; and Marguerite's husband, Jim. Mr. Ward is a widower." She now wore a smile that simply wouldn't be frowned away. "We will be moving to Mr. Ward's house after the wedding."

But Norvia couldn't summon a smile in return. The thought of a supper with the Wards did not cheer her in the least.

Instead, her mind kept returning to Pa, to the horrible moment, months earlier, when she had refused to say goodbye to him the day he left for Flint. She vividly recalled standing on the staircase, digging her fingernails into the newel post instead of looking at his face. The image of Pa turning toward her, his hand on the doorknob, lingering, hoping she would speak, was now burned into her mind's eye. . . . Still, she had done nothing. She would have, if only she thought that saying goodbye would *do* anything. But it wouldn't—nothing she could do would ever mend her splintered feelings—or reverse this dreadful change.

At the last second, she had decided to speak anyway. But, of course, by the time she did, she was too late. Pa was already closing the door. He left without a word from her. And she regretted that every day.

Ma, however, was thoroughly content with her own choices. "I would also appreciate it," she added thoughtfully, "if you four did not mention our—our *background*—in front of the Wards."

A leaden stillness descended.

"Our background?" Elton repeated, as if daring her to clarify.

Ma was up to the challenge. "Our Indian blood," she said. "I don't feel it needs to be discussed with our new family."

Norvia was reminded, suddenly, of what had happened to Migizi, and the realization did not comfort her.

Elton let out a low, humorless laugh. "They can't tell just by looking at us? I know the younger kids don't particularly come across that way, but you and I sure do—and the Marys, too."

Ma pursed her lips. "I don't wish to discuss it any further," she said. "Can you refrain from mentioning it?"

They dutifully mumbled yeses—all except for Dicta. "But I want to tell my future stepfather *all about* how our people sailed in birch bark canoes by the shores of Gitchee Gumee—"

Ma did not listen to the end of Dicta's sentence. Having informed her children of the impending marriage, she said with an excited flush blooming on her cheeks, "I'll need a new traveling dress for our wedding journey"—then went to her sewing room to sift through patterns, bolts of colorful fabric, and spools of thread.

Norvia was left standing on the porch, feeling more lost and alone than ever. Ma was so different now. She had *heard* the name Ward, of course: Ma had done some dressmaking for his grown and married daughter. And before this announcement, Norvia had to admit to herself, Ma had spent much of her time wandering through the house whispering to herself, sometimes crying, and always seeking new advice from her mother and grandmother.

Norvia followed Ma to the sewing room, not sure what else to do. Old Mary and Young Mary had bustled in after her, chattering away in rapid French. Young Mary tended to speak French only when she was agitated, while Old Mary spoke nothing else.

"But, Angélique—this man has children, doesn't he?" asked Young Mary, a tinge of worry in her voice. "A young boy?"

"Yes," said Ma, smoothing a bolt of cream-colored silk fabric. "A son named Vernon. You will be great friends with him, Norvia," she added, turning to her oldest daughter with a smile.

"Have you met Vernon?" asked Norvia, pulling at a loose thread on her sleeve.

Ma shook her head. "Not yet," she admitted.

Norvia wished his name wasn't Vernon. She had grown up hearing about the *Vernon*, a ship that had sunk years ago carrying passengers from Beaver Island—just like the *Rouse Simmons* had met with an untimely demise two years after Pa had stopped sailing the Great Lakes. It felt like bad luck.

"That boy will be trouble. I predict it," said Old Mary, echoing Norvia's feelings.

Everything will be trouble, not just Vernon, thought Norvia with rising anxiety. Living with Mr. Ward, moving to yet another new place, facing an entire new existence filled with uncertainty—away from the Marys this time, away from Pa...

Tears gathered in Norvia's eyes, and a sob settled in her throat. The fabric, the Marys, and her mother blurred, and Norvia hurried out of the sewing room. She bumped into Casper as she rushed blindly to the staircase.

"Why didn't you back us up?" he demanded hotly. "You could have said, 'Don't marry that guy.' But you just stood there and hardly said a word!"

"It doesn't matter what I say," gasped Norvia, swallowing hard. "And—and it doesn't matter if they get married or not."

"What do you mean, 'it doesn't matter'?" said Casper. "At least we're better off here than living with some stranger and his strange kids!"

Struck by the truth of his words, Norvia realized that he was correct. Change brought nothing but hardship. When Ma and Pa had moved them to Boyne City from Beaver Island three years ago, they had traded fir forests and sparkling waters for this small, rickety house on a hidden street. And after Pa had left them for Flint, they'd suffered more financial trouble than ever before. Who knew what would happen after Ma married Mr. Ward?

"Well, things *are* easier if they stay mostly the same," she admitted, chokingly. "But there's nothing we can do about it."

The reality of this irrefutable fact dawned on her more heavily than ever. First Pa made the choices; now Mr. Ward would. How could she be happy when nothing she did mattered? The shape of their lives was out of their hands.

Seeing the tears pooling in his sister's eyes, Casper reached into his pocket. "Say," he said, his voice taking on a forcefully light tone. "I found a fifty-cent piece on the sidewalk yesterday." He spread his palm so she could see the tantalizing coin. "Why don't we go to the motion picture show? It'll…take our minds off it. You know."

Norvia didn't hesitate. "Yes, let's," she said with relief. The mid-August sun would be hot as they walked to town, but anything was better than staying here.

"I want to come, too," said Dicta. Neither Norvia nor Casper objected, even though the limp in Dicta's left leg would slow them down as they walked. Everyone only wanted to leave.

CHAPTER TWO
A PIECE OF HOPE

A seventy-foot clock tower stood like a sentinel over Boyne City, calling out the time with regular bongs, and beyond it the high school—the school of Norvia's dreams—rose like a massive castle. She couldn't help admiring it, even as she, Casper, and Dicta hurried to the theater. Chaotic voices and the snorts of horses intermixed with the cool air wafting from Pine Lake. Casper let out a cry of excitement when he saw a dark-green automobile pass a few yards in front of them.

"You see that?" he crowed. "That was a Willys-Overland. They've got such powerful motors—and all these electric features! Wish we had one."

Norvia loved the sleek look of automobiles—especially this green one. "I wish we had one, too," she agreed.

Once Park Street merged into Water Street, the world consisted solely of brick and frame buildings, cheerful striped awnings, and masses of busy passersby, mostly women in summery white dresses. The occasional call of a seagull squealed overhead, and Norvia smiled at this sweet reminder of Beaver Island. She pictured the island in her mind's eye—dotted with forests as green as the Willys-Overland—and felt a pang of homesickness.

"Hurry up, or we'll miss the start of the show!" Casper urged.

Finally they reached the cinema, paid for their tickets, and rushed to find seats. Low murmurs threaded through the crowd of moviegoers as pictures began to flash on the screen, and the pianist in the corner tapped out a plinking melody. They saw a western called *The Great Divide*, then sat glued to their seats during the war newsreel.

(Dicta kept complaining about her arms sticking to the seats, but nobody paid attention to that.) The newsreel was fascinating—an archduke in Europe had been killed at the end of June, and a war had broken out between Germany and France, with the British Empire backing France.

"Maybe America will get in on the fighting, too," Casper whispered, leaning forward.

"America doesn't go to war anymore," Norvia whispered back.

"We did the year Elton was born."

"That only lasted a few months, and besides, *this* is going on across the Atlantic. It has nothing to do with us," said Norvia with finality, hoping that she was right. "A big war would never happen nowadays."

"Canada's sending soldiers."

Again Norvia had a swift answer. "Only because Canada's tied to England. We're not under the rule of the Crown. That was the whole reason for the Revolutionary War, you know."

"I thought that was 'cause some tea got dumped out of a ship or something." Casper laughed. People behind them began to shush them, so they quieted down for a time.

Casper could not stay silent for long, however. "Say, isn't that Kittie?" he hissed.

Norvia followed his pointed finger to a redheaded girl a few seats away. From the back of the head, this young lady *did* resemble Katherine "Kittie" Sloane, age fourteen. Kittie used to attend their grammar school before the Sloane family moved to Petoskey. Norvia remembered her as the sort of girl who always stood on the outskirts of games—and always contributed to conversations she wasn't involved in. Kittie was, in short, the opposite sort of girl to Norvia's best friend, Helen Haney, who was generally well-liked wherever she went.

"Where? I don't see any kitty!" said Dicta, and before Norvia could shush her, Kittie was craning her neck to catch a glimpse of the

Nelsons behind her. She flashed a silly smile, and Norvia knew they were doomed to speak with her after the movies were over.

Kittie caught up with them as soon as they left the theater.

"It's so good to see you," she gushed. "I'm so glad we've come back to live in Boyne City. We haven't seen each other in a couple of years!"

"It *has* been a long time," agreed Norvia, even though eleven months was hardly a couple of years.

"Oh, heavens, yes." Kittie grinned at Casper and Dicta. "My, you've grown a lot, haven't you?"

"Not me," said Dicta. "I'm short."

Kittie gave Norvia a big, squeezing hug. "I heard about your mother and father. I'm so sorry!"

Casper made a face. "Our ma's getting married again. Some man named Virgil Ward."

Kittie covered her mouth with her hand. "Really? I know him! Some say he went *mad* after his wife died, but I don't believe that. I think he's lonely. I always feel sorry for lonely people, don't you?" A random giggle escaped her mouth, but she managed to control herself. "He has two daughters, but they're both married now. The older one—Julia—lives someplace far away. Detroit maybe. I can't quite remember."

"Do they have cats with fleas in Detroit?" asked Dicta, apropos of nothing.

"I don't know," said Kittie, considering a moment before continuing. "Well, anyway, the younger daughter, Marguerite, married Jim Rockford. He's a third or fourth cousin of mine, but we've never been on good terms with the Rockfords—something to do with a land-grab scheme in the nineties. Oh, and Mr. Ward has a son, too! People say the boy has a kind of *disease*, but nobody knows for sure. My mother thinks he's consumptive, but you'd think he'd be in some sort of sanitarium then, wouldn't you?"

"I don't know," said Norvia, feeling rather numb.

"Anyway, that's about all I know, other than Marguerite Rockford's got the most stylish clothes of anybody, except for maybe the Beardsley girls. I think it's because of her brother's health that they don't come to church every Sunday—we go to the same Presbyterian church, you know."

In Norvia's mind, *stylish* equated to *snobbish*, and sickness spelled disaster. She mulled over Kittie's words, wondering if they were rumors, exaggerations, or—worst of all—the truth.

That night Norvia immersed herself, as she often did when anxious, in memories of her childhood on Beaver Island: surrounded by all her family; playing on lush banks dotted with wildflowers; watching the ships sail by.

The Nelsons had lived on Beaver Island until Norvia was eleven years old—not long after Pa had sailed on the *Rouse Simmons* in disastrous weather. It was that same year that Grand-père had passed away and they'd moved to the mainland.

Norvia couldn't help thinking that if they'd only stayed on Beaver Island, everything might have been all right.

Boyne City was wonderfully picturesque, but Norvia still preferred her old home. They had all been together there. In her island daydreams, she envisioned Herman standing beside her, grinning in that special older-brother way—the grin that made all her worries blow away like dandelion seeds in the wind. They had always been good friends, the two of them.

But Herman had left—just like that. Before the divorce, even. He had grown weary of home life, of Ma and Pa's arguing, and he'd gone to the Upper Peninsula to seek work.

Hugging a pillow to herself, Norvia turned toward the darkened window, where she could see the first evening stars flickering in the deep-blue sky. She had noticed something about stars. Whenever she looked at them directly from her bedroom window, they disappeared.

Just vanished. She could see them—distantly glittering—out of the corner of her eye, but if she adjusted her focus and stared right at those selfsame stars, it was as if they never existed. She often lay in bed now, wide-awake, trying to catch a firm glimpse of the stars above. But they flitted away, like lightning bugs too quick for childish hands.

So many things had a way of escaping her grasp.

"Norvie, are you awake?"

"Shh, Dicta. Go back to sleep."

"I had a dream," Dicta said, ignoring Norvia. "I dreamed that my eyeballs fell out of their sockets. Do you think that could ever happen in real life?"

"No," scoffed Norvia.

Dicta raised herself up on one elbow. Somehow, even in the dark, her little sister's eyes could sparkle, and a faint wisp of moonlight illuminated her brownish-blonde hair and pixie face. "Do you think I could ever be a famous actress like Mary Pickford? That was my other dream."

Norvia gave her a half smile. "I don't think so. Go to sleep now."

"*Elton* never went to bed," Dicta protested in a soft whisper. "I didn't hear him come up. He's still downstairs!"

The little cuckoo clock in the hallway chirped that it was eleven o'clock. A pinprick of concern prompted Norvia to slide out of bed and look for her sleepless brother.

A few minutes later, she cracked open the lazy screen door to the back porch. Elton sat on the steps staring out into the dusky summer night, a lantern lighting up a small space around him. Norvia sat on the step beside him, wondering if there was anything she could say that would help.

"It'll be all right, eventually," she said, although she didn't believe it.

"I hope so, Nan," said Elton, using the pet name he'd created long ago from her initials—Norvia Ann Nelson. "But that doesn't help right now, does it?"

She reviewed what Ma had said about Mr. Ward, trying to think of a possible piece of positivity to brighten Elton's mood. *Mr. Ward is a Christian. He values education.*

"Maybe—" Norvia caught her breath, and a beautiful thought unfolded itself before her in the dim light. "Maybe Mr. Ward will let me go to high school this fall. Wouldn't that be grand?" *Oh, what if she really could attend Boyne City High School with Helen Haney, just like in her daydreams? She'd be a heroine surrounded by hordes of friends—perhaps she could even be the first one in the family to make the bold and brave expedition into higher education—*

"I wouldn't count on it," said Elton.

Norvia deflated. He was almost certainly right.

She noticed the book spread over Elton's lap, and, hoping to divert the conversation to more pleasant things, asked, "What's that? It looks sort of fun."

"Oh, these are just finances. It's my ledger. I'm trying to figure out how to afford the things we need with my paycheck," he explained, tapping the lonely columns of sporadic numbers with his pencil.

Norvia leaned her chin on her hand. "Don't the Marys help?"

Elton shook his head, still tapping the ledger with his pencil. Even the sound of the tapping seemed somehow forlorn. "Just a little. Taking in laundry doesn't pay for much, not when there's so many of us. That's why Ma does her dressmaking, and I work at the broom factory. And I don't know how it'll change with this—this *new husband* coming into the picture. Will he contribute to the household? What if he's just—just a do-nothing?" Elton glanced back down at his notes. "Or a gambler? Or worse? I could try to work another shift at the factory...."

A newspaper clipping slipped out of his ledger; it was from a recent edition of the *Charlevoix County Herald*. Norvia's gaze fell on a dramatic account of wolves in Escanaba, but the column that Elton had circled was titled Harvest—Bouncing Crop of Alfalfa Hay.

"Why are you reading that?" she asked.

Elton crinkled the paper closed and stuffed it back in his ledger. "Oh, just wishful thinking. It says old Mr. Redgrave has a nice alfalfa crop this summer. He's looking for somebody to help him on the farm now that he's getting on in years, and he asked if I'd help."

Norvia glowed. "You should! You would love it! You've always loved growing things!" On Beaver Island, Elton had been most helpful in their old kitchen garden: the strawberries, peas, and salad greens he grew every year had always been perfect. He had a gift.

"He wants a sort of apprentice. But he can't pay," Elton explained, the joy fading from his eyes. "It would be the best experience, learning all his methods and how to really work the land . . . but I can't spare the time from the factory. I have to earn a living."

"But—" Norvia's voice wavered. "Maybe you could find a different job. One that took less time, so you could help Mr. Redgrave."

Elton patted her knee, smiling at her in a defeated sort of way that was not like him at all. "Not that easy, Nan. Jobs are scarce now that most of the logging in this area's done."

Norvia looked away, unable to bear the sight of his resigned face any longer. There was a little potted plant on the edge of the porch— its healthy vine trailed out into the grass below. Elton had grown it, of course.

Norvia sighed with admiration. "It's so lovely," she whispered, reaching out to stroke its soft ferny leaves.

"Well, it's one thing I can grow—unlike money," said Elton, and he grinned. It was not an extra-special grin like Herman's, but it was a middle-brother grin that gave her a twist of hope inside.

Norvia thought of the little vine when she went to bed later— thought of it with all her heart and soul. But try as she might, wish as she might, that she could change things . . . make her brother happy . . . say goodbye to Pa . . . somehow become filled with joy . . . it just wasn't so simple.

"Why don't you want to live with Mr. Ward?" asked Dicta, her tiny voice piping up.

"Shh," Norvia warned again. "We have to go to sleep."

"But it'll make us all happy. You have to be happy sometimes, Norvie! *Mary Pickford* is always smiling, and I'm just like her," Dicta added with satisfaction.

If only it were that easy.

It was unfair, she thought as she drifted off, that even though he now lived hundreds of miles away, Pa was still dictating her happiness—and so was Mr. Virgil Ward, a perfect stranger.

CHAPTER THREE
SUPPER WITH THE WARDS

Dear Norvia,

Florida is a simply magnificent place! Everything here in Tarpon Springs feels so charmingly exotic compared to Boyne City. We're staying at a lovely inn with a wide porch and white pillars, in a town on the Gulf of Mexico! It isn't like home and Pine Lake. I wish you and I were together so that we could talk about anything and everything.

We're having supper with old friends of Mother's tonight. They've recently returned from Paris, which they had to leave because of the war sprouting up—isn't that a terrible shame? I cannot wait to hear all about the fascinating sights they've seen. France is very cultural, you know. I want you to teach me to speak French, because then we could speak fluently with any Parisians we meet. (Because someday we will meet more, of course, when we're deliciously grown-up and on our own.)

Farewell for now! Au revoir! Mother is calling me.

Love,

Helen

Norvia read Helen Haney's letter in the last fleeting minutes before the Ward family arrived for supper. It was a scrumptious letter, just the chatty sort that Norvia liked best—it made Helen's voice come alive, somehow—but she couldn't read it with slow carefulness, drinking in every syllable as she preferred to.

She took a deep breath, shoved the letter under her pillow, adjusted the ribbon in her hair, and marched out of the room. It was time to get the evening over with.

Mr. Ward came into the house with a hesitant sort of expression. He wore an ivory suit, the sort that looked both sophisticated and dashing. At least, it *would* have been dashing if he hadn't been so tall and angular and middle-aged. Still, Norvia had to admit that Mr. Ward was slim and debonair with an infectious smile; she could guess why Ma liked him. But his son, Vernon, who wore a gray suit and had a sullen face to match, didn't say a word as everyone gathered in the entryway.

Mr. Ward's daughter Marguerite wore her chestnut-brown hair twisted into a high knot, and her myrtle-green gown was made of luscious silk taffeta, with becoming ruffles and buttons down the front and quarter-length sleeves. (Norvia felt quite dowdy in her blue linen dress that wrinkled if she sat a certain way too long.) Marguerite's husband, Jim, wore a red-striped suit and a straw boater, and the two of them linked arms and laughed as they entered, as if the world was far more amusing to them than anyone else. They looked young, almost too young to be a married couple. But then Ma had married Pa when she was only sixteen.

"It certainly is a glorious night, isn't it?" said Mr. Ward, motioning toward the window. "Such a golden sunset out there."

Golden sunset... What a lovely phrase, Norvia thought, then halted herself. Flowery language was just empty talk.

"Yes, glorious," Ma agreed, linking her arm with Mr. Ward's, as if mimicking Marguerite. "Now I suppose some introductions are in order. Children, this is my fiancé, Mr. Virgil Ward. Virgil, these are four of my children: Elton, Norvia, Casper, and Dicta."

Norvia wished that Herman was here. But, no, her oldest brother was off gallivanting in the U.P.—well, working on the railroad, anyway—and had abandoned them all at the worst possible moment. What would he say when he heard about Ma's engagement? Norvia decided to write to him the minute this was over and tell him the truth of what was transpiring in his absence. He may have left, but he had *always* known what to do.

"It is a pleasure and an honor to meet you all," said Mr. Ward with great gravity.

Norvia wondered whether he was joking or serious. And could he guess their heritage simply by looking at them, as Elton had thought?

Dicta unabashedly stood on her tiptoes and held out her hand. "I'm Mary Benedicta Nelson, but everybody calls me Dicta. I was named after both my grandmothers *and* the most important woman in all the world, the Virgin Mary, mother of Jesus—*and* I was named 'Benedicta' after a courageous, selfless nun on Beaver Island, *and* it's Latin for 'blessed,' so I really have the most sacred name in the whole entire universe." She attempted a crooked curtsy. "My curtsy would be prettier, but I have a lame leg. It happened when I was a baby, and I fell on a ship and injured myself irrevocably. I'm *very* glad to meet you."

Norvia wished she had a convenient cave to crawl into.

"And I'm very glad to meet you, Mary Benedicta," said Mr. Ward, smiling above Dicta's head at Marguerite.

"I'm eight years old," Dicta chattered on, "and Casper is thirteen and Elton sixteen and Norvia fourteen."

And a half, Norvia added silently. She could not bring herself to say it aloud, but she found it difficult not to be perfectly exact about dates and ages.

"And this is my son," Mr. Ward continued, gesturing to the slender boy who stood in the corner, away from everyone else. The boy's eyes flitted briefly to Norvia before they fixated on the floor. "Vernon is thirteen."

"And a half," said Vernon suddenly. He had the palest skin Norvia had ever seen, devoid of any healthful color, and his dark hair and eyes created a stark contrast. She found herself smiling at his correction in spite of herself.

"I'm pleased to meet you, dear," said Ma, transferring her smile from father to son. "Your father has told me so much about you. I'm Mrs. LeBlanc Nelson."

LeBlanc Nelson! Her maiden name, too? As if plain old Nelson wasn't good enough!

"Quite charmed to make your acquaintance." Vernon sounded remarkably like an aristocratic earl. Norvia inched a step away.

"I, of course, am not a blood relation, just a pesky in-law—Jim Rockford's my name." Jim laughed, gazing at Marguerite with adoration. "And of course you already know that Mistress Margie is Mr. W.'s flamboyant daughter and my very charming wife."

"I am so pleased to meet you, Mr. Rockford," said Ma in her new, girlish way. "And it's a delight to see you again, Marguerite."

"Oh yes! But Jim made it sound as if I'm the only one of the Ward girls, and I'm not. Julia is the oldest, but she lives in Detroit with her husband and children." Marguerite explained this with a smile that extended to everyone in the room.

Vernon was the first to move into the Marys' modest parlor, where he gazed around at the tired furnishings and faded wallpaper. A knot of anger twisted inside Norvia. How dare he stand there gawking, openly judgmental?

But an odd sentence popped out of his mouth. "They haven't any bookshelves in this room," he remarked, turning to his father.

Mr. Ward started to say something, then paused and made his own cursory inspection of the room. "Well, I'm sure they don't have to spend as much time dusting as we do," he joked lightly.

Norvia could feel her cheeks turning crimson. "We don't really have any books," she blurted out. She blinked hard to prevent her stinging eyes from betraying her.

Mr. Ward turned his gaze toward her, and a flicker of . . . annoyance? . . . sympathy? . . . flashed across his face. She busied herself retying Dicta's hair bow.

"May I invite you all to the table?" asked Ma, smoothing over the moment.

Norvia had spent all afternoon helping the Marys cook the engagement supper: cream of vegetable soup, lamb, peas, baked potatoes, and buttered cauliflower. Ma hadn't helped; she was too busy admiring herself in the mirror, spritzing Djer-Kiss perfume everywhere and trying on dresses (she had finally chosen the wool challis that made her look like a movie actress). When Ma sat at the dining room table beside Mr. Ward, Norvia felt a twinge of sadness. It was sweet, yet all wrong.

"I'll sit next to you, Margie," said Dicta, claiming the chair beside Marguerite.

"Dicta," Ma reprimanded. "Say 'Mrs. Rockford.' "

Marguerite gave Dicta's hand a brisk pat. "It's all right, Mrs. Nelson. I do like getting on a first-name basis straightaway. Keeps things friendlier."

Well, aren't you perfect, thought Norvia—but then she blushed at her own unkindness.

Norvia somehow ended up sitting between Old Mary, who stared shrewdly at Mr. Ward, and Vernon, who took great pains to use perfect table manners—he even spooned soup *away* from himself, rather than *toward*. She found herself dabbing at her mouth with a napkin, chewing with her mouth closed, sitting up as straight as an arrow—things she wouldn't usually think about in ordinary company. But if Vernon meant to show off his quality, then she must, too.

If only the other Nelson children would do the same! She wished Casper wouldn't poke every single pea with the prongs of his fork—you'd think a thirteen-year-old would start to heed a few table manners, but he hadn't even combed his wild black hair. Dicta had fashioned her bread into a boat and was pouring gravy into the hollow. Elton wasn't eating at all.

"Excellent meal, Mrs. N.," said Jim Rockford, grinning at Ma.

"Thank you," said Ma in her most affected manner, "but I actually didn't prepare this supper. My mother and grandmother did."

"With Norvia's help," said Old Mary.

Norvia hoped this would be the end of any supper table discussion, but Jim had the audacity to inquire, "So, when's the wedding?"

Ma opened her mouth to recite the date, but Mr. Ward spoke first. "Anytime two families come together, it's a difficult transition," he said, twirling cauliflower on the end of his fork. "Angélique and I considered that perhaps making the change quickly would be better and less taxing on everyone. But there are advantages to"—he hesitated a moment—"long engagements."

Vernon stabbed his portion of lamb with his fork so abruptly that Norvia jumped.

"Marry in haste, repent at leisure," quoted Dicta with a sunny smile. Old Mary smirked behind her napkin.

"Well, I think it's a grand idea to go ahead!" said Marguerite, leaning forward. "An end-of-summer wedding, right away. Skip a fancy ceremony; just go to Judge Walters, save your money, and then you two can enjoy a lavish wedding journey."

Norvia almost swallowed her milk the wrong way, but she managed to recover without a fit of coughing.

"Where would you go on a wedding journey?" demanded Vernon.

Mr. Ward was unmoved by his son's accusatory tone. "We haven't discussed it yet."

Angélique (for she was Angélique tonight—Norvia could no longer imagine her as "Ma") leaned forward like Marguerite, her dark eyes catching the dancing lights of the chandelier. "I was thinking of Canada."

"Niagara Falls!" Marguerite clasped her hands together.

"Romance with a capital *R*," said Jim, who *did* choke on his milk and had to be slapped on the back for the next minute.

Young Mary frowned as she began stirring the vegetable soup for no reason. "This idle conversation hardly seems suitable for the young people," she said. "Let us move into the parlor. The children can eat their dessert here."

And so the Marys, Angélique, Mr. Ward, and the Rockfords took their coffee cups, saucers, and plates of chocolate cake into the parlor, leaving the door just slightly ajar. Elton was almost a man, and he wavered for a few moments before opting to stay in the dining room.

"I honestly can't listen to all that drivel," he muttered, throwing his napkin onto the table.

"You'd think Mr. Ward was some lover in a play," Casper chuckled, and burst into a rendition of "Sweet Adeline"—changing it to "Sweet Angélique"—before Norvia elbowed him.

"That is my father you're speaking of," said Vernon, one of his eyebrows arching higher than the other.

Dicta, with a rim of chocolate around her mouth, began to question Vernon. "Is your father old? He doesn't look very old."

"He's forty-eight." Vernon sniffed.

"How old is your sister?" pressed Dicta.

"It's exceedingly impolite to discuss a lady's age, but she is twenty." Vernon blinked. "And three quarters."

"So, your mother died," Dicta continued, licking her plate to snag every last cake crumb. "She's not still alive, like our father is. Was your mother like Ma?"

Vernon's complexion was paler than ever. "No, and I would thank you not to mention my mother."

"I just want to know what her name was," insisted Dicta.

"Did you not hear what I said?" Vernon snapped.

A wave of irritation washed over Norvia. Why did he have to be so rude? Of course, if his mother was dead, he must miss her, but he could at least be civil to Dicta. After all, she was only eight! And now they would have this boy for their stepbrother.

Again, so many feelings welled up inside Norvia: anger, frustration, sadness...and there wasn't anyone to turn to.

"*Je souhaite que cette journée soit finie,*" said Vernon, pushing his plate of cake away.

"*J'aurais aimé que vous ne soyons jamais venus,*" Elton retorted.

Norvia had to smile behind her napkin at the look of surprise on Vernon's face.

After everyone had consumed their chocolate cake—or rather, not consumed it; no one touched it except Casper and Dicta—Mr. Ward came into the room and asked for "a moment with the children." This did not include Vernon, who began murmuring in a low tone to Marguerite. Close confidantes, no doubt. After they went home, Norvia was certain that those two would never stop gossiping about their undesirable stepsiblings.

Mr. Ward led the way to the front porch, with Elton, Norvia, Casper, and Dicta following in an uneasy line. They sat on the steps, and fireflies began to zigzag around them.

"I know this is hard," began Mr. Ward.

"Look, sir," Elton started, but Mr. Ward interrupted him.

"Please, let me finish. I don't want you to feel as if you had no voice in our decision to marry. I do love your mother—and this would make us very happy. But if you want us to wait, we will wait. Tell me the truth about your opinions."

It was on the tip of Norvia's tongue to say, "Don't marry my mother." She fought to release the words, to let them fly from her dry lips. But even *if* she said them, he wouldn't listen—not really. He would only say in a calming but persuasive voice, "It will be best for all concerned—don't worry your little head about it." Just as Pa would have, before he patted her head and went off to play poker with the other sailors.

She remained silent.

"I want you to get married right away if you're going to," Dicta declared. "I like getting things over with." She smiled up at Mr. Ward.

Casper shrugged and mumbled, "Whatever you think is best."

Elton stared off into the distance. That golden sunset had dimmed, and the sky was fading to a dark, becoming blue. "If that's really what Ma wants," he said eventually, his voice rusty.

"So, you would rather we waited," said Mr. Ward patiently.

Elton heaved a sigh. "Not if it means she's just going to be miserable for months."

"Truly," said Mr. Ward, "I know this will work out in the end. We'll have a wonderful life together, you'll see." Suddenly he glanced up at the awning of sapphire sky. "The Cygnus constellation," he announced. "Look at that."

Norvia followed his gaze to the first stars of the night—the stars that formed a crane—and then to the Milky Way that Grand-père had called the Spirit Path. She felt strangely comforted by the night sky, and by the knowledge that Mr. Ward was on a first-name basis with the collections of stars that Grand-père and Migizi had loved.

If he's friends with the stars, Norvia thought, *he might be a tiny bit nice.*

True to her word, she put pen to paper as soon as she was back in her bedroom.

Dear Herman,

I really miss you so very much. I hope you're having a nice time in the Upper Peninsula. (This was a kind white lie, for she would have much rather he didn't like life in the U.P. and returned home.) Something has happened that I want you to know about. I assume Elton's going to write to you about it, but you ought to hear it from me, too. Ma is remarrying.

She wants her new husband to be this Virgil Ward person (oh, it felt good to refer to him like this) and they're going to be married right away, at the end of this month.

Norvia tapped her pencil against the desk and considered how to phrase her desperate plea.

Can't you find some way to help us? ... I don't know how, but I'm so worried about things and I want everything to return to the way it used to be. I really don't see how you can change anything, but if you can—please try to think of a way.

Please write back soon.

Love,
Norvia

The woods of Beaver Island were a magical place to Norvia. She loved playing among the ferns that speckled the forest floor, the multitudes of rocks (some shiny, some covered in soft moss), the white pines, and the hornbeams. Today she, Herman, Elton, Casper, and Dicta were berrying together, heading far enough out that no one could see them—a truly delicious feeling.

Norvia snapped a twig with deliberate skill—a young, two-pronged twig—and then for good measure she snapped a second. The berry bushes awaited them, but she didn't want to get lost. Twig snapping absolutely ensured that the Marys could find them again, because they could follow their trail. It was one of the old ways.

"It's 1796," Norvia improvised, choosing a date that sounded foreign and ages old. She liked to pretend, sometimes, that she was living in the time of her ancestors. "We have to sail in our birch bark canoe across the waters...hoping to reach land before the stars come out and the night turns cold...."

Dicta, who was only four years old, picked up a stray leaf and twirled it between her fingers, uninterested in the events of 1796.

"Only we're not allowed out on the water by ourselves," Elton pointed out, sitting down on a skull-shaped rock to examine an arrowhead he'd found.

"They never let us do *anything*," Casper complained, flopping down on the pine-needle ground. "I bet I could paddle a canoe *by myself*. It's easy."

Herman was busily carving plus signs on a birch tree to indicate stars. Grand-père had taught them this was another Ojibwe method to keep travelers from turning the wrong way. "We could try to make a small canoe," he mused. "We could at least see if we could."

"Let's!" Norvia agreed. "A little one, anyway. I know how."

She hurried to the birch tree where Herman was carving. It was a slim, elegant tree with a smooth skin, unlike the rough maples and firs. Grasping an already-peeling strip of bark, Norvia tore it off the trunk, then sunk to the ground to fashion their canoe. For several minutes she labored over her project, bending the papery bark, populating it with woods-people (a few handy pine cones). These represented their ancestors.

"Our Indian ancestors," Norvia announced, relishing the sound of the words as she adjusted one of the pine cones.

"I don't think that will float," said Elton. "Let me try it."

After some more fiddling and fixing, the siblings tramped to the shoreline and sent their voyageurs out onto Lake Michigan. It was a good day for a voyage—the lake sparkled fresh and blue in the sunshine, and the berries sprouting everywhere in the woods promised deliciousness. "It's the Berry Moon," Old Mary had said this morning, as the children had gathered their tin pails. "It's a good time for gathering."

They watched their canoe float lazily away, as if in no hurry at all. "If that little canoe was *actually* full of old-time voyageurs, they'd be going much faster. They'd be trying to get to a fort to deliver furs," said Herman knowledgeably.

"I want raspberries," said Dicta, already bored with the game.

"Old Mary asked us to get blueberries," Norvia reminded her.

Herman laughed. "Let's get both!"

Surprisingly enough, when they reached the best berrying spot—a thorny, weedy kingdom of juicy riches in jewel tones—they saw a dog. Norvia's heart ached for the poor animal, who was skinny and had matted fur, probably from the downpour of rain two nights earlier. He was of a medium size and stared at them with great dark-brown eyes, wagging his tail hopefully.

"Lost doggy!" Dicta squealed.

"Oh, poor puppy!" cried Norvia.

"Wait," said Herman quickly. "You have to be careful around strange dogs. It's safer that way." He advanced toward the dog slowly, cautiously. The dog continued to wag his tail, and not once did he growl. Herman reached out a gentle hand and patted the dog's head, gingerly at first, then more confidently. "He's not wild," he decided at last. "I mean, it's likely he was lost fairly recently. But what a bad condition he's in!"

Norvia untied her apron from her waist and draped it over the dog's back. "In case he's cold," she explained.

Herman reached into his pocket and pulled out a length of string, tying it loosely around the dog's neck. "I'm taking him home," he said firmly. "A dog like this can't be left alone."

An awful suspicion crossed Norvia's mind. "You're not hoping to keep him, are you?"

"Pa will never let you," Elton warned.

"If no one claims him, of course I will keep him," said Herman importantly. "Pa can't say no to a miserable dog like this."

But he did say no. As soon as they arrived back at the cottage, dog in tow, Pa took one look at him and said, "No."

"But, Pa," said Herman incredulously. "Someone needs to keep him!"

"Dogs are always needing things," said Pa. "He will be far too much bother. You've got your head in the sky again."

"Clouds, you mean," Casper corrected absently.

Pa gave Casper a glare that made Norvia wish they were still back in the woods on their merry berrying expedition. "Of course you must find him a home, but his home will not be with us. Do you understand?"

"Yes, sir," said Herman, frowning. "But it may take time to find him a home...."

"Ask your uncle Eugene" were Pa's final words on the subject.

So Herman took the dog to Uncle Eugene, who was dependable and even older than Grand-père and loved animals, but who lived over on Hog Island. Sometimes Norvia wondered about that dog over the years. What might have happened if Pa had let them keep him, instead of sending him away? Perhaps, over time, the dog might have sweetened Pa's disposition more than a pailful of fresh berries ever could.

CHAPTER FOUR
LIGHT AND SHADOW

Norvia lay on her bed, staring up at the low, slanting eaves. Her mind was far away, catching glimpses of beauty, living in her usual enchanting world of daydreams. When she finished planning them out to her fullest satisfaction, she reached for her notebook and began to transpose her thoughts into the most beautiful sentences she could conjure up.

"How do you learn these things so quickly?" a very Dashing Young Man was asking her as he carried her books down the crowded hallways of Boyne City High School. "Whatever is your secret? You're at the head of every single class."

"It just comes naturally to me," Norvia replied, smiling in a genuine, carefree manner. The Dashing Young Man gazed at her, as if he had never seen such beauty before. He was probably thinking that she was perfectly ideal with her soft, round face, voluminous brown hair, arched eyebrows, and perceptive chocolate eyes....

"I can't wait to live on McKinley Street," Dicta interrupted, bouncing on their bed. "It's so close to downtown, and we'll be able to go to the movies *all the time* because Mr. Ward is very wealthy and lenient and generous." She wound a strand of hair around her smallest finger. "I think those words suit him and his money extremely well. And Vernon can teach me how to say all things regal and important, and we'll wear fancy dresses all the time like Marguerite's, and we'll live happily ever after."

Norvia decided she would be wearing a peach-colored gown at the very first dance she attended with the Dashing Young Man. "Perhaps we'll stay here. Perhaps Ma will decide that we shouldn't move to McKinley Street at all," she said, clinging to her last hope.

"Of course we will. Mr. Ward doesn't want to leave his house to come live with our grandmothers." Dicta, lying upside down now, was trying to reach the ceiling with the tip of her shoe. "Did you hear Ma talking about her honeymoon?"

Why do you think I'm hiding up here? "What did she say today?"

"She said they talked about going to Detroit to visit Mr. Ward's daughter Julia, but they decided to go to silly old Lansing instead. Isn't *Julia* the dreamiest name? I mean it's not as gorgeous as Mary Benedicta, but it's not disgusting. Julia has a husband named Walter Robertson. He's got a wart on his nose. Ma didn't say that, but my friend Gilma did," she added, rubbing her own spotless nose. "Her family used to be friends with the Robertsons before they got all big-headed and moved to Detroit. Did you know that? Julia has a daughter named Emaretta and a son named Ian. If I wasn't named Mary Benedicta, I would like to be called Emaretta." She stopped for breath and assumed a thoughtful look before resuming. "Remember what Kittie was saying the other day, about her family and Marguerite's husband's? She says they've been on the outs for *years*. Something about a land-gab scream in the nineties."

Norvia exhaled a sigh of frustration. "Land-grab scheme."

A look of concern appeared on Dicta's face for the first time throughout this conversation. "Do you think Mr. Ward will let us bring Peggy to live in his fancy house?"

"Peggy will want to stay here, with the Marys," Norvia reminded her.

Dicta stroked the sweet cat with one sad finger. "I think she would rather stay with me."

Later that week, Marguerite invited Ma and Norvia and Dicta to a luncheon at her house. Norvia dreaded it. Having to sit with this stranger and say polite things, all while anxious shyness wound up inside her... It wasn't fair. It was easy for Marguerite to be gracious and say the wedding was all right: *She* lived in her own home, with her own husband.

But, of course, there was no escaping the invitation. So Norvia went.

Marguerite lived in a cheerful yellow bungalow set amid lilac bushes and rustling maple trees. Walking up the front path, Norvia fleetingly found herself hoping there might be lilacs at Mr. Ward's house. Chickadees sang their morning songs like delicate chimes whistling on the breeze.

"Please, come in," said Marguerite in a courteous hostess manner, opening the front door. She was wearing another immaculate dress, this one a rich yellow that matched the shade of her house to perfection. Why *was* she so happy that her father was remarrying? Perhaps she was simply putting on a convincing façade, but Norvia was almost sure that it was genuine. What must it feel like, having your mother replaced by a perfect stranger who flaunted your father's first name and talked of romance and wedding journeys? Norvia knew how *she* would have felt.

"Oh, I'm so glad you could all come," said Marguerite, leading her guests through a parlor decorated in a rose-and-gold color scheme with leafy patterns everywhere. But it was when they entered the dining room that Norvia saw the most breathtaking wallpaper: sea blue and sprinkled with nautical scenes, with large prints of waterbirds framed on each wall—the type of birds they used to see on Beaver Island.

Norvia's intention had been to remain as silent as possible during this unhappy gathering, but she took one look at the perfect room and cried out, "This is so *beautiful!*"

Marguerite's smile shone as bright as the morning sunshine. "Do you really like it? Jim thought my decorating was a bit much, but personally I adore the prints and the paper. Some people call them loud, and maybe they are . . . but they do speak to me."

They sat at the dining room table, which was clad in an elegant white-lace tablecloth. Fresh flowers smelling of summer air sprung from a glass vase, and tiny sandwiches—crusts removed—awaited their appetites, along with a shining silver teapot. Dicta cooed and began to pour herself a haphazard cup of tea.

"Vern picked these for me," said Marguerite in a cheery tone, pointing to the vase of goldenrod and black-eyed Susans. "He didn't really feel like attending our girls' confab, so I gave him his luncheon earlier. He's out reading," she added with an indulgent laugh, glancing out the window.

Intrigued by the very word *reading*, Norvia couldn't resist following Marguerite's gaze to the backyard, where Vernon lay sprawled in the grass, stroking a kitten while reading a slim brown-velvet volume. Norvia squinted to read the golden text on the front cover—*Robert Browning,* it said.

Oh, if only Pa had let us read like that—but Norvia squashed the thought.

"Are you wealthy?" asked Dicta, fondling a trinket on the sideboard.

"Dicta, that's impolite!" Ma reproved.

Marguerite began to serve the food on blue china dishes that clinked in harmony. "We're not a bit wealthy, but we're more or less comfortable."

Ma took a sip of tea. "I take it that Vernon stays with you each day while Virgil is at work?" she inquired.

"Mm-hmm." Marguerite broke off a piece of cookie and tossed it into her mouth. "Lots of nights he just stays here if Papa's working late. We're grand pals, and he's always gotten along with Jim."

"I'm grand pals with my friend Gilma," said Dicta. "Gilma and I were both born in January, so we're practically twins, except that she has brown hair and a snub nose instead of dark blonde hair and a perfect nose like me."

Norvia thought of Helen Haney, still away in the south with her family. She couldn't wait for her return—it would be so wonderful to confide all her troubles to her friend. Why didn't Helen write more often? She'd had only a handful of letters all summer. And, for that matter, why didn't Herman write at all? Perhaps if they wrote to her more often, she wouldn't feel so miserable.

"That's so nice that you take care of your brother," Ma said, beaming. Was she hoping that Vernon would continue to spend most of his time with Marguerite? "But, of course, I suppose you'll be glad when he goes back to school in a few weeks."

Norvia felt even more uncomfortable listening to Ma and Marguerite speak so warmly. She tried to think of Beaver Island as she drank the tea, which tasted like bitter water. Perhaps if she stirred it, the tea would improve. She envisioned a flock of swans alighting on the waters, their wings glistening in the sunlight.

"Oh, no," said Marguerite with a distracted smile, as she wiped up Dicta's spilled tea. "Vern doesn't go to school. Papa and I teach him. He's so prone to headaches and stomachaches that we just let him study at home."

Norvia held her spoon a little tighter, feeling a sudden stab of pity. "That's too bad," she said softly. How disappointing it must be for Vernon to have a father who approved of education, and yet not be able to take advantage of it!

Again her sparkling vision flashed into her mind—her cherished dream of attending high school. Mr. Ward might let her go—mightn't he? Perhaps there would be one good thing about this marriage, at least.

That night, Ma went to supper with Mr. Ward at Kerry's Restaurant and Soda Parlor—the same restaurant where Pa used to take Ma on special occasions. Norvia pictured them dining by candlelight at those low tables with their white tablecloths, sipping champagne and admiring the polished countertop where the soda jerk served ice cream and winked at girls. Perhaps he would wink at Ma, and Mr. Ward would challenge him to a duel.

That would happen in a romance serial, but probably not in Boyne City.

Ma was excited by the prospect of dining at Kerry's again, so she primped in the mirror, put on rouge, and arranged her raven-black hair just so. She hummed a ballad from Beaver Island as she glided gracefully down the stairs. Norvia could hardly wrap her mind around the fact that this was her mother.

Mr. Ward, dapper as ever, came to call for Ma. As usual, he looked pleased but serious. Norvia stood in the shadow of the banisters, unwilling to watch but somehow unable to stop herself.

"You look wonderful, Angélique," he said with grave sincerity.

"Thank you, Virgil," said Ma with a demure smile.

"Aren't you going to say that Mr. Ward looks dashingly handsome?" Dicta asked, standing between the lovers.

Ma gave a trilling laugh. "Dicta, dear."

"Well, he does," Dicta insisted.

"Angélique, I've brought you ... here," said Mr. Ward, slipping a black box from his pocket. For once his poise lapsed as he fought for words. "This will be your wedding ring," he managed, after a significant pause.

Without hesitation, Ma snapped open the box. "Oh, Virgil, it's exquisite!" She slid the ring onto her finger—the finger bereft of its old golden wedding band. Now her hand sparkled with the stunning diamond.

Dicta's eyes grew enormous. "Did that ring belong to your dear departed wife?"

Mr. Ward shook his head, very patient. "No, this is a family heirloom—it belonged to my mother. And it just so happens that I have these as well." He pulled out two more boxes, one blue and one brown, and he handed these to Norvia and Dicta.

Inside the boxes lay silver necklaces, shaped like birds and shining in the lamplight. Dicta squealed and began struggling to fasten the chain around her neck; finally, Mr. Ward did it for her.

"I look like Empress Carlota, or Cleopatra, or Queen Zenobia," said Dicta, rushing to admire herself in the hall mirror.

Norvia tried her best to sound delighted. "Thank you," she said, although her words came out more stiffly than she'd intended.

"Do you need help putting it on?" Mr. Ward asked kindly.

"I can do it." Again Norvia's voice was sharper than she had intended, and she wished she could present a calmer façade. She fiddled with the tiny hook before it finally clasped together. She didn't want to wear it—it would be like saying she approved of the marriage, that she *wanted* them to marry! It would be like wearing a fib! But she couldn't be rude.

"You look splendid, Norvia," said Ma, flashing Mr. Ward another smile.

"I thought that perhaps you two would like something to commemorate the occasion," said Mr. Ward in his gentlest voice. "My mother was actually my father's second wife. And I remember hearing a story from my older half sisters—that when my mother married my father, she gave each of my sisters a necklace."

For a moment, Norvia was disarmed. It was a nice idea, and he had been kind to think of it. Maybe she could keep her necklace in the special seashell box that Herman had promised to bring her from the Upper Peninsula.

"It's too bad this isn't a locket," said Dicta, still twirling in the mirror. "Then I could put one picture of you and one of Pa in it. So I could have both my fathers in my locket."

That brought Norvia back to reality—and she couldn't remain

there another second. She ran upstairs, ignoring the fact that Ma was calling her back down.

By eight o'clock, Ma had still not returned, and Elton had yet to come home from the factory. Norvia started downstairs to ask the Marys why Elton was so late, but she paused on the steps when her ears were met by a strange conversation.

"It's good for Angélique to have things to occupy her mind," Young Mary was saying in French. "Without a book club, her old acquaintances, or the church ladies, she's been so lonesome."

"Strange how one man could make up for all the friends she has lost," said Old Mary, "but love can do many things."

Norvia sat motionless on the step, wondering. Ma hadn't lost any friends. Mrs. Hampton, their next-door neighbor, still came to borrow eggs once a week. It was true that Ma hadn't attended any book club meetings lately, but then, she had never been a regular member. As for the church ladies, well, of course Ma didn't spend time with them now. Norvia still remembered the day that Father McKay came to visit after the divorce procedures began—after that, Ma had stopped attending Mass. So, yes, naturally the church ladies wouldn't visit anymore, either.

"Those old biddies think they've led such model lives." Old Mary sniffed. "Remember that rumor about Mrs. Greeley?"

"Don't I!" cried Young Mary.

Norvia couldn't stand on the stairs in limbo anymore, so she hurried down and looked out the front window to see if Elton was coming up the road. The Marys behind her in the parlor murmured *"pauvre enfant,"* which meant they were feeling sorry for her now.

After a lengthy wait, Norvia saw Elton walking slowly up the pine-lined street, wearing his dusty factory clothes. He was a short but strong young man with dark skin, and it was sometimes hard for her to believe that he was only sixteen. Lately, he had looked so much older.

"Hi, Nan," he called out.

Worry flooded her heart. "Why are you late? Are you all right?" she asked him, her gaze intense.

He looked at her with tired blue eyes and forced a sort of smile. "Mm-hmm," he said, but he was hiding his right hand.

"You hurt yourself!" she blurted.

"Not really. Just cut my hand a little. It's nothing." Elton's smile brightened artificially. "Really," he added firmly, seeing her face. "Listen, don't mention it to Ma. I'll swipe some antiseptic on it and do the bandaging. It'll be fine."

"Can you do that with your left hand?" Norvia asked hesitantly.

"I think so."

She warned herself not to look at the wound. *Don't look, don't look*, she chanted inside, but she quickly wished she possessed more willpower, as it was bloodier than she expected. She winced.

"Does it hurt?" she asked, her voice barely above a whisper.

"Not much, Nan," he reassured her as he walked toward the mailbox.

He told beautiful lies.

Elton opened the box with his left hand and peered inside. "Guess nobody looked in here today. There's a letter from Herman."

The fading duskiness of the night became beautiful in an instant. Joy surged into Norvia, despite poor Elton's injury—if only Herman would remember them every week!—and she let out a squeal as she dove for the little wooden box to pull out the envelope. It was battered, but the precious contents were still in good condition.

"It's addressed to both of us!" Norvia said.

"I'm going to go fix my hand up," said Elton, "but you can go ahead and read it. I won't be long."

Norvia sat down on the front steps, unwilling to go inside and allow Dicta's excitement and Casper's questions to bombard this moment. In the yellow glow of the porch light, she unfolded the letter, smiling at an enclosed picture of Herman standing in front of an enormous rock.

Elton & Norvie,

Hope you like the picture. It's from when I visited the Pictured Rocks here in Munising. I think this name comes from the word minis (remember Grand-père telling us it meant island?). It makes me feel not so alone to think of that.

It's very pretty up here. I like Lake Superior best of all, much more than Lake Michigan. You two would certainly appreciate the beauty of this place. Sometimes, looking out at the water or walking in the woods, I even get ideas for grand old stories like we used to dream up when we were kids. What do you think, should I become a famous author?? (Ha ha.)

I got Norv's letter yesterday, and I don't think I like this. From what I judge, Ma is desperate to find a husband and she picked the first one who came along. No telling if he's the right man for her, or the right man to be the father of a big family.

So I think you should come to Munising. I'm guessing Ma would never let Casper and Dicta come, but she might let you two. I stay at a nice boardinghouse run by a motherly lady, and she'd be happy to take you in. I could probably find work for you both. There's some logging in this area that Elton could do, and for Norvia, Mrs. Gregory here at the boardinghouse could use a girl to help out with chores.

Let me know what you think—you're welcome here. Miss you both. Je t'aime.

Herman

For a brief moment, Norvia imagined herself walking the beaches of Lake Superior, free from the Ward family...but she recoiled as soon as she remembered that going to Munising would mean moving farther from Beaver Island than ever.

And her family! She would be leaving so much behind! Images of Ma and the Marys floated through her head, and a lump rose in her throat.

Perhaps, though, Ma was so enamored with Virgil Ward that she didn't care about her children anymore? Maybe she would even be glad to see them gone!

Deep down, Norvia knew this wasn't true, but for some reason it felt good to wallow in self-pity. Oh, what was wrong with her? Why couldn't she be happy about the wedding, like Dicta was?

Then her perennial daydream surged back into her mind.... She envisioned herself standing in front of Boyne City High School—a heroine heading off on an educational adventure. A heroine just like the ones in the *St. Nicholas* magazine short stories that she borrowed from Helen. A heroine whom everyone liked.

Norvia gave the letter to Elton once he had bandaged his hand. He scanned it quickly.

"What do you think?" he asked, a bit doubtfully.

She closed her eyes. She had stared at the note so long all she could see was Herman's unkempt handwriting.

"I will stay with Ma—and Mr. Ward," she announced.

CHAPTER FIVE
A NEW HOME

The carriage ride to Mr. Ward's house was uneventful, despite Casper and Dicta singing "Come Josephine in My Flying Machine" all the way down Lake Street. In the gathering darkness, people were lighting summer bonfires: children were playing and laughing, and the air was full of voices and smoke. Norvia felt closed off from reality, barely able to speak or hear a word.

Everything had happened so quickly: Elton wrote to Herman to tell him they would stay in Boyne City. Dicta asked to bring Peggy to the Ward house, and Mr. Ward miraculously agreed. The matter-of-fact wedding took place at the justice of the peace, followed by the long wait for Ma and Mr. Ward to return from their wedding journey to Lansing. And *oh*, the way they looked when they came home to the Marys' house! Mr. Ward seemed younger, somehow, as if a weight had been lifted from his shoulders—and Ma, so carefree and contented. How could two people be so jubilant when they had tangled up every thread of life?

They'd been back for only a few minutes when Ma announced that it was time to go to their *new* home, Mr. Ward's house on McKinley Street. Norvia knew it would be dreadful—stuffy and sophisticated, not a *home*—but she had no choice.

And the worst of it all? The Marys weren't coming. Mr. Ward had invited them in the most gracious of tones, but they had declined.

"We would only be in the way," Old Mary had said. *"Nous ne sommes pas nécessaires."*

"We're fine here," Young Mary had added, her face staid and

determined. "With just the two of us, we'll be able to keep house nicely this winter. Don't worry. We have our laundering."

Norvia felt abandoned. The Marys were always so comforting, so—*necessary*. Was it because they disliked the Wards that they insisted on staying?

Her mind snapped back to the present with a jolt as the carriage pulled to a stop. "Well, this is it," Mr. Ward announced.

Norvia caught her breath. Before her stood a stately white-frame house surrounded by whispering poplars and a prominent lilac bush. It boasted two stories, decorative adornments, and—best of all—an *upper-story balcony*. Why, this was a veritable mansion!

Mr. Ward carried Ma over the threshold of the door, like young lovers on their honeymoon.

"Good grief," Casper muttered.

"Don't injure your back, Papa," said Vernon.

"Peggy wants to go over the threshold, too," said Dicta, carrying her cat into the house.

The house was dark at first, but then Mr. Ward turned the knobs of a few lamps, and light came flooding into the foyer. It really *was* a foyer, not just a glorified entry hall: there was a grand mirror and an oak staircase with carpeted steps in a herringbone pattern.

"Welcome home," said Mr. Ward, taking a deep breath.

"*Bienvenue dans notre humble demeure,*" Vernon muttered in his slightly sarcastic way. Norvia caught her anxious expression in the mirror and tried to smile.

Vernon dashed upstairs so suddenly that Norvia wondered if he was planning to slam a door in fury. Instead, within seconds a dog appeared at the top of the stairs—some sort of hound with an ancient gray face and a tentatively wagging tail. He stayed beside Vernon as they came down and then proceeded to sniff each of the newcomers in turn. Norvia backed away as he came toward her—what if he bit her?

"This is Mr. Bingley," said Vernon, looking scornfully at the way she retreated.

"He's *enchanting*!" Dicta exclaimed, ruffling her hands through the dog's short fur without hesitation. She plopped Peggy onto the hall carpet beside the dog, and while Peggy bristled instantly at being thrust in front of a stranger, the dog merely sniffed Peggy's ears and walked over to Casper.

"He's been with us a long time," said Mr. Ward, as if the dog were an old family servant. He reached out to give one of Mr. Bingley's ears a scratch. Casper and Elton just stared at the dog with dumbfounded expressions, and in an instant Norvia realized why: this dog looked *remarkably* like the one Herman had brought home years ago on Beaver Island. Yet Vernon had been able to keep *his* dog!

Even Ma was impressed by Mr. Bingley. "Virgil, you didn't tell me you had such a lovely animal," she cried. Mr. Bingley sniffed Ma's dark-blue skirt, decided it was acceptable, and wagged his tail once more.

Dicta began wandering through the downstairs, cooing. "Ooh, look at the carpets! Look at that ugly rug! Ooh, look at the chandeliers! Are they really glass? How much did they cost? Is this Vernon's piano? Ooh, is that your first wife? Look at the pictures!"

The parlor was positively opulent. There was a gleaming upright piano with three pedals and intricately carved woodwork; a tall, antique secretary in the corner; and a golden harp with enticing strings (Dicta and Casper immediately began plucking them). A grand bookcase sat in the corner, filled with—to Norvia's surprise—a number of novels, in addition to leather tomes on dull, intellectual subjects. Plush armchairs and a velvet settee were arranged cozily around the fireplace.

But it was the enormous oil painting above the mantel that caught everyone's attention.

The painting depicted a young woman who appraised them with a soulful stare. She had auburn hair, curly without being frizzy, cascading like waves. She wore a white dress, and her eyes stared out of the painting with a desolate expression—as if she knew of some impending doom. Not that this girl wasn't pretty—she was, but not a raving beauty. She didn't have Ma's beautiful eyes or demure mouth; in fact, this girl's mouth was rather pouty. But her nose and ears were flawless, and Norvia knew firsthand that ears were not often attractive (she and Dicta had both inherited Ma's elfish ears).

"Is this your mother?" asked Dicta curiously.

"No, we keep portraits of strange women in our parlor," Vernon replied sardonically, shooting a silencing look at Dicta. "Of course this is my mother. Celestia Amanda Barnett Ward." The melodic syllables rolled off his tongue.

Mr. Ward spoke in a hushed voice. "This was Celestia's favorite room," he explained. "She decorated it with gifts from her parents and things she picked up on her journeys abroad."

"Very lavish taste," said Ma, glancing around at the darkly patterned walls and old-fashioned drapes. Norvia wondered if Ma was already redecorating the house in her head.

"The other rooms aren't as nicely furnished, I'm afraid," Mr. Ward apologized. "However, I think you'll find the house comfortable enough."

Comfortable? Norvia followed her siblings from room to room in rapture, admiring the wall hangings, the treasure trove of paintings, the rounded porcelain lamps. Most of the furnishings, she judged, were not really that expensive, but they had an impressive air. Even Elton looked a little awed by their new surroundings—Norvia noticed him swiping a gentle finger across one of the golden picture frames.

But Casper was bored.

"You said you brought us presents from Lansing," he reminded them.

"That we did," said Mr. Ward, stepping away. "I'll go fetch them."

Everyone fell silent in Mr. Ward's absence. Norvia closed her eyes and imagined that she was standing before Boyne City High School, preparing to make dozens of new friends and conquer the world of higher education. But she opened her eyes again when she heard Ma remark, "Your mother was a pretty woman."

Vernon stared at Ma with distaste in his eyes. "She was uncommonly beautiful," he informed her.

Before Ma could respond, Mr. Ward returned with an array of fascinating packages, all white boxes wrapped in colorful ribbons. "We shopped at a department store," said Ma, tapping a blue-ribboned box. "The size of that place! They had a golden elevator! It was marvelous."

"Did your stomach feel funny?" Dicta giggled.

"Is it true that your gravity gets thrown off when you go down an elevator shaft?" Casper asked.

"Which one belongs to me?" Vernon asked, reaching for a thick, book-shaped parcel.

Mr. Ward proceeded to distribute the packages, but he did not place the book-shaped gift in Vernon's hands. Instead, he gave it to Norvia. The parcel felt cold and smooth and exciting in her perspiring palms.

Dicta, being the youngest and least patient of the family, opened her box first. She untied the pink ribbon, stroked it as if she were petting Peggy, and announced, "I'm going to keep it forever and ever till death do us part." But the ribbon fell to the floor as soon as Dicta opened the box, for between folds of tissue paper lay an elaborate Japanese fan. "I'm a queen!" she declared, batting her eyelashes as she waved her fan. "A coquettish queen. The whole kingdom is madly in love with me."

Elton and Casper each received jackknives, horrifyingly sharp silver blades with pearl handles. "I could stave off any rapscallion with this," said Casper, brandishing his knife with a flourish. "I bet I could win the European war all by myself."

Vernon's gift was a few selections of sheet music—pages dotted with dancing black symbols. The "William Tell Overture," Mendelssohn's "Spring Song," "Chopin's Funeral March." "Thank you, these will be quite…" The delighted words died on Vernon's lips as he saw the last book of sheet music in the box: "When the Midnight Choo-Choo Leaves for Alabam'."

"I chose that one for you," said Ma, leaning forward. "Your father's been telling me how well you play the piano. I'm looking forward to hearing it."

"Thank you," Vernon repeated, but the warmth had faded from his words.

Norvia had saved her present for last—partially because she didn't know how to accept it. She wouldn't read this book, whatever it was. The feel of it in her hands brought back one of her worst memories from three years before: when Pa had caught Elton reading a biography of Benjamin Franklin when he was supposed to be doing his chores.

"Why do you want to read books?" She could still hear Pa's voice demanding, contempt lacing his thick Swedish accent. "What will you ever do with them? You're filling your head with things you don't have the need to know."

Elton had tried to defend himself, and the book. "I like reading and learning things—we do it in school."

"School," Pa had sneered, "is a waste of your time. You are the son of a poor man…. You are an Indian. What future is there for you in education? What hope is there of getting a good job?"

That was the extent of her memory of the conversation—along with the way Elton had closed his eyes against the onslaught of hurtfulness and put the book away. She knew that he had never again picked up another book for pleasure. He simply read schoolbooks until he finished the eighth grade, and that was all. It had been a challenge for Ma to convince Pa to allow the boys even that much schooling.

Since that day, Norvia had never read any books that weren't required for school, either—even though she had longed to discover the stories within their fascinating covers. Magazine stories were all right, but novels—never. She had always dreaded receiving that same lecture from Pa. She simply could not have taken it without her heart breaking in half. And now, despite the fact that the book in her hands brought all her literary longings to the surface, she just *couldn't* read it.

But I could open it, at least, to be gracious, thought Norvia, since all eyes were on her.

She lifted the lid of the box to reveal a brown hardbound book— *Patty Fairfield* by Carolyn Wells. A novel. The cover depicted a quaint house with smoke curling into the sky—a house that almost resembled this one.

"Thank you," Norvia whispered.

"I hope you like it," said Mr. Ward gently. "I thought you would enjoy a book, but your mother seemed to think you didn't care for novels."

"It was just that . . . Pa didn't think—" Norvia started, chokingly.

"—Anders said books were 'frivolous,'" Ma broke in. "But don't worry about that now, Norvia."

Did she dare read it?

Pa was gone. He was in Flint now, and there was only Ma and Mr. Ward.

The novel felt perfect in Norvia's hands; it enticed her with a wonderful new-book smell and thick, creamy pages. She cracked open the cover and the first lines jumped out at her: *"How old are you, Patty?" asked her father, abruptly. "Fourteen, Papa,—why?"*

She was the same age as Patty Fairfield! Norvia closed the book slowly, savoring the feeling of its luxurious pages.

"Is something wrong?" asked Mr. Ward.

"Oh. No! Thank you—thank you very much." Norvia's voice was a soft squeak of pleasure. Perhaps she *would* read it—read about Patty Fairfield and her papa, who doubtlessly encouraged her to read books.

Norvia sat on the velvet settee and read *Patty Fairfield* until it was time for supper. It was a brilliant diversion, especially so because she wouldn't have to speak to Mr. Ward or Vernon while lost in her brand-new book. She had just arrived at a fascinating scene in which Patty was meeting her disagreeable cousin Ethelyn when Ma called them to the table.

Supper was odd. Mr. Ward asked them all to join hands while he prayed—a strange ritual to which they reluctantly surrendered. Norvia ended up between Vernon and Dicta; Vernon's hand was clammier than her own.

Mr. Ward's prayer was different from the one Old Mary said, and since they were all holding hands, they couldn't cross themselves as they always did. Elton still crossed himself at the end anyway, and Norvia wondered if she ought to follow his direction—until Ma gave Elton an almost disapproving look.

"Why do you pray different?" asked Dicta. "Is it because you're a Presbyterian? We were raised Catholic. That's why my name is Mary Benedicta, the most sacred name in all of Catholicism."

"Yes, we are Presbyterians, and we do things differently," said Vernon in that same condescending tone that Norvia despised.

But Dicta wasn't finished yet. "Mr. Ward, what will we call you now?" she asked out of the blue. "We can't call you Pa because we already have a pa."

Mr. Ward glanced from Ma to Dicta and back again. "Well, what would you like to call me?" he asked.

What other option is there, besides calling him Mr. Ward? Norvia thought in horror. She would never, in a billion centuries, think of him as her father.

"We could call you Daddy," suggested Dicta, looking virtuous.

"No, you will call him Uncle Virgil," Ma corrected. "That is the only proper thing."

Elton and Norvia's eyes met across the table in mutual displeasure.

"Uncle Virgil," said Dicta, with clear enunciation. "*Un*-cle *Vir*-gil. Un-*cle* Vir-*gil*."

Norvia attempted to conjure up mental images of a calming Beaver Island landscape—of high school—of Marguerite's cheery dining room—anything to take her mind off this unbearable conversation.

"And Vernon must call me Aunt Angélique," Ma continued, giving Vernon's hand a pat. He recoiled from her touch, and Ma's face fell.

After supper, the family sat around in the parlor under the watchful eyes of Celestia Ward. Was it just Norvia's imagination, or did Celestia have a new expression of disdain on her face?

Ma's gaze kept flickering to her haughty predecessor. Elton cracked his knuckles half a dozen times. Dicta and Casper began pointing at a bizarre clay statue on the piano and giggling. Norvia felt tense—so very tense she began tingling. First her smallest fingers, then her hands and forearms, then her nose, then her cheeks, as if her whole body was starting to fall asleep in order to get away from this horrible atmosphere and that portrait of the queenly figure above the fireplace.

"I am going to bed," Vernon announced. "I should not have eaten Mrs. Ward's cake."

Ma smiled. "*Aunt Angélique*, remember," she reminded him. "Didn't you like the cake?"

"It was delicious; rather, I have a weak digestive system," he said, looking distant and almost pitiful. "I cannot consume rich food."

"He means his stomach hurts," translated Dicta, already an authority on Vernon's oddities.

"I think that's a good idea, son," said Mr. Ward—no, *Uncle Virgil*. "You'll feel better once you lie down."

He sighed a little as Vernon hurried off. Was he already regretting this hasty marriage?

"In fact, why don't all of you head to bed?" suggested Uncle Virgil. "You'll need some time to settle in. Norvia, Benedicta," he said, addressing his stepdaughters in a formal tone, "your bedroom is the white one at the top of the stairs. My Julia and Marguerite used to sleep there before they were married. Elton, Casper, I've moved some beds for you into Vernon's room."

"There's an extra bedroom, of course, but it's for guests," said Ma, who had evidently already taken inventory of the rooms and catalogued their possible uses. "You boys will have to share."

Uncle Virgil gave Elton and Casper an apologetic glance. "It's a bit of a tight squeeze, but I hope it'll be all right."

"I'm sure it will," said Elton stiffly, rising from the sofa.

All of them dashed for the stairs.

"Say, what's that room?" asked Casper abruptly, yanking on Vernon's sleeve to get his attention. Norvia followed Casper's pointed finger to a closed door at the far end of the foyer.

Vernon gave the door a cursory glance. "That is my father's study."

"Why's the door shut?"

"He always keeps it closed," said Vernon, before turning and climbing the staircase.

Norvia half expected Casper to barge right through the door, but perhaps he assumed it would be just a bit too presumptuous on their first day in the house.

"My theory," Casper announced in a whisper, "is that he keeps ancient talismans in it. That statue on the piano—that was one of them!"

Norvia was fairly certain it was just a regular study with a multitude of papers and a desk, but then, one never did know for sure. She followed the others upstairs.

The white bedroom proved to be the house's greatest treasure of all. Cozy eaves, blue-and-white floral wallpaper, seascape paintings on the walls. How charming—how *elegant!* Norvia felt a rush of satisfaction despite the musty, closed-up scent that pervaded the room.

For a time, she basked in the sumptuousness of her brand-new bed, while Dicta bounced and giggled in the opposite bed. She *did* feel like a proper heroine in this sea-inspired haven, in this room that was larger than any bedroom she'd ever slept in before. Ma came in to say good night, a glow of delight still on her face, which made Norvia glad in spite of herself.

But as she lay there trying to relax and enjoy the room, she remembered with discomfort that this bed had been either Marguerite's or Julia's, once upon a time. Suppose Uncle Virgil had not washed the sheets since they had slept there? Maybe one of them had some terrible disease at one point, a digestive disease like Vernon's, and now Norvia would catch it. Marguerite seemed healthy, of course, but who knew about Julia? She tried in desperation to think of something else.

Dicta was still bouncing on her new bed, singing at the top of her lungs. *"A bed for Dicta, a bed for a queen, a bed for Dicta, a bed that's a dream, a room for Dicta, a room for she, a room for Dicta, a room for me.* Isn't it scrumptious, Norvie?"

Norvia squeezed her eyes shut. She heard the creaking of bedframes and the squeaking of mattress springs as her brothers got into their new cots in the next room. Casper was joking, making up dialogue for the people in the painting on their bedroom wall. Eventually they quieted down, and Elton knocked on the wall and called good night. Casper echoed his sentiments, but Vernon remained silent. He was probably already asleep, what with his delicate stomach and all.

"That picture of Uncle Virgil's wife over the fireplace is kind of spooky, don't you think?" asked Dicta.

Norvia considered. "She looks like—like she's staring at you."

Dicta pulled her quilt up to her chin and stared at the ceiling. "I remember once Aunt Belle told me about this book called *Jane Eyre*, where this man's wife was supposed to be dead, but she was really a madwoman locked in the attic. Do you suppose that's where Uncle Virgil's wife *really* is?" she whispered, pointing upward.

A chill ran through Norvia's body. "*Dicta!*" she hissed. "This house doesn't even have an attic!"

"Maybe she's locked in the Study of Secrecy. Or maybe she's a ghost!" Dicta continued, a glint of mischief in her expressive eyes. "Maybe when all the lights go off, her ghost will slip out of the portrait and wander through the house, tucking in any children she—"

"*Stop it*, Dicta. Go to sleep."

Dicta gave one last giggle and finally grew silent. Norvia tried to convince her racing heart to calm down. Dicta's suggestions unnerved her, and the mental image of a spook in this strange new house gave her unreasonable shivers. She could vividly picture that creepy woman sort of gliding down the hallway. . . .

Stop! Just stop thinking about it.

The harder Norvia tried to push the unhappy thoughts away, the faster they rushed forward, and with a greater vengeance. Ghosts. Stepsiblings. Secrets. Living with the Wards might be absolutely dreadful—who could tell? If only she could go back to Beaver Island. . . .

What am I going to do? Utter desolation knocked on the door of Norvia's heart, and she could do nothing but lie in her beautiful new room and cry. Even her imagination deserted her, and she could not think of any consoling imagery from her distant childhood. She began to cry as softly as she could, so Dicta would not hear and call Ma, prompting an investigation. But she discovered it was nearly impossible to cry quietly, so she stifled her sobs as soon as she could.

She heard footsteps, soft ones, creeping toward her door. A ghost? *Don't be silly*, she scolded herself. The door creaked open, and Ma stood there, her expression much different now.

"Norvia, are you all right?"

How did Ma know? But then mothers always seemed to know such things instinctively.

"Yes," said Norvia, wiping her tears on the edge of the quilt.

"I know it's hard—I know," said Ma, sympathy clouding her eyes. She sat on the end of Norvia's bed. "But this is going to be a wonderful new beginning for all of us. It will do you good to have a father again—a caring father—and I know I can make Virgil and his son happy." Although her smile was determined to be cheerful, Norvia noticed a fleck of worry on her mother's face. "At least, I hope I can," Ma added.

Norvia's voice sounded more confident than she felt. "Of course you'll make them happy! And you're prettier than his first wife, anyway," she added with a giggle.

Ma laughed, too, and Norvia felt a bit of a weight roll off her chest. After Ma said good night and left, Norvia's thoughts turned back toward this opulent home, this brand-new backdrop for her life. As much as she hated to admit it, this was the perfect place for a budding heroine; a girl destined for high school and—and *romance*, just like Ma had found. It was a grand, elegant home befitting of a pretty, well-liked young woman. Like Marguerite! Like Patty Fairfield!

Starting to feel calm, Norvia drifted off to sleep.

CHAPTER SIX
GOSSIP AND A VICTORY

In the morning, Norvia awoke to filtering piano music, light and lilting and jovial. The notes drifted up the stairs and down the hall, filling the house with unsought joy. For a moment, she felt strange, opening her eyes to a sunlit, alien room, but her gaze fell upon the seascape painting on the opposite wall, and she found her heart lifted to match the vibrant music.

She dressed as quickly as she could and slipped downstairs to find Vernon playing away, his fingertips alighting like butterflies on the ivory keys. He wasn't looking at sheet music; instead, his eyes were fixed on a picture of his mother. Not the portrait above the mantel, but a bluish snapshot of Celestia Ward posed with a bicycle, wearing bloomers and flashing a coy smile. Norvia thought that it was a rather daring photo to put right on the piano top for the entire universe to see, but she did not say so.

"Why are you staring at her?" Vernon asked, without halting the waltzing melody.

"She was—very pretty," said Norvia, grasping at the first compliment available. (Of course, she did not add that Ma was prettier.)

"My sisters take after her in appearance, but I inherited her affinity for music and literature."

Norvia had no idea what her response was supposed to be. There was no sheet music on the rack, which gave her an inspiration. "What song are you playing?" she ventured, hoping to divert the subject from the all-important Celestia.

"*Grand valse brillante in E-flat major.* Chopin. 1834."

"It's—very pretty, too," stammered Norvia.

"Thank you," said Vernon, still without looking at her.

Irritation rose inside Norvia. He could at least glance at her! But no, he kept his eyes transfixed on Celestia. Did he intend to ignore her—and all of them—forever?

With a sudden flourish, Vernon concluded his Chopin and darted from the room like a frightened rabbit. Such a strange boy!

At breakfast, Dicta was her usual fluttery self, although everyone else was silent. "My new room is the prettiest room in the whole wide world," she chatted. "Prettier than Gilma's, even though she has a vanity with pink bows on the cloth. But my room just doesn't *feel* like my room without my little glass cat or my patchwork quilt. My *Beaver Island* patchwork quilt," Dicta added. "Can we put it back on my bed, Ma?"

"Oh, we'll have to do some redecorating in this house," said Ma, smiling at her new husband. "Right now, it's unmistakably a bachelor's residence, and I'll consider it a challenge to work in some femininity."

Vernon looked up from his bowl of Post Toasties cereal. "You can't redecorate!" he exclaimed.

Uncle Virgil spoke up in a determined voice. "Why don't we all go to church this morning? I would like to acquaint you with the Presbyterian church that my children and I attend. I think you'll enjoy the services."

A deft change of subject, Norvia observed—but then the full realization of his words toppled down upon her. Attending a different church! The idea had never even occurred to her. Next he would want them to change their surname to "Ward."

"Of course," said Ma. "That sounds wonderful." But her voice sounded somewhat doubtful.

The Presbyterian church was, quite simply, the most frightening place Norvia had ever seen. (Well, except for the chemical plant where

57

Pa used to work with methane gas and combustion chambers after he stopped sailing. But this came second.) Unlike the modest-sized Catholic church she had attended for years, this sprawling, towered structure was dark, with arched stained-glass windows. It was, in a phrase, ecclesiastically imposing.

"It looks spooky," said Dicta, and her hand clasped Norvia's. "Like ghosts should come out of the windows."

"There are no such things as ghosts," Norvia chided, but a chill shuttled down her back nonetheless. The image of Celestia Ward floating down the hallway still upset her.

A domed ceiling and a massive pipe organ characterized the inside of the church, which was packed with people—unfamiliar faces, mostly; a few were semi-recognizable, but there was no one comforting. Norvia wished she was sitting through a sermon given by Father Leary from Beaver Island, or—at the very least—Father McKay from their old church.

"The text I have chosen this morning is from the Book of Matthew," said the minister. Unlike Father McKay, this mustachioed man had kind eyes, and his square face almost resembled Pa's. "The words *seek and ye shall find* have become so ubiquitous that we don't often stop to dwell on what they actually mean. . . ."

My, but there are lots of people here! Norvia began to count. Twenty in front, at least, just on her side of the room, and probably thirty in back—maybe *forty*.

"Norvia, sit still," Ma hissed.

Norvia snapped her head back to attention but found her eyes still wandering the room. People looked bored. One elderly gentleman toward the front was actually falling asleep, and his wife kept poking him. A little boy was being pacified with peppermints and gumdrops from a benevolent older woman beside him. Dicta began rocking a loose tooth back and forth, forth and back. Casper was staring at the ceiling, studying the architecture.

Still the minister spoke, and Norvia couldn't understand half the words in his expansive vocabulary.

"Therefore, if you do not search for joy, peace, and security, you will never attain them," concluded the minister. "You cannot wait for those fruits to fall into your lap."

That was a sour note, thought Norvia. *Why couldn't the minister say something positive and uplifting at the end of his sermon? Oh, well. At least it was over.*

Norvia sucked in a large breath of fresh air when they emerged. The churchyard was trim, if not large or lush. How good it was to be outdoors again on a cool, sunny day!

But her joy evaporated with the realization that *other* churchgoers had stopped to mingle on the lawn as well. Hordes of them. All of them. Norvia slipped behind Elton.

Ma was carrying a white silk parasol—an extravagant gift from Pa five anniversaries ago, bought after he'd happened to win a few rounds of poker. "Here, girls, come under the shade with me. We don't want to get freckles, now, do we?"

Norvia did not really care whether she had freckles or not, and Dicta rather preferred them, but they didn't argue with their mother. The only snag was the parasol itself, which refused to open.

"Let me try it," said Elton.

"No, I can manage," Ma insisted, but she couldn't. She was still fiddling unsuccessfully when Uncle Virgil reached out to assist.

"Please, allow me," he offered, and in one swift motion, the parasol unfurled like the feathers of an ivory peacock. "Umbrellas enjoy being perverse, in my experience," he said. Oh, the way he looked at Ma! So caring and genuine and happy. Norvia wondered if anyone would ever look at her that way. Perhaps they truly *were* in love, Ma and Uncle Virgil.

Three women clustered around them—two older ladies and one young woman who smiled in an odd way at Uncle Virgil.

"Ladies, I would like to introduce you to my new wife, Angélique," said Uncle Virgil, who removed his hat with courtesy. "And these are her children. Angélique, this is Mrs. Jeremy Fox, Mrs. Horace Curtis, and Miss Lila Morton."

Ma extended a white-gloved hand. "It's a pleasure."

"Oh, the pleasure is mutual," said Mrs. Fox, gazing at Ma with scrutinizing eyes.

"Miss Morton came to tea once. She sat on my sheet music," Vernon whispered to Norvia. "I know I oughtn't to have left it on the sofa, but..." His voice trailed off. Norvia was surprised he would confide in her this way.

"This is *quite* the surprise," said Miss Lila Morton, flashing Uncle Virgil a dazzling but oddly manufactured smile. "My dear Virgil, if I'd known you were on the market, I'd have had a stab at you myself."

Both Ma and Uncle Virgil laughed. Norvia wondered if either of them actually found her words funny.

"Aren't you Angélique *Nelson?*" Mrs. Curtis inquired, adjusting her pince-nez to see with more clarity. "Oh yes, of course. I remember hearing something of your...situation."

Ma's face fell, and she glanced at Uncle Virgil as if for support.

"Ladies," said Uncle Virgil again, nodding at the women before leading Ma away. The children followed, but Norvia hung back for a moment, unable to stop herself from listening to the women as they gathered in a gossipy circle.

"I truly cannot fathom his marrying a divorcée," said Mrs. Curtis, "*especially* after seven years of mourning. It's unseemly."

Mrs. Fox agreed. "And so sudden...I heard they were married by Judge Walters. No proper ceremony at all!"

"What else can you expect from a woman like *that?*" asked Miss Morton, shrugging her narrow shoulders. "*I* feel terrible for Celestia's son. What a blow this must be to him—the sacred memory of his poor mother desecrated in such a way...."

"Well," said Mrs. Curtis with a sniff, "I certainly won't be calling on any of the Wards from now on, let me tell you that."

A turmoil of anger, worry, and doubt swirled inside Norvia. Just like last night, every time she tried to push unhappy thoughts aside, they kept returning, stronger and stronger. How could she endure it if everyone in town was gossiping about her family?

As soon as she reached home, Norvia sat on the parlor sofa to read *Patty Fairfield*—first making sure there was no sheet music under her—and allowed the story to sweep her away to a land of enchantment, a land far removed from the Presbyterian church. At first, she feared that reading might be too difficult with so many people around, but Uncle Virgil read his Bible peacefully in a nearby chair, and Vernon's harp-playing wasn't too distracting. But she had only finished a few chapters when Dicta strolled in and sat on the rug near Uncle Virgil's chair.

"Uncle Virgil, how close is this house to my new school?" she asked.

A stab of pain pierced Norvia's heart. Dicta and Casper would be going back to grammar school next week. What would happen if she didn't attend high school? She would be stuck in this house with no amusements, only endless chores, for there would be no Marys to do most of the work. They had often turned down her offers of assistance because they couldn't "let their bones turn brittle with disuse." But here she might be expected to toil about in endless choredom (which wasn't an actual word, Norvia knew), especially with the redecorating Ma wanted to do. . . .

"Actually, the school you'll be attending is just at the end of the street," said Uncle Virgil, closing his Bible. "That big square building with all the birch trees. It was built last year."

Elton was sitting at the antique secretary in the corner, writing numbers in his personal ledger. (He was a very careful accountant when it came to his wages.) Now his eyebrows knit together. "The kids aren't going back to the same school?" he asked. "Their old one?"

Uncle Virgil reassured him. "This school will be much closer for them. In fact, you can see it from here—"

"Are you *positive* it's not too far for me to walk?" persisted Dicta, holding out her left leg. "I'm quite lame, you know, Uncle."

Norvia buried her face in her book.

"What's the school like? I bet it's awful," said Casper, turning to Vernon.

"I would not know," Vernon said. "I have never attended school, what with my ill health. Papa and Marguerite have always taught me at home."

Dicta lolled on the carpet. "So you don't know anything? Do you know multiplication tables? *I* do. I know all the times tables by heart. And I'm the best speller in Boyne City. *I* can even spell *hippopotamus* backward. It's s-u-m-a-t-o-p-o-p-p-i-h.'"

"How useful. If only I had been publicly educated," said Vernon with a dry smile.

Elton closed his ledger with a firm *thunk*. "Sir, my mother tells me you are in favor of women's rights. Do you approve of higher education for girls?"

Norvia's wits deserted her.

Elton taking a stand like this! Bearding the lion in his parlor! Her breath caught in her ribs like a caged bird.

Uncle Virgil glanced around the room for a moment, taking stock of each expression around him. "I believe women have as much right to be educated as men, if they wish," he said firmly. "What's on your mind, son?"

Elton hesitated. "Perhaps we could speak in private," he said, with all the grace and poise of a gentleman. Where had he acquired these manners, this way of speaking? Maybe he'd been listening to Vernon.

"Certainly," said Uncle Virgil. "Let's go into my study."

Norvia, Casper, and Dicta proceeded to watch with eager anticipation as Elton was ushered into the Study of Secrecy. Uncle Virgil left the door ajar, and the three of them clustered close. One couldn't see much through such a thin sliver, but they tried.

"My father didn't allow my older brother and me to attend school past the eighth grade," Elton began with complete honesty. Norvia's knees shook. "He thought high school was a waste of time, seeing how we'd probably end up laborers anyway. And I guess maybe he was right. But I'd like my sister to have a good education. She's very bright, sir, and she likes learning."

Norvia's cheeks felt warm. Elton was too kind to her. She didn't deserve this praise, and she *didn't* enjoy learning outside of tidy arithmetic lessons and English. Did she?

"She has told you she wishes to go to high school?" asked Uncle Virgil.

"She's mentioned it a few times. She's not complaining," said Elton. "But she'd like it. Our father wouldn't have let her, but I am hoping that you'll feel differently. I—I don't want my sister to have to settle for a factory job like mine, or some other position where she'd be unhappy."

Uncle Virgil's voice was gentle. "What makes you think your sister will have to work for a living? I keep a job myself, and my children and I have always lived comfortably. And in any event, she'll be getting married herself one day, and then—"

"I don't know about that, sir," Elton broke in. "With my mother and father, and what happened—I just don't know. I want her to have a good education, so she can make a nice life for herself."

Norvia felt slightly dizzy now. Images of the three ladies at church floated into her mind.

"I see," said Uncle Virgil, after a pause. "Well, my daughter Marguerite attended high school, as did my older girl. Julia didn't wish to finish, but Margie graduated from Boyne City High School just a few years—"

"*Ah-choo!*" Dicta sneezed.

A terrible silence followed. Then Uncle Virgil closed the door of his study, leaving Norvia's fate unknown.

"Why'd you do that?" Casper moaned. "I want to hear if Norvia's going to school!"

"I can't control what my nose does!" Dicta snapped.

A few desperate minutes passed. Norvia grew more and more anxious to know what they were speaking of behind those closed doors, and she paced back and forth, crossing her fingers and inhaling unevenly.

Vernon finally left the parlor to investigate. He stood in the foyer, staring at them with his dark, inquisitive eyes.

"You act as if your life depends on what my father decides," he said incredulously.

Well, doesn't it? But Norvia would not dignify his remark with a response. She sat down on the lower steps of the staircase and knit her hands together.

Vernon put his ear to the keyhole, listening intently. "It doesn't sound as if they are talking about schooling," he said dubiously, standing upright again. "Why does school matter so much? I have never gone. I am alive."

"Perhaps for now, but you're very sickly," Dicta pointed out.

Vernon didn't laugh, although amazingly, his mouth looked as if it wanted to. "I only mean that even if you *don't* attend high school, I think you would be all right.... Surely you might adjust..."

To never being happy again. Norvia completed his unfinished words in her mind. Without high school, she would remain forever a nobody—worse, an outcast!—in the eyes of the world...and she would have to live with that same old feeling of shunned despair, not able to make her own happiness.

After what seemed like an hour, Elton emerged from the Study of Secrecy with a bewildered grin on his face.

"Well? What'd he say?" asked Norvia, leaping up and taking him by the arm.

"First, he said I could quit the factory," said Elton, still dazed. "He says he'll take over all the expenses of—well—of everything."

Of us, thought Norvia guiltily . . .

. . . but then Elton's words registered in her mind. *Quit the factory!*

She clasped his hand and squeezed it hard. "Oh! That's *wonderful*," she cried, delighting in his spreading smile.

"I told him he didn't have to," Elton continued, shaking his head in disbelief. "But he kept saying it was all right, that he was happy to handle the finances . . . and he asked me what I really wanted to do. He talks so sort of genuine—like he actually cares. So I told him. And now I'm going to see if old Mr. Redgrave still needs help on the farm. And . . ." Elton paused for effect, the boyish grin widening on his face. "He says you can start high school next week."

"*ELTON!*" An elated shriek of hysteria echoed in the wallpapered hallway, and Norvia threw her arms around her dear, kind brother, a champion of a noble cause.

"See, Nan, sometimes you just have to get up and do something," said Elton, winking at her.

Norvia barely heard him. Her mind was already whirling with blissful eagerness and firm resolve. She would attend high school, and it would fling open the doors of her new life as a stylish, happy heroine.

The lighthouse at St. James Harbor was a slim, graceful brick pillar standing proudly beside a white house with dark roofs. To Norvia, the light was a symbol of refuge, and she suspected her mother felt the same way.

But tonight, all she felt was a chill under her skin.

Ma led the way inside, hurrying up the spiral staircase, her skirts swishing. Norvia followed—Elton close behind—feeling intensely cramped within the narrow corkscrew.

When they reached the tiny circular upper level, where the lighthouse keeper kept his watch, Ma wasted no time. "Have you seen anything?" she asked him, her words tight. She was shivering in her shawl. "You haven't seen any distress signals?"

"Not a one," said Ernest Schmidt, taking a sip of his coffee. The keeper's thick German accent had a way of calming Norvia, perhaps because it was so similar to the Swedish lilt in Pa's voice. Mr. Schmidt's small daughter Olga sat beside him, her head on his shoulder. That was the sort of comfort Norvia longed for on this cold wintry night. She looked out at the dark horizon and wished it was *her* father who studied the sea and sky from this perch above the world, with the Fresnel lens spreading its crimson beams of mercy across the night waters.

When Norvia spoke, she frightened herself with the intensity of her voice. "Don't you think . . . Don't you think the ship should have been back by now, Mr. Schmidt?"

"Yes and no." He pulled out a map of the Great Lakes, wrinkled with age and coffee stains. "Look here at all these islands—this is where we are, of course." He tapped Beaver Island. "See? There are many places a ship could come into harbor, if she got off-course."

"But lots of islands means lots of places they could've gotten wrecked," Elton shot back. Norvia was shocked by the sudden tears in his eyes.

"Shh," said Ma, placing her mittened hands on his shoulders. "We don't know anything yet."

"That we don't," agreed Mr. Schmidt. "But if a ship is late, it doesn't mean she's foundered."

They lingered at the lighthouse for another few trifling minutes, watching, waiting, listening to nothing. Finally Ma said, "We won't take up any more of your time."

Norvia and Elton and their mother left behind the reassurance of the lighthouse and the sounds of the happy Schmidt children preparing for bed. A sprinkling of neighborhood lights guided them on the road toward home, up the path to the winsome pinprick on the dark hill that was their cottage. The distance was not really far—it only seemed so on cold, empty nights such as this.

Back at home, Grand-père was whittling away at a small block of wood as he sat before the familiar fire. Peggy the cat sat on the hearth, glowing-eyed, knowledgeable.

Norvia settled herself on the rag rug beside the cat. "Tell me about when I was born," she said quietly. At least the shadows of the room could never overtake the orange and yellow of the fire and the lamplight—never.

"Oh, dear! What a night!" said Ma, firmly hanging her scarf and coat on the corner hook. "It was cold and dark. We were having such a nasty blizzard."

Grand-père leaned close to Norvia's ear and whispered, "It wasn't quite a blizzard, but your poor, dear *maman* perceived it to be one...."

Ma pretended she had not heard this. "And then after you were born, around nine o'clock, all the snow and clouds cleared away and it was a beautifully starry night. I could see the stars from our window...."

Norvia was enraptured by this image. "Which stars?"

"Let me think," said Ma, hesitating. "Well, the moon was nearly full. I remember that."

"It was just beginning to wane," Grand-père corrected, a thoughtful look on his face. "There was the Wintermaker, too, I recall—*Biboonke-o-nini*. They used to say that he brings the cold weather."

"You remember more than I do," said Ma, flashing him a smile of amusement. "Perhaps the crane was out..."

Grand-père lit his pipe. "No, not the crane—that's in the summer. And the moon would have been too bright to see *Mishi-Biizhiw*, but *Ikwe'anang*—the Women's Star—that was out."

"The Women's Star?" Norvia repeated.

"Also known as Venus." Grand-père smiled.

Ma sat in a chair beside her father's, close to the comforting flames of the fire. "And then when Dicta was born, of course, Sister Benedicta happened to be visiting...."

Grand-père nodded. "And it was a good thing she was, too. *Très chanceux.*"

"Why?" Norvia asked, although she knew perfectly well. She'd heard the Marys discussing this before: how Ma had a difficult time delivering Dicta, and the capable visiting nun had known just what to do. So of course they decided to name Dicta after the Sister.

Ma did not answer, possibly because she felt such a story was unfit for children, and Grand-père wisely said nothing either, instead opting to change the subject. "The crane," he said thoughtfully, repeating the erroneous constellation Ma had mentioned. "You know there are different Ojibwe clans?"

"Oh, yes," said Norvia, "but tell me again."

"The Crane Clan is one of them. Another is the Reindeer Clan, of course—the one Migizi belonged to. It means that we value stories, and we bring people together, and we have grace, just as the reindeer do. But our gracefulness isn't on the outside—it is deep within us, how we treat people, how we approach life."

Value stories... bring people together... have grace... Norvia loved the sound of these inspiring words. She felt herself being lulled to sleep by the crackling fire and the sounds of the lake's waves, which had calmed to a soothing lap.

A gentle sea is a lullaby to a sailor's child. Norvia had heard this phrase passed around the island many times before, and she knew just how true it was. She closed her eyes.

Grand-père was singing now, ever so quietly. Norvia dimly recognized the words as her great-grandmother's Ojibwe song, left over from the days when her ancestors camped along the lakes every summer.

Agwaa'amaazo... She comes ashore singing....

Biidaasamishkaa... She comes in a boat....

Grand-père broke off. The song had evidently reminded him of something, for the storytelling look was on his face. "Once, long ago," he began, "a *memengwaa* led my great-great-grandmother's family to the perfect place to make their camp for the warm season. Did I ever tell you about it?"

He had, of course. But that didn't matter to Norvia. "Tell me again," she implored. And so he did.

CHAPTER SEVEN
OF REDECORATION AND READING

The next few days were a flurry of activity. Elton left the house whistling each morning. Butterflies chased each other around Norvia's stomach every time she thought of high school, but it was an exciting feeling. Ma quickly whipped up a few fashionable dresses for Norvia to wear to school, of which the cheerful blue sailor suit was Norvia's favorite. Ma had wheedled Uncle Virgil into giving her a corner of his Study of Secrecy for her sewing machine, and he'd also given her the money for new fabric. Ma spent hours making dresses for her daughters and shirts for her sons, and Norvia had never seen her mother look so pleased as when she finished each new piece.

Ma began to add her own touches to the Wards' house, placing little trinkets from home in various places. First she gave everything a thorough dusting, too, and then she got rid of the old damask drapes and hung white muslin and lace curtains. The photo of Celestia on the bicycle surreptitiously disappeared from the piano top.

But this light cleaning was nothing compared to what would come.

"My mother and grandmother are coming to help me redecorate the house today," said Ma one bright morning at breakfast. She poured a cup of coffee for Uncle Virgil and set it gently on the embroidered tablecloth before him. "We're going to put new wallpaper in the parlor and rearrange the furniture. The children can help."

Norvia recoiled at the sound of such goings-on. She wanted to make plans for high school, or reread *Patty Fairfield*, or play with Dicta—not shuffle foreign objects around this enormous house. But at least the Marys would be there. . . .

"You cannot rearrange the furniture," said Vernon, finally looking up. He hadn't even tasted his buttered toast—he'd only pulled off the crust. "If you move my pianoforte, the acoustics will be altered."

Uncle Virgil smiled at Ma. "You can move anything you like except Vernon's piano."

"And my mother's portrait," Vernon added in a whisper.

Stop arguing with Ma. Stop! Norvia silently ordered him. She didn't dare say the words aloud, but she couldn't listen to him another second. So she burrowed into her daydreams and pictured a Dashing Young Man, a proper hero, inviting her to waltz with him at a dance.

"Is something wrong, Norvia?" asked Uncle Virgil.

Pulled out of her reverie, Norvia answered him with a quick "no" and then drank her milk so she wouldn't have to say anything else.

"Norvie's *imagining* things," Dicta explained. "Things like knights in shining armor."

Too embarrassed to respond, Norvia drank another sip of milk and avoided looking at Uncle Virgil. Before this, she had been planning to work up enough courage to ask him for another book to read—one like *Patty Fairfield.* Oh, how glorious that story was! And how she longed for an experience like that all over again. But now she felt so embarrassed she didn't know how she could even look in Uncle Virgil's direction.

But then, unbidden, she could almost hear Grand-père's voice encouraging her.

We value stories, he had said so long ago.

Hadn't Grand-père said that their clan placed great significance on storytelling? Perhaps that was why she longed so much for books—and how would she ever get another book if she didn't say something?

Norvia swallowed hard and felt for her voice.

"Could I have another book, please?" she blurted, still not looking at her stepfather but instead at his blue-and-white china plate.

Uncle Virgil paused for a brief second before inquiring, "Are you enjoying the novel we brought back from Lansing?"

"Oh—yes," said Norvia, almost unable to process the question in her trepidation. "I finished it."

"I'll see what I can do," said Uncle Virgil pleasantly, tossing his napkin down on the table as he rose to leave.

After Elton and Uncle Virgil left for work and Casper dashed outside to search for grasshoppers—his latest insect obsession—the Marys arrived for their wallpapering party with sponges and pails and other supplies. Mr. Bingley watched them with curious eyes, thumping his tail against the floor.

"This won't take a bit long," said Old Mary with confidence.

"Ooh, can I try?" Dicta clamored.

Norvia watched as Ma rolled out the beautiful pale-pink paper covered in stripes and delicate flowers. "Isn't it marvelous? I found it at Bergy's—oh, I think it will do wonders for this room."

They pulled all the furniture to the middle of the parlor and then stood around, staring up at the faded walls. Norvia wondered how Vernon would react to seeing the old walls covered by fresh new paper. (He had vanished upstairs as soon as the Marys arrived.)

"Well, get out the paste! We do not have all day," said Old Mary, flapping her hands.

Just as Ma began to press the first piece of paper onto the wall, the doorbell trilled and Marguerite waltzed in, wearing a green dress and her usual engaging smile.

"Oh, goodness! Doesn't this look industrious? I admire your initiative." Marguerite stared up at the walls, too—her smile waning a little. "This will be very nice. It was all getting too old, I think," she added quickly. "You see, after Mama died, Papa didn't bother redecorating or changing anything, so this is exactly how the room has looked for eight years. Longer than that, even."

Norvia felt another twinge of sympathy for Marguerite. She must be sad to see her mother's favorite room redecorated. Was that how Vernon felt? But he seemed stubborn and resentful, not sad.

Marguerite picked up one of the framed pictures that Ma had discarded in an uneven stack. "This is my older sister, Julia," said Marguerite, turning the frame so that everyone could see. "You can't see it in this photograph, but she has the loveliest auburn hair. Just like Mama's." Celestia's portrait sat sideways on the floor.

Ma continued to smooth down the wrinkled new wallpaper. "I hope to meet Julia soon."

"She doesn't visit much anymore," said Marguerite, setting the picture of Julia back down. "She's hardly come at all since she married Walter. I think after Mama...well, she hasn't been herself for some time now." Her face brightened then, and she pulled a chair toward the wall and stepped up onto it. "Do you need any help? If I just stand on this chair, perhaps I can reach—"

"*Margie!*" Vernon's scandalized voice made Norvia jump. He rushed into the room, taking ahold of Marguerite's hand as she balanced atop the chair. "Papa says you're not to exert yourself."

Marguerite flashed an indulgent smile at the Marys and Ma. "He worries too much, really," she said, but she gripped Vernon's hand as she stepped down. "Thank you, Sir Lancelot."

With a flash of excitement, Norvia realized the reason behind Vernon's warning. How happy for Marguerite! How utterly splendid!

Unfortunately, Dicta was not so intuitive.

"Why can't she stand on the chair?" Dicta demanded, turning to Vernon.

Vernon fiddled with the cuff of his sleeve. "It's nothing," he said with a dismissive wave of his hand.

"Tell me! Tell me! Tell me!" Dicta insisted.

"It is...a rather...delicate situation," he said, his face coloring as he glanced at Marguerite.

"She's going to have a baby," Norvia hissed in Dicta's ear.

"Oooooh," said Dicta.

Norvia was glad that Marguerite looked amused instead of insulted. And while Marguerite did not climb on any more chairs, she did help to unroll the wallpaper in a most efficient manner. Casper came in partway through the process and produced his terrifying new knife.

"Need me to cut off any paper for you?" he offered, slicing the air with his blade. "If so, I can offer my services to save the day."

"Do not kill yourself, boy," Old Mary warned. "The world may need more heroes, but we don't need any more dead fools."

Ma laughed. "I think we have the situation well in hand."

After a long interim of difficult work, Norvia stepped back to admire their progress. Marguerite stood beside her and appraised the same view.

"I think it looks brilliant," she declared, with a smile that was somehow both genuine and fragile.

Norvia summoned up a few ounces of courage. There was something about Marguerite that made her want to be friends, despite herself. "I'm going to high school," she confided quietly, a rush of exhilaration heating her cheeks.

Marguerite nodded at her with shining eyes. "I think that's a splendid idea," she said, as if Norvia had decided this life-altering course all for herself. "You'll love it—I adored my time at BCHS. That's where I met Jim, my handsome graduate." She laughed. "But there's so much they don't tell you—things you're simply expected to understand. Let me help. You'll begin the school year with a meeting at Assembly Hall, with old Mr. Holthrope leading the way." Marguerite giggled like a child. "He's the principal and very hard of hearing. You'll love the Social Room—I did. And English with Miss Patterson! Oh, there are *so* many things to learn!"

It was meant kindly, she knew, but actually it was rather annoying, Norvia discovered, to hear Marguerite carry on about the school this way. Now, experiencing those things for herself would be spoiled, because Marguerite had done them first and was explaining them all in great detail. But she did not say this.

"That's good to know," said Norvia, several times.

Ma had just (reluctantly) returned the portrait of Celestia to its place of honor, and Marguerite fixed her gaze on it. "I've always loved that painting of my mother, but it doesn't half do her justice," she murmured. "Mama was an angel, and her face reflected so much light and joy. Life wasn't easy for her," she added, glancing back at Norvia. "She had a hard time of it when her own mother died. But nothing deterred her, really—at least that I know of. She went to a women's college in the east, and she traveled abroad, and *oh!* When she came back to the Middle West, all the boys were crazy about her!"

Norvia could not hold back a smile. "Really?" she said, wishing she could glean a clue as to why the boys liked Celestia.

"Oh, yes, because she was so glamorous and mysterious, flinging around foreign phrases and wearing the most fashionable clothes. Papa once said she just had a 'way' of talking to men that intrigued them. Say," said Marguerite suddenly, as if a brilliant idea had just occurred to her. "I know what we should do. I haven't been to Kerry's for an ice cream soda in ages. What if we all go tomorrow? You and your siblings and me and Vern. Wouldn't that be a fun outing?"

Norvia hesitated, waffling between yes and no. Ice cream sodas were a rare treat, of course, and a day in town would be a refreshing escape from this house—but did she really wish to spend so much time with her stepsiblings?

We bring people together, Grand-père had told her, *with grace.*

She couldn't seem to shake his words of wisdom from her head, She had always felt obligated to honor him whenever his guidance came to mind.

"Of course," said Norvia cheerfully, hoping that her acting skills were convincing enough.

The papering job took up most of the morning, and it took all after-noon to relocate the furniture to more tasteful positions. Long after Marguerite and the Marys went home and Uncle Virgil and Elton returned from work, Ma kept on working, scrubbing windows and rearranging chairs and sweeping the floor. Norvia helped wherever she could, especially with putting away Celestia's souvenirs from all over the globe.

Only three tall stacks of books remained—books that Ma had taken off a lovely oak shelf she was wiping down. Norvia took the chance to have a good look at them. Several were glorious novels with fascinating titles, a few of them gold-edged. Norvia longed to hold them, to caress their pages.

"Those are mine," said Vernon, pointing an accusing finger.

"Well, why don't you put them in your room?" Ma suggested. "I don't care for the appearance of books in this sort of setting."

"But they've always been here," Vernon insisted.

By now a little crowd had gathered around them: Casper, Dicta, and Uncle Virgil. "Golly!" Casper whistled. "Where'd you get so many books?"

"I never wish to run out of reading material," said Vernon, selecting a copy of *Great Expectations* by Charles Dickens from one of the stacks. Mr. Bingley licked the edges of its pages until Vernon made him stop.

"These books all belong to you?" Dicta exclaimed, running jelly-stained fingertips along their spines.

"Of course," said Vernon, regarding his new stepsiblings as if they came from a peculiar planet devoid of literature. He brushed Dicta's fingers away from the books. "I have a vast collection of books in my home library. I've noticed that you don't."

How dare he make fun of their lack of literature! *He* had never had to work, or launder, or cook, or do anything else—he had never wanted, he had never *worked*!

And yet...Norvia knew she should be angry, but she only felt a spreading sense of curiosity as Vernon sorted through his beloved volumes. The next book he pulled out was *The Hound of the Baskervilles* by Sir Arthur Conan Doyle. "This is a Sherlock Holmes story," Vernon explained, noting their intrigued expressions. "Have any of you read *A Scandal in Bohemia*?"

That sounded rather...scandalous. "No," said Norvia, sitting up taller.

"Incomparable wit, Doyle." Vernon removed another volume, this one with a well-creased spine: *Do and Dare: A Brave Boy's Fight for Fortune.* "Horatio is an old friend of mine," he said with great affection.

Ma sounded impatient. "I understand you like your books, dear, but why don't you move them somewhere else?"

"I must sort them before I can decide where," declared Vernon.

Other selections in his library included a Bible (which contained at least fifty bookmarks), *Ivanhoe* by Sir Walter Scott, *Around the World in Eighty Days*, and a compilation of Tennyson's poetry.

"This one," said Vernon, holding up the poetry book, "belonged to my mother."

Casper flipped through *Ivanhoe* and, upon finding no illustrations, tossed it back onto the stack. "What'd she die of?" he asked.

"Casper!" Ma cried. "Don't say such things!"

Vernon blinked. "She was fragile, like I am, constitutionally speaking." From his vagueness, Norvia wondered if he even knew the cause of his mother's death. She glanced at Uncle Virgil, whose face was drawn and blank.

"Ooh, what's this?" asked Dicta, pulling out a small, tantalizing black notebook from one of the stacks.

"Stop touching my things!" Vernon grabbed the notebook from her. "Is it too much to ask that you all leave me to myself?"

"Fine! Who cares?" Norvia spat out, unable to think of anything better to say. She, Casper, and Dicta all scattered from the parlor, and

Norvia stomped upstairs, making as much noise as possible and feeling justified in it. Why did her stepbrother have to be so petulant and bossy? Yet, when she reached her bedroom, banged the door shut, and collapsed on the bed in a heap of disgruntlement, she felt only regret.

Only a few minutes had passed when Uncle Virgil called up the stairs.

"Norvia, would you come down here a moment, please?"

Norvia's stomach twisted in knots. Was he angry with her for snapping at Vernon? She shouldn't have been so harsh. What would Uncle Virgil say?

He was waiting for her in the foyer, under the glittering chandelier. He carried a stack of books, some thick and tightly bound, some thin as pamphlets—perhaps some of Vernon's precious volumes. Casper stood beside him with a wary look on his face.

"I was just wondering," said Uncle Virgil, "if you two would like to read some books."

Casper's eyes lit up, but he said nothing—as if he was afraid to speak. Norvia understood completely, as she felt the same way. She hadn't expected this at all.

Uncle Virgil blew on the stack to clear away a layer of dust. "Here you are, Casper. These are stories about boys your age, and biographies of famous men. Books about nature. Some about the discoveries of comets and constellations. One or two on automobiles. I think you'll enjoy them."

"Really?" Casper blurted, his eyes fixed on the books. "I mean... You don't mind if I read them, sir?"

"No, I don't mind," Uncle Virgil replied with a smile.

Casper let out a low whistle. "Thank you! This is so swell—"

Ma stepped into the foyer as soon as she heard a word of slang. "Don't say *swell*," she reprimanded.

"It's grand, then," said Casper, glowing.

Norvia stood for a moment, staring at the books—hoping—

"Come into my study," Uncle Virgil invited, and Norvia felt another thrill. *The Study of Secrecy!*

Norvia followed her stepfather into his oak-doored den, fully prepared for darkness and dust. Indeed, a musty, closed-up scent greeted her nose, the same scent that was so prevalent in her new bedroom.

Uncle Virgil flicked on a lamp in the corner—a magnificent lamp with crystals hanging from its shade—and the room bloomed with a cozy glow, revealing an entire wall of books.

Hundreds of books!

Norvia couldn't hold back a gasp of surprise at the treasure trove of stories.

Uncle Virgil smiled with immense pleasure. "This is my collection, as you can see. It's rather nice, isn't it? Come over here." He led Norvia to a tall bookcase stuffed with books of all shapes, sizes, and colors. He pointed to two particular shelves: "These belonged to my daughters. And," he said, stopping to draw in a bit of a deep breath, "some belonged to my late wife."

"Can I," Norvia began—then caught herself. "I mean, *may* I read them?" she asked, her voice just above a whisper.

"Of course," said Uncle Virgil.

Norvia gathered the books into her arms, one by one, reading the titles as she stacked. *Little Women. Anne of Green Gables* and *Anne of Avonlea. What Katy Did. Emma. Rebecca of Sunnybrook Farm. The Secret Garden. The Little Girl Next Door. Under the Lilacs. Daddy-Long-Legs. Dandelion Cottage. Clover.* Half a dozen *Patty* sequels. *Pollyanna. An Old-Fashioned Girl. A Little Princess. The Story Girl.*

"Oh—thank you," she breathed.

Norvia carried them upstairs with great reverence, as if she were transporting precious jewels. She arranged the novels on her bedspread, so she could look at each cover and revel in its individual glory.

"*I get to read them all,*" she said to no one in particular—and then let out a spontaneous squeal of joy.

CHAPTER EIGHT
IN WHICH NORVIA LOSES A FRIEND
AND FINDS A STAR

"'A thing of beauty is a joy forever,'" Marguerite quoted blithely as they walked down the sunny sidewalk leading to Kerry's Restaurant and Soda Parlor. It was one of those too-good-to-be-true mornings, with a sky so blue it crowded out the clouds, and sunshine that was warm but not overpowering. Norvia almost felt like skipping along the sidewalk, she felt so delighted with her life and its sudden bookishness. She had already started reading *Patty at Home.*

Marguerite was wearing her most stylish navy-blue coat with a white collar. Norvia suspected that the reason for the coat—which she did not need in early September—was a way to be discreet about her coming baby, as it was a bit oversized. But the coat didn't make Marguerite frumpy, as it might have other women—instead, she looked lovely.

"You're quiet," Marguerite remarked, slinging her arm around Vernon's shoulders. "All that redecorating is taking its toll?" She spoke teasingly, but Norvia still didn't appreciate the inference. Ma was making the house brighter, cleaner, and more comfortable than it had ever been.

"No. Only eating an ice cream soda might be too rich for me," Vernon observed.

"Ice cream has never bothered you!" said Marguerite, very definitely.

Vernon fell silent. Norvia smiled as she realized how effectively Marguerite had settled his protests. "How are your Latin and geography going?" Marguerite continued. "Do you need me to come help you with them?"

"Well—Mrs. Ward tries to help me, when Papa is busy," said Vernon slowly.

Next, Marguerite turned to Elton. "My father says you're interested in farming," she said brightly. "Our aunt and uncle have a farm downstate, with fruit trees and absolutely endless rows of corn. Is there any particular crop that interests you?"

Norvia caught the look of surprise on Elton's face, which was quickly replaced by embarrassment. "Well, I like...all vegetables," he said at last. "Potatoes would be good."

"Definitely," said Marguerite, nodding. "Do you like farming, Casper?"

"Gosh, no," said Casper fervently. He was dawdling along behind everyone else, playing with the various blades of his new knife. "I'd like to work on cars or join the navy."

"I'd like to be a motion picture star like Mary Pickford," Dicta chimed in, linking her arm through Marguerite's. "I want to wear a wig with long golden curls and be saved from burning buildings by handsome rogues."

Marguerite laughed. "Oh, I think your hair is already film-worthy. And as for the rogues, they're probably not so fascinating in real life."

Kerry's was a marvelous place, with a carpeted floor, sweet-looking chairs with thin-wired backs, and an arched ceiling. A tall, ornate Victrola stood in the front corner, and the tinny tune spilling out was "Can't You Hear Me Callin', Caroline?"

"What shall we order?" said Marguerite briskly, as they settled onto the stools in front of the gleaming countertop. "I myself like a good pineapple soda. Norvia?"

The menu was so full of delicacies that Norvia had difficulty choosing. "I'll have the Movie Sundae," she said at last, because it contained strawberry ice cream.

Dicta couldn't decide between the banana split ("It sounds like something all *tropical*") or the Cupid's Dart Sundae ("Will it make me fall in love—*today*?"), but she eventually chose the latter. The boys proceeded to make their decisions in quick succession: Casper chose a root beer soda, Elton picked lemon, and Vernon finally decided on the Sundae De Luxe, which was possibly the richest thing on the menu and cost a whopping thirty-five cents. (Norvia found she felt sorry for the items on the menu left unchosen, despite reminding herself that ice cream sodas didn't have feelings.)

A young woman in a silk poplin dress and velvet hat approached Marguerite. "Out with your brother?" she asked with a smile, glancing at Vernon before fixating her attention on Marguerite once again. "Margie," she continued in a low voice, "is everything all right? Dad just told me that your father was removed from the Board of Elders at church."

"Oh," said Marguerite, all her poise and ease melting away with one syllable. "Yes, of course everything's all right—Papa knew that was going to happen." In a clearer, more confident voice, she turned and put her hands on Dicta's shoulders. "These are my new brothers and sisters! Dicta, Norvia, Elton, and Casper. We thought we'd have a nice little outing together. Everyone, this is my friend Mavis."

Suddenly Norvia realized what had happened. This young woman had not realized that the other patrons at the counter were her friend's new stepsiblings.

Poor Mavis looked miserable and guilty. "I—I'm so glad to meet all of you," she said with false brightness. "It's really a pleasure. Sorry to horn in, Margie."

"We'll talk later," Marguerite promised in a whisper, waving her gloved fingers as Mavis scurried out of the shop. The overhead bell jingled in agitation as the door swung shut.

When the white-capped soda jerk presented Norvia with her

Movie Sundae, somehow she found that her appetite had faded away. She pushed the decadent dessert around with her spoon aimlessly.

Once they were back in the fresh air and on their way home, Norvia hung back from the others until she and Marguerite were more or less alone on their portion of sidewalk. "So you knew that before?" she asked, too curious to be cautious. "About—your father and the church board?"

"Yes," said Marguerite with a nod.

"But . . . why did they do that?" asked Norvia, with a sinking suspicion that she already knew the answer.

Marguerite heaved a little sigh and avoided meeting Norvia's eyes. Instead, her gaze flitted all around the busy streets, settling on horses and carriages and ladies with their arms full of shopping boxes. "People are . . . well, they don't want to appear as if they condone something like . . . a man marrying a woman who was divorced. They worry what their friends will think."

"But why is it supposed to be so bad?" asked Norvia.

Because it is? It certainly felt bad to Norvia. Everything had changed because of the divorce.

"Well . . . it's hard," said Marguerite, shaking her head now. "And I'm sorry it has to be this way. I wish that people could be a little bit more open-minded. But they're not. Divorce happens, of course, and it's not so rare as it used to be, but still: this isn't New York or Chicago. It's a community where everyone knows everybody else and people end up gossiping about those who make—unconventional choices. I think most women would rather endure a husband who doesn't love them, simply to avoid all the talk and—and shame that a divorce would bring."

A memory flashed into Norvia's mind of a wintry day long ago on the island, when her mother had cared very much what other people thought. But Pa had scoffed at her about it—even though other people's opinions mattered even more to him.

Norvia realized she had fallen silent as she thought it all over. "Ma doesn't usually mind what other people think," she said finally. "Not anymore."

Except when she asked them not to mention their Indian heritage...

"So she has a thick skin," Marguerite agreed.

"Yes. And..." Instead of feeling the need to defend her father as she once did, she found herself defending Ma. "It isn't because Pa... stopped loving Ma. It's because he started leaving when he was angry. Sometimes for days." The words rushed out before she could stop them. "He would always come back. But..." But those absences were too much like his long days on the lakes back on Beaver Island. Ma hadn't been able to stand it any longer.

Marguerite listened carefully before speaking. "Then I think that, in this case, it seems like she made the right decision. She was trying to do what was best for all you children, as well as herself. So let's try not to think too hard about what other people think, hmm?" She clasped Norvia's hand and began swinging her arm, humming the tune from the ice cream shop.

The afternoon before her first day of high school, Norvia started to reread letters. They were the letters she had received from Helen Haney over the summer, sent during Helen's trip to Florida. But she hadn't received a letter from Helen in weeks now. Not since the night of that dreadful first supper with the Wards!

Surely Helen should have written since then....

Norvia read through the letters with care, wondering if they would yield any clues to her friend's silence. Perhaps she was having such a grand time that she didn't have a chance to sit down and write about it? Or perhaps Helen had been waylaid by a hurricane? Norvia checked the newspapers to see if there had been any reportings of southern hurricanes, but she found nothing.

However, no news might be good news. Perhaps it meant that she would arrive home soon! And wouldn't Helen be surprised to learn that her best friend could attend high school after all?

High school had always been one of their favorite topics. Norvia remembered splendid afternoons where they would put a phonograph record on Helen's Victrola and spin around the room, imagining that they were attending a high school dance. They had promised each other that once they were freshmen and meeting students from all over Boyne City, they would make a social splash! Norvia had relished those plans—those dreams and fantasies. She'd always felt so alone at school, so shy, except for Helen's companionship. And while Helen had never been awkward like Kittie Sloane, she had never belonged to the best crowds of girls, either. But things would change in high school.

Norvia decided that she would try to teach Helen to speak French, just as she'd requested in her last letter. Speaking French phrases would intrigue the other students, with certainty. Perhaps the boys especially?

Setting Helen's letters aside, Norvia reached over to her latest book, *Anne of Green Gables*. Now that she had fascinating books to read and high school to look forward to, Norvia hardly even needed to write her own daydream-laced short stories. She was whizzing through *Anne* instead, delighted to find that Anne Shirley went to a school called Queen's—which Norvia imagined to look just like Boyne City High School.

But as Norvia flipped back through the pages of the long novel, she wondered how Anne seemed to make such a winning impression everywhere. She had even made a good start at her small Avonlea school before moving on to Queen's, despite the incident in which she smacked Gilbert Blythe with her slate. Most of the girls in Avonlea liked Anne very well. In fact, Norvia's eyes landed upon a particular line of Rachel Lynde's: *Anne seems real popular among them, somehow.*

Popularity! That was what made Anne such a sparkling character. It was the key to enjoying school, and to enjoying life as well! No wonder she and Helen had never been one of the popular girls—they hadn't tried to mold themselves into chatty, witty, amusing, carefree heroines. Heroines were *always* popular.

If Anne can be a heroine at school, so can I, she decided with a snap.

She just needed to figure out how Anne managed that, and then she could apply it. Norvia opened her black-and-white composition notebook, settled onto her crisp eiderdown, and began to write.

To Do in High School.

She wanted to add *"Things that will make me a real heroine"* but she refrained, because Dicta might find the notebook and read it aloud to everyone. At the moment Dicta was dumping her paper dolls on the bedroom carpet, shaking them out of a box. Peggy curled up on top of several of the dolls and began cleaning her face in utmost contentment.

"Dicta, don't make a big mess," Norvia warned.

After all, who knew what Uncle Virgil might do if his new stepchildren went around being sloppy and careless? He had been extremely patient so far, but Norvia didn't want to press her luck. Pa had never been able to tolerate things strewn across the floor.

Dicta ignored the warning. "Casper, come play with me!" she shouted.

Casper bolted into the bedroom, waving his knife. "Need anything cut up?"

"Not yet. This is Ma," announced Dicta, selecting her favorite Gibson Girl paper doll. "And this is Uncle Virgil," she added, choosing a mustachioed gentleman cut unevenly from a cigarette advertisement.

"Uncle Virgil doesn't have a mustache," said Casper, ignoring the fact that the paper doll man was missing half an arm. "And Ma's not as skinny as that girl."

"*Shh!*" Norvia hushed them. "Ma is right downstairs!"

Doubling over with giggles, Dicta made Gibson Girl and Cigarette Man stand close together, gazing into each other's papery eyes. "*Dearest, darlingest Angélique of my heart,*" she intoned in a deep imitation of Uncle Virgil's voice, "*we shall sail far away in a pea-green boat, and I will give you anything your heart desires. Fame, fortune, a parakeet that sings 'Moonlight Bay.'...*"

Norvia had to bite her tongue to keep from laughing, but her cheeks burned at the idea that Ma might hear. "Dicta, stop," she ordered through gritted teeth.

"*Oh, yes, my Virgilest of Virgils,*" said Dicta in a fairyish lilt, "*I shall be happy to the ends of the earth, if only you give me a clever bird that sings sweet music. Je t'aime beaucoup!*" Gibson Girl threw her arms around Cigarette Man as well as she could, considering the limitations of paper doll mobility.

"*Dicta!*" Norvia half giggled, half shrieked.

"Oh, fine." Dicta relented and sent the newlyweds away on a journey "to Borneo, in search of the perfect parakeet."

Vernon appeared in the doorway, and Norvia held her notebook a little tighter. Suppose he had heard? He *must* have heard—had he been in the next room, listening to every ridiculous word that Dicta uttered?

"That is not how my father sounds," he began solemnly, but then his lips twitched into the beginning of a smile.

Dicta must have noticed the smile, too, because she patted the carpet invitingly. "Come play with us," she urged.

Vernon opened his mouth, then glanced at Norvia—and she glanced away, wishing he would leave. She heard him say in a cool voice: "No, please go ahead. I have no intention of interfering." And he left just as quietly as he had arrived.

Norvia returned to her list.

To Do in High School:
1. *Be popular. (Anne made lots of friends at both the Avonlea school and Queen's, and Patty had a wide circle of devoted chums. This is the most important step.)*
2. *Find a beau. (Like Anne's Gilbert and Patty's Kenneth, and all the boys who were crazy about Celestia.)*
3. *Be charming and exciting. (I expect this to be the hardest of all, but if girls in books—and Celestia Ward—could do it so well, why can't I?)*

Norvia awoke early the next morning—far too early. She stole out of the house and sat on the front porch to finish the second installment in the Patty series.

Patty was popular, mischievous, attractive, and decorous, and everyone adored her, even the unpleasant characters. (Well, except Cousin Ruth, but who cared what that unpopular girl thought?) More than ever, Norvia hoped that she would be well-known in high school; "a favorite" with the young people.

"If Patty can do it so easily, so can I," she muttered to herself. "I just have to try."

As she closed the covers of the book, the clock tower announced to all of Boyne City that the beginning of high school was nearly here. Norvia couldn't decide if she was more nervous or excited.

She dressed, breakfasted with the others, and then left the house with her younger siblings. Her anticipation arose when she had to leave Casper and Dicta at the big square building at the end of the street.

"Now, be good, and don't get into trouble," said Norvia, smoothing Dicta's skirt and straightening Casper's collar.

"Aww, I can take care of myself," said Casper, but he smiled at her.

Now she had to walk to the high school alone. As she started off, a large portion of her courage began to desert her. The tree-lined street took on an unfamiliar tinge, and she cringed at the sight of oncoming horses and carriages. Everywhere she looked was a stranger, and she would soon arrive at a place she had never been, to meet scores of new people. Why had she dreamed of high school? It would be just as lonely as her old school had been—

The rumble of an automobile sounded behind her. Norvia instinctively jumped to the very edge of the road, for she harbored a secret fear that she would someday be run over by a crazed driver. Clutching her notebook, she turned to stare at the oncoming auto.

It's the Willys-Overland, thought Norvia, pleased with her ability to recognize the green auto Casper had pointed out in town. It was sleek and glossy, like a well-shined shoe. She realized the driver was a young man, maybe seventeen, with a handsome face. She could not help but think of Item Two on her to-do list: *Find a beau....* For a brief, hopeful second, she dreamed that he would tilt his cap to her as the car sped by—and, to her amazement, he did.

Norvia gazed after the automobile and its wondrous driver until it disappeared from sight.

"Ooh, I can't wait to meet him," exclaimed a voice behind her. Norvia glanced around to see a trio of chattering girls: one redhead, one brunette, and one the sort of blonde Dicta envied, with truly platinum hair.

"Is it true his family just moved here from the French Quarter?" the brunette inquired.

"Is that near Paris?" asked the redhead with a swooning sigh.

"No, it's in Louisiana," said Norvia—before she had time to think of the consequences of admitting to eavesdropping.

The trio of girls stopped and stared at her.

"Louisiana?" said the blonde. "That's down south, isn't it?"

"Yes," said Norvia, wondering how anyone could be so geographically uninformed. "The French Quarter is in New Orleans."

"Oh, what a shame," said the brunette, and the trio kept walking, leaving Norvia to wonder why New Orleans was so incredibly un-thrilling compared to Paris. But the redheaded girl *had* looked with admiration at Norvia's new sailor dress, so overall she considered the encounter a success.

I will be popular, and everyone will like me, Norvia vowed. *And I won't be shy. I will be charming and exciting.*

She trotted to catch up with the girls again.

"Say, who *was* that boy in the auto?" Norvia blurted out, cheeks reddening at the sound of her own affected voice. "The one that just passed?"

"That's Louis Behren," said the brunette, patting her hair. "He's a *senior*, you know—he even works at the lumber company after school. My brother's in some of his classes, and he says no one ever sees Louis outside school because he's always in *such* a hurry to get to the office."

A senior—that meant he *was* only seventeen! Not so much older than her.

It must be interesting to do office work. That was the sort of position they gave to people who were good with arithmetic and writing and small details. *Like me*, she found herself thinking. But she didn't know any women who worked in offices.

As Norvia reached Boyne City High School, looming over the town with its elegant cupola, she realized she had never stood before its doors until today. She caught a glimpse of the gleaming green car parked outside but looked away. Realizing that there were two entrances—and that the boys and girls had split into groups—Norvia rushed after the girls and into the expansive cloakroom.

And then the troubles began.

Masses of students, all in that gangly stage of growth Norvia recognized in herself, were milling around, somehow knowing just where they were supposed to be in this educational institution. There was no guesswork here, no lone sheep searching for its place in the flock. Except Norvia.

Assembly Hall, that was first, she thought with confusion. Marguerite had mentioned a Social Room, too. *Why isn't anyone helping me?* Norvia paused to examine her reflection in a nearby mirror amid coat hooks and shelves. She looked blank—sort of whitish, big-eyed, and overwhelmed. No wonder everyone else ignored this ugly duckling among a thousand silver-winged, self-assured swans. Perhaps people were avoiding her because she looked ill.

Could she summon the courage to ask someone a question? She scouted the cloakroom for a friendly face, hoping to recognize someone from grammar school. At last she saw Ophelia Farris, a black-haired girl who used to share peppermints with her during supper hour when they were little girls. After a few false starts, Norvia approached her with a thudding heartbeat.

"Hello," she said in a squeaky hush. "Are we going to Assembly Hall now?"

"Yes, of course," said Ophelia, rearranging her hair before the mirror. "You'd better fix your hair fast before the gong sounds."

Norvia's hand flew to her head. "It is fixed."

Only then did Ophelia look her square in the face. "Oh," she said, but that was all. And then she walked, with a somewhat slouchy posture, over to a massive flight of stairs and disappeared.

For a moment Norvia was too flabbergasted to move, or to think clearly at all. Ophelia didn't like the way Norvia's hair looked. *Do I like the way my hair looks?* She stared at herself in the intimidating looking glass, once again trying to see herself as others might. She saw a girl with two impossibly long, thick braids of dark-brown hair. Did she look too much like an Indian with her hair this way? She should have worn her hair down, with just a ribbon—but there was no time to change the style now.

Assuming there was strength in numbers, Norvia clung to the

group that moved up the stairs and down toward the Assembly Hall, chattering and gossiping and laughing over secret jokes. One girl whispered the word *divorce*, and another looked back in Norvia's direction. She caught sight of Louis Behren—most definitely a Dashing Young Man—but the crowd separated them.

Assembly Hall was a reverberating cavern of voices; the raucous hoots of boys mixed with the shrill whispers of girls. Norvia weaseled her way into an empty seat toward the back of the auditorium, trying hard not to meet anyone's gaze. Two boys settled into seats behind her, a blond boy and his dark-haired companion, and she realized with a pang that they now had an extremely good view of the back of her hair—her subpar hair. At least the auditorium seats themselves were beautiful. Norvia ran her fingers along the smooth iron curlicues on the edge of the row, which brought back an evocative memory of the staircase of the St. James lighthouse.

"Not a bad place," a boy whispered somewhere.

The principal was a gentleman who might have been tall and good-looking once, but was now stooped and wizened. He appeared as if he'd seen a thousand high school assemblies and this was, quite frankly, old hat.

"I see many students here today," said the old principal—Mr. Holthrope, Marguerite had called him. "Many students. I am glad to see it; for this is one of the finest institutes of learning in all of . . ." He hesitated. "In all of . . ."

"*Michigan*," prompted some of the upperclassmen.

"Michigan, yes, thank you," said Mr. Holthrope with an enormous, gratified smile. "Now . . . let me see, what was I saying? Oh, yes! The glories of studying here, at this great high school . . ."

"Ever seen such a sad face on a pretty girl?" muttered one of the boys sitting behind Norvia. "You'd think she'd never had a speck of fun in all her born days."

"She's just trying to look like a motion picture actress," the other boy retorted. "I like the girl in the striped dress, way over there."

The first boy said in a confidential undertone, "I fancy dark-haired girls, myself." And suddenly he was whispering in Norvia's ear. "*Is that your real hair color or is it dyed, m'lady?*"

Norvia whirled around to face this inquisitive boy, and he started laughing, as did his obnoxious friend. A joke. It was a joke. But why? It didn't even make sense. Norvia turned around to hide the tears mounting in her eyes.

"Heck, Aylmer, now you've got her crying," moaned the second boy.

"She's not crying. She's laughing," said the blond Aylmer lightly, but his voice dropped an octave as he leaned in again and murmured, "You're not really crying, are you? It was only a joke, I swear. Any fool can see your hair's natural."

He sounded honestly remorseful! But Norvia wouldn't let him see her cry. She kept her face turned away, focused on whatever the principal was rambling on and on about, and didn't make a sound. Listening to the principal was for the best, anyway. What was he saying?

"And, thus, it is a great privilege and a sterling opportunity for you all to be able to learn here, at this fine school we call . . . that we call . . ."

"*Boyne City High School!*" the upperclassmen roared.

"That's the spirit!" Principal Holthrope chuckled. "Good old BCHS! May God bless you all!"

Finally, his speech was over, and students began to file out of the auditorium. Still avoiding the gaze of Aylmer and Company, Norvia's eyes searched the throng for Helen Haney, but she couldn't see her among the roaming masses of students. Why *hadn't* she written lately?

"Well, time to go get registered," Aylmer announced to his friend with a sigh of mock weariness. They had somehow appeared ahead of her. "Sign away our lives forever."

Norvia followed the crowd into a room down the hallway that was labeled REGISTRAR'S OFFICE. A young woman in a white shirtwaist sat behind a colossal desk, gazing at the incoming students with a professional smile.

"Name, please," she said to a girl at the head of the line.

"Ernestine Talbot," the girl replied, smoothing her own flawless hair.

"Date of birth?" The woman continued.

"December twentieth, 1899," said Ernestine, as if reciting the birthdate of a famous personage.

"Your parent or guardian's name."

Ernestine replied primly, "Orville Talbot."

A sense of enchantment rose up inside Norvia as she watched this proceeding. This young woman, sitting coolly behind her desk and jotting crisp notes on pieces of lined cardstock, was some kind of secretary. Instantly Norvia envisioned herself in the very same position, greeting new faces with encouragement, writing down information in flyaway cursive. *This* was what she wanted to do, if she was able to stay in high school long enough to become proficient in that type of work. It would be just like the work Louis did. . . .

But *would* she ever be able to get a job like that? Pa would have said it was a foolish notion.

Now the registration secretary had started to assist Aylmer, who was giving his address. Norvia gathered her courage and stepped forward once he had moved aside.

"Name, please," the secretary repeated evenly.

"Norvia Nelson."

She wrote this down on a new sheet. "Date of birth?"

"January seventeenth, 1900."

"Name of your parent or guardian?"

Norvia froze, realizing how closely she had come to announcing

"Anders Nelson" just as plain as anything. But he didn't even live here anymore—and he certainly wasn't in charge of her. "Mrs. . . ." It was difficult to wrap her tongue around the awful truth of her mother's new name. "Mrs. Virgil Ward," she said at last, hoping no one else had overheard.

But the secretary didn't object to the discrepancy in the surnames: Nelson, Ward. She merely wrote down Norvia's information, proceeded on to her address, the school she had previously attended, and finally today's date.

"You will have to choose your first-year subjects now," the woman informed Norvia, handing her a slim pamphlet. "We provide all our students with lists to choose from. You will have to select four of your six courses. English and algebra are the only requirements for freshmen, and of course one of your self-chosen courses must be in the domestic arts."

A cloud of panic descended on Norvia as she hastily glanced through the pamphlet. How was she to choose in a matter of mere minutes?

But the idea of the secretary's poise and sophistication had stirred her, as had the realization that her father was no longer around to say they were Indians without prospects. Besides, Elton had said something about how she might get a job someday. *He* believed she could. Mightn't she, then? If she had the education?

Seizing upon this inspiration, Norvia looked up from the pamphlet and said, as firmly as she could, "I will take bookkeeping and typing." Then, remembering the homespun harmony of the March sisters in *Little Women*, she added: "And music and sewing." (Ma could help with her sewing, and for music—but she did not relish the idea of receiving pointers from Vernon. Well, she could muddle along without his guidance.)

Having taken care of her classes, Norvia exited the registrar's office—and gasped.

"Helen!" she exclaimed, her feelings transformed in an instant. How wonderful Helen Haney looked, with her shiny brown hair and new georgette dress! "Why didn't you tell me you were back?"

Norvia rushed over to hug her friend, but the hug didn't last long. Somehow it didn't feel quite...authentic.

"Hello, Norvia," said Helen, a weak smile forming on her lips. "We only returned from our journey last week, you see."

"Last week?" Norvia repeated. "You didn't tell me! You should have visited. I would have loved to see you!"

"Oh, well, it doesn't matter," Helen said in a hushed tone. "Of course I'm—glad to see you. It's just that...that..."

A chill swept over Norvia. "Helen, what's wrong?"

Tears flooded Helen's eyes, and the jeweled bracelet on her wrist sparkled as it caught the rainbow light from the window. "Well, Mother had a letter from one of our neighbors while we were in the south, and now Mother says I ought not to...that I shouldn't..."

For a moment, Norvia stood speechless, but Helen finally found her words. "It isn't anything against you personally, Norvie," she blurted out. "We've always been the best of chums. But Mother won't allow our friendship any longer. She's dead set against it."

This was too much—far too much for anybody to withstand.

And to think that these terrible words were coming from Helen— her very best friend, her longtime comrade. Norvia's stomach grew tight, and her mouth became dry.

"Is this because of my—?" But Norvia could not bring herself to finish the sentence. Her head rushed with dizziness.

"Don't put words in my mouth," begged Helen, her eyes darting down the hallway beyond Norvia. "We'll still see each other at school... but if I want to have *any* friends this year, we have to part ways."

And without so much as a goodbye, Helen slipped away.

At that moment, Kittie rushed by and knocked all the books from Norvia's arms.

"Oops! Sorry! I'm so clumsy. Everyone says so. But we're officially freshmen!" Kittie crowed, retrieving the books and squeezing Norvia's hand. "Shall we go to Kerry's for a soda later to celebrate?"

Norvia looked over Kittie's shoulder. A cluster of other freshmen had surrounded Helen, all asking her questions about her summer in the south, admiring her dress, laughing like old chums. She looked like Patty Fairfield. Everyone in the hallway seemed to be in some sort of group or friendly trio. Only Kittie stood beside Norvia.

She could almost hear her grandfather's voice, his low, gentle voice, speaking of the Reindeer Clan: *We bring people together....*

But her life was torn apart, and she could not put anything back together. "I—I think I'll just go—h-home afterward," Norvia murmured. She took off running down the hall.

It was a blessing that Boyne City High School dismissed its freshmen early on the first day. A waterfall of tears was bursting to fall, and Norvia had to wait only through a brief introduction to each class before the gong rang again and school was over. Those tears impeded her ability to see as she slowly walked home, but she didn't care. Nothing mattered. Only getting home mattered.

And there was her pretty, new house, patiently waiting for her—such a soothing white color, encircled by the green leaves of lilac bushes. Right now, Norvia's only thought was to escape to the sanctuary of her bedroom. When she reached it, she promptly collapsed on her bed, sobbing into her pillow.

And *this* was exactly why life never mimicked books—why a girl in the real world could never be a proper heroine! *Although Celestia did it*—Norvia reminded herself—*Celestia Ward had been a heroine, a popular girl admired by everyone.*

But her parents had not been divorced.

After a while, Norvia rose, dabbed water on her face, and tried to think of happy, delightful things, like books and beaux and *Patty Fairfield*—stupid, popular Patty!—and the promise of next spring's lilacs. She dried her eyes, and, with as much courage as she could muster, went downstairs.

Norvia was subdued all afternoon, and everyone knew she should be dancing on air. Dicta, perhaps recognizing the signs of a disappointing school day, brought Norvia a faded aster and a crayon picture entitled *Mary Benedicta: Queen of the Third Grade.*

"I made a good impression on the teacher," Dicta chirped. "It's my goal to be the teacher's pet at this school. Miriam Morrison was the teacher's pet last year, and she got all the monitor jobs and the gold stars when *I* did more gold-star work than she did. It's a good thing we switched schools."

It was difficult to stay in the doldrums after that confident announcement. But all throughout supper, Norvia found that eating her food was a challenge—every mouthful felt tasteless. As she ate her mashed potatoes, she glanced over at Mr. Bingley, who was sitting by the back door of the kitchen—she could see him through the open door from the dining room.

"Why is he sitting out there?" Norvia asked, making a monumental effort to divert her thoughts from school and Helen.

Vernon sipped his milk. "Because that is where my mother used to feed him."

"They say that old dogs can't learn new tricks, and I'm afraid they're right," Uncle Virgil said with a laugh. He scraped his chair away from the table. "Let's go out to look at the stars."

Vernon jumped up from the table, speaking a mile a minute. "May I be excused? I'll get the telescope straightaway. Don't forget your coat this time, Papa; it's bitterly cold tonight."

"Come, Angélique. It's a beautiful night," said Uncle Virgil.

"I have dishes to wash," Ma apologized. "Take the children. They would love to see the stars."

Norvia rarely went outside at night anymore. She had no reason to, without Grand-père to tell stories of the stars and their Indian names. But she followed her stepfather out back and allowed her eyes to focus on the sky instead of the ground.

It was a cold, wonderful, mesmerizing evening. The crisp air of early autumn made Norvia catch her breath, which came out in clouds before her. The majesty of the heavens soared above the stargazers, rendering their personal worries and woes almost insignificant. A sense of refreshment and relief washed over Norvia.

The stars didn't disappear. She could stare at them as long as she pleased, and they glittered like flecks of jewels pasted onto a black panel of sky.

"Isn't that Ursa Minor—the Little Dipper?" asked Casper, pointing to the constellation in these moonless heavens that brought so many memories pouring back into Norvia's heart. She remembered those beautiful days on Beaver Island....She recalled her grandfather's deep, easygoing voice, his words of wisdom, the way he asked her if she remembered the loon in the sky, one of Migizi's favorites.

It was on the tip of her tongue to tell Uncle Virgil and Vernon about the Ojibwe interpretation of this constellation, but she couldn't. Not without alluding to their forbidden heritage.

"Yes, and that's the North Star," said Uncle Virgil, indicating the biggest, brightest star in the Little Dipper. "It's the only star that doesn't move. Throughout the night, all the other stars rotate around it. But the North Star is always there, waiting for us." Norvia recalled the words Grand-père had used for "North Star"—*Giiwedin'anang.*

"'I am constant as the northern star,'" quoted Vernon, smiling at his father.

Uncle Virgil smiled back. "'Of whose true-fixed and resting quality there is no fellow in the firmament.'"

Vernon continued whatever they were quoting as he adjusted the telescope. "'The skies are painted with unnumbered sparks; they are all fire and every one doth shine.'"

"'But there's but one in all doth hold his place: so in the world,'" concluded Uncle Virgil.

"Did you just make that up?" gasped Dicta.

"No," said Uncle Virgil, laughing a little. "It's from *Julius Caesar.* Shakespeare!"

Norvia was not thinking of Shakespeare, but of *Patty Fairfield* and *Anne of Green Gables,* books where houses had their own names—like Villa Rosa, the home of Patty's wealthy aunt and uncle, and—naturally!—Green Gables.

"You are now christened 'North Star,'" she whispered, glancing back at the now friendly white house that she hoped would also be her constant light.

CHAPTER NINE
DICTA'S PLAY

Norvia awoke with a start. She had been dreaming of Beaver Island, but the sounds of the lake and the gulls faded away as soon as she opened her eyes. Hurrying footsteps met her ears, but the night was pitch-black except for a weak light beckoning from the boys' bedroom.

Norvia slipped into her dressing gown and padded to the doorway of the boys' room. Elton and Casper—who could sleep through anything—were unconscious to the world around them, but Vernon was awake, sitting up amid a stack of downy pillows. Mr. Bingley sat at the end of Vernon's bed, his worried face on his paws. Uncle Virgil was doling out medicine from a blue bottle, while Ma stood by with her hands knotted together.

"What's the matter?" Norvia asked in a groggy tone.

"Vern's just got a bad headache, that's all," replied Uncle Virgil with a reassuring smile. "Nothing to be alarmed about."

"Papa, don't go," Vernon protested, the instant his father rose to leave. "I feel much better when you're here."

"I'll stay with him," Ma volunteered.

"No, it's all right. You go back to bed," said Uncle Virgil, massaging Vernon's forehead with great gentleness, brushing back his dark hair in comforting, rhythmic strokes. Witnessing the scene made Norvia feel very calm.

Ma picked up the blue medicine bottle. "Are you sure there isn't anything I can do?" she asked. Norvia felt a pang of sympathy for her poor, useless mother.

"No, he's just fine," Uncle Virgil repeated. "He's used to head-aches, aren't you, son?"

Vernon gave a sort of murmuring response, but it was clear he was already half-asleep.

In the morning, Vernon was still achy and refusing food. He did not come downstairs, and Uncle Virgil announced at breakfast that Vernon would be spending the day in bed.

"I don't think you need to baby him," said Ma, sounding less sympathetic than she had last night. "He's thirteen years old. Casper wouldn't lie in bed all day simply because he had a headache."

"I'm tough," declared Casper, who had spent half an hour groaning over a paper cut the day before.

"Vernon feels better after a relaxing rest," said Uncle Virgil, ending the discussion by giving Ma a kiss. Norvia glanced away.

Dicta *kerthunked* upstairs to Vernon's room after breakfast, and Norvia followed out of curiosity, although it was hard to tear herself away from the joys of *The Little Girl Next Door*—her latest selection from the stack Uncle Virgil had given her. The sisters found Vernon lying flat on his back in bed, staring at the ceiling and clutching his coverlet with white fists.

"Are you all right?" Norvia asked in a wisp of a voice, for he really did look uncomfortable.

"Oh, yes. I'm better now. The headache is fading off." He drew a deep breath and managed to smile up at Norvia. "Headaches aren't so bad, anyway. Sometimes I pretend I'm suffering from malnourishment or *la grippe* in an old English debtor's prison. It's quite riveting, really."

Much to her chagrin, Norvia felt a pinch of interest. Here was someone else who pretended things and lived in his imagination! "Why...do you do that?" she asked slowly, because the question seemed to be expected of her. She knew the real answer—because sometimes, imagination was the only place that felt like home.

"It takes my mind off the pain, for one thing," said Vernon slowly, "and imagining something ten thousand times worse than your actual situation makes everything better."

"Why'd you get sent to prison?" asked Dicta.

Vernon took a sip of watery tea. "Because my father didn't pay his bills." His eyes flashed with imagination. "And we—my nine brothers and sisters and I—were starving to death, but our cruel landlord didn't care. Now my father and I have been imprisoned, with no chance of outside help, and our last friend in the world, an elderly pedagogue, has died of the Black Plague—"

"I don't think the Plague was part of the Industrial Revolution. That was much earlier," Norvia said.

"This is *my* game," he replied, sitting up in bed. "Anyhow, now I shall die an early death from lack of care, but I shall bear the burdens without complaint—as I promised my dead mother that I would be brave."

Dicta looked impressed. She sprang into action, running from the room and returning a moment later with a damp dishcloth. "I'll nurse you back to health. I'm the prison nurse," she explained, flopping the cloth on her dying patient's forehead. "You're going to get better, or my name isn't Mary Benedicta Nelson."

In an instant, Norvia forgot she didn't like Vernon; forgot she was a sophisticated high school freshman. "Your name isn't Mary Benedicta Nelson," she cried. "It's Sister Benedicta. You're a nun, and I'm the wife of the jailer. I've allowed you to come help this poor, sick child."

"Young man," corrected Vernon, adjusting the wet cloth. Two trails of water drops rolled down his temples. "I'm not a child anymore. You may address me as John. Everyone was named John back then, from the beggars to the gentry."

"Hush, patient!" said Sister Benedicta, who evidently did not bother with the Christian names of lowly debtors' offspring. "You must be silent, for noisiness will not cure you of what ails," she added.

"I thought all nuns were kind," John the pauper boy grumbled.

"Sister Benedicta only wishes you to have a complete recovery," the jailer's wife murmured with sympathy.

"I'll never be cured," John mourned. "I am beyond saving."

Sister Benedicta waved a hand. "Do not fear, child. I have saved billions of lives on the battlefields of . . . of . . ." The nun faltered, being unfamiliar with the locales of battlefields.

"Of Valley Forge," said the jailer's wife.

"No. Calcutta," objected John.

"We're going to be late for school," Casper yelled from downstairs. "Come on!"

Dicta burst out laughing at the interruption, and Norvia and Vernon couldn't help laughing, as well. But after Dicta ran off downstairs, Norvia's uneasiness returned. He really looked terrible—his face was so pale, his eyes smudged with lack of sleep. She didn't know how to leave. Should she say, "I'm sorry you don't feel well"? Was that the right thing to say? Would it irritate him—if he thought she was pitying him? She couldn't bear the thought of him suddenly being angry with her.

But she had thought too long.

"Why do you stare at me?" asked Vernon, a trace of irritation in his tone.

"I wasn't," said Norvia. "I mean—not like that," she added, confused.

"I know I look dreadful. But it's not my fault, and you don't have to stand around *staring*." Vernon threw his blankets over his head like a five-year-old.

"I was just—" Oh, how could she explain what she was thinking? That she felt an ache of indecision over every tiny incident? That she was afraid of how people might make her feel, or how she might make them feel?

In the end Norvia said nothing—after all, she had to get to school.

I'm sorry, Grand-père, she thought, miserable and angry at the same time. *But I don't have any grace at all.*

Norvia's first class was English with Miss Patterson. She tried hard to focus on her textbook, but the blond boy—the one called Aylmer—kept glancing in her direction from the corner of the classroom. Norvia shouldn't even have noticed, but somehow her eyes couldn't help traveling toward his corner, and almost every time she looked, he stole a glance back at her. She wished he wasn't quite so observant.

After the class ended, she remained at her desk longer than necessary, hoping that Aylmer would leave the classroom with the rest and she could have a few moments of peace. As she flipped through her textbook aimlessly, she found herself wishing that history had been one of the required classes instead of English. Perhaps she could have learned more about Ojibwe Indians from a history textbook—

"Is it not bad enough that they have Indian blood—now they must learn all about it?"

Her father's words of yesteryear sprang back to her, and she suddenly felt foolish for seeking out stories like Grand-père used to tell. She should have known better.

In algebra, Aylmer sat right in front of her, straight and confident and silent, while she hunched in her seat and worked out angles and *x*'s. He kept passing notes to her. Yesterday the note said:

Is your hair naturally wavy?

Today the note said:

Might you deign to tell me your name, m'lady?
—from your Humble Servant

Norvia shoved the message in her desk along with the first one. Why did he feel the need to tease her? Everyone else ignored her— why couldn't he?

Aylmer was not in her bookkeeping class, at least. In fact, she hardly recognized any of the other students in the room, but the teacher was a pleasant young woman named Miss Darnell. Norvia was fascinated by the idea that a woman not much older than Marguerite could teach a subject like this.

"This class is going to be challenging, as well as highly enjoyable," Miss Darnell announced, smiling at her students. "We'll be setting up a school bank. Each student will put a little money into our bank, and then the top students in this class will act as the cashiers and take charge of that money."

Norvia felt a deep thrill at the thought of being entrusted with such responsibility—but at the same time, the potential for mistakes overwhelmed her.

"But right now, we're going to launch into learning single-entry bookkeeping, before we move onto double-entry later in the year."

Norvia took out her pencil and poised it above her paper, feeling immensely capable. She was good at math and at writing, after all. Perhaps she would be good at bookkeeping, too.

When she returned to North Star that afternoon, she found Dicta lying on the patterned rug in the parlor, swinging her legs back and forth in the air as she scribbled on a tablet. Casper was doing homework on the sofa next to Vernon, who was lying beneath an afghan with his eyes closed.

"Guess what, Norvie?" Dicta squealed. "I'm a playwright."

Norvia smiled. "I thought you were going to be a nun."

"Well, we're Presbyterians now. Anyway, nuns can't fall in love, and I want to kiss at least five different boys when I grow up. No, I'm writing a *wonderful* play. It's called *Love's Lovers Lost*." Dicta flipped to the front of her tablet, where this glorious title was proclaimed in bold capitals. Underneath she had written, *by Mary Benedicta Nelson, age 8.*

"This sounds rather sad," Vernon observed.

"It's a tragedy. They're more popular than comedies. Everybody likes crying over fake things." Dicta hugged her tablet to her chest. "I shall play the young queen, whose name is Arabella Montmorency de Plainero, Esquire. Norvia, you'll play the part of my maid, Bertha, and Casper can be a page. Elton can be the Evil Whiz-Bang, and Vernon shall portray my knight in shining armor, Prince Dudley Porter." She flung a smile at him. "Ma will play Miss Mollusk, my spinster aunt, and Uncle Virgil can be my father, the old, retired king. Young Mary will be a townswoman, and Old Mary can be a witch. I'll write out all her lines in French."

"I don't want to be in it," exclaimed Norvia, blushing at the mere notion of appearing in some ridiculous play.

"What's a page?" asked Casper with suspicion.

"Kings don't retire," Vernon pointed out. "They either die of disease or they're beheaded by revolutionists."

Dicta let out an elongated sigh, as if amazed by such stupidity. "I know *that.* But Ma already said there can't be any dying in my play."

"Then how can it be a tragedy?" Norvia asked.

Momentarily stumped, Dicta bit the end of her pencil, and then admired her evenly spread teeth marks. "The love parts will be tragic enough," she decided.

"I'd prefer to play the background music for your dramatis personae rather than play a role," Vernon continued. "I could perform some Bach on my harp. 'Ave Maria,' perhaps—"

"No one else can *possibly* play the prince," fussed Dicta. "Prince Dudley Porter is supposed to be fragile and pale. I don't know any other boy who looks like that."

Norvia darted a worried glance at Vernon, who closed his eyes again.

"You all have to study your parts and memorize the lines as soon as I'm done writing it," Dicta continued. "I don't want anyone to forget what to say halfway through the big performance. Our audience mustn't be disappointed."

"Who's our audience?" demanded Casper.

"Whoever buys tickets."

Norvia was not allowing that. "You can't sell tickets, because we're not doing it."

"We are so."

"We most certainly are not."

"Girls," warned Elton, who heard all the commotion and came to investigate.

"Ladies, I am still suffering from the after-effects of my headache," Vernon sighed. "Please refrain from arguing in such a repetitive manner."

Dicta cleared her throat. "Listen to this. *Act I, Scene I. Queen's Quarters at Castle Rilamont. Arabella enters, faints, and revives in time to speak to her maid, Bertha. Bertha: 'Queen, you are looking ill as a dog.' Arabella, wearily: 'Pray don't speak to me suchly, for I am decidedly under the weather.' Enter King of Rilamont, Retired. King: 'You are looking lovely, my dearest Bella-boo.' Arabella: 'Pray, don't speak to me on such matters, Daddy Dearest, for the kingdom is in such turmoil, and I cannot bear the progress of monuments and edification.'* I found those words in the dictionary," Dicta added. "They're real."

"I shudder to think what the Evil Whiz-Bang gets to say." Elton chuckled.

"Say what you will," said Dicta, shrugging. "The play will be performed next Saturday. And we will have an audience. So there."

Two days later, Dicta's script was finished, and she announced her aspirations to the entire family at supper that night.

"My play will be on Saturday at three in the afternoon," she declared.

"May I see the script?" asked Uncle Virgil with a grave expression, holding out his hand.

Dicta handed the sheaf of crumpled, ink-blotted papers to him across the table. (She had been sitting on them to enhance her height.) "You're the Retired King. You have an attack of apoplexy near the end, but you recover in time to see your daughter, me, happily married to Prince Dudley, Vernon."

Norvia's cheeks felt hot as she watched their stepfather read Dicta's work. She had read some of the script at intervals when Dicta wasn't looking and was thoroughly embarrassed by the play. Her own lines weren't so bad, but she was left cringing for everyone else. She couldn't help thinking of certain ludicrous selections as Uncle Virgil paged through the script, making "hmm" noises.

"I think that this shows good effort," said Uncle Virgil, as he smoothed the wrinkled papers with slow, deliberate palms. "I might suggest, however, that you rushed the ending. And some other sections."

Hope fired Norvia's soul. Perhaps Uncle Virgil would find a kind way to cancel the performance?

"It needs some revisions. I would be happy to help. Then, I think it could be performed," Uncle Virgil added. "Perhaps Norvia can also help you with it."

"*Love's Lovers Lost* doesn't have any rough spots," Dicta argued under her breath.

Norvia saw a loophole and leaped through it. "You said the tornado scene could have been better. Maybe we should wait and perform the play another time," she suggested.

"Well, just change some of it, then," said Dicta, much aggrieved. "Cross it out and add in what you want. We're still performing on Saturday. Here, take it," she said, thrusting the script into Norvia's hands.

Feeling somewhat akin to Jo March, who was always scribbling stories, Norvia read the script in its entirety that evening and tried to figure out why the play was so dreadful. It wasn't simply the absurdity of the dialogue. It was the story itself. Absolutely nothing happened at all over the course of the play: Queen Arabella fainted a few times, bemoaned the illness of Prince Dudley, and mumbled to herself. The final scene included a coronation, a wedding, and a plea of repentance from the old witch. Queen Arabella, however, was teary-eyed and worthless from beginning to end.

Sometimes you just have to get up and do something, Elton had told her, and Norvia hadn't forgotten it. Perhaps his advice would apply here.

She began to experiment with revisions. She took out several "yes-eths" and half a dozen fainting spells. She gave Arabella a backbone, transforming the young queen from a person of inconsequence to a suitable leader for her kingdom. Arabella no longer moaned insensibly; she slashed taxes, fought down a rebellion, and convinced the witch to surrender. A smile blossomed on Norvia's face as she wrote with increasing eagerness, making Arabella do things she could never do herself.

Once Norvia was finished, she found herself thinking again of the March sisters in *Little Women*, always writing scripts and performing plays (and how later, even Laurie had joined in on their fun). She ran her finger over a line of text in the old worn volume—a volume that had *Celestia A. Barnett* written in the front—"*What good times they had, to be sure! Such plays and tableaux; such sleigh-rides and skating frolics; such pleasant evenings in the old parlor, and now and then such gay little parties at the great house.*"

She ached inside, wishing that she still had a best friend to "frolic" with. Suppose she asked Helen Haney to come visit sometime, for an afternoon of listening to the Victrola or talking about school? Suppose...But Helen would never come, not if her mother forbade it.

Norvia was still wistfully thinking of *Little Women* as she walked toward her algebra class the following morning. She felt confident in algebraic formulas so far, and found x and y to be easy allies. She had wondered if algebraic equations would be a hurdle too high to leap over, but they were like solving a puzzle. Her daydream of leading the class had come true for algebra, English, and bookkeeping—she had some of the highest grades. *Wouldn't it be wonderful if I could do something with my talent for working with numbers?*

Aylmer fell in step with her on the way to the classroom.

"Care if I join you, miss?" he asked in a playful tone.

"I'm going to algebra," she informed him primly.

"Lucky! So am I," he teased. Of course he was: he sat in front her. "Any good at it?"

Norvia wished with all her heart that Helen, or anyone for that matter, would come along and distract him. "Sort of," she said, and quickened her pace.

"I can carry your books for you, if you'd like." Aylmer reached out to take them just as Norvia swerved sharply around the corner of the hallway, and everything in her arms slid and clattered to the floor.

Aylmer whistled in regret as he stooped to pick them up. "Deepest regrets, my duchess. I didn't mean to send them sprawling. My name's Aylmer, by the by. Emrial Aylmer. A beast of a name, eh? I must have been born under an unlucky star."

Norvia frowned. "I thought Aylmer was your first name."

"My friends call me by my surname." He hesitated, then grinned. "You can, too, if you like."

"Um..." Norvia began—then, in a flash, she remembered Marguerite's story. Didn't she want all the boys to be crazy about her, like they had been about Celestia? She quickly thought of how Patty Fairfield behaved around boys—even if they weren't dashing potential beaux.

"Oh, gorgeous!" she declared in a more definite manner, attempting to sound thrilled by his attentions. "Yes, *do* take my books. I think it would be lovely!"

Aylmer stared at her for a second—as if startled by her sudden transformation—but he obediently accepted the books that he had offered to carry.

They reached the algebra classroom. Helen was in her corner seat, her glossy brown hair catching the morning sunshine so that it looked almost ruby-red. She was giggling with a boy—the dark-haired boy who was friends with Aylmer. Norvia felt a twinge of envy at the scene: Helen didn't have to try anymore to be likeable, not like she used to. How had she changed so much? She was certain that Helen never felt as foolish as she did when trying to be vivacious, and that her exclamations never came out sounding so forced.

Dicta didn't hold any rehearsals for the play, but she kept asking if they had studied their lines. Norvia memorized hers one quiet evening after her homework was finished, and Casper learned all his "Of courseth, madams" with great gusto. Norvia wandered into the boys' room one afternoon because she heard Vernon reciting something over and over, but it turned out he was only whispering, "Aunt Angélique, Aunt Angélique" to a blank wall. She hoped the disease wasn't spreading to his brain.

Dicta was all aflutter on Saturday morning, scribbling last-minute backdrops onto large sheets of foolscap and pinning them together. But at noon, she disappeared without a word to anyone, and Norvia began to feel anxious as three o'clock approached. Was Dicta out trying to sell tickets?

"Poor little thing, it will break her heart if she can't find someone to watch her play," Ma said, pushing aside the curtains to glance out the window.

"I asked Jim and Marguerite to come," said Uncle Virgil. "There'll be a small audience, at least."

"Well, when she's ready to perform, you and I will just join them in the audience." Ma laughed softly. "She'll be so wrapped up in the excitement that she won't mind if we don't participate. Norvia and Casper can do our parts as well as their own."

Uncle Virgil gave her a strange look. "I'll do the part she gave me, Angélique. It may be a child's play, but she has a child's trust in me. I won't disappoint her."

Ma blinked. "I thought you wouldn't care to join in her little..." Her voice trailed off—and then suddenly the most beautiful smile appeared on her face, and she looked positively radiant. "I love you," she whispered.

Dicta returned to North Star only a few minutes after Jim and Marguerite arrived. A boy about her own age trailed behind her, dragging his feet. "He bought a ticket," Dicta announced grandly. "Sit *there*, Valentine. Yes, there. He was named Valentine because he was born on Valentine's Day. That's February fourteenth. Sit, Valentine. Right there. No, *there*."

Despite the small size of their audience—and the comical cast of characters—butterflies besieged Norvia's stomach. She fought to eradicate them by taking deep, relaxing inhales, but they kept returning in full force. Presently she heard Vernon starting up the overture, Debussy's "Maid with the Flaxen Hair." The Marys brushed imaginary dust from their impeccable black dresses, Casper practiced his "yes-eths," and Elton sharpened his sword (which was, of course, his knife).

And then it was time for Act I, Scene I.

"All right, Dicta, go out and faint," Norvia whispered.

Dicta smiled with perfect confidence and marched out on stage. Norvia followed, to stand by as meek Bertha, the maidservant.

"Go ahead, Dicta," she whispered.

But Dicta stood still, white, and silent, staring at the three-member audience.

Norvia wondered if she had forgotten the lines. "Queen, you are looking ill as a dog," she prompted, remembering to give Queen Arabella an inquisitive but respectful glance.

Dicta stared at Marguerite, Jim, and Valentine, her mouth tight. Then she burst into tears and ran from the room, careening past the curtains and actors and rushing for the stairs.

"What is wrong with the child?" Young Mary exclaimed, flabbergasted.

"I suppose I won't be playing the witch today," Old Mary chuckled.

Norvia raced upstairs after Dicta, who had flung herself on the bed and was sobbing into her pillow. "Dicta, what happened?"

"Go away. Make them go away! I can't look at them. They're all *staring at me!* They're making me feel so—so *silly!*"

Ma and Uncle Virgil and the others congregated in the doorway.

"Did you turn chicken, Dicta?" Casper snickered.

"Are you ill?" Vernon asked with a worried frown.

"Just go away!" Dicta howled.

"Dicta, it's all right," said Ma. She sat on the bed and began rubbing Dicta's back sympathetically.

Uncle Virgil's smile was sympathetic, too, but it was also faintly humorous. "Mary Benedicta," he chided, "you're stronger than that. Why don't you go back downstairs and tell them the show is indefinitely postponed?"

"What does that mean?" she whispered.

"It means you'll do it later, once you're ready."

Dicta dabbed at her eyes with a handkerchief. "Well—all right," she said, tilting her chin up. "I mustn't disappoint my audience."

Jim and Marguerite were kind enough to protest the postponement, but Valentine didn't seem concerned by the announcement. "Now can I have the gumdrop you promised me?" was this critic's response.

That night, as Dicta snuggled under her covers, she told Norvia in confidence, "I would have done the performance, but I'm a very temperamental actress. I bet you wish you were temperamental."

Norvia didn't dignify this with a response. She merely turned off the lamp and stared into the darkness, thinking of—strangely—Queen Arabella. If it was so easy for fictional girls to take charge of their lives, why did real life sometimes seem so hopeless and unchangeable?

JUNE 1907
Giniiwaanzo | PINK

It always seemed to Norvia that her father was happiest when he was alone.

Of course he was happy when there was a gathering of some sort, or on a ship with a group of cheerful sailors, or even sitting down to a meal with the Marys and Grand-père. At those times he smiled, joked, and helped Herman with the arithmetic problems that the nuns at school gave him.

But he could sit alone, for hours, and be perfectly contented. That morning he was sitting on the beach with a gold-edged book in hand. Later, Norvia would think this over, trying to puzzle out how he could condemn books to his children and yet be so satisfied with his own reading material. Of course he had only this one book, this evident treasure trove, with its covers so worn there was almost nothing left of them. Norvia once tried to look inside to see what the story was about, but the words were in mystifying Swedish.

He wasn't only reading: he was watching the boys flying kites on the shore and shouting out the occasional suggestion for maximum altitude. Norvia was gathering daisies, and Ma was sitting nearby with tiny Dicta in her arms. But for all that, it still seemed as though Pa was lost in his own private world, a rich sanctuary to which Norvia could rarely find the entrance.

The rays of the sun warmed Norvia's long hair, her hair that was so much like Migizi's, while the seagulls and sandpipers swooped and swirled in the air. Near midday, Pa beckoned to Norvia, and she tumbled down onto the forgiving sands beside him, sinking into their grainy goodness. She fingered a seashell she had discovered, staring at its beauty.

"Listen to this," said Pa, inviting her into the world of his book for a fleeting moment. "Who has divided a stream to flow over water, or a road for thunder?" He read slowly, savoring, feeling his way through the darkness of translation. "To let it rain on the earth, where no man is; in the desert, where there is none; to satisfy the wilderness and the wasteland; and to let the tender herb bud spring up?"

He closed both his eyes and the gold-edged book simultaneously. "*Det är vackert.* Do you hear the poetry in these words, Norvia?"

She did—the words soared as high as the seagulls. Her fervent "Oh, yes" brought a smile to Pa's face. Realizing he was in a good mood, Norvia clasped his hand. "Can we go to Salty Malloy's to see the fairies?"

"Can we go to see the fairies," Pa repeated in a most meditative way. "*Yes!*"

And off they went to the hillside in back of old Salty's place, where the fairies were said to flit. The elder ladies of the island—including Old Mary—insisted that they'd seen the fairy folk on this hill in years gone by, dancing, bobbing, glowing. Norvia had always longed to witness these rites of dancing sprites.

"Perhaps if we're very quiet," said Pa, "the fairies will come out."

Norvia held her breath, chin on her hands, determined to catch a glimpse of gold-dusted wings fluttering on the breeze. Deep down inside her, she knew she did not *truly* believe in fairies. But a tiny, whimsical hope kept springing up, and she felt certain there was *something* to the ladies' tales.

"Pa," she asked in a whisper, "do you really believe in fairies?"

Pa smiled. "Do you really believe those old Indian stories your grand-père tells you? Like the one about the beaver and the muskrat exchanging tails?"

Norvia had to admit she did not. "But Grand-père makes it seem like *he* believes them, and that makes them special."

"So it is with us and the fairies, eh?" said Pa, looking at the grassy hill stretching below them.

CHAPTER TEN
AN INSPIRED IDEA

Uncle Virgil made an announcement one evening that caused Norvia's heart to jump most startlingly. "I've invited some friends of mine for supper on Thursday night," he said to Ma, before adding with a light laugh, "they're very old friends, so you don't have to go to great lengths to impress them."

But Ma did not pay heed to this. For the next two days she scrubbed and polished and mopped and even made minuscule repairs to their best lace tablecloth. When Thursday morning came, Norvia watched in amazement as Ma prepared dish after dish, scouring the cookbooks for ornate recipes and executing them to perfection. (At least, *most* of them were perfect. Norvia tried to forget about the burned biscuits.)

"Are the Rayburns escaped royalty from Russia?" Dicta asked Vernon that afternoon, popping a cherry into her mouth that hadn't made it into Ma's cobbler.

"Of course not," said Vernon, not even glancing at Dicta as he sat studying some sheet music. Mr. Bingley lay beneath the piano bench, twisted up like a contortionist yet sound asleep. "Mr. and Mrs. Rayburn are my godparents," he explained, as if this fact alone cleared them of any foreign connections.

It was then that Norvia realized: the Rayburns were not only *friends*—they were like *family*. They mattered to Uncle Virgil. No wonder Ma was so anxious to make the supper a success.

"It's too bad stories like Cinderella aren't real. Then you'd have fairy godparents," said Dicta dreamily, evidently envisioning the Rayburns flying to supper on silver wings.

Vernon gave a little snort. "Mr. Rayburn is a physician."

"Did he deliver you like Sister Benedicta delivered me?" Dicta asked eagerly.

"Yes. And my sister—" He broke off and stared idly at the first page of notes for a Chopin nocturne. Norvia felt uneasy, wondering what sudden thought had stilled his tongue. But before she or Dicta could ask, he briskly shut the piano lid and walked away. Mr. Bingley rose groggily from the floor and lumbered after him.

Norvia felt even uneasier as the evening drew nearer. The old thrill of people coming to visit—cultivated by Beaver Island isolation—had not entirely died out, but it was very faint. She wondered what she should wear; what made sense? If Mr. Rayburn was a physician, he might be wealthy—his wife could even wear a silver fox stole around her neck. Hastily Norvia sifted through her wardrobe, half hoping that some miraculous silk dress might have appeared overnight. (Sent by a fairy godmother, perhaps!)

In the end she pulled out the blue plaid dress that Ma had made for her last month. It was somewhat plain but still in excellent condition, and it didn't have a hole in the skirt like her muslin did.

"If they're such good friends of your old man's, why is this the first time they've been here since we came?" Casper was talking loud and clear in the boys' bedroom; anybody could hear him. A shiver of horror went down Norvia's spine. *Your old man!* What if Uncle Virgil overheard!

"They live in Eveline now," said Vernon stiffly. "They can't come as often as when his practice was in Boyne City."

"I guess they'll probably hate us," Casper replied, a bit too casually to be convincing. "Horning in on you Wards and all."

"They're perfectly nice," Vernon insisted.

But what if Casper's assessment of the situation was correct?

With mounting apprehension, Norvia slipped down the staircase, wearing the blue plaid. The door to Uncle Virgil's study was ajar, and in the evening lamplight she could see him writing something—or drawing. What could he be—

But she did not have a chance to wonder any further, for the sound of an automobile rushed toward the house, and lights flashed across the yard. Uncle Virgil emerged from his study and swung open the front door.

"Come in!" he called out, his voice much heartier than usual.

Norvia's shyness dropped over her like a blanket, and for a split second she was deathly afraid of even saying hello. She wished she could hide somewhere, anywhere, away from godparents in flashy cars who might not approve of their closest friend marrying a divorcée. As she stood in the shadows of the staircase, a new thought occurred to her: perhaps Uncle Virgil did not want her here at all, greeting the Rayburns at the front door as if she were his real daughter and not a stepchild?

"Virgil," said a man with graying hair and a mustache, throwing his wool overcoat on a chair by the door. "Good to see you! And how is the bride, may I ask?"

Uncle Virgil grinned, and for one instant Norvia knew precisely what her stepfather looked like as a boy. "Wait until you meet her," he promised, helping the woman out of her coat (which had a collar of some unidentifiable fur that Norvia hoped was not beaver). She did not have a fox stole, but instead a long pearl necklace to complement her black dress. "I am eager to meet your new wife," she said pleasantly.

At last they seemed to notice Norvia hiding frozen in the shadows.

"Norvia, this is Dr. and Mrs. Rayburn," said Uncle Virgil kindly. "We've known each other a long time. Douglas, Rita, this is Norvia Nelson. Angélique's older daughter," he added after a second's contemplation.

"A pleasure to meet you," said Dr. Rayburn.

"Very happy to know you," said Mrs. Rayburn.

Norvia opened her mouth to say something in reply, but they had not looked at her for more than two seconds before their eyes flicked back to Uncle Virgil. "Where is Angélique?" Mrs. Rayburn inquired.

"I'm sure she'll be along shortly," said Uncle Virgil brightly. "She's a whiz in the kitchen."

A whiz? Since when did Uncle Virgil use words such as *whiz*? Why did the mere presence of other people transform him into a different person?

But she had noticed that with Pa, too. With the sailors he was jovial, laughing, with a joke for everyone and a perennial song on his lips. With Ma...

Instead of clambering down the stairs in her usual haphazard fashion, Dicta descended the steps with mincing, regal movements, wearing her best navy corduroy. "You must be Vernon's *baptismal sponsors*," she said elegantly, extending her hand when she reached the second-to-last step so she was on roughly the same level as the adults. "I am Mary Benedicta Nelson, named in honor of..."

Norvia ducked out of the room, scarlet embarrassment on her face.

She found Ma standing in the kitchen in front of the gleaming silver stove, closing her eyes and taking gigantic breaths. "Ma?" asked Norvia nervously.

The prompting seemed to snap Ma out of her trance. "Please tell Virgil I will be there shortly," she said, her voice strangely light yet insistent.

Ma really did look marvelous tonight. When she took off her white cooking apron, Norvia realized how lovely her mother's dress was: it was wine-colored with three-quarter sleeves and lace frills, the pinnacle of what she could do with her sewing talent when given the time and money to pursue it properly. Pa had never appreciated Ma's ability to whip up a Paris-inspired creation for profit—Norvia clearly recalled the twinge of resentfulness in his face one day when Ma gave him the small sum she'd earned from sewing. But all of that was behind Ma now, and she looked like the woman in the Campbell's soup advertisement, dining by candlelight with the gentleman in the black suit.

Uncle Virgil wore a black suit tonight, fittingly. And they were to dine by candlelight, although the many-crystaled chandelier still glimmered with the reflection of the flames. He pulled out Ma's chair for her—an act of chivalry that Pa had rarely performed—and Dicta elbowed Casper until he did the same for her.

"You've grown since we last saw you, Vernon," said Mrs. Rayburn.

"Not really," said Vernon, staring intently into his teacup as if reading his future in the leaves.

"Virgil didn't say where you were from, Mrs. Ward," said Dr. Rayburn pleasantly. "Have you always lived here?"

Ma shook her head ever so slightly, her delicate diamond earrings from Uncle Virgil jangling. "We're imports," she said with a laugh.

It took Norvia a minute to realize that Ma was not going to say where they were from. Beaver Island, evidently, wasn't good enough.

After supper, Ma entertained Mrs. Rayburn in the parlor while Uncle Virgil and Dr. Rayburn went into the Study of Secrecy with their cigars. Unsure if she was welcome during this portion of the evening, Norvia began to head upstairs after the other children, but in the downstairs hallway she realized she could hear the men's voices.

"When you first told me about this, I have to say I was skeptical," said Dr. Rayburn, his strong voice penetrating the walls of the study. "But she seems a lovely woman, in spite of it all. People are talking about the two of you quite a bit."

"I know," said Uncle Virgil with a heavy sigh.

"Of all the women in Boyne City, why her? That's what I don't understand, Virgil. You were so happy with Celestia. Why, I come into this house and I half fancy I can hear her singing at the piano. Her very soul is in these rooms. And you mourned her so long. . . ."

Uncle Virgil sounded almost angry, and the edge in his voice sent tremors of fear into Norvia's heart. "Douglas, this house was empty. Vernon and I were completely alone. I married Angélique because I love her." His voice grew softer again, but Norvia could still hear him. "I saw her on the shore one day. I was sketching. . . . She was walking along Pine Lake, so I sketched her, too. She looked so sad that I wished I could do something to help her. Then—quite providentially—I went to Margie's house a few weeks later, and who was there but Angélique? She was making a dress for Margie."

"And you fell madly in love with her," said Dr. Rayburn with a smirk in his voice. "Virgil, she isn't some heroine in one of your old Russian novels. This is your life, and I can't imagine your son has appreciated this. . . ."

"Angélique's children are my children now, too," said Uncle Virgil. "You know how I feel—I've always wanted a large family."

Dr. Rayburn fell silent at this. For a long minute Norvia heard nothing more, although she had crept forward to sit on the steps so she could catch any further remarks.

"You know how sorry I am, still," the doctor murmured.

"I know . . . I didn't mean to . . . ," Uncle Virgil replied.

"As I said," Dr. Rayburn continued, still speaking quietly, "she is lovely. I'm sorry I spoke out of turn, Virgil. But we've known each other so long I felt I could be honest with you. Rita and I have talked about this a great deal because we've been concerned that you made a rash decision based on—nothing more than a passing infatuation."

"I know you want me to be happy," said Uncle Virgil. "But trust my judgment on this. And please give Angélique a chance."

"That we will," said Dr. Rayburn.

They moved on and talked of other things: work and the doctor's patients and funny stories and whatnot. Norvia rose from her uncomfortable position and retreated to her seascape bedroom to think it all over. Uncle Virgil sounded as if he truly loved Ma. It gave her an odd—and not altogether unpleasant—feeling inside.

"Your name is Norvia Nelson, correct?" asked Aylmer.

Norvia was in the back of the Social Room—a communal space for the popular high schoolers, for the students whose parents were still in love, and for the people who were never self-conscious or shy— or only pretending to be popular. Aylmer's arms were folded, and he looked at her with an almost amused curiosity.

"That's right," she said, giving him a fatigued glance. "I thought everybody knew who I was." Everyone at school seemed to know all about her—or rather, about her parents' divorce. She was surprised that Aylmer still wanted to talk to her.

"I didn't know. But I thought I'd heard your name mentioned," said Aylmer, folding his arms. "You know, I only recently moved to this fair village. I was born in Chicago, but these past few years, I've lived in New Orleans."

Suddenly Norvia recalled the conversation of the trio of girls that first day of school—the same girls who were currently dominating all the Social Room conversation and flirting shamelessly with half a dozen young men. (Patty Fairfield, glamorous though she was, never flirted.)

"Some of the girls think the French Quarter is in France," she whispered to him, confidentially.

"Good joke!" Aylmer grinned with an appreciative nod. "Shall we go over and reveal their ignorance to the world?"

For one dreadful moment, Norvia was afraid Aylmer would do just that, but he stayed in the corner with her, just smiling.

Helen and the French Quarter Trio stood in the doorway to the Social Room, laughing about nothing and pointing to various boys in the room. Still, when Norvia approached the door to leave, the expression on Helen's face altered; she looked almost sympathetic. That look gave Norvia a spark of hope. Perhaps things *would* work out, given the right circumstances. If she could only make herself popular, then Helen would change her mind—and Helen's mother would, too.

As Norvia slipped out of the Social Room, she caught a glimpse of Kittie walking toward her, but she darted away. Making friends with Kittie would not help her cause.

Norvia walked home that afternoon in mild weather, with the crisp squelching of early leaves under her shoes and the sweet scent of apples in the air. She inhaled deeply, deciding to focus on her beloved books instead of Helen's brush-offs. She couldn't wait to go home and spend time with Bab and Betty in *Under the Lilacs*—or maybe she would stop at Sunnybrook Farm to visit Rebecca Randall—or sneak into *The Secret Garden* with Mary Lennox while Vernon played his harp. (She tried to read whenever Vernon played the harp; it lent such a golden etherealness to her reading experience.)

She had not walked very far before Aylmer caught up to her. "Would you like me to walk you home?" he offered.

Norvia fought to sound carefree and flattering, like Patty. A popular girl, after all, would sound like Patty. "Thank you! You have *such* a way with words." She plastered on (what she hoped was) an enchanting smile.

As they continued to walk, however, her thoughts drifted to another novel, *What Katy Did*. Aylmer occasionally had to guide her out of the paths of other passersby.

"You are very absorbed, m'lady," he remarked, pulling her toward the correct road—she had been about to walk down Pine Street instead of Cedar Street. "Methinks your silence could only be caused by a demanding profession, an inheritance, or another fellow. Considering you're a girl of only fourteen . . . and you don't seem to be mourning any dead relations . . . I suspect that the former two are incorrect. So, who is he?"

"You talk a mile a minute. I can't even understand you," said Norvia, pulling herself back from Burnet, where Katy Carr was languishing with paralysis. "I have a lot to think about. I don't have a fellow yet, and if by that you mean beau—"

"Putting words in my mouth. I merely wondered if somebody else was carrying your books for you," said Aylmer.

"No, of course not."

"Then allow me to seize the honor!" Aylmer grinned and shuffled her books into his own arms. If only this was Louis Behren showering her with such attentions! Then Norvia would have her very own hero—that vital missing component to becoming a heroine. Aylmer simply did not measure up to her idea of a Dashing Young Man.

A clinging fog descended, wrapping the world in a veil, and the scent of wet, decaying leaves strengthened in the air. Norvia kicked a stone along McKinley Street as they walked.

"You still seem distracted," said Aylmer.

Norvia glanced at him. Would he understand?

"I'm thinking about Katy Carr," she admitted. "She's a character in a book I'm reading." Slowly, her voice warmed with enthusiasm. "This girl Katy, she's twelve, and she's very rambunctious—but she means well, most of the time." She quickened her steps. "One day she falls from this swing in a shed she wasn't supposed to get into, and she gets a sort of fever in her back and can't walk anymore. But she has a cousin Helen, who's almost like an angel, and she broke off her own marriage years earlier when she was hurt in a similar way—"

Norvia broke off, realizing that Aylmer's eyes had glazed over, and now *he* was the one kicking the stone.

"Well, it's an interesting book," she said, quieter now. "I only have a few chapters left."

"Hmm," said Aylmer.

And somehow, the fact that he was not interested in this fascinating book rubbed away a bit of Norvia's joy for *What Katy Did*. A sudden regret enveloped her, and she wished she hadn't said a word about it—now the book would be forever tainted by his disinterest.

Before she knew it, they had arrived at North Star, that now-familiar beacon. Norvia wrestled her books clumsily from Aylmer's arms, the two of them dropping only one pencil in the process. "Thanks," she said, suddenly hoping he would just leave. Kenneth Harper certainly would never drop Patty's things—he was more sophisticated: a college boy who liked tableaux and critiquing art.

But Aylmer was back to bantering. "I believe it is customary among today's youth to invite a boy in for a bit of refreshment at the end of a hard school day. May I come in, m'lady, or do you prefer I wait on the step?"

"Oh—I guess you can—come in," said Norvia, too flustered to remember her manners. "Just—wait in the hall." *Foyer*, she corrected herself bitterly. *Why did you say "hall"? "Foyer" sounds ever so much grander. Goodness, why is it so exhausting to behave properly?*

Dicta happened to be sitting at the foot of the stairs when the high schoolers came in. "Ooh, Norvie! A beau!" she breathed, clamping her hands over her mouth.

"Not a beau," Norvia corrected. "He's Emrial Aylmer."

Dicta rushed forward to clasp Aylmer's hand. "May I call you Rial? Or RiRi? Is *Emrial* a French name? Can you speak French like us and our grandmothers and our stepbrother? My stepbrother, Vernon, can speak French almost as good as the Marys, plus Latin and some German. I think he's a genius, like me—we're the last of our kind. My name is Mary Benedicta Nelson, the most sacred—"

"—I'll get you some cookies," Norvia burst in, cutting off the stream of Dicta's monologue.

Aylmer smiled. "I can speak French, *mon amie*. I went to school in New Orleans. Of course, my folks think education is a waste of time, but I got something out of it anyhow." Aylmer let out an unpleasant laugh—not at all the cheerful chuckle Norvia was used to hearing. But the shadow vanished from his face as soon as Norvia returned from the pantry with a few buttery sugar cookies. "Bliss for the stomach," he pronounced them. Peggy the cat stared at him with intense scrutiny from the top of the stairs.

That evening, Aylmer was the only subject on Dicta's tongue. "A *boy* walked Norvie home from school today," she announced. "A real live boy from the French Quarter who says *mon amie*. He looked at her with *snoogly* eyes!"

"And what," inquired Vernon, "does 'snoogly' mean?"

"I made it up. That's how he looked." Dicta demonstrated an expression that looked nothing like any face Aylmer had ever displayed. "He was *just* like the man in the 'buy four Chambers novels' advertisement."

"Do you like him?" Ma asked with a glimmer in her eyes.

"Is he on the football team?" asked Casper.

"Where's the French Quarter?" asked Elton.

Before Norvia could answer anyone, Uncle Virgil spoke, a serious expression on his face. "What sort of boy is he, Norvia? Do you know him well?"

In an instant, Norvia felt defensive—and far too warm. "I don't know him very well," she admitted. "But—he's a *very* nice boy," she added, unable to keep a note of triumph out of her voice. She liked the idea of everyone else imagining her to have a beau, even if she didn't have one yet. Sometime she would catch Louis Behren's attention....

"I'd like to meet this boy sometime," said Uncle Virgil.

Norvia kept waiting for him to say something else—he looked as if he wanted to—but nothing came.

That evening, Norvia finished *What Katy Did* and lay back on her pillows with a bittersweet sigh. Downstairs she could hear Uncle Virgil teaching Ma to play the piano. They were going slowly: Uncle Virgil would play a few bouncing chords, and then Ma would try to replicate them. Sometimes it sounded pretty, and other times Norvia could hear Vernon's groans of displeasure from the boys' room.

Norvia picked up the third volume in the Patty series, which quickly proved to be almost as perfect as its predecessors. It simply wasn't fair that Patty's life was so full of gaiety and sparkling amusement when Norvia's life paled in comparison—all because of a divorce.

But *could* Norvia force the other girls to forget about that deplorable fact, if she did something clever enough to gain their attention and admiration?

A party! Norvia sat up with a start.

Halloween was only a week away. Cheery jack-o'-lanterns, spooky invitations, and an autumn feast waltzed through her mind. Why, Helen herself had even suggested hosting a Halloween party this year—before her mother discontinued their friendship.

No matter, thought Norvia, as a jubilant smile sprang to her lips. A chummy Halloween party seemed the ideal excuse to invite some of the most popular girls at BCHS to her house for a night of delight. She was certain that despite the fog of gossip and rumors that swirled around her, none of the girls could resist such an invitation. Norvia snuggled deeper into her bed and dreamt of her wonderful plan.

In the morning she realized one tiny snag, a pinprick of a flaw. She would have to ask Uncle Virgil's permission before she planned an enormous party with a myriad of guests. But what would he say? Would he be angry at the idea of a horde of young ladies descending on his domain?

Norvia approached Uncle Virgil in the Study of Secrecy the next morning before breakfast. He was wearing his reading glasses and perusing a book called *The Brothers Karamazov*.

She fixated on the thought of being popular and drew on her courage.

"May I have a party here on Halloween for some of my classmates?" she blurted out.

Uncle Virgil adjusted his eyeglasses and searched for a bookmark to slide between the pages of his massive volume. Norvia's eyes flitted to the books lining the shelves behind him—books by authors named Melville and Brontë; history books like *The Decline and Fall of the*

Roman Empire, and—she had to blink several times to believe it—*History of the Ottawa and Chippewa Indians of Michigan.*

Norvia longed to page through the book, to remind herself of Grand-père's stories—but she could not. It might give away the heritage she had promised Ma she would hide.

But... if Uncle Virgil kept such a book in his personal library... did this mean that he wouldn't mind if his stepfamily was Indian?

"A party sounds enjoyable," said Uncle Virgil. "Which of your classmates?"

Norvia felt as if coiled springs inside her were twisting even tighter. "Um—my friend Helen Haney—and some of her friends."

"Including the boy who walked you home from school?" Uncle Virgil tapped his desk with a pencil. "Aylmer?"

Why did it matter *who* came to the party? Norvia felt more and more tongue-tied, more and more interrogated—almost as if Pa was asking these questions. Uncle Virgil was probably a great deal like Pa, beneath the surface. She should keep that in mind.

"No—it's just a girl's party," said Norvia in her quietest voice.

Uncle Virgil smiled. "I think it's a good plan. I don't mind at all."

"Oh, thank you!" Norvia cried, joy surging into her. At last he had agreed!

She fully intended for this party to be the most memorable gathering any of the girls had attended. *Helen will love it*, she told herself firmly.

CHAPTER ELEVEN
A HEROINE FOR HALLOWEEN

Miss Norvia Nelson requests the pleasure of your attendance at her Halloween Party on the eerie night of October 31, 1914, at half past seven. Prepare to have your fortune foretold by a Great Clairvoyant, with games to follow.

"It sounds so wonderfully frightening!" Dicta shivered. "It's really too bad we don't have a black cat." Her eyes lit up. "Ooh, I know! Valentine has a white cat. We could stick him in the fireplace, and he can get all sooty!"

"No black cats," Norvia said immediately.

Dicta spun in a crazed circle. "If you're going to be a fancy French fortune-teller, you need a cape."

Norvia thought about this. "I could use the fringed shawl on the piano," she mused.

"No, you mustn't. It was my mother's," said Vernon, a look of alarm flashing across his face.

They did not utilize the sacred shawl—one of Old Mary's shawls from Beaver Island would have to do, instead—but Norvia and Dicta spent a wondrous afternoon scavenging for apples to serve, candles to place in strategic locations, and various accoutrements for their party games.

"We need a pumpkin to carve," said Dicta, looking around the parlor as if she expected a pumpkin to walk through the door on her command.

"Elton might be able to give us some," Norvia suggested. "I'll go to the farm tomorrow and see if we can borrow a couple."

She set off for the Redgrave farm after school the next day, sometimes skipping along the way. A sprinkling of bright-colored autumn leaves littered the road, crunching pleasantly underfoot; maple trees waved banners of red and yellow, and cattle and horses grazing in the distance completed the picturesque scenery.

The views of the sprawling farm were worth the effort of walking so far out of town. Four snow-white swans glided gracefully in a dark-blue pond beside the pasture; enormous pumpkins dotted the front field; and lumpy, quirky gourds of blue and green lined the entrance to the house. Norvia could understand why farming meant so much to Elton—to share in a part of this beauty, and to receive such stunning fruits from your labor!

Fortunately, it didn't take her long to find her brother. He was carrying two rather filthy buckets of water across the barnyard.

"What are you doing out here?" he asked, setting down the buckets with a slosh. "It's four-thirty. Shouldn't you be getting home?"

"I need a pumpkin for my Halloween party," said Norvia breathlessly. "Or two pumpkins. Actually, three might be better."

"Why not forty?" Elton grinned. "Come out to the field, and we'll pick out a fine one."

They trekked into a wide, sunny field of gold and green. Norvia stared at the pumpkins with amazement—they ranged in size from tiny to gigantic.

"You helped with these?" she asked.

"A little," said Elton. "I helped with the watering. It's a tough job, but I rather like it."

"Hey, Nelson!"

"Behren, come on over!" called Elton, waving in the distance to someone on the roadside.

Norvia turned and squinted, shielding her eyes with her saluted hand. It was the Willys-Overland! And there sat Louis Behren in his automobile, waving back at Elton!

"You *know* him?" She gasped.

Elton gave her an amused look. "Why shouldn't I? His folks have a beautiful farm not far from here. He's been giving me pointers."

But this Dashing Young Man was supposed to work at the lumber company—how could he be a farmer?

"Here, this looks like a nice one," said Elton, hoisting an oddly shaped pumpkin. "Kind of lumpy, but that might work best for Halloween, don't you think?"

"Yes, yes," Norvia agreed, her eyes still fixated on Louis as he jaunted up the path to the pumpkin patch.

Elton stuck out his work-worn hand to shake his friend's. "Good to see you. How's your folks' harvest going?"

"Really well, considering," replied Louis, nodding. "I help whenever I can, but they're doing well on their own." Then, in a wonderfully cataclysmic moment, he turned toward Norvia. "Care to introduce us?"

"Nan, this is Louis Behren," said Elton in his most gentlemanly manner, gesturing to each of them in turn. "Lou, this is my sister Nan—well, Norvia," he corrected himself.

"It's a pleasure," said Louis, offering to shake her hand as well.

"Oh—yes," Norvia breathed, accepting his hand, her eyes darting from his face to the fresh earth below. His eyes were such a fine deep-blue, and he possessed such a nice nose.

Elton picked up the pumpkin again. "Can you carry this, Nan, or should I?"

For a split second, Norvia struggled between making life easier for her brother and presenting a damsel-in-distress façade for Louis. She chose the former, even though grappling a ghoulish gourd was hardly the vision she wished to convey.

Louis sighed. "Well, I just stopped in to say hello. I'd best be going on home. Have a good harvest, Nelson."

"You, too," said Elton.

"Goodbye, Norvia," Louis added.

"Goodbye," she echoed.

And then he smiled at her.

Norvia waltzed off with her pumpkin, feeling so much like Cinderella that she almost believed it might turn into a magical carriage.

That evening was quiet. Vernon felt ill after eating one of Ma's brownies, and he had taken to his bed. Uncle Virgil had gone to visit Marguerite and Jim, and Elton was working late at the farm. Dicta and Casper were off playing a game somewhere, softly, so as not to disturb Vernon. Norvia sat hunched over by the fireplace crafting invitations for the party as Ma hemmed one of Dicta's dresses.

"You're lost in thought," observed Ma.

Norvia couldn't keep the excitement out of her voice. "I hope all the girls can come to my party," she confided.

"That would be nice," said Ma. She leaned back in her chair, staring at the flickering blue and orange flames in the fireplace. "Good times with friends are not easy to come by."

For a fleeting second, Norvia wondered if Ma, too, was longing for companionship. As she watched the fire, she thought of their old life, when Ma had a multitude of friends.

Her heart ached to do something to fix her mother's friendships—but instead she found herself saying ever so quietly, "I'm sure that sometime you can find new friends..."

She broke off, realizing that her mother was no longer paying attention. Instead, Ma was staring at the portrait of Celestia above the mantel.

"Is something wrong?" Norvia asked.

"Hmm? Oh. No, nothing," said Ma absently, forcing her eyes

away from the painting and back to her sewing. "I keep thinking of Virgil's first wife."

"You're much nicer," said Norvia, laying her hand atop Ma's.

Ma gave her a faint smile. "Thank you. I just wonder if Virgil would agree with you. It's difficult to do my housework with that woman staring at me all day. Every time I see her, I wonder if I could be doing more. Being a better wife, a better mother. The other day, I couldn't stand looking at her any longer, so I started to take the portrait down. But Vernon wouldn't allow it. He was angry with me."

That must have been the day Vernon had spent all afternoon playing the darkest of piano sonatas. "He... he just needs time to adjust," said Norvia, unsure of what else to say.

"I'm afraid he views me as a wicked stepmother," said Ma with a bit of a rueful laugh. "I try to help him—tend to him, mother him, help him with his schooling like his sister does—but he won't have any of it. He barely speaks to me."

Norvia wished she knew the proper comforting words to say. "Well, he doesn't know what a good mother you are."

"I suppose," said Ma, patting Norvia's hand. She put aside the hemming project and stood up from her rocking chair. "I'm going to check on Vernon."

Norvia followed her mother upstairs, waiting outside the boys' room where Vernon was curled in a ball under a thick white quilt. "Do you feel any better?" Ma murmured, rubbing his back.

"A slight amount," he said in a muffled voice. "I still feel ill, ma'am."

"I'm sorry, dear. Do you want me to read to you?" Ma asked gently.

"No, thank you. You won't want to"—he paused—"sit here with me."

"Shh, don't say that. I can stay here."

"No. It's all right."

It was hard for Norvia to listen to this, so she slipped away. Why did things have to be so complicated? Life would be so simple if there were fewer people involved.

The day before Halloween, Norvia scurried into the Social Room with her handful of carefully addressed invitations: Helen Haney, of course, along with Imogene Cullens, Ernestine Talbot, and Violet Van Pol (the trio of girls whom Helen monopolized). She chose not to invite a few people—like Ophelia Farris, who was far too intimidating—but after a long mental conversation with herself, Norvia added Katherine Sloane to the stack. Kittie might hear about the party later on and be disappointed that she hadn't been invited, and Norvia still couldn't shake the idea that she should "bring people together" with grace. It was easier said than done, she felt—probably it had been simpler to do in the olden days of her ancestors.

"Here," said Norvia in a small voice, approaching the cluster of girls and thrusting the letters at Helen. "These are for you. They're for my Halloween party. I hope you can come." *Be vivacious, be like Patty!* "I'd simply love it if you could," she added, attempting a sophisticated way of speaking.

"Will this be at *your* house?" inquired Ernestine, the queenly brunette. She held Norvia's invitation between her fingertips. "Your... stepfather's house?"

"Yes, naturally!" said Norvia, hoping to make a sparkling impression. "We're going to have heaps of fun."

Violet examined her invitation with care, while Helen glanced at Imogene as if wordlessly asking her opinion.

They'll come. Helen will remember how much fun we've had together, and she'll convince her mother to let her come. Then all the other girls will follow suit!

She hurried away before they could say another word. The most prominent guests invited, Norvia handed Kittie her envelope.

"I hope you can come," Norvia told her.

"Oh, my! Scrumptious! I'd be tickled," said Kittie, her face turning pink as she clutched the invitation. Norvia wished that Kittie wouldn't make such a scene out of every little thing. She ought to be more dignified, like the other girls.

Halloween dawned crisp and sunny, but by seven thirty that night, all was black outside. A naughty wind picked up, whistling through the walls and sending leaves scuttling across the yard. Norvia and Dicta pushed aside the parlor curtains to revel in the darkness beyond.

"It *looks* like All Hallows' Eve," whispered Dicta.

"They should be arriving soon," said Norvia, her voice full of hope.

Although Norvia had tried hard to engineer the house into emptiness on Halloween night, it did not work out that way. Ma would be home, of course, but so would Uncle Virgil (who promised he would be in his study reading most of the time). She wished he had simply gone to work late in his blacksmith shop as he sometimes did. Elton was working at the farm, and Casper was reading one of his new books in his room, but Norvia's efforts to steer Vernon to Jim and Marguerite's house for the night were to no avail. "I have been planning to practice Brahms's Piano Quartet No. 2 tonight, and I will do so," he had informed her. Norvia couldn't help feeling annoyed.

Soon the table was ready, laid with orange paper napkins and mysterious poems beside each plate of applesauce—a very Halloween-ish food, the sisters had decided. Yesterday, Young Mary had suggested making fry bread, a delicious Ojibwe food, to serve at the party. With a sinking heart, Norvia had appealed to her mother once the Marys had gone home.

"You don't have to do that," Ma assured her. "The refreshments we've prepared will be more than enough."

Norvia had breathed a little sigh of relief, even though it made her feel guilty to discard her grandmother's idea. But, after all, what would the girls think if she served Indian food at her glamorous gathering?

Her hair had been another similar concern—she couldn't help remembering the way Ophelia Farris had looked at her braids with such disdain. After far too much consideration of varying styles, Norvia simply left her braids the way they were. They would have far too much fun tonight to think about her hair!

At precisely 7:35, a sharp knock rapped on the front door, but it was only Kittie, blowing warm air into her hands.

"It's chilly outside!" She stamped her feet on the mat and hurried into the foyer. "My, doesn't this look festive?" And it did: crepe paper dangling from the chandelier, Norvia bedecked in Old Mary's black shawl, the toothy jack o' lantern with its lopsided grin welcoming them all from the foyer table.

"Come in and sit down," said Norvia, patting the sofa cushions and feeling pleased that the rest of the household was keeping their distance. Ma was in the kitchen, Uncle Virgil in his study, Casper and Vernon up in their bedrooms.

"This is so...*festive*," Kittie repeated, knocking over a stack of books in her haste to sit on the sofa.

Dicta ran back to the window. "Why don't the others come? We have to tell Helen she's going to meet a monk at sunset on Saturday."

"Oh, Dicta, we can't tell fortunes like *that*," Norvia said.

Kittie guffawed. "I think it's funny."

The sound of the door knocker reverberated triumphantly through the house. It had to be the rest of the girls! Norvia bolted to answer it, smoothing her skirt as she prepared to welcome them in.

She swung the door open to reveal Helen, Imogene, Violet, and Ernestine standing on the porch, wearing crisp drop-waist dresses and enormous bows in their hair. For a second Norvia was so delighted that speech failed her.

"I'm so glad you're here," she cried, ushering them in. "Come sit down—Kittie's already here, and that's my sister, Dicta—"

A happy smile appeared on Helen's face, but Imogene's eyes flashed with pure curiosity. "Where are your parents?" she asked in an undertone, glancing around the room as if she expected them to be hiding behind the furniture.

"This party is properly chaperoned, isn't it?" asked Ernestine, instant disapproval in her voice.

"Of course it is," said Norvia, still attempting to sound light. "My—mother is here."

"And your stepfather?" asked Violet.

"What about your real father? Where's he?" asked Imogene, sitting beside Kittie but ignoring her completely.

A barrage of emotions—hurt, anger, and embarrassment—all piled up inside Norvia, but she managed to remain calm and gracious on the outside. "My father is in Flint. Mr. Ward is in his study."

"I call him *Uncle Virgil*," Dicta broke in, swishing her skirts as she spoke. "He's very wealthy and tall and gives us everything we want."

"This is such a nice home compared to your old one," said Helen, fingering the strings of Vernon's harp as she looked around at the new wallpaper and the portrait of Celestia (who seemed gratified). "My mother almost didn't let me come, but I told her that your mother had married an upstanding man. I'm glad I was correct."

Torn between anguish and pleasure, Norvia glanced at Dicta. "Shouldn't we get our fortunes told?" she said, clasping her hands together. "Won't that be terribly gorgeous?"

"Oh, yes, gorgeous," echoed Kittie. Ernestine shrugged her shoulders indifferently, while Helen and Imogene and Violet settled comfortably on the carpet with expressions of intrigue.

After that, the party progressed admirably. With mounting satisfaction, Norvia proceeded to give out a bevy of bizarre fortunes (whispered in her ear by Dicta), ranging from "You will have a conversation with a parakeet" to "You will grow up to be the wife of a counterfeiter."

"Norvie! I didn't know you were such a howl," cried Violet.

"Actually, my sister was responsible for the fortunes," Norvia admitted.

Imogene smiled at Dicta and gushed, "Your little sister is absolutely priceless!"

"Isn't she darling?" Norvia agreed, hoping that Dicta would not become impossible.

Next came their supper of chicken, deliciously cool applesauce, mashed potatoes, and decadent chocolate cake. After that, Ernestine dashed for the Victrola in the parlor, opened its lid, and fished a smooth black record out of the bag she'd brought. "We must have music," she declared. "What's a party without a few songs?"

A sliver of panic seared through Norvia. If Vernon overheard a speck of music that he did not like coming out of the Victrola, she hated to imagine what would ensue.

Norvia hastily glanced at the title of the record—"When You and I Were Young, Maggie." Well, the title was not as silly as it could have been. And when the song came alive in all its scratchy, melodious glory, it sounded both sweet and melancholy at once.

"This is so slow," Imogene complained.

"It's *beautiful*," Ernestine corrected her.

Through the open doorway to the foyer, Norvia watched as Vernon came down the stairs and joined the girls around the source of this unclassical music. He hardly looked at any of them, just at the slowly spinning record.

"My mother liked that song," he announced.

"Who's your mother?" asked Violet.

"Celestia Ward." Vernon spread his hands in the direction of the illustrious portrait.

This was dreadful—Norvia could not stand this another second—Vernon, taking center stage to talk about his mother!—but Kittie unwittingly saved the day. "She was so attractive," said Kittie. "Could you tell us about her?"

Kittie's distraction of Vernon allowed Helen to draw Norvia aside. "How strange it must be to have such a mixed-up family now!" whispered Helen, her eyes wells of sympathy. "But then, what can one do?"

"Nothing," Norvia agreed.

Perhaps because his mother's favorite song had put him in a good humor, Vernon did not take over the piano with any heavy-handed Brahms as he had threatened earlier. Instead, once the record had finished, he created a soft, pleasant accompaniment to their after-supper conversation—some light Chopin.

"Your stepbrother is quite good at making music," remarked Ernestine, once they were all sitting around on the rug again in a sociable circle. "They say Emrial Aylmer is musical, too—or at least that he can carry a tune. Surely you've heard him sing, Norvia."

"Not yet—but I would love to," said Norvia, achieving almost as gushy a manner. "He is one of the cleverest boys at BCHS. I wish he would join the glee club and share his voice with everyone!"

Ernestine smiled. "You should really meet Stanley Collins. *He* is the cleverest. I can't imagine anyone not falling for his charms."

Norvia tried her best to sound fascinated. "Has he ever walked you home from school? And carried your books?"

"Dozens of times," Violet declared. "Ernestine's practically been inundated by his attentions!"

"I've been inundated by attentions from Valentine, my future husband," Dicta contributed eagerly. "He's always bringing me lollipops and things and saying I have the best vocabulary of any girl in the universe."

During this confab, Norvia grew aware of the fact that Vernon was halting his music occasionally to turn and give her an odd, almost confused look. Was it because she was acting so much like the other girls? The popular girls? But what difference did that make? It was good that she was growing out of her shyness.

The riotous conversation surrounding every boy in BCHS and every juicy little bit of gossip was a success. As the party wore on, Norvia began to feel a sense of complete confidence that she had never felt before. The girls liked her. They confided in her. They were laughing at *her* jokes and enjoying *her* party.

But the best part of the evening was still to come: the cellar game. Dicta had found this idea in a book she had borrowed from Valentine entitled *Games for All Occasions*.

" 'The Cellar-stairs test is where a girl boldly goes down the cellar stairs backward, holding a mirror, and trying to catch in it the features of him who is to be her mate,' " Norvia read from the book, giggling.

"That sounds—interesting," said Kittie.

"Oh, goody!" shrieked Imogene.

"I hope mine is handsome," said Dicta, brandishing a small hand mirror.

"Be careful," Ma warned them from the kitchen.

They clustered at the cellar door. Dicta inched backward down the steps, thumping one by one with her limp. When she reached the bottom, she let out a grumpy sigh. "I didn't see anybody," she muttered, returning and thrusting the mirror at Kittie.

Kittie, always game for anything, thundered down the stairs with dexterous speed. But she, too, came back with feigned disappointment. "Maybe I saw his nose," she said doubtfully. "But nothing more than that."

The other girls tried—Helen, Imogene, Violet—and all of them came up laughing and joking. Ernestine descended the steps happily enough but returned mildly disgruntled (she had tripped on the last step).

Norvia, when it was her turn, edged down the stairs, making sure she had a firm foothold on each slippery cement step. She reached the bottom and held up her mirror—

Louis Behren!

She screeched and jumped around, stunned at the *very real* sight of Louis Behren, her Dashing Young Man, laughing at the foot of the steps. Elton popped out of the shadows, too, also laughing.

"The look on your face!" cried Elton.

"I hope we didn't scare you too badly," said Louis in a voice tinged with concern.

"No—no," Norvia stammered, unable to recover from the shock.

"Who are *you?*" Dicta exclaimed, limping down the stairs.

"I'm Louis Behren," he said. "And you are . . . ?"

Dicta stood tall and put on her most Dicta-ish smile. "I'm Mary Benedicta Nelson, but everybody calls me Dicta. I was named after the most *sacred* of women in all of Catholicism—and every other religion, too, I expect—*the Virgin Mary*, mother of Jesus. And I was named after my grandmothers and a famous nun, too."

Louis appeared to be charmed by this unorthodox introduction. He shook the hand of the sacredly named child before him. "I'm pleased to make your acquaintance."

"He doesn't have much of a chin," whispered Dicta.

"*Dicta!*" Norvia hissed.

Elton wiped tears of laughter from his eyes. "Ma said you'd be playing this game tonight, so we decided to hide out. I brought Lou over, figuring we could play a good joke. Actually, it was all Aylmer's idea!"

"I confess," said Aylmer, also crawling out from the shadows. "It was my plan, yes, but alas, I could not quite bring myself to scare you out of your wits, m'lady. So we made Lou do the dirty work."

"Aylmer!" Kittie scoffed, climbing down the stairs. "You were not invited."

"You most certainly were not!" agreed Helen, laughing.

"I heard you talking in the Social Room," said Aylmer, flashing her an obnoxious smile. "Thus we lads all joined forces."

"Pretty sneaky," said Norvia with a disapproving frown, but her heart danced a jig at the sight of Louis Behren smiling in her cellar. Who needed a pumpkin carriage?

After Louis and Aylmer said their goodbyes and left North Star, a joyous feeling settled into Norvia's heart. Louis was well on his way to becoming her beau, and all the girls had enjoyed her party!

However, the boys' departure seemed to signal to the girls that it was time to leave. "We've had a perfectly scrumptious time," said Violet, squeezing Norvia's hand.

"Thanks ever so much for inviting us," Imogene added.

Ernestine donned her gloves and coat and smiled at Norvia. "See you at school!"

"It was a lovely affair," Helen assured her.

"I'm so glad you could all come," cried Norvia. Recklessly she added: "Would you like to come here again for—another party?" *We could invite boys next time! If Uncle Virgil lets us—*

"Oh, wait," said Ernestine, looking around the foyer in dismay. "Where on earth did I leave my bag? And the record I brought?"

"They must still be in the parlor. I'll fetch them," said Norvia, hurrying away.

She found the round black record in the parlor and smiled at its adorable label of a puppy listening to a Victrola. She grabbed Ernestine's bag and headed back to the foyer...

But before she reached them—while she was still out of sight—Norvia heard them exchanging whispers.

"I'm not going to her next party," Ernestine was saying in a quiet but flat voice. "You three can do what you wish, but I don't want to get the reputation of being friends with a divorcée's daughter. I only came because I wanted to find out if she likes Aylmer—I think I can steal him away from her. I've liked him ever so long."

Norvia swayed with dizziness. She leaned against the parlor wall for support.

Imogene giggled softly. "I came just to see what it was like here. I was so curious to see her mother and her stepfamily. Do you think it's true that they're Indians? That's what Mrs. Ferguson said. Her brother really looked it, didn't he?"

"Too bad we never got to see her stepfather," Violet whispered. "That would have been interesting."

"Well *I* had a very nice time," said Kittie staunchly. These words penetrated Norvia's grief, sending in a ray of hope. If a mere acquaintance like Kittie would support her, Helen certainly would.

"And you, Helen?" Ernestine prodded. "What do you think of your friend now?"

Norvia froze, waiting, unable to breathe.

Helen hesitated for a moment. "My mother would probably have a fit if I came to another of Norvia's parties," she admitted. "She thinks it's improper for me to socialize with them. You're probably right—we really shouldn't spoil our reputations."

"What do you mean by that?" Kittie asked, almost defiantly.

Ernestine's voice came out dry, almost sarcastic. "Must I spell it out, Katherine? Norvia's mother is a *divorcée*. That means she's not fit for *real* ladies to socialize with. Because if we did, our chances for a good place in society—and *suitable beaux*—will dwindle to absolutely nothing."

"Take Louis and Aylmer, for example," said Violet. "Why would they want to involve themselves with a girl who will undoubtedly take after her mother? Norvia won't make a good wife someday. She's liable to leave her husband, too!"

Tears clouded Norvia's eyes, blurring her vision. She had to give Ernestine her things—but she had to get out of here; she couldn't stand this another second longer. Would they see the tears in her eyes? Norvia rushed into the foyer, stuffing Ernestine's bag in her hands.

"Here you are—thank you for coming," she said, without looking squarely at any of them. "I—I'm going to bed. Good night."

"Good night, Norvia!" they all chirped in cheerful unison, slamming the door behind them. Did the door-slamming make the house shake, or was it just the pulsating of Norvia's throbbing heart?

She bolted up the stairs, almost crashing into Casper on the way.

"Is your party over already?" he asked.

Norvia could not answer—she knew she would break down crying if she did. Vernon began to climb the stairs behind her.

"May I ask why you were acting so—*different* tonight?" Vernon inquired. "You seemed—not quite like usual."

Oh, now he's going to start picking at me. Norvia couldn't stand another word.

"I'm trying not to be shy," she said in as fierce a tone as she could muster through the lump in her throat. "I am trying to be a—a good heroine."

Vernon looked nonplussed. "But...that is not how it works," he said slowly, sounding almost confused. "The best characters in books do not act like all the other people simply to be—well-liked. They merely become a better person by the end of the story, through—proper means. In the words of Shakespeare—'to thine own self be true.'"

This time Norvia just ran into her room, where she gave in to the racking sobs that clutched at her throat. She cried for her lost friend and her hopeless popularity—but mostly she cried for herself.

Why am I always at everyone else's mercy? Why does everyone else get to decide what happens to me and how I feel? She cried inside, asking herself questions that she could never answer.

Norvia dabbed at her eyes, trying to come to grips with the situation. So they all viewed her as an oddity, a curiosity to be gawked at and whispered about. That was the only reason they had come. Now she knew how Vernon had felt that day when he thought she'd been staring at him.

Is this how *everyone* viewed her—and her family? Perhaps that book on Uncle Virgil's shelf was only there because he saw Indians as a *curiosity*—not because he would relish a connection to them.

What hurt the most was thinking of Louis and Aylmer. Louis probably had no idea she was the daughter of divorced parents—but as soon as he found out, that would be the end of his friendliness. But surely Aylmer had heard? He was always in the Social Room picking up bits of gossip, unlike Louis, who hurried from class to class and left BCHS as soon as the bell rang.

Does he feel the same way the girls do? Does he think I'm just a curiosity?

CHAPTER TWELVE
FRAGILE HEARTS

"What are you reading today, my looking-glass lass?" Aylmer jogged along the road beside her, looking pleased with himself.

Norvia glanced up from *A Little Princess*. She had buried herself in it; sympathizing with Sara Crewe's miserable life smoothed a balm over her own sadness. "This one," she said, holding it up so he could see the title. She didn't have the heart to tell him anything about the plot. She had felt sad from the moment she woke up—especially when she put her hair determinedly in a rolled-up knot with a bow instead of her usual braids. *No one* was going to think that Norvia looked like an Indian on top of being a divorcée's daughter.

"Looks dull to me," Aylmer remarked. "Say, are we going to that football game against Charlevoix? Together, I mean, for two is always better than one."

This puzzled Norvia. Could it be that Aylmer was not as well-versed in school gossip as she thought? If he knew the truth, he would never wish to be seen in public with the daughter of divorced parents.

He must not know!

To her own surprise, she found herself wishing that Aylmer would never find out the truth. Even if she did not want him to be her beau, he was at least a friend—one even the popular Ernestine approved of. And a good heroine had plenty of friends—like Sara Crewe.

But could she really risk attending the game? Wouldn't the other girls be there? She couldn't bear the thought of facing them. Would they tell him everything?

"I—I don't know," Norvia hesitated. Oh, she *wanted* to make him happy—she wanted to be a good friend like Sara, to say yes and agree to go to the game with him. But what would such a decision cost her? If any of the girls noticed her and started gossiping among themselves—how could she stand it?

"Well—I suppose so," said Norvia finally.

A warm, spreading glow washed over her as Aylmer grinned jovially in response. "Grand, m'lady! See you then."

As they parted ways, Norvia entered the school and saw Kittie hurrying along the hallway, and for once she was glad to see her. Kittie had stood up for her—but Norvia's cheeks burned at the recollection of the party. How could she ever be around Kittie again without remembering that hideous conversation?

But Kittie ran up to her, gregarious as usual. "Are you and Aylmer going to the game against Charlevoix, I hope?"

"Yes," said Norvia reluctantly.

"Splendid! Cal Evergreen is taking me. Yes—I managed to snag a soph!"

Even Kittie was more popular than she was these days. A sophomore was willing to go with her! And all the girls weren't gossiping about *her*. It struck Norvia that perhaps it wouldn't be so detrimental to become better friends with Kittie.

Boyne City High School was abuzz that week, with the hallways full of snippets of talk about "the big game" and "Charlevoix High" and "this Saturday." A cluster of tall boys kept saying things like, "We're gonna trounce 'em!" and "We'll show 'em who's got the goods!"

Norvia felt disconnected when she overheard such conversations, especially when the silliest of girls chimed in with, "You're all so *strong!*" and "You'll *easily* beat those Charlevoix boys." Was Vernon right? Had she been as silly as those girls? But what bothered her most of all was the fact that those girls doing the talking cared nothing for her—and never would. *She* would never be admitted to their inner circle of popularity.

That day in the Social Room, Norvia looked for Aylmer to ask what time the game was. She found him with a group of friends, slouched against the walls and sitting astride chairs, playing cards and gabbing about the war. The scene reminded her of Pa playing poker with his friends years ago—only these boys were not betting. If only Pa could have played without gambling, too.

"You hear about Brussels and Antwerp?" Aylmer asked, studying the cards in his hand.

"Nasty business," agreed his dark-haired companion, tossing down a discard. "The Germans have those siege guns and now submarines."

"France is half murdering 'em, but they won't give up," Aylmer said, shaking his head. "Wonder if Wilson will ever let us get in on the action. I'd easily quit school and go into uniform."

"We can't for a couple years yet," another boy said, resting his head in his hand. "And even then, you'd have to get your folks' permission to join up, I'd bet."

"That ought to be easy for me, then," said Aylmer dryly. "My folks would sign off anything to get me out of the way. Gin," he concluded, laying down his cards with a flourish. Catching Norvia's eye, he excused himself from the game. "Something you need?" he inquired.

Norvia wished she could call off the entire thing. "What time is the game?"

"Let's see; Cal's going with Kittie, and they're both coming by to pick me up—and Cal's borrowing his father's carriage. I tell you what, we'll all be by at about one o'clock. Marvelous, eh?"

"Marvelous," said Norvia weakly.

She could hardly concentrate in bookkeeping class later on, and she made frightful mistakes. Was she not intelligent enough to become a professional working woman after all? Perhaps not, if she couldn't focus on which column to place which number.

"I know it's not easy," Miss Darnell sympathized. "But if it's any encouragement, you have an excellent memory, and that comes in handy."

Typing class went a bit better. Norvia loved the feel of the smooth metal keys under her fingers, and her spirits rose a bit as she worked.

All that evening, Norvia worried about the impending football game. She would be a misfit—everyone would be talking—and what if Ernestine approached Aylmer during the game and said something about Norvia's divorced parents? After all, Ernestine wanted Aylmer for herself. She could just picture Ernestine hurrying up to them at the game and asking, "How is your stepfather?"—or something to that effect—and Aylmer would want to know why she had a stepfather....

Her heart thrummed every time she envisioned it.

Kittie, Cal, and Aylmer were punctual. They reached North Star at precisely one o'clock, and Norvia could hear them outside, calling for her with wild hoots of impatience. It was Norvia who delayed their departure for the football game, suddenly overcome all over again with paralyzing fear. She fixed her hair again and smoothed her striped dress.

"Norvie, there's people outside waiting for you," Dicta announced.

"I know."

"Are you sure Aylmer isn't your beau?" Dicta asked in a thrilled tone, gazing out the window.

Norvia pushed the curtain aside to see Aylmer with his hands in his pockets and Kittie linking arms with a brawny, bespectacled boy—evidently Cal Evergreen.

"No, he's not," said Norvia firmly. Gathering her wits, she hurried outside, trying to stand up straight and assume a pleasant expression.

"Norvia! Here's the soon-to-be-conquering hero of BCHS!" hollered Kittie, smiling up at Cal, who towered above all of them. "Won't it be fabulous when we beat Charlevoix? They're a cocky lot, so sure they'll win everything! Oops, I forgot to make the introductions—I'm such a scatterbrain. Norvie, this is Calvin Evergreen, and Cal, this is Norvia Nelson. She's a freshman this year."

"Excited about the game?" Cal asked, a smile warming his face.

Norvia nodded, returning the smile faintly.

Aylmer offered his arm to Norvia. "Shall we, m'lady?"

The football game was difficult to understand, despite Kittie's hurried explanations in between cheering and waving to Cal out on the field. Once, Norvia caught sight of Helen Haney, who was walking along with a good-looking boy—a sophomore, no doubt. She scrunched further down in her seat.

Aylmer sat beside Norvia, eating one sandwich after another, often stuffing a few pretzels into his mouth along the way. Apparently, he was one of those boys with unlimited appetites, like Herman, who had not written in over a month. What if Herman was ill? Or worse... Railroad work could be dangerous....

"So, you know nothing about football?" Aylmer asked, brushing crumbs off his patched jacket and onto the ground below. "I mean, absolutely nothing? Some girls pretend they're dense about men's games just to win the honor of a long conversation elucidating every detail. You one of those girls?"

Torn between offense and amusement, Norvia fixed him with an arched eyebrow but didn't say a word.

"*Ahh*, my friend is coy. So be it." Another pretzel disappeared down the hatch. Aylmer crumpled the paper bag in which he had brought his snacks and leaned back on the wooden benches. "What, then, are your early impressions of the noble sport of football?"

"It—looks dangerous," admitted Norvia.

"Sometimes danger is courageous," said Aylmer. "Like those soldiers in France. Somebody's got to defend the people, or else the kaiser and his army will conquer them."

"Yes, but football's not like that." In a rush of honesty, she added, "I think it's silly to jump all over each other and get bloody for no reason."

Aylmer chuckled. "I'll tell 'em you said so."

"Don't you dare!" Norvia cried, but Aylmer just kept laughing.

Norvia began to watch the game closely, although she didn't understand any of the action or the rules. Aylmer assured her that BCHS was beating Charlevoix handily, and it was rather fascinating to watch him bellow and clap at random intervals. She began to feel a bit better—the sun was shining even though it was November, and it felt nice and warm. Everyone around her seemed happy, especially Kittie—and somehow Norvia got the feeling that she should be happy, too, even though nothing was going her way.

And there was Ernestine, inching her way through the crowded benches toward Norvia and Aylmer. She was going to make trouble—she was going to tell him about the divorce to try and make him lose interest in Norvia.

"Could we leave?" asked Norvia suddenly.

"Game's not over yet," said Aylmer, not even glancing at her.

"I know, but—*please*," Norvia insisted, a ring of desperation in her voice.

A look of disappointment—or hurt—flashed across Aylmer's face. "Tired of sitting with me, I guess?" he asked.

"No—I just—I . . ." Norvia could not conjure up a proper answer.

"It's just that Norvia is probably feeling very exhausted and overwhelmed, this being her first football game and all," explained Kittie, rushing to offer an explanation and flashing an encouraging smile in Norvia's direction.

Aylmer sighed. "All right," he consented. "I'll walk you home."

Norvia gave Kittie what she hoped was a look of immense gratitude as they walked away.

As soon as she reached North Star and had closed the door on

Aylmer, Norvia was filled with a sense of relief. Strangely, this feeling did not last long—it was quickly replaced by a stab of grief.

"Back so soon?" asked Uncle Virgil.

"Yes," said Norvia, hastening upstairs.

She wasted Saturday evening toiling away on homework—she hardly even had time to read *A Little Princess*. Sunday consisted of church and listening to Vernon play Liszt's *Liebesträume,* which he claimed was "of a religious nature, *d'une grande beauté.*" The piece had a moody sound—not exactly somber but not particularly upbeat, either. Liszt and his religion floated through the house for a good hour while Norvia read her book and Uncle Virgil read his golden-paged Bible in the corner of the parlor.

After the fourth time Vernon played *Liebesträume,* Ma set aside her knitting and asked him, her eyes pleading a bit, "Couldn't you play something else, dear? Something sprightlier. I feel as if we're at a funeral."

Vernon gazed at her with a dark frown. "My mother is listening to it."

Ma blinked several times and glanced at Uncle Virgil before she vanished into the kitchen.

"Vernon, would you please play something cheerful?" said Uncle Virgil, without looking up from his Bible. "We brought you that new sheet music from Lansing."

"I prefer to play something that will honor the Lord," said Vernon in an even tone, "as it is the day of worship."

"There's nothing sacrilegious about Tchaikovsky's instrumentals. Play that finale one I like."

Vernon sat more erect than ever on the piano stool. "You mean the third movement of his *Piano Trio No. I in A Minor.* Papa, it only sounds proper with at least a violin accompaniment, and without Marguerite, I fear it should sound discordant."

However discordant the *Piano Trio* might have sounded with only a single piano, Norvia never knew, for at that moment Casper entered the parlor with a paper.

"I got this on Friday. I was supposed to give this to my father, but I guess I have to give it to you now," said Casper ungraciously, handing the paper to Uncle Virgil. "It's a note from my teacher saying you're supposed to come to talk to him on Monday."

Norvia's chest tightened. The ticking of the grandfather clock grew ominous with its everlasting *tick...tick...tick...*

Uncle Virgil unfolded the stiff note. After a few moments of silent perusal, he asked, "What did you do, son?"

"Hardly anything."

"What did you do?" Uncle Virgil repeated the question, more firmly this time.

"Robbed a bank," suggested Dicta, bouncing up and down for no reason. "Cheated on a test."

Casper shrugged. "I was playing cards with some other boys in class before the teacher, Mr. Ritter, came in. He got a bit sore about it, but I don't see what's so wrong. Pa played cards all the time."

"There is nothing inherently wrong with card-playing, unless there is gambling involved," said Uncle Virgil, after a moment's pause. "But if you knew this was a defiance of the rules, you shouldn't have done it, and you ought to be reprimanded."

"I didn't know it was against the rules at *this* school," Casper stressed pointedly.

Norvia cringed at this flimsiest of excuses. In the background, Vernon began to play a slow, edgy, mysterious song—the kind that might have been played at a courtroom trial, if music were played at such events.

"Did you suspect it was the wrong thing to do?" asked Uncle Virgil, sounding very much like a courtroom judge.

"I thought it might be, but I didn't know for sure," Casper shot back. "Anyway, that's not the real problem. Mr. Ritter has it in for me, 'cause I'm a dunce at school. I get *F*s all the time."

"Do you study hard and try your best?"

"No. There's no point. Someday I'll work in a factory like Elton used to, and then it won't matter if I got an *E* or an *F*."

Uncle Virgil shook his head. "That isn't the best attitude, son."

"It's my attitude," said Casper. "It's my *father's* attitude."

"What sort of work do you want to do when you grow up?" asked Uncle Virgil in a curious, conversational tone. Norvia began to feel a little better. . . . Perhaps they would have a nice talk, and this terrible tense feeling would melt away.

Casper gave his stepfather an odd look. "I'll do whatever comes along. I mean, I guess if I had to choose, I'd—you know, work with autos and things like that. Or I'd go to sea."

Uncle Virgil thought a moment. "Why don't you apologize to your teacher on Monday and tell him that you won't play cards again? Explain that you didn't know for certain that it was against the rules, and you won't—"

Casper interrupted, his face flushed with anger. "I'm not apologizing, and you can't boss me around. And you're not my father—so stop calling me *son*."

At that, silence reigned over the room.

Vernon began to rearrange booklets of sheet music, and Norvia braced herself for the inevitable explosion. She felt as if her heart was stretched thin and taut—Uncle Virgil would be so angry—he would yell—it would be horrible. Norvia darted a glance at Ma, who looked as if she might cry.

But the explosion didn't come. Uncle Virgil merely rose from his velvet armchair, put down his Bible, and left the room.

Dicta's eyes grew round as translucent marbles and twice as bright. "Casper, you shouldn't have said that. Now he's on the warpath. He might whip you. He's probably going to get a birch bark switch."

157

"Papa doesn't believe in corporal punishment," said the proud product of this disciplinary method.

Uncle Virgil returned with a pencil, a paper, and a calm demeanor.

"What if you came to help me in my blacksmith shop after school?" Uncle Virgil suggested. "If you want to learn a trade, I will teach you a trade, and I'm called upon to work on automobiles from time to time. However, the law insists that you must have schooling—"

"*He* doesn't have to go to school," Casper interrupted again, jerking a thumb at Vernon.

"You know he is too ill to attend school," Uncle Virgil replied. "But education is compulsory for most young people, and I think that's a good thing. You need an education these days to get ahead, to advance yourself. If you try your best at school, I'll teach you my trade."

Casper stared at him—then his eyes shifted to the pencil and paper in Uncle Virgil's hands. "What are those for?" he asked with suspicion.

"For the apology letter you will write to your teacher. If you write it and leave it on his desk tomorrow morning, I will talk with your teacher, and we'll say no more about it."

Norvia felt weak and limp with relief, and she saw a bit of relief creep into Casper's eyes, as well. Perhaps he realized now how dreadfully he'd behaved.

"Yes, sir . . . I'll do it," he murmured, accepting the paper. "Thanks."

Uncle Virgil put a comforting hand on Casper's shoulder, and Norvia detected a tinge of sadness in his eyes. But before she had a chance to ponder this any further, Casper pulled another envelope out of his pocket—one that bore familiar handwriting and a Flint postmark. His voice sounded painfully casual.

"Oh yeah, and this came yesterday from Pa."

NOVEMBER 1909
GIIZHIGAANZO | BLUE

Norvia gazed out over the waters surrounding Beaver Island, ever-shifting in their lapping cascades of aqua and azure. A breathtaking expanse of sky stretched out, reaching to the moon over the fir-starred hills on the far end of the island. It was on nights such as these that Norvia really understood that the world was round—she could see the curve of the earth like it was a miniature globe on a revolving stand. (Or at the very least, she could *pretend* she saw the curve, and that was enough to satisfy even Norvia's demanding imagination.)

"The stars were a comfort to our ancestors," remarked Grand-père reflectively, looking up with thoughtful eyes at the cloud-speckled sky, which was like a bolt of dark-blue sateen fresh from the general store. "Of course, they understood them. In the old days they looked to the North Star to find their way. . . . *Giiwedin'anang*. There it is up there—so reliable. It's the *maang*, the loon, that makes up that collection of stars."

Norvia looked up, searchingly. A bright star met her eyes, a tremendously pretty one.

"I like that," she said, looping her arm through her grandfather's. But a creeping melancholy darkened the edge of her consciousness, giving her an unease that quick thoughts could not dispel. She leaned against the thick flannel sleeve of Grand-père's coat. "What if Pa keeps"—she fumbled for words that sounded casual and lightweight—"playing poker, and gambling, and going off during stormy weather and—"

Grand-père studied her face, listening intently. His interest gave her confidence.

At last she burst out, unable to contain the words another second: "Why can't he find a *nice* job? An easy job, like—like Laura McDonough's father? He's a butcher. Or he could keep a lighthouse like Mr. Schmidt!" Norvia loved to imagine her father perched above their little island with his beacon of light wafting over the world.

"There are only two lighthouses on Beaver Island," said Grand-père gently. "And their keepers do not intend to retire anytime soon. Schmidt has young children, you know, and he needs the money."

But Norvia's frustration would not easily be placated. "I want him to stop sailing," she said firmly.

"The sea gets in a man's blood. Not easy when it takes hold of you—*c'est une obsession.*"

This was not the real truth. Norvia recognized it instantly, and Grand-père knew that she knew. But he gave her such a sad smile of sympathy that she didn't care, because she knew he understood her heart.

And then all she thought was that it was a marvelous feeling to be walking beside her grandfather in the blossoming blue of a winter night.

"Let's go home," she whispered.

At home, snug in the little cottage, Norvia and Dicta crawled into their bed. Dicta was cradling her rag doll, Corky, in her arms, while Norvia lay staring at the ceiling. Ma had gone to the lighthouse, as usual on waiting nights like these, and Old Mary had fallen asleep in her rocking chair with a basket of mending in her lap.

So it was Young Mary who opened the hope chest at the foot of their bed with a comforting creak and lifted a thick, homey quilt from the mothballs, spreading it over her granddaughters and tucking them in. The room was all comfortable shadow mingled with honied lamplight.

For Norvia, the quilt was like an old friend. It was so familiar, with its bright-green patches and crimson folds. There were other colors, too: blue and black and pink and yellow and purple and white. "This quilt tells a story," Young Mary told the girls. "All important things do. This piece," she continued, indicating a square of blue broadcloth in the middle of the quilt, "came from a dress that Grand-père's grandmother wore when she was a young girl. In those days handsome gifts were given to the Ojibwes by the Indian Agencies—silver jewelry and ribbons of many colors—and this cloth was one of the things given to her family. For years Grand-père's mother—"

"Elizabeth," said Norvia, recalling the genealogy. "Lisette for short."

"How well you remember!" said Young Mary warmly, smoothing the last few lumps in the quilt. "For many years, she saved different scraps of fabric, from her own family as well as her husband's, in order to make a quilt. But she never quite got around to it—raising thirteen children on an island isn't easy. And then she passed away. So my mother and I took over the quilting of it, and we added our own scraps to the mix."

Norvia vaguely remembered Great-Grandmother Lisette. Not her looks so much, but her voice: deep yet soft, singing a lullaby in Anishinaabemowin, every syllable safe and soothing.

"Lisette couldn't write, but she drew pictures of each square's origins, and I keep that old list in a drawer." She pointed to a tiny red dollop of fabric. "*Miskwaa*—that's 'red' in Anishinaabemowin. And blue, the color of the sky, is *giizhigaande*. It is funny how colors can mean feelings—when someone is 'feeling blue,' they are sad." Young Mary smiled thoughtfully as she continued to study the red scrap. "This is from Acadia, back in the old days. It was—let me see now—a good hundred and fifty years ago. The LeBlancs had to get out quickly and shove off to Boston, leaving their beloved land behind." Young Mary's eyes sparkled sadly as she looked at Norvia. "This bit of crimson cloth was part of a shawl that one of your great-greats—fourth-great, if I'm thinking it through correctly—wore, as she was forced onto the boat leaving for parts unknown."

"And why did they have to leave?" asked Norvia, dumbfounded by this tale as she always was. She could never get it right in her head—why her Acadian ancestors had been forced to flee, to board ships and live in exile.

"Well, because the British rule Canada, of course, and the Brits and the French didn't get along so well back in the day. The two nations were almost always at war! They were afraid there'd be trouble if there were too many French living in Canada, you see, so they wanted the Acadians gone."

"The world is always quarreling," Norvia observed, stroking the red cloth. Imagine that this had been worn by one of her foremothers, so long ago! "The Acadians were French?"

"Yes, indeed; French immigrants who'd made their home in Canada, but it did not last as long as they hoped." She paused, as if still considering the days of those long-ago people and the beauty they left behind. "It's a troubled world, but a pretty one."

"But they were able to get back to Quebec," said Norvia, anxious for a happy ending. Dicta had already dropped off to sleep.

Grand-père, passing the door on his way down the hall, called in: "After a time, yes! But first they were sent off to Boston, even though the Bostonians didn't want them. Nobody wanted us," he added with a laugh that made Norvia giggle.

Ma came home then—Norvia could hear the front door swinging open and shut, and then Ma's light footsteps as she tripped up the staircase. Untying the shawl from her head, she came into the girls' bedroom and whispered, "You didn't all have to wait up for me."

"Norvia was keeping me company," said Young Mary, patting the end of the bed. "Sit down."

Ma sat obediently. "I just can't sleep at night when he's away. I try, but I can't." She let out a little sigh as she fingered the fringe on her shawl. "It isn't fair of him."

"Shh, now," Young Mary said.

"He'll be home soon," said Norvia confidently.

Ma flashed her a meager smile. "I hope so. It's just that..." Ma stood up and went to the window, staring out into the shimmering black night. "Sometimes I wonder if he's going to come back."

"God will watch over him," Young Mary assured her.

"I mean, what if he *stays* in Chicago or Milwaukee? What if one day he simply decides he's tired of us?"

"Questions, questions without answers! Stop your fussing. He's your husband, and he is a good man." Young Mary opened her sewing basket made of brown wicker, one of the sturdiest things in their possession. "Start on your mending. You said you wanted to patch your gray dress before church."

Ma sat on the bed and set to work sewing up the little hole in the sleeve of her best dress. Norvia watched in mesmerized fascination. Ma was an accomplished seamstress, the finest on the island, better than her mother or grandmother. Sometimes she talked about making dresses for other women and trying to earn money for it, but she never discussed this when Pa was around.

"Ma," whispered Norvia. "When Pa comes back—" She paused, allowing her words to linger on the air.

"Yes?" said Ma.

"Everything will be perfect."

Ma smiled. "For a while, anyway," she agreed.

Pa brought them gifts from the mainland—beautiful gifts. Norvia and Dicta each received a porcelain doll robed in finery, and Ma a long dress the color of apricots with frills galore.

"You've been gambling again!" Ma accused him.

"So I played a hand or two," said Pa casually. "The important thing is that I won. Won't you wear it to the Donovans'?"

Norvia expected Ma to say no immediately, to throw those words back in his face. But she was running her fingertips up and down the folds of the silk dress, and a tiny smile of pleasure had come to rest on her lips. "Oh, Anders," she whispered. "It's so elegant.".

"You'll look like an angel," he murmured.

"But I can't wear it." Ma grew resolute, staid, the prim and proper self she often was. "No one else has anything like this! It would be such showing off. I couldn't bear to have them think that I am putting on airs."

"I'm tired of everyone thinking my family has nothing. That I can't provide for you. That—that you're just the usual half-breeds."

Norvia cradled her doll closer and wished that Pa did not have such a knack for making them sound so...undesirable.

CHAPTER THIRTEEN
A CONFLICTED LIFE

Ma took the letter first. She took it matter-of-factly, as if receiving letters from Pa was an everyday occurrence. "Let me see that, Casper," she said briskly, and she studied the envelope. Everyone except Uncle Virgil crowded around to see the letter—Elton even came down from his bedroom, and Vernon and Dicta craned their necks—and Norvia felt a chill of loneliness blow through her.

To Angélique, the envelope said. No last name. *To Angélique, Boyne City, Michigan.* Norvia marveled at the postal workers for knowing who "Angélique" was—until she realized that *everyone* knew who her mother was now. But why hadn't Pa put down the address of the Marys' house? Or Ma's old surname? As far as Norvia knew, he had no idea of the marriage.

"I—I didn't expect Anders to write," Ma faltered. She still hadn't opened the envelope. "I told him . . . He gave me his address in Flint. I wrote and told him—everything. But I said I didn't expect an answer, or desire one."

Now Uncle Virgil was the one trying to keep his voice light-hearted. "Well, I think it's only natural for him to respond if you wrote a letter. It's courtesy, after all."

"But I told him not to," insisted Ma.

Since when had that ever mattered? Norvia wondered. Pa had always done exactly what he wanted. She couldn't stand the suspense another minute—she wished she could open the letter herself—

"Here," said Casper, slitting the envelope with his pearl-handled knife.

"Why didn't you tell me yesterday that this letter came?" Ma asked, pulling out the paper with nervous hands.

Casper fixed his gaze on the dark, patterned carpet. "I don't know," he muttered.

Norvia knew why: because he had wanted to avoid this moment as long as possible.

For a long time—too long—Ma read the letter in complete silence, leaning against the piano under the eyes of Celestia Ward, who looked as if she were trying to read over Ma's shoulder.

Ma stuffed the letter back into its jagged envelope.

"Your father only wishes for you children to write to him," she said, stiff and formal.

Norvia couldn't believe it. "That's all?" *That was all he said?* He didn't rant about her sudden marriage to a total stranger? He didn't say anything about how sad he was, or how much he missed them? He didn't warn her not to let his children further their worthless educations?

"That is all," said Ma, glancing away toward the window where the November sunshine streamed through.

Uncle Virgil cleared his throat. "Well, that doesn't seem like an unreasonable request. I think every father likes to hear from his children when they're apart." He said this in a strange way—as if he was hurt.

"I'll write Pa a big, long letter all about my play and Gilma's new dress and how Vernon is a musical genius," Dicta chattered, already searching for a piece of stationery for her missive.

When Norvia went to bed that night, she didn't try to catch a glimpse of any disappearing stars, and she didn't think of walking along the shores of Lake Michigan with Grand-père. Her heart had felt heavy ever since Ma read Pa's letter. A piece of her wanted to reach out to him—to write, to tell him about everything that had transpired since he left, like Dicta—but just like the day he left for Flint, she felt that anything she did simply wouldn't change anything.

166

Nothing I write will fix anything or make me feel better.

Norvia picked up *A Little Princess* and lost herself in the story.

The following afternoon felt sleepy, with lazy rain drizzling down the windows. Vernon had played a dreary Rachmaninoff piece until everyone made him stop, and now he was reading *Oliver Twist* on the settee amid a mountain of cushions. Casper and Dicta flopped on the carpet, staring at the portrait of Celestia, while Norvia finished reading *A Little Princess*. Peggy and Mr. Bingley were, unbelievably, sitting side by side on the floor.

"I'm bored to tears," said Dicta.

"I'm bored beyond tears," said Casper.

Vernon closed his book and sighed. "I wish my life had *one-sixth* the spice that Oliver's did. Not that I want to be orphaned—or hungry—or a juvenile criminal—but I wouldn't mind an edge of adventure, a good lark or two. Just think: if my father *had* died as well as my mother, and if I *hadn't* any sisters or aunts or uncles, I might have ended up as Oliver did." His eyes seemed to sparkle with the prospect. "*Cela semble si excitant.*"

"We all know what you're saying, so there's no point in speaking French to impress us," Casper said with disdain.

"My *mother* spoke French," Vernon replied loftily.

"I want more excitement, too," said Dicta, sitting up. "I want to have an interesting life, like a motion picture actress, a battlefield nurse, or a *spy*."

"I'd like to be a spy, too," said Casper. "We could start a whole ring of spies."

"With passwords and a mystifying handshake and messages with jumbled letters that no one can decipher," said Vernon, his words tumbling over each other with enthusiasm.

His fervor made Norvia want to join in. "Our ring of spies would need a mysterious name." She laughed.

"We could call ourselves the Black Knights," said Vernon, to honor *Ivanhoe*.

"The Blue Knights," said Casper, to be silly.

"The Blue Knights of Champagne," Dicta concluded with a rapt expression.

Norvia set aside her book. "Do you even know what champagne is?"

"It has a good ring to it," Dicta said stubbornly.

Celestia Ward almost seemed to be laughing at them in that portrait above. Norvia realized that it had been a long time since the portrait seemed to stare at her with appraising eyes, and she grew aware of a strangely comfortable feeling. Somehow it felt right to joke around with Vernon, to include him in lighthearted sibling conversation. Somehow it made her feel better.

"Is this the first time you've read *Oliver Twist*?" asked Norvia, venturing her question with only a hint of timidity in her voice.

Vernon's unusual smile faded, and his expression returned to a frown. "No, I've read it before. Papa used to read it to me, in the evenings. Before—everything," he said, gesturing around at his stepsiblings.

Norvia felt that same old twist of irritation with him and didn't say anything more.

By the end of November, the hallways at BCHS grew full of excited students, congregating to discuss plans for Thanksgiving. The conversations reached their peak on the Wednesday afternoon before the big day, as everyone gathered their coats and scarves to leave school.

"Me and my folks are headed down to my grandfather's farm in Muskegon," boasted Cal Evergreen. "We'll go back for Christmas, too. Chop our own tree from his private forest."

"My father and mother were married on Thanksgiving, so we always have their anniversary celebration with cake and candles on the table," said Ophelia Farris, tossing her flawless hair behind her shoulder. Her hair was not thick like Norvia's—everyone probably thought Ophelia's was much prettier.

"Simply *loads* of my relatives are coming from the East," Helen Haney added.

Even Kittie was bouncy and gleeful. "I just love Thanksgiving. Don't you, Norvie? It's so sort of . . . *peaceful*. And silent. And happy. Oh, I can't describe it; I've hardly got half a brain. But you know what I mean!"

Norvia did know. In her heart, she held a picture of past Thanksgivings, past Christmases, with all the family gathered around the fireplace of their Beaver Island house: Herman drawing lifelike sketches in charcoal pencil, sitting on the hearth; Dicta having a wedding for her dolls on the ottoman; Elton and Casper arranging dominoes on the parlor carpet; Ma and Pa sitting together on the divan, speaking in low voices, the reflection of the fire in their warm eyes; her grandparents laughing together; herself, basking in the presence of her family. Such a beautiful scene . . .

The memories choked her. Kittie, Cal, Ophelia, and Helen grew blurred in Norvia's vision—wavy and dizzy—and she just had to escape.

Brushing tears from her eyes, Norvia ran. She ran out of the hallway, down the stairs, out to the schoolyard, down the road. She paused for breath when she reached the end of the street, gasping, barely noticing the pretty swirls of snowflakes that floated from the heavens. This was the first snow, and here she was sobbing.

I should be happy. I should, Norvia told herself. *The holidays are coming, and everything should be happy—*

"Excuse me. Norvia, isn't it?"

That voice! Norvia turned, wiping her eyes with the sleeve of her coat. Louis Behren, wearing a flattering gray suit, with depths of concern in his dark blue eyes, had leaped out of his Willys-Overland and walked over to her.

Just like a hero in a novel!

"Yes. That's right. I—I didn't know you would remember my name," she said, giving him a watery smile.

A slight smile altered the frown of anxiety on Louis's face. "I'm rather good at remembering. It's part of my job."

Norvia tried to behave as if crying was a perfectly ordinary thing to do. She dabbed at her face with a linen handkerchief. "And...you work at the lumber company?" she ventured, just to make conversation as she covered her nose with the handkerchief.

"Yes, I do their bookkeeping. Not all of it," Louis added. "Still learning from the old bookkeeper. He's showing me the ropes until I can take over permanently. But it's a start." He broke off, offering a larger, less-dampened handkerchief from his own pocket. "Is there anything I can do?"

"Thank you," she mumbled, half wondering if she should have refused such a kind gift from an unknown, albeit perfect, gentleman. Or did Louis Behren count as a stranger? Elton knew him. Either way, it felt lovely to encase her miserable nose in the folds of such a clean, voluminous handkerchief. Did it smell of lavender? Norvia had no idea that boys cared about such beautiful scents! Perhaps only *gentlemen* did. Again, she fought for something clever or witty to say. What would Jo March or Katy Carr say?

"Bookkeeping sounds interesting," said this uncertain heroine. "You must know a lot of things." *Don't be so dull!*

"For sure," Louis laughed. "But it's fairly easy to me. I've always been good at keeping things in order, and I do some stenography for them as well. Anyway, they taught me well at BCHS—I took classes in bookkeeping in my freshman and sophomore years."

She longed to confide, *I'm taking that class, too!* "How long have you been doing it?"

"About a year now. I want to go on to college, but..." He gave a sort of shrug. "I don't think that will be possible."

Norvia could not scrape up enough courage to ask any more

personal questions, although she desperately wished to inquire more about the art of bookkeeping, to tell him how the idea of becoming a bookkeeper or a stenographer filled her with a glowing excitement. She had imagined this same sort of work for herself! She wanted to ask him if he thought a woman could do the job just as well as a man, and if he also liked the feeling of jotting down numbers in tidy rows, of typing on a pristine machine—

Without warning, Pa's words from years earlier snapped back to the surface and stabbed her. *You are an Indian. What future is there for you?*

"Are you on your way to the lumber office now?" she inquired, shakily.

Louis nodded. "Yes, I can't hang around school like everyone else—I have to get going, so I can—"

"Hey! Behren!"

Another young man approached—this one from the opposite direction—driving a smart-looking carriage. "What's taking you a year?" he called out, pulling to a stop before them. "Old Man Heathrow's having a fit, just about. If school's out, why aren't you at work?"

"I'm coming, but I was waylaid by a damsel in distress," said Louis, smiling as if he had all the time in the world.

"Well, you'd best hurry up," said his companion.

"I'm all right," Norvia told Louis, her voice stronger now. "My house is just up ahead."

"Chin up, Miss Norvia Nelson. There's daylight left yet," said Louis, giving her a wink before he swung himself back into his automobile. "And I find there's usually a silver lining to every cloud of gloom. Take care," he added.

As she started to walk away, waving a few shy fingers, she overheard the other young man ask, "Who was that girl?"

"Just a sister of Elton Nelson's. She's a good kid," she heard Louis reply.

A good kid!

Norvia stood in the street feeling as if her heart were driving away without her. So that was how her Dashing Young Man viewed her—as a "good kid," a mere child.

That heavy, foggy feeling of sadness clouded over her again. She took a few steps farther up the road and then stopped. She didn't want to go home feeling miserable, but what else could she do?

Maybe Elton will cheer me up, she thought, her spirits rising slightly. Elton was always in a good mood. *Maybe I'll go to the farm and see him.*

Norvia raced to the Redgrave farm, her footsteps creating imprints in the freshly fallen snow.

Today Elton was leading an enormous Clydesdale horse to its snow-dusted pasture. Norvia slowed and walked to him, trying not to frighten the horse. "Can we talk?" she asked hopefully, looking around to be sure that no one was watching. Mr. Redgrave was in the distance with another horse, thankfully out of earshot.

"Sure," said Elton, but his voice was heavy. Norvia looked closely at him and saw tears in his eyes. Her strong, brave brother reduced to tears—Norvia's heart shattered.

"What's wrong?" she cried out. Not Elton, too! Was this terrible sadness everywhere?

"Nothing."

"Something is!" insisted Norvia.

"I don't know why it bothers me. It has nothing to do with me," said Elton, unhooking a halter from the majestic Clydesdale with great care. "It's just—when you get to be my age—well, it'll never get that far, I hope. Anyway, I was just reading a bit in the paper at lunch…and Mr. and Mrs. Redgrave were talking about it….Just shook me up, is all. That war going on overseas, the missiles…I just…I just hate hearing about it." He attempted a smile. "Don't you wish everything would just stay the same?"

Yes, Norvia whispered inside. But she didn't say it.

Her mind sifted through possible comforting replies, but they all sounded so trite. She didn't know of anything that could fix how Elton felt. The war was a terrible thing, if the snippets she'd heard were any indication. *There's nothing any of us can do about it.*

"I'm sorry," she murmured finally.

"Aw, don't worry about it." Elton gave her shoulder a reassuring pat. "What did you want to talk about?"

Norvia shook her head. "Oh—it was nothing. I just—felt like talking." But now she wished she had never come.

When Norvia opened her eyes on Thanksgiving morning, a flood of emotion hit her all over again. But North Star was largely quiet.

As soon as Norvia dressed and slipped downstairs, she could smell the tantalizing Thanksgiving scents: creamed turkey, brussels sprouts, and cranberry ice. No one was up—only her mother was bustling about in the kitchen. Ma wore a smile on her face as she tended to the beautiful foods, and she hummed softly to herself. Norvia hated to disturb her.

"Happy Thanksgiving," said Norvia. "I'm going for—a walk."

"All right," said Ma, glancing up from her cooking. "But don't be too long."

Norvia buttoned up her coat, stepped out the door, and closed it with a thud, looking out into the snow. It was inviting this morning, a blank sheet of paper just waiting for her—

"Norvie! Wait for me!"

She turned to see Dicta struggling into her boots on the porch, her coat flapping in the wind. Adjusting her bulky winter hat, Dicta hurried down the steps to Norvia as fast as she could (which wasn't particularly fast). To Norvia's immense surprise, Vernon followed her out the door—despite the fact that he had once said he "despised going outdoors in foul weather." Casper emerged from the house as well.

"What are you all doing?" she asked, staring at them as they gathered around her.

"It looked like ideal snowball weather, that's all," said Casper with a wicked grin—and before she could think fast enough, he'd pummeled her with a giant ball of snow.

Norvia brushed the snow off her coat without saying a word. She'd simply go back in the house if they were going to be silly—

Smack!

"Casper, stop that!" Norvia commanded, growing more irritated by the second.

"It wasn't me that time, it was him!" Casper shouted, jabbing a thumb in Vernon's direction.

"It's only that you seemed unhappy, and I thought this might cheer you up," said Vernon innocently, already packing the next snowball with his mittens.

But Norvia had thrown snowballs all her life—far more often than Vernon, she guessed—and she was quicker and craftier. She packed a snowball almost faster than the eye could follow, and then, with more force than she knew she had, Norvia hurled it—but Vernon ducked in time.

The fight was on.

As the merciless snowballing continued, Norvia *did* hit Dicta (who couldn't hit anyone because she had no aim whatsoever). Only after three successive attempts did Norvia manage to get Vernon, but she could never come close to striking Casper—her main target. He was a master dodger.

By the time they had exhausted themselves—and gotten thoroughly coated in snow—it was time for breakfast. Norvia felt much more lighthearted.

"You look somewhat improved," declared Vernon.

"Norvie's never happy," Dicta remarked carelessly, as she limped toward the front porch.

Vernon gazed at Norvia with—pity? No, it was more like sympathy, as if he understood how she felt. "Sometimes it is hard to be happy," he said, turning to Dicta—as if he was speaking to her instead of Norvia. "But it is always—worthwhile." He hesitated, as if wishing to hold back the words, but plunged ahead anyway. "The Bible is full of verses about being joyful."

Norvia walked ahead of him, hurrying to reach the door and escape into the house before Vernon did.

That evening, after their massive Thanksgiving supper, Vernon complained of another headache. "It must have been something I ate. I hate to be a bother, but could you fix me a cup of chamomile tea?" he asked, turning to Ma.

"Oh, I don't think chamomile tea does much for headaches," said Ma. "Some chocolate would probably make you feel better, though."

"I do not eat rich food," said Vernon, interlacing his fingers in agitation. "My mother always fixed me chamomile tea when I had a headache."

Ma's eyes flicked toward the portrait of Celestia, and her voice came out impatient. "That may be so, but tea doesn't fix headaches. If you'd like chocolate, I can find you some."

But Vernon still refused and excused himself to the parlor, wasting no time as he retreated to the sofa with *Great Expectations*.

While Norvia washed the dishes that night, she mulled over what Vernon had said earlier. As she thought about him, her thoughts turned to his mother, and she found herself contrasting his experiences with her own. In a way, Vernon was like her—he wanted everything to be the way it used to be, to make him feel better. And yet he had cast his own comfort aside to make *her* feel better.

Once the dishes were done, Norvia prepared one cup of weak chamomile tea and brought it to Vernon on a tray. "Here," she said simply.

Vernon stared at the teacup as if it were a gift from heaven. "Thank you," he said, his voice surprisingly warm. "This is...most appreciated."

"I hope you like it," said Norvia, a bit anxious that she had ruined it somehow.

The tea connoisseur took an experimental sip, and a smile bloomed on his colorless face. "It's delicious," Vernon declared. "Very much like my mother used to make. Thank you, Norvia."

She was so pleased she could barely speak, but she managed to mumble, "You're welcome," before slipping away upstairs.

Was this the kind of grace that Grand-père had meant?

CHAPTER FOURTEEN
SHARDS OF EMOTION

Vernon's fourteenth birthday was in December. "I do not need any gifts," he announced the day before. "I only want to be left to myself."

But Norvia was beginning to wonder if his desire for solitude stemmed simply from a wish to avoid awkwardness. Did he feel just the way she did—*shy*? He had been so delighted by the tea she prepared for him—he had laughed with Dicta over silly games and followed Norvia out to throw snowballs—perhaps it was simply *uncomfortable* for him to seek out companionship? He was sort of like Colin in *The Secret Garden*, Norvia judged: he only *thought* he wanted to be alone.

It was while Norvia was thinking over this conundrum in the hallways of BCHS that she heard the French Quarter Trio—plus Helen Haney—whispering and giggling over something. She almost didn't stop to listen, but some unwitting magnet pulled her toward them.

"Did you hear? The Valentine's Day Dance is going to be *girls ask the boys*," Ernestine hissed.

"What a spot to put us in!" Violet whooped.

Norvia's mind whirled. Who would *she* invite to the Valentine's Dance in two months' time? There was Louis—but he only thought of her as a "kid." If she asked him, he would probably laugh and think it was all a good joke.

But how could she ask Aylmer? Even if he was perfect "beau" material—which he was *not*—there was the terrible chance he would find out about the divorce if he came to her house to pick her up. She could see it now: Aylmer would arrive, Norvia would sail down the stairs to greet him, Uncle Virgil would be hovering nearby to see who was taking her—and then she'd have to introduce them. "Aylmer, this is my *stepfather.* . . ."

Norvia pushed the vision away. She had to get home early to prepare for Vernon's party, anyway (he had said he wanted to be alone, yes, but that didn't mean Ma and Uncle Vernon were going to let the day pass totally unremarked). Marguerite, Jim, and the Marys were all coming.

Aware that it was impolite to stare but unable to resist, Norvia and Dicta gazed in rapture at Marguerite's altered physique as she entered the house. Surely the baby would arrive any day now! They wished that the impending infant would surface as general conversation, but of course it did not.

Old Mary wore a shawl, as was her customary winter garb. "I am always cold," she claimed to anyone who questioned its necessity. "Too long living on Beaver Island. The water gets in your blood."

"Is that what my teacher meant when he said lizards are cold-blooded?" Dicta inquired.

"How have you been enjoying high school?" Marguerite asked at one point in the evening, when she and Norvia happened to be alone in the parlor.

Such a simple question, yet Norvia was at a loss to answer. Yes, she enjoyed the English assignments, and she loved algebra with all its reliable numbers fitting neatly into place. Yes, she loved typing, which made her fingers hurt but was so satisfying, and yes, Miss Darnell had just promoted her to cashier of the high school bank in their bookkeeping class. But the gossip, the snubs from the other girls, the problem of Louis and Aylmer . . .

"I don't know," she confessed. "It's so different. It's not what I expected, and—"

"A bit overwhelming, isn't it?" said Marguerite. "So many things to learn—both in and out of the classroom."

Norvia lowered her voice in hopes that no one else would overhear. "The first dance of the new year will be in February. It's the Valentine's Day Dance, and the girls will invite the boys."

"Horrific," Marguerite agreed.

"I don't know who I should ask."

I want to ask Louis Behren—even if he thinks I'm only a child. Norvia squashed the thought, refusing to allow such nonsensical notions to enter her head.

Marguerite gave Norvia's shoulders a squeeze. "You've got plenty of time to decide. Is there more than one boy who's caught your fancy?"

In a rush of honesty, Norvia blurted out, "Just one, but he's a senior."

"Well, isn't that exciting!" Marguerite sounded thrilled—or perhaps she was good at feigning it. "An older man. The very words have a sort of bookish ecstasy to them, don't you think?"

Norvia giggled. *"Very* bookish."

"My advice for who to ask is…" Marguerite's voice trailed off, and she stared at the portrait of Celestia Ward on the parlor wall—who almost looked sympathetic today. "Think about it for a good long while before you set your heart on any one boy. It's important not to hurry into things like that." Marguerite suddenly looked away, over at Uncle Virgil, who was standing in the parlor doorway. An odd look passed between father and daughter, and Norvia felt vaguely unsettled.

Norvia and Dicta had made birthday cards for Vernon, which they presented to him at supper. He slit the envelopes with one studious finger and unfolded each one, careful not to tear or bend the thin notebook paper. Norvia's was neat and simple and succinct; Dicta's overflowed with higgledy-piggledy letters, balloons, and hearts.

"I appreciate your sentiments," said Vernon, tucking the cards back into their envelopes. A sting of disappointment pricked at Norvia's eyes, but she blinked it away.

"Mine was the best," Dicta declared.

Ma didn't bake a cake, being afraid of Vernon's delicate digestive system, but she did produce some plain sugar cookies and a cupcake. Atop the cupcake sat one lonely striped candle.

"For your wish," said Ma.

"Close your eyes," Norvia said.

"Make it a good wish," said Casper.

"Give it some lung power," Elton advised.

"Don't spit all over it; I want a piece," Dicta added.

Vernon closed his eyes, paused for a brief interim, and then blew out the flame. It vanished in a swirl of birthday-scented goodness.

"What'd you wish for?" asked Dicta.

"I cannot divulge," he demurred.

Presents came next: Marguerite and Jim bought Vernon a new phonograph record of waltzes by Strauss and Berger ("precisely what I wanted," he assured them), and the Marys had knitted him a sweater ("very warm, I'm sure"). Uncle Virgil handed his son a small bookish package, which turned out to be a Horatio Alger story. Vernon's face colored with pleasure. "Thank you, Papa. I did want this one."

"Here is my gift," said Ma, producing another envelope—this one plain and white. "I didn't know what to give you, so it's a bit of money. I thought about sheet music, but you didn't learn the one I gave you before, so I assumed you would like to choose your own."

The pleased pinkness of Vernon's cheeks faded, and his face became ashen white once again. "Thank you, Mrs.—Aunt—ma'am," he stammered. "It is always beneficial to have—cash—financial aid—*argent—geld—pecuniam.*" Having rattled off this string of foreign words, he scraped his chair from the table. "May I be excused, sir?—thank you," and he bolted from the dining room.

Norvia wandered upstairs after their guests went home. She found Dicta standing outside the boys' bedroom, staring at the closed door. "I think he's crying," said Dicta, raising tragic eyes to Norvia.

Norvia listened. She didn't hear any dramatic sobs, but there were a few moist sniffs coming from within.

The sisters looked at each other and knew exactly what they had to do. They knocked on the door.

Vernon murmured "come in" indistinctly.

They did. He rubbed at his eyes and straightened.

"Thank you for the cards," he said, sitting up even straighter. "I—I—really liked them. It was—kind." And he broke down crying again, but it didn't matter—didn't matter for a second, because Norvia and Dicta were there with handkerchiefs and comfort, patting his back and murmuring that everything was quite all right.

As Norvia pulled out a handkerchief to offer Vernon, she noticed the initials monogrammed in the corner:

L.A.B.

Louis Behren! She should have returned it to him ages ago!

Norvia spread the handkerchief on her bed, smoothing it with her palms, admiring the embroidery of the initials. L.A.B. For what, she wondered, did his A stand? And how delightful that they shared a middle initial! Ann and . . . oh, Arthur, perhaps. Or Anders—like Pa. Or Aylmer.

No, there was only one Aylmer.

She would have to return it—there was no question about that. And Norvia could not help but admit that she relished the task. Perhaps if she composed herself and returned it with a graceful manner, he would realize that she was a grown-up young lady and not a "kid."

But Norvia had no idea how to return it, because she hardly ever saw him at school—there were no guarantees she'd ever run into him in the hallways. Should she ask somebody where Louis Behren lived? No. That would be unseemly. And she couldn't very well just arrive at his doorstep with a hanky, anyway. She would look ludicrous. And if she asked Elton, he would bombard her with embarrassing questions.

I could mail it, thought Norvia. *Stuff it in an envelope and put "Louis Behren, Boyne City" as the address.* There couldn't be more than one Louis Behren in town.

Then Norvia remembered a wonderful thing. Louis worked at the lumber company. Perhaps she could go to his workplace and return the handkerchief there!

No! Norvia shuddered. What was she thinking? She could never do anything so bold and rash and forward. If she did that, it would be the absolute end of her reputation. People would find out that she'd gone to the workplace of an almost-stranger to get his attention.

No, she wouldn't return it—and he probably wouldn't miss it all. L.A.B. probably had a dozen lavender-scented monogrammed handkerchiefs.

But if she didn't capture his attention somehow, then he could never be her escort for the Valentine's Day Dance.

There's always Aylmer, thought Norvia with a sigh.

"I think it might be a nice idea to read a book together for the next few weeks," Uncle Virgil announced at supper one night, his expression brightening. "We'll take turns reading it aloud in the parlor each night."

Vernon dropped his fork. "Papa!" he exclaimed, as if wounded by the suggestion.

"I thought you enjoyed our tradition," said Uncle Virgil.

"Yes—it's only"—Vernon opened and shut his mouth twice before finishing—"it's *our* tradition."

"And I'm sure that the others will appreciate our tradition as well." Uncle Virgil took a serene sip of water.

"Are we reading a Christmas book?" squealed Dicta. "I know. *A Christmas Carol.*"

"My son knows his Dickens by heart. I think we'll pick something a bit less familiar," said Uncle Virgil.

I hope he won't expect me to read aloud, Norvia thought with terror. Yet she wondered what book he would choose. She hoped he wouldn't pick something like *War and Peace,* a thick and dull book she had seen on Vernon's well-stocked shelves.

The next evening, Uncle Virgil came home to North Star with a thick volume entitled *Jack and Jill.* Norvia immediately recognized the author's name: Louisa May Alcott. "She wrote *Little Women,*" Norvia blurted out as soon as she saw the book.

"And did you enjoy it?" asked Uncle Virgil.

"Oh, yes," said Norvia, blushing at her own enthusiasm.

Vernon had been "hopelessly ill" again that day (as he phrased it) and had lolled on the settee the entire afternoon, a cool cloth applied to his forehead. He was not too ill to chew minty gum, however, and he was still chewing in annoying fashion when Uncle Virgil began to read *Jack and Jill* aloud.

"This isn't a girl's book, is it?" asked Casper, looking up from a copy of *Motor* magazine.

"If it was a girl's book, I don't think the name *Jack* would be in the title," Dicta retorted.

"But if it was a boy's book, the name *Jill* wouldn't be in the title," argued Casper.

"I'm sure the story will suit both of you," said Ma.

The book, in fact, suited them all. Norvia was soon immersed in the wintry world of Harmony Village, in which cheery gangs of children sledded down hills, spoke in a friendly fashion toward one another, and got into dreadful mishaps, only to emerge as brighter, stronger people. She fell in love with almost every boy in the book, especially Frank Minot—even though he made terrible mistakes—and she found herself admiring the spunk and spirit of Jill Pecq, who, like Katy Carr, became a quieter and gentler person due to her paralysis.

Uncle Virgil read aloud the first five chapters that night—his voice was quite well-suited for reading aloud, being warm and humorous and natural. He used different tones and mannerisms for each character, like a one-man theater, and everyone objected when he closed the book.

"You can't stop before we find out what the surprise is," protested Casper.

"I'm sure Chapter Six will reveal all," said Uncle Virgil, smiling.

The next night, he asked Dicta to read aloud—an invitation she accepted with great gusto.

"*It seemed as if nine o'clock would never come, and Jill, with her*—I mean, *with wraps all ready, lay waiting in a fever of impatience for the doctor's visit* (he's a quack doctor), *as he wished to super*—in—superintent—*superintend the moving.* What does that mean?"

Dicta read only two chapters before she was removed from the position of narrator—by Vernon, who accused her of "stumbling."

"Fine, you read it, if you've got such a gilded tongue," said Dicta, shoving the book at Vernon.

"I'm sorry, I only meant I wanted Papa to read it," apologized Vernon hastily. "I'm sure I could do no better."

The charming read-aloud continued all week, but it didn't make a great impression on Norvia until the chapter where Merry Grant revitalized her home life: brightening up her somewhat dreary house, encouraging her lazy brothers to adopt more gentlemanly habits, and forcing herself to be cheerful despite imperfect circumstances.

I wish I could change things, thought Norvia. *I wish I could be brave and help my family, like Merry Grant. But I can't.*

The next morning, Vernon began playing a dramatic Bach piece on the piano before breakfast. Norvia found it depressing, but she wouldn't dream of saying anything of the kind to sensitive Vernon. Ma, however, did not harbor such anxieties. She came downstairs in her freshest shirtwaist and black skirt, a dark cloud on her face.

"Vernon," she said, her voice weary. "I've mentioned this before, but I would prefer it if you played happier songs. I really would. Anything a little less like a funeral will do."

"I *must*—play it," he replied, halting as he spoke.

That was the extent of their conversation, but Norvia heard them both sighing with irritation afterward.

As Uncle Virgil continued to read *Jack and Jill* aloud, Norvia recalled another storyteller—Grand-père. She remembered long nights by the fire or under moonlit skies, listening with rapture as he spun tales and enumerated the stars. More than ever she longed to recapture those moments—perhaps then she would feel a sense of renewed normalcy.

Uncle Virgil had that tempting book of Indian history in his study. What would be the harm of borrowing it? She couldn't *ask*, exactly, for he could not know why she was interested, but she could quietly take and then return it. Merry Grant would have made a decision like that and acted on it. And Grand-père would have approved of her seeking out those stories, she was certain.

So Norvia stole into Uncle Virgil's Study of Secrecy one evening, feeling a bit like a criminal instead of a girl on a quest. She was glad for the soft carpeting that muffled her footsteps as she tiptoed across the room to his unending bookshelves, all glossy spines and delicious titles. For a moment she felt dizzy; there were so many books, it would be difficult to locate the volume she sought. Luckily, Norvia's memory served her well—there was the thick book right where she remembered seeing it: *History of the Ottawa and Chippewa Indians of Michigan*. She reached for it . . . slid it out . . .

"Do you need help finding something?" Uncle Virgil's voice interrupted the stillness.

Instantly frightened, Norvia spun around and lost her grip on the book—which then smashed into a violet-colored vase on Uncle Virgil's desk.

The look of startled pain on his face hurt Norvia's heart. He rushed over to the scene of the disaster, staring at the shards of broken glass on the floor.

"Are you hurt?" he demanded.

"No—no," said Norvia, who felt as if all the wind had been knocked from her. "I—I'm so sorry!"

"No, sweetheart, it's all right," he said with a gentleness that astounded her.

A mental image of Pa clouded her mind—the memory was so sudden and so potent that she began to cry. She could practically hear him calling her *min dotter* in his most soothing tones, holding her closely during a frightening storm. He may have been set in his ways and strict and shortsighted, but until now Norvia had not realized how much she missed his fatherly affection.

"I—I didn't mean to," Norvia said in a quavering voice she barely recognized.

"I said it's all right—it's all fine," Uncle Virgil reassured her— but she detected the sadness in his eyes, the deep-rooted regret as he stared at the broken bits of purple glass.

It had probably belonged to Celestia. And now she had ruined it.

"Step away from the glass," Uncle Virgil instructed, motioning for Norvia to circumnavigate his desk to avoid the sharp pieces. Norvia obeyed, watching in helplessness as he attempted to sweep up the mutilated remains of the vase. It felt wrong to leave, so Norvia stayed, hovering in the doorway.

"Did you need something?" he asked, realizing she was still there. "Did you find the book you wanted?"

"Yes." Now she was terrified lest he ask *which* book it was—

Uncle Virgil squinted at the volume in her hands. "Something for school?"

And now here was the perfect opportunity to lie—but her conscience wouldn't allow it.

"No," she whispered. "I—"

Dicta galumphed into the room. "I heard a crash! What's that? Ooh, a book about *our people!*" she cried, snatching the big book from Norvia before continuing to prattle on heedlessly. "Uncle Virgil, did you know our grandparents are *all* Indians—"

"Dicta! We have French ancestors, too!" Norvia cried desperately. "And—and Pa is Swedish!"

Uncle Virgil said nothing. Oh, this was dreadful—now he knew they were Indians and he would *never* see them the same way, *ever.* Why had she tried to borrow this book? Why on earth couldn't Dicta have kept her mouth shut?

"I'll put it back," Norvia began.

"No—please don't," Uncle Virgil halted her. "You can go ahead and read it. I'll clean this up."

But it was too late, for the damage had been done.

Boyne City High School closed for Christmas vacation on the Friday before the twenty-fifth, and evidently it was an old tradition for students to exchange gifts in the Social Room on the day before vacation. Cal Evergreen gave Kittie a box of chocolate candy. Helen and Ernestine received even larger boxes of candy—as did Ophelia Farris, who received boxes from four different boys.

Oh well, I'm not really a candy sort of girl, thought Norvia.

It seemed especially insignificant in light of the fact that Uncle Vernon now knew of their heritage. She expected him to grow cooler and cooler by the day, until finally he was nothing but ice. If only she hadn't gone for that book! She couldn't even bring herself to read it.

"Merry Christmas, Norvie!" squealed Kittie, embracing her exuberantly. "I was absolutely going to give you a present, but I forgot it at home. Isn't that just like me? I haven't a brain in my head. Anyway, you'll love it! I'll bring it by your house, if I can remember where I put it! It's a new book bag for your books—I noticed your old one was getting worn. I made it myself! You've been such a good friend, and I want you to have it."

For a moment, Norvia stood there, gazing into her friend's merry eyes. "Thank you, Kittie," she finally said. "Thank you so very, very much. That was nice of you—but you didn't have to do that."

"I wanted to," said Kittie, squaring her shoulders in triumph.

Guilt settled inside Norvia, and she wished that she had thought of giving Kittie a gift. But it had never crossed her mind.

"Would you like to go get ice cream sodas at Kerry's?" asked Kittie hopefully.

It sounded so inviting—so relaxing—but Norvia pictured the scene and inwardly shuddered. How could she go to the ice cream parlor when that was the typical hangout of all the popular girls after school? What if she overheard them whispering about her?

"I would," Norvia began slowly, "but..." Try as she would, she could not think of any suitable excuse. She watched the happy light fade from Kittie's friendly face.

"That's all right," said Kittie softly. "You don't have to. I understand. I know I'm not as fun as the other girls." She turned away before Norvia could stop her.

"Wait, Kittie!" said Norvia, but Kittie did not turn around.

"Mind if I interrupt with glad tidings of great joy?" Aylmer stepped toward her, smiling. He was wearing an old brown jacket with plaid patches on the elbows, and he held out a small, promising box.

Norvia eyed the box with immediate excitement. A boy giving her a present! Just like something that might happen to a real heroine! It was too small for candy, and jewelry would be inappropriate. What could it possibly be?

"This is for you, and with best wishes for a bright new year," said Aylmer, bowing in deep deference.

Norvia's fingers trembled as she lifted the lid. He really liked her, liked her so much he would buy this lovely—

"*Oh!*" Norvia screamed, dropping the box and leaping backward, her heart thumping. A tiny brown mouse scurried out of the box and into a crack in the wall.

Aylmer was laughing—actually, howling—doubled over and leaning against the wall. "It's only a mouse," he gasped. "Not a rat. It wasn't even full-grown."

A charge of guilt smashed her chest. That poor little mouse! Thrown to the ground like that! It was the last thing she'd been expecting. Norvia swallowed several times before she said, "I'm sorry. I was surprised. Do you think it will come out of the wall? Is it lost?"

"No. I found him inside the building. He's at home!" Aylmer wiped tears of laughter from his eyes. "Methinks that surprised you, m'lady. I shall hereafter refer to this incident as the transgression of the unwanted rodent and its uncouth messenger. Quite the lark, eh?"

Bewilderment and hurt commingled inside Norvia, fighting for supremacy. Hurt won out—and tears welled up in her eyes as she stood staring at the place where the mouse had escaped. What hero would ever do this to a heroine?

"Hey," said Aylmer, a bit of the laughter leaving his eyes. "It's just a joke."

Norvia knew she ought to laugh—she should have let silliness win out over the same old exhausted, hurt feelings. But this—this was too much.

"You can't ever take a joke, can you?" said Aylmer, starting to walk away. "You can't ever just be happy!"

But Norvia barely heard him. As he left her—his angry footsteps reverberating in the jumbled, crowded hallway—she realized that her last hope of an escort for the dance had just disappeared.

Ma met her in the foyer as soon as she reached North Star. "We've had a letter from Herman!" she exclaimed, a brightness radiating from her face that sent a pang of happiness into Norvia's heart. "At last!"

Norvia could hardly believe it. Herman hadn't written in *months*! "It's postmarked Cheboygan—he's not in the U.P. anymore!"

"Read the letter," said Ma eagerly.

Dear Ma and Norv and everybody,

I'm coming home for Christmas! Can't wait to see you all. I have lots of things to tell you, and a big surprise. I hope I can find your new house without trouble. My, aren't we fancy, living right in town?? Sorry this is so short, but I've got a lot to do to get ready to come. I'll be arriving on Christmas Eve, if all goes smoothly. Don't bother meeting me at the station; I'll walk. You know how I like walking.

Love,

Herman

"He's coming!" Norvia shrieked.

He's coming! My brother is coming home to North Star! He would bring stories of life in the Upper Peninsula, of working on the railroads, of surviving alone with no one to make his bed, mend his shirts (she had learned how in Sewing class), or fix his favorite lemon meringue pie.

Well, they would simply *lavish* him with lemon meringue pie— make it every day he was home. Oh, what if he stayed a *month*? He probably wouldn't, but perhaps a week. Oh! To spend a joyous week with her brother, taking wintry walks and talking about everything under the sun and joking all the old jokes.

And the surprise! Why, what else *could* it be? The seashell jewel box! She would put her jewels in it—when she got some. Oh, when he came back everything would feel so deliciously *normal*. It would be such a change to feel normal and comfortable—like the old days.

CHAPTER FIFTEEN
HERMAN'S HOMECOMING

"Norvie? Wake up! It's Christmas Eve!" Dicta jumped onto her, shaking the bedframe.

But Norvia didn't need to be awakened by anyone. She had woken with the earliest light—which was quite late, considering it was December—and she had lain awake for a half hour in her excitement over Herman's impending arrival.

"Merry Christmas Eve!" hooted Casper, rushing into their room. "Get up, girls!"

"I'm awake, I'm awake!" Norvia cried.

Casper began fumbling with his shoelaces. "His Majesty is still asleep. Or praying. Or he's got a headache—but never mind him. Let's go downstairs straightaway. Elton will be back soon from the Redgraves'—he got up early to help with the milking."

Elton came home smiling, a light dusting of snow on his coat, looking as if he'd found a miracle on the road home.

"The perfect Christmas tree," announced Elton, blowing on his purple fingers, "is waiting outside. Mr. Redgrave was kind enough to let me take home one of his small pines. Take a look!"

They rushed out the door, not bothering with boots and scarves and coats, to behold the most Christmassy tree in all recorded history—tall, but short enough to fit inside the house, scented with an ecstasy of piney fragrance, perfectly triangular, with low branches like outstretching hands of joy.

"An enchanted tree!" Dicta's eyes grew starry.

"How'd you find one so *perfect*?" Casper asked.

"Magic. Christmas magic," said Elton, grabbing Dicta's hands and twirling her in circles.

"Well, let's decorate the tree before the noon meal," Uncle Virgil said, putting his arm around Ma.

Elton, Casper, Norvia, and Dicta stood quite still. To decorate the tree in the morning would be sacrilege. This was not a Nelson tradition by any stretch of the imagination.

"We can't do it like that," said Dicta. "We absolutely can't."

"But we always string the popcorn and hang the ornaments right after supper," said Norvia, the words gushing forth before she could think twice. "It's the way we always do it."

"Papa and Marguerite and I always do it before the noon meal," announced Vernon.

"Let's compromise and do it this afternoon," suggested Elton.

Norvia would have minded, but she was sure that Herman would be coming any minute. When he did, it would truly feel like Christmas—and all her problems would dissipate.

Norvia spent much of that morning waiting on the porch steps, despite a temperature of only fifteen degrees.

At last he arrived—wonderful, *normal* Herman—unchanged! Same piercing blue eyes, slicked-back hair, and bright expression— but, Norvia realized belatedly—the young woman walking along with him was not simply a passerby going in the same direction.

"Norv!" Herman called out, quickening his pace and grinning from ear to ear. "Come meet my wife!"

Norvia joined him across the snowy yard as if she were walking in a dream. His wife—*his wife?* He wasn't married. He *couldn't* be married. He was supposed to be an adventurous bachelor—he was only seventeen—he was her *brother*!

"No, let's go on inside—it's so cold! Then we'll tell you everything!" Herman said, his face alight with pleasure.

Later, Norvia could never recall how she'd made it back to the foyer without crying or demanding why on earth he was married. All she knew was that somehow she'd followed Herman and the girl into the house, where the entire family congregated around them.

"Allow me to introduce you to my wife," said Herman, his arm around the slender, sweet-faced girl beside him. "Ma, meet Bernice Porteous—I mean, Bernice Nelson!" he corrected with a laugh.

"We're so—delighted," said Ma, torn between elation, amazement, and confusion. "My goodness. When did all this happen?"

"About a month ago. Aren't I the lucky one?"

Oh, he looked at Bernice with such *devotion*—in fact, he barely looked at anyone else at all. Norvia received one quick, squeezing hug that couldn't hold a candle to the embrace he gave Bernice afterward, for what appeared to be no reason whatsoever. He only gave one meager scratch on the head to poor Mr. Bingley, who was industriously sniffing Herman and Bernice. (Herman passed the test with a quick once-over, but Bernice required a lengthier check—her high-heeled boots in particular were fascinating.)

"How old are you?" Dicta cried, grabbing Bernice's hand.

Bernice shook Dicta's hand. "I am seventeen," she said as a smile tugged at her lips.

"It is a pleasure to meet you both," said Uncle Virgil, in a tone that was kind yet laced with reservations.

"It is indeed," said Herman, offering his hand to Uncle Virgil. "And it is a fine place you have here, Mr. Ward."

Vernon hissed in Norvia's ear, "You didn't tell me he had a—a *bride*."

"He didn't tell *me*," Norvia hissed back.

Ma gathered her composure. "We have a beautiful guest room where you can stay—"

"Herman, why don't we stay at the Wolverine Hotel? That lovely place with the big pillars," suggested Bernice. "We don't want to impose."

"Anything you like, Bernie," said Herman, a doting look on his face.

"Tell us about the wedding, the wedding," chanted Dicta, leading them into the parlor. Herman and Bernice followed her, arm in arm, but they stopped short under the penetrating eyes of Celestia Ward.

Herman let out a long whistle. "Who's that beauty?"

"What a wondrous painting," cried Bernice, running her index finger along the edge of its golden frame. "I wonder if it was done by a famous artist?"

"That beauty," said Uncle Virgil, a rather amused smile on his face, "was my first wife. And the artist was me."

No one said a word—Vernon flashed a rare grin—and they all sat down.

"My wife and I had a wonderful trip," said Herman, leaning back on the sofa with the air of an old married man. Couldn't he stop saying *my wife* already? "It wasn't so hard to keep the secret, though of course we did want to write and tell you."

"We wanted it to be a wonderful surprise," said Bernice, squeezing Herman's hand.

For a few minutes, the conversation lagged and dragged with endless talk—of the snap decision to marry. Of their elopement. Of the exciting secrecy. Of the idea for a surprise visit...

Norvia listened to every word, but she stopped absorbing after a while, specifically once Herman began to drone on about the various sightseeing expeditions of their impromptu honeymoon. She began to assess her sudden sister-in-law, feeling mean to be so scrutinizing but too angry to care much. Bernice would have been a plain-looking girl had it not been for her dazzling eyes. Deep, endless wells of black. Flirtatious eyes. Eyes that could easily persuade. And her poor gullible brother had been the victim of that persuasion!

That's cruel. You don't even know her, Norvia told herself. *She seems perfectly nice. You're just jealous because you want him to pay attention to you and not her.* But it was more than that. Herman was part of her old life—and now even that shred of familiarity was ripped to pieces, exchanged for an immense shadow of the unknown, the unfamiliar.

"How did he propose?" Dicta demanded. She settled herself between the two lovers, almost in Herman's lap, and her eyes kept darting between husband and wife. "Did you get down on one knee? Was he terribly romantic, Bernie? Did you buy her a ring, Hermie? Did you recite Shakespearean sonnets?"

Herman's smile was contagious—so contagious that Norvia found herself smiling, and she tried to look pleased at her brother's good fortune.

"It was such a whim, I barely remember the details. Happened so fast!" He looked at Bernice with proud eyes. "Well, I was working with her father on the railroad, and he showed me a picture of his daughter—what a looker, I thought! So when he invited me down to their place in Cheboygan, I couldn't resist going."

Bernice laughed. "*I* wanted a big wedding; *you* were the impatient one."

"Anyway, after we got acquainted, I knew she was the girl for me. So we went out to this little restaurant. There had to be thirty other people in the dining room that night—a cheap violinist, arguing couples, about fifteen kids running around the place. Pure chaos. Well, somehow it was just the right atmosphere, so I asked her to marry me then and there."

"But you *did* get down on one knee?" Dicta prodded.

"I would have, but there was no room. It was not a large dining room."

"I did receive this," said Bernice, and she held out a pale, slender hand, bejeweled with an aquamarine ring.

Casper's mouth dropped open. "That must have cost a fortune! Why'd you spend it on *her*?"

Herman and Bernice laughed as if it was the most amusing thing they'd ever heard, and all the others laughed, too, in order to smooth

Casper's stupid comment into a hilarious joke. "Just wait till your turn comes, son," said Uncle Virgil.

"I'm never getting married," said Casper. "It changes a guy."

"Enough," muttered Elton, and he rose to shake his brother's and sister-in-law's hands. "I guess congratulations are in order! I'm happy for you both."

"Yes, very happy," Norvia echoed, plastering a smile of good humor on her face.

"Thank you," said Mrs. Herman Nelson, giving her groom a kiss.

Herman and Bernice stayed for luncheon—a luncheon that seemed to crawl on forever—but right afterward they left for the grand Wolverine Hotel, a place where Norvia had always dreamt of staying. She and Herman used to joke about sneaking in sometime to give themselves a free, secret tour. . . .

"Surely you'll stay to help us trim the Christmas tree," Ma had protested in vain.

"I want to go sightseeing," Bernice insisted, "and I want to explore the hotel. It looks simply magnificent, and they've decorated the grounds for Christmas."

Norvia retired to her bedroom the minute the newlyweds left, utilizing Vernon's perennial excuse—that she didn't feel well. (Which was absolutely true. She felt as if she had the makings of a bad cold, runny nose and all.)

She had never felt so lost, so alone. She lay on her bed staring at the ceiling, feeling as if her heart had a giant stone on top of it. She fought the tears, but they came anyway, squeezing the life and every last drop of joy out of her.

She enumerated her problems in her head, agonizing over each one: the endless gossip ensured that she would never be a heroine. She had lost Aylmer's friendship. She had irreparably injured the feelings of the only girl who liked her—Kittie. She would never be able to ask

Louis to the dance. And now that he knew of their ancestry, Uncle Virgil would grow to be ashamed of them, just like Pa—Pa, to whom she would never have a chance to bid a proper farewell.

Now, to top it all off—nothing would ever go back to the old way.

She had no gift for bringing those she loved together; she possessed no gracefulness. She had missed her opportunities; she had bungled her relationships; and everyone in her life had twisted her entire world around, bent it out of shape, and handed her the mess.

But the ruined world kept turning. Dicta came up the stairs after her. "We have to decorate now!" she called out.

It was the very last thing she wanted to do, but her family would start asking questions if she stayed away much longer. Norvia reluctantly followed Dicta back downstairs, where they began the great trimming process. They crafted ornaments from paper, and Uncle Virgil found some beautiful glass ornaments, which apparently Celestia Ward had collected. The rest of the family—the ones who didn't have their worlds twisted apart—had a wondrous time snacking on the popcorn they were supposed to be stringing. Mr. Bingley weaved around them, wagging his tail at the goings-on, while Peggy gave the tree a disdainful look. Uncle Virgil had to lift Dicta up so she could place the angel on top.

"Is that how your mother looks in heaven?" Dicta asked Vernon, pointing to the serene white angel with her blonde hair.

"Ye-es," said Vernon hesitantly, "although I think she still has auburn hair even as an angel."

Elton looked fairly happy while he worked on stringing the popcorn. He hummed carols and smiled at everyone and looked as if he'd completely forgotten that such things as wars existed. But Norvia caught him staring at the tree a little while later with an expression of pain on his face.

Norvia barely said a word during the decorating, and as soon as it was over, she returned to her room to hide away from the gaiety.

She stood at her bureau, studying a postcard Herman had sent her from the Upper Peninsula, before he met Bernice. She held it in her hands, savoring the colorful photograph on the front and the fascinating stamp on the reverse, remembering how she had tried to eke every tiny detail from her brother's dashed-off message.

Norvia closed her eyes. She couldn't look at it another second.

The sound of light footsteps in the hallway alerted her to someone's nearby presence. Norvia opened her eyes to see a note sliding under the door in a slow, hesitant manner. In exquisite cursive were these words on the front of the note:

> To Miss N. Nelson: Please excuse my forthrightness but you seemed rather upset earlier, and I wondered if I could be of any assistance. These are particular favorites, which I turn to when I am under the weather.
>
> I feel I must say something else, as well. When Marguerite married Jim, I rather despised him for taking her away and changing our situation at home. But my loathing of Jim only bothered me, for I never let him see I despised him and I never informed Margie of my feelings. My own self-inflicted pain became a dreadfully heavy burden. At last I forced myself to begin to like him and to adapt. Thus we are good friends now. So you see I do understand . . . but you must give people a chance.
>
> Do not think I know everything—I am still learning this myself. The past months have been difficult for me. But the Lord tells us to be happy, so I do not give up trying.
>
> Cordially, Vernon Ward

Norvia unfolded the sheet and found a series of Bible verses:

The sufferings of this present time are not worthy to be
compared with the glory which shall be revealed in us.
Romans 8:18
Fear not: for I am with thee. Isaiah 43:5
Then shalt thou call, and the Lord shall answer; thou shalt
cry, and He shall say, Here I am. Isaiah 58:9

She was a bit fuzzy on the meaning of the first one, but the last two were absolutely clear. As she read them, over and over, she felt a warmth settle over her.

But her thoughts still swirled with secrets . . . and jokes . . . and old times . . . and change . . . and an aquamarine ring that had been bought with money meant for a seashell jewel box. . . .

DECEMBER 1909
ZHOOMINAANZO | PURPLE

It was the night of fiddling and dancing at Roddy Donovan's, and Norvia had a song in her heart. Pa and the rest of the crew of the *Betsy Hammer* had finally returned from Chicago, and their reunion called for a celebration. Some nights they held dances indoors, but this one was outside, in the blissfully fresh night air with cold caressing winds sweeping up from the waters.

The meal had come first, with king-size plates of potatoes, fish, and vegetables, along with apple cider to drink. The Marys contributed their own maple syrup, gathered in the spring, to drizzle on the food.

The scents of the refreshments were deliciously overpowering, but for Norvia, there was so much more to take in than merely food. They ate at long tables set out on the grass, and afterward they moved out to dance around the bonfire, which sent crackles of sparks into the sky and made Norvia's eyes sting. Elderly ladies sat on chairs at the edge of the commotion (Old Mary never danced—she claimed her "bones were too old"—but she kept in time with rhythmic clapping), while children played and squealed and ran around in the middle of everything. Lights glowed from the interior of the Donovan house, where the womenfolk scurried in and out carrying dishes and laughing.

The men rosined their bows before beginning to play the old, beloved tunes on their fiddles, while other men took out their accordions. The carefully choreographed action of the evening and its camaraderie all took place around the bonfire, the roaring orange centerpiece of the party; the lifeblood. All that music, alive in the night, made Norvia feel uplifted and giddy and full of fun.

Pa loved to dance—he was known as one of the best waltzers on the island. He was less enthusiastic about the square dances that others preferred, but he still partook in them with zeal. She loved to watch them waltz, Pa and Ma together...in those moments, Ma seemed so young and delighted. And they laughed together during the square dances, the allemande, and the circling and rejoining of hands, the endless forming of bridges.

"When Anders and Angélique dance," said Grand-père, "it always reminds me of when they were courting. They danced often then."

Norvia clung to tidbits like this. "Pa always liked Ma best, didn't he? Of all the island girls?"

"Always. He danced with Maggie Gallagher once—but never again, not after he danced with Angélique." He paused, watching the dancers, and then added: "It's good to see him dancing with her—that's good. I only wish he would admire her other talents."

All the old songs stacked up through the night and came alive with color and zest: the infectious "White Cockade" and the hauntingly luminous "Whiskey in the Jar." Norvia only spilled her apple cider twice.

Herman was even dancing with another girl his age—Molly Dunlevy. He was twelve years old now, and Norvia knew he'd be getting married inside ten years. No doubt he and his wife would raise a family who were properly Irish instead of Indian.

Christmas came a few weeks later in all its finest glory: a holiday of peace, with snow sloping across hills of wintry pines. Beaver Island was already sealed off from the rest of the world every winter—or at least as long as the ice held the island imprisoned—but Norvia *loved* the feeling of frozen wonder and perfect solitude at this time of year. (Of course she would never admit that she enjoyed snowfalls, because Ma and Pa thought they were dreadful nuisances. In fact, it was one of the few things the two of them wholeheartedly agreed upon.)

After supper on Christmas Eve night, they decorated a small tree's thin, feathery branches with strung popcorn. The Marys brought out molasses candy made from their maple syrup, and finally, Pa lifted Dicta up to place the star atop the glistening Christmassy pine.

They sang all the songs, the ancient ones that spoke of Bethlehem and joy and Jesus. The Marys sang a carol in French, and even though it wasn't a Christmas tune, Ma sang a haunting Acadian song from the old days that Grand-père had taught her. Christmas Eve night also meant church services with Father Leary.

"Will you come with us, Anders . . . please?" asked Ma, staring at him pleadingly with deep-brown eyes.

Pa was sitting in his favorite chair with Dicta on his lap. He frowned a little at the mention of church. "No . . . I'll stay here," he said slowly.

Norvia was suddenly filled with empathy for her father. She found herself putting her arms around him. "Don't you like church?" she murmured. "It's so beautiful on Christmas Eve."

Pa kissed her cheek. "I suppose it is, *min dotter*. But—but I don't . . . I don't belong in a church," he said finally.

"Why not?" demanded Elton.

But Pa could not put his feelings into words. Norvia understood this. It was from Pa that she had inherited her terrible gift of inexpression. She squeezed his hand and followed her mother out into the cold, swirling blizzard of Christmas.

CHAPTER SIXTEEN
A VERY SPECIAL CHRISTMAS GIFT

The Marys came for Christmas Eve supper, wearing black, as usual. Their cheerfulness made Norvia want to crawl in a hole to mourn in seclusion. "Angie, you never decorate the tree before supper," observed Young Mary. "What brought about this change?"

"I suppose you won't be making fig pudding this year, either," said Old Mary with a smirk. "Anders's favorite."

"Would you help me in the kitchen?" Ma asked in desperation, avoiding Uncle Virgil's eye. Norvia wondered if he knew enough French to understand what Old Mary had said.

Jim and Marguerite came over, too. Jim held his wife's arm gently as she walked into the house looking huge and tired.

"I thought the baby would be here by now," said Dicta, hands on her hips.

"Well, James Rockford Jr. is a bit of a slowpoke," replied Marguerite with a soft smile.

Even in all the bustle, Norvia kept turning Vernon's note over in her mind—in spite of her great unhappiness, she couldn't keep it out of her head. The words permeated her soul as much as the Christmassy environment and scent of pine needles. There were such riches around her—and yet she couldn't enjoy them. She felt like Sara Crewe, looking in on the home of the Large Family in the neighborhood, longing to enjoy their warmth and togetherness—but always miserable, unable to take part.

Norvia caught her breath, remembering how much she had longed to be a good friend like Sara. She knew that Sara would never have hurt Kittie as she had. Perhaps she could make amends?

I just know that Kittie will never forgive me—there's no purpose in it. . . .

But Norvia was tired of thinking that. Somehow she had a strong feeling that Kittie *would* forgive her. Wasn't she the only one who had defended Norvia at the Halloween party? She felt ashamed of herself, remembering it as she threw on her overcoat—there might be time before the evening meal. She rushed to Uncle Virgil.

"May I have fifty cents, please?" she asked quickly. "I'd like to go to the bookstore before supper."

"For a gift, I assume?" said Uncle Virgil, reaching into his pocket. "Here you are. I hope you find the perfect present!"

Through the falling snow and the merry shouts of passersby, Norvia dashed to King's Bookstore, where she purchased a luscious copy of *Anne of Green Gables*. It was one of her very favorites of all the marvelous books she'd read, and Anne Shirley resembled Kittie in many ways. They were both talkative, impulsive, and superb friends—and both had red hair. Norvia all but flew to the Sloane house, despite the iciness of the roads and the frigid air.

The Sloane house, characterized by crumbling shingles and a sagging porch, was bright with light on this gray day. Mrs. Sloane answered the door with a wide smile. She was an older version of Kittie: wiry, nervous, and cheerful.

"Come in, dear! Come in! You're Norvia Nelson, aren't you? Kittie went to your Halloween party. She had such a wondrous time—oh dear, don't step there, I spilled some flour—just step—there. That's right!" Mrs. Sloane beamed and gave Norvia a firm, squeezing hug. Kittie bounded in before Norvia could get a word in edgewise.

"Norvia!" she exclaimed, a look of unmistakable surprise on her face. "What—what on earth are you doing *here*? I thought—" Kittie could not finish.

Norvia's cheeks blazed. "I—I came to say I was . . . I have a present," she stammered, thrusting the book out to Kittie.

"Why, thank you!" Kittie opened the book's cover and flipped through a few pages with reverent fingers. "It's beautiful. I've been wanting to read this! How scrumptious! Sit down, will you?" She thumped a torn cushion on a nearby divan.

"Thank you," said Norvia in a soft tone.

Norvia sat and took in her surroundings with wordless awe. Five bouncy children, ranging in age from twelve to two, danced around the cramped house in a frenzy of festivity. And Mrs. Sloane was baking, sweet-scented bread that made Norvia's mouth water.

"That smells delicious," she complimented.

"Oh, it is! Mama's a fabulous cook," Kittie assured her. "She cooks for the Bergmanns on Terrace Street."

Mr. Sloane approved of his wife having a job, earning part of the family income? Norvia marveled at this. "Your father doesn't mind?" she whispered.

A shadow crossed over Kittie's face, but it vanished a moment later. "Oh—my father is dead."

In that instant, Norvia understood. Images of Pa swept through her mind, crowding out everything else.

"Oh—Kittie! I'm so sorry. . . ."

She knew too well what it was like to miss a father, but . . . to never be able to see him again? To only be able to *remember* him, like Sara Crewe? To know that you would never be able to even—write him a letter?

"It's all right, really," said Kittie with a brave smile. "I'm just glad we're friends. Aren't you?"

"Yes," said Norvia—and she meant it. Why, Kittie was a *real* friend, an authentic one, not a flimsy one like Helen who would drop a friendship at the first whiff of trouble.

As she stepped onto the porch to leave a short while later, Norvia wished she could say something that might comfort Kittie about her father—but the words would not come. They never would, it seemed, when words mattered most.

"Thank you for stopping by," said Kittie, her face bright red in the cold.

"You're welcome," Norvia replied. Hesitating just a moment, she reached out to give Kittie a warm hug. "I'm sorry about—how I acted," she whispered at last. She had behaved just the way Helen had—trying to push away a girl who might ruin her popularity. A perfectly wonderful girl.

"It's all right! Everything's grand!" Kittie assured her, waving goodbye with a frenzied hand.

Norvia rushed home through swirling snow. At North Star, the Christmas Eve supper was an unparalleled feast. While fig pudding was indeed absent from the table, Ma served baked ham, scalloped potatoes, hot rolls, and cranberry ice cream.

Festivities followed the meal; Uncle Virgil read from the Book of Luke, and they lit candles, admired the majestic tree, and sang carols around the piano. Vernon played "O Little Town of Bethlehem" followed by all the old standbys: "Silent Night," "Jingle Bells," and "Angels We Have Heard on High." It was that carol that made Norvia feel a little more uplifted—peaceful and wrapped in a feeling of Christmas splendor.

> *"Angels we have heard on high*
>
> *Sweetly singing o'er the plains*
>
> *And the mountains in reply*
>
> *Echoing their joyous strains*
>
> *Gloria in excelsis Deo!"*

Norvia felt more confident in her singing than she used to, thanks to the music class at high school. She loved the last line of this carol, the sustained "Gloria" in the triumphal ending flourish.

"Gloria in excelsis Deo!!"

After the second refrain, Marguerite laid a hand on Jim's arm. "I don't feel well," she confessed.

Instantly, the atmosphere in the room shifted.

"Is it time?" demanded Uncle Virgil. "I can telephone Doctor Rayburn—"

"It's only a false alarm, isn't it?" Vernon said, twisting his hands together.

"What exactly do you feel?" Ma wanted to know.

"Is the baby finally coming?" Dicta shrieked.

The Marys took charge. "Don't you worry your head about a thing," said Young Mary, rising from her rocking chair. "We'll take care of everything. No need to call any doctor; I've delivered a few dozen babies on the island!"

"We brought Angie's entire brood into this world," added Old Mary, nodding toward Norvia and her siblings. "Come with us, dear."

Jim was wringing his hands. "Oughtn't I to telephone a doctor, or—"

"Nonsense, boy! We have the matter well in hand," said Old Mary, helping Marguerite move slowly toward the stairs. "Virgil Ward, step lively! Boil some water on the stove. Angie, look alive, get some clean sheets. Children! Don't be underfoot—"

Norvia's entire being swelled with exhilaration. The baby—Marguerite's baby—a Christmas Eve baby!—and it was happening *right now!*

Once it began, the wait was interminable. Norvia, Dicta, and

Casper sat in a row on the sofa, staring at the tempting packages under the Christmas tree as anticipation mounted. Elton stood in the doorway, cracking his knuckles, while Herman and Bernice busied themselves looking at a photograph album stuffed full of Celestia's relatives. Vernon sat hunched at the piano and stared at Celestia Amanda Barnett Ward herself, who stared back with a countenance of concern. Jim, his face taking on a greenish tinge, was led into the kitchen by Uncle Virgil. Norvia wished that the miraculous Sister Benedicta was here.

And so much noise—people moving back and forth, talking. Marguerite, in particular, seemed rather loud. They all jumped a mile whenever she shrieked. Mr. Bingley, after attempting to run upstairs nine times, finally took refuge under the piano.

Ma came downstairs, pushing loose wisps of her hair back into place.

"Is the baby born?" Dicta cried.

"No, not yet," said Ma. "Everyone says I'm only in the way." She sat down, under Celestia's nose, and gave the portrait a rather wretched glance.

Vernon began to pace the room, never stopping to look at anyone.

"Please calm down," said Ma shortly.

"I cannot," said Vernon. The look that passed between them was almost too much for Norvia to stand.

Merry Grant would know what to do. Merry, who pieced her home life back together when things weren't going quite right.

The thought frightened her . . . but then, when she really thought about it, it was far more inspiring to emulate Merry than it was scary.

She waited until she could speak with Vernon in private—he had gone to the kitchen to see if there was any chamomile tea around. Perhaps this wasn't the time or place, but still. She must try.

"I—I've been thinking about—Ma, and everything," said Norvia, a bit tentatively at first. Out of thin air, Grand-père's words from years earlier sprang back into her mind: *we bring people together*. This was her ancestry, their clan's precedent. Perhaps this *was* in her blood.

The words burst forth in a rush: "I think she feels—I think she feels that she doesn't quite fit in. I think she has a hard time living up to your mother."

Vernon's face flushed. "I can't help that," he said, his voice lowering along with his eyes. "And she is always bothering me about the pieces I play—it's as if she doesn't care for me at all. I play the pieces that my mother loved. She had a passion for the rich melodrama of Bach and Liszt and Rachmaninoff."

"Then why don't you tell her that?" asked Norvia, slowly warming to her subject. "Explain to Ma that—that the songs have a special meaning for you, because your mother loved them." But that, she realized, might make matters worse. "And you could try to learn a song that Ma might like, to make her feel that—that you care about her, too." *Oh,* this was so hard, and her words were coming out all wrong. Norvia felt as if she was standing too close to the kitchen fireplace, and her heartbeat drummed relentlessly.

"I—I do care about her." Vernon fidgeted with an empty teacup. "It's only that—" He closed his eyes. "It is so hard to talk to her. She doesn't understand."

"I think Ma would understand a lot more about you, if you just . . . confided in her," said Norvia, her voice low and sympathetic. "I think . . . I think perhaps that's what she's waiting for."

Vernon jerked his head up to look at her square in the face. He didn't say a word, but somehow Norvia felt that meant much more than an entire Shakespearean soliloquy.

The clock ticked onward, and time dragged on.

Footsteps continued overhead; noises drifted down. Ma went to the foyer and stood at the bottom of the stairs, waiting.

"Ma," said Norvia, going to her. She was almost too embarrassed to begin. "I sort of think that—Vernon would like it if you . . . if you . . ."

"If I what?" prompted Ma.

"Well, maybe if you . . . just . . . well, tried to understand about his mother," she finished, her cheeks bright red. "Maybe?"

Again she received no response, but Ma gave her a long look before returning to the parlor, where Vernon still paced endlessly.

The grandfather clock announced that it had been four hours since Marguerite had gone into labor. Norvia began to feel tired despite all the excitement. She had tried to mend things, to help things, but she still felt as if a heavy burden lay on her heart, preventing her from fully taking part in the goings-on around her.

Four hours and ten minutes.

"How much longer will it be, do you think?" asked Norvia.

"It's her first. It may take some time," said Ma.

Vernon may have been ashen-faced before, but now he was pure white—bloodless. "Oh, please, Lord, please let her be all right," he gasped, as if unaware that any other soul was present. "Please let Margie and the baby be all right, Lord, please."

"Vernie, calm down," said Ma, reaching out to touch his shoulder. He jerked away.

"Don't call me that!" he snapped. "That was my *mother*'s name for me—don't say it." He swiped at his eyes, then stared blazingly at the grandfather clock. Four and a half hours.

Then, he turned back to face Ma, giving a great shuddering sigh.

"I am sorry. It's only . . . my mother—" He was so choked with emotion that his words failed him. "My mother . . . died in childbirth. The baby was a little girl. She was so still . . . and she didn't have a name. Papa called her . . . 'The Little Angel.' " He inhaled. "Only he hardly speaks of her now. And Mama . . ." His eyes brimmed with fresh tears as he glanced about the room in terror. "I didn't even get to say goodbye—oh, what if it happens *again*?" A waterfall of tears— a young lifetime of worry and grief—cascaded down Vernon's face, pouring free with the relief of confession.

"Oh—Vernon—" Ma didn't cry, although anyone could see her eyes were clouded. She put her arms around him, embraced him close to her, and pressed her cheek to his forehead. "You don't have to think about that. Marguerite is strong! She's young and healthy and brave. Your mother was a delicate woman, and much older." She pulled away from him and stared into his forlorn eyes. "Margie will *live*, Vernon— she and the baby will survive, you'll see. You have to be brave, and have faith. Can you do that for her?"

He nodded—a nod that lasted a century. But he didn't make any efforts to leave the comforting sanctuary of Ma's arms.

Norvia wasn't so brave. Tears streaked down her cheeks, stung at her eyes. How much she wanted to wrap the entire world in a warm embrace—but she didn't know how. What must it be like—for someone you love to leave—*and to know you never had the chance to say goodbye*? It might be like having the chance to say goodbye—and not doing it.

Four hours and forty minutes.

Norvia began to wonder if this night would ever end. She longed to put all the feelings of the day behind her—but she kept thinking of Herman and Bernice, and the pain stabbed her afresh whenever she glanced at them.

But the scene with Vernon and Ma kept replaying in her mind. *I helped them—I gave them ways to help each other.*

From the front window she watched as Jim left to take a walk— evidently he had too much nervous energy to remain in the house any longer. Norvia could see Uncle Virgil sitting on the porch steps, despite the cold, despite the fact that he was alone now.

She bundled a scarf and coat around her before slipping outside and, to her own surprise, joining him on the top step. His face was drawn with tension, but he managed a warmhearted smile for her.

"I've been through this half a dozen times," said Uncle Virgil, staring at the stars—but all the constellations were enshrouded by wintry clouds. "Five with my own children—we lost two—and once with my daughter Julia's baby. She's had two of her own—but I wasn't there for the second child's birth. Sometimes I wish Julia still lived here—still kept me a part of her life."

"I know how that feels," Norvia whispered.

Uncle Virgil hesitated. "You feel that way about Herman, don't you?" he asked softly. "Are you sad that he's gone? Or sad he got married?"

"Well...both," she said.

"Isn't it strange how people can change so quickly?" said Uncle Virgil, shaking his head. "How—*life* can change so *rapidly*. Especially when there are families involved. You probably pictured him the way Angélique did: still a boy, still the same as when he left. But he's different now, as anyone would be. Norvia, you just—you can't expect people to stay the same. You can't expect them to always be what you want them to be."

"It's as if he didn't care about me at all," said Norvia, dabbing at her nose.

"Oh, he does care, Norvia," said Uncle Virgil in the gentlest of tones. "But right now he's preoccupied. He's got a wife, and a whole new life to experience," he reminded her, staring into the distance. "You just weren't expecting that. And how could you? He didn't tell you. But—you have to realize that life *does* change. Things will be different, always. There's only one thing you *can* control."

"What?" Norvia murmured.

"The way *you* handle those changes. You're in complete control of yourself and how you adjust and respond. And," said Uncle Virgil, breaking off and smiling, "there *is* Someone on whom you can always rely—completely. He will never fail you. Christmas is a good time to remember that Jesus is always there for us, caring for us."

Norvia stared into the sky, discovering that her great pain was beginning to subside to a small ache. She reached into the pocket of her dress and unfolded the note that Vernon had given her, mouthing the verses once again. They *did* make her feel better. She took a great, deep breath.

Life can change so rapidly, especially when there are families involved. Had he ever spoken truer words? But then, he must know what he was talking about.

In a flash Norvia remembered what Marguerite had said on the redecorating day, about how Julia didn't visit often anymore. *She's hardly come at all since she married Walter,* Marguerite had said. Had Julia wanted to distance herself from a splintered family, too? Just like Herman? But those actions didn't fix anything—they only hurt the people left behind, the people who were forgotten—and the people who were ignored when they tried to reconnect.

Norvia's heart swirled with emotions as Jim returned from his walk, hands shoved in his coat pockets.

"Anything happen?" he asked, his usually jovial voice now tense.

"Not yet. Why don't we go back inside?" suggested Uncle Virgil.

Norvia followed them into the house, where the sweetest sound of humanity followed: the first cry of a new life.

They rushed up the stairs.

"Mother and child are doing perfectly," announced Young Mary, still brisk.

"It's a girl," said Old Mary, squeezing Dicta's cheek.

"Her name is Olivia Celestia," whispered Marguerite. She lay back on her pillows, white and exhausted but happy, the baby cuddled in her maternal arms.

"She's—she's *wonderful*," Vernon breathed.

The grandfather clock bonged again, twelve times.

"Merry Christmas, Mrs. Rockford and daughter," said Jim, kissing his wife.

After a long, lovely while of soft chatter and congratulations and Dicta insisting on holding the baby, the house began to wind down for the night. Norvia crept down to the kitchen to fetch a glass of milk to make her sleepy, and she met Elton on the stairs. She studied her brother, wondering if she would find the pain on his face again. In the light of the pale moon, he seemed all right.

"Elton," she said in a quiet voice, for she did not want to disturb the newborn Olivia.

"Yeah, Nan?" he asked.

"Uncle Virgil told me something tonight." She paused, searching for words. "He said that even though . . . life changes, all the time, and the world changes . . . there's still one thing you can control."

Elton's brow furrowed, a great indication that he was listening with care, which gave Norvia courage.

"It's the way *you* handle change. You're in control of yourself—*you* choose how you respond to things. And . . ." Could she get out those final, most important words? "You can always depend on Jesus."

Elton stared at her, then he nodded. "Mm-hmm," he said—and that was all he said. But he walked slowly upstairs as if each of his steps had new meaning.

Norvia went to her room as soon as she drank her milk—it was very late, after all. Out of the corner of her eye, Norvia saw the North Star outside her window—and it didn't disappear when she gave it a direct look. It remained, so bright and vivid and beautiful. She remembered the verses Vernon had given her.

Then shalt thou call, and the Lord shall answer; thou shalt cry, and He shall say, Here I am.

"Thank You for being here," whispered Norvia. "Thank You for never leaving me or forgetting about me."

As she crawled into bed, she felt a strange new sensation of joy and satisfaction and restoration. She glanced over at the book on her nightstand: *Pollyanna.*

Now *there* was a wonderful heroine. Not only because she was always searching for gladness, but because she knew her own mind—and she pursued the things she wanted. Why, she even befriended a couple who had planned to get a divorce... until Pollyanna changed their outlook on life.

Norvia's mental monologue broke off. Pollyanna was sort of like Anne Shirley, in that respect. And Pollyanna and Anne were both similar to Jo March, and Katy Carr and Merry Grant and Sara Crewe and Patty Fairfield—*all* the heroines knew what they wanted, and they didn't let obstacles or fear stop them from being bold and decisive.

But most of all, heroines didn't languish in dreariness. Maybe they did at the start of their troubles—Anne certainly did—but they always managed to pull themselves up. And they did so by bringing people together... by valuing stories... by having grace.

See, Nan, sometimes you just have to get up and do something, Elton had said. Because if not, Dicta's silly queen would still be waiting for her world to improve instead of getting up and fighting for the kingdom. And nothing would ever have happened in any of Norvia's favorite novels.

Isn't there more to becoming a true heroine than simply being popular?

Herman and Bernice left two days later. They had to visit Bernice's grandparents in Ann Arbor and deliver the news of their marriage. A twist of despair gnawed at Norvia's heart as she watched them readying to leave, hand in hand, laughing over some private joke.

She stood on the stairs as she watched everyone else say their goodbyes. Ma hugged Herman with tears in her eyes, wishing him all the best. Dicta danced around the two of them excitedly, offering name suggestions for their future children. ("I think *Harold* or *Hortense!*") Even Elton was smiling and wishing them a good trip—

Norvia waited.

Then she stepped off the stairs and gave her brother a hug.

"I love you," she whispered. "See you soon!"

January 1, 1915

TO MR. ANDERS NELSON, FLINT, MICHIGAN

Dear Pa,

I am writing to wish you a very Happy New Year, and to say I love you very much. I hope you will write back to me. I'm in high school now, and I'm actually doing rather well. I've discovered that education can be quite a wonderful thing... and not only the education you receive in school. I feel as if I've learned so much this year!

We're all well. I hope you are, too.

Love,

Your Norvia

P.S. Please write back.

P.P.S. Vernon, my stepbrother, gave me this. I thought you might like it....

"The sufferings of this present time are not worthy to be compared with the glory which shall be revealed in us."
—Romans 8:18

CHAPTER SEVENTEEN
TO FIND A HERO

Norvia washed the handkerchief in warm water and ironed it carefully, smoothing out the creases. It was fairly early in the morning, before breakfast even, but Norvia was getting a head start on a momentous day. As she worked, she listened to Vernon practice "When the Midnight Choo-Choo Leaves for Alabam'."

"Norvia, what on earth are you doing?" Ma asked, staring in bewilderment at the ironing board on the kitchen table. "I didn't ask you to iron any handkerchiefs."

Norvia prayed her mother would understand. "This belongs to—to Louis Behren. I'm returning it." She hurried through the most difficult passage. "I was sort of upset one day after school and he gave me this—because I was crying. It was nothing—I was just being silly, but he was nice, and anyway I feel bad about keeping it." *There.* She had told the truth and the story in its entirety, and she had been a bold heroine in doing so.

She had decided that if Louis Behren was going to escort her to the Valentine's Day Dance, she had to make it happen herself. And he *had* to escort her—because all *real* heroines had their own heroes—even Jo March ended up with Professor Bhaer! (Although he wasn't exactly dashing.)

"Louis Behren," repeated Ma. "I don't know the name. He's your age?"

"No, a little older. Seventeen."

Ma's brow furrowed. "Do you know where he lives?"

"No."

"Then how were you planning to return it?"

Norvia explained her idea about visiting the lumber company, but Ma shook her head. "You're far too young to be out and about by yourself. Your stepfather will make inquiries and return it himself."

"He's Elton's friend," said Norvia in desperation. "He came to play that joke on me at Halloween, remember?"

Ma pursed her lips. "Oh, that boy? Yes, I remember. But your stepfather will make the inquiries himself."

So much for romance and initiative!

That day at school—the first day of school in 1915—Norvia hurried to algebra, hoping to catch Aylmer before he went into the classroom. Her heart pounded—she hated awkward apologies—but she had to do it.

Finally he emerged through the crowd of high schoolers, carrying his books with a somewhat sullen expression. Norvia bolstered her courage and approached him.

"Aylmer," she said softly, "I—I just wanted to say that I'm sorry if—if I overreacted to your—" She wavered between calling it a "joke" or a "present" and ended up with "poke."

He stared at her blankly.

"I mean your joke present," said Norvia.

Aylmer shrugged, and a faint smile appeared on his face. "Well, I shouldn't have done it. Forgiven and forgotten all around, eh, m'lady?"

Norvia smiled, and they went into class together.

That night Ma relayed the situation with the handkerchief to Uncle Virgil at the supper table. "Ooh, Norvie's got a beau," Dicta cooed.

"I do not," Norvia said.

"Yes, you do! His name is *Louis*, which rhymes with *gooey*," chattered Dicta.

Vernon smirked. "And now that our lesson in French pronunciation has been neatly explained..."

Norvia flushed. "We don't know that he's French."

Vernon pierced his cauliflower with the elegance of a knight. "Think of the long succession of French kings named Louis. Alas, poor France, having to face the kaiser's army," he lamented.

"Louis Behren isn't French," said Elton. "He's German. The Behrens live on a big farm in the German settlement on the outskirts of town. I know him fairly well, and he seems like a good guy to me."

Norvia glanced at Uncle Virgil and Ma. Would they dislike Louis because he was German? After all, Germany was England's enemy in the war.

"You say the boy works for the lumber company?" asked Uncle Virgil. He had that look on his face again—a sort of severity that wasn't typical for him.

"He's a bookkeeper," murmured Norvia, her chest tightening.

"I don't recall the boy having an accent," said Ma doubtfully.

"Louis and his siblings were all born here," Elton said. "They're as American as we are. It's only their parents who were born in Germany, but they're naturalized citizens."

Uncle Virgil folded his hands, and now his face showed a man in great thought. "I would be curious to meet a boy willing to leave the family farm in search of a more lucrative position. One that requires a higher education. That kind of a transition takes courage. Although I do wonder at his choice, considering most families would be glad of an extra helping hand...."

"He attends my high school," Norvia added, hoping to keep Louis in a positive light. "And—and he was very kind to me. I just want to give him back his handkerchief—and *I* should be the one to do it. I borrowed it."

"I wonder if it was clean when he gave it to you," said Dicta. "Imagine stuffing your face in a hanky covered in someone else's—"

"*Dicta!*" roared her family.

Another idea was at the back of her brain—and Norvia knew she had to admit it, or it would seem like she had an ulterior motive. "And I wondered—I wanted to ask him—I know he probably won't want to—but I want to ask him if he'll be my escort at the Valentine's Day Dance."

There.

Uncle Virgil turned to Norvia and spoke in a low and serious tone that sent pangs of anxiety into her heart. "I think, Norvia, that it would be wisest to let me return the handkerchief to this young man. I know that you like him, but he is older than you, and I don't feel that you should ask him to your dance."

Why couldn't he just let her do it? Why did he have to involve himself in something that didn't concern him? Norvia swallowed down the hard lump in her throat. Was he afraid that people would gossip about her visiting Louis, and it would reflect badly on him as a stepfather?

"I don't think it matters very much," said Norvia in a whisper. "He'll say no. I won't take up much of his time—I just want to give the handkerchief to him and—and ask him about the dance." *I can handle it.*

Uncle Virgil rubbed his forehead, covering his eyes as if he was getting one of Vernon's headaches. "Let me give it some thought," he said finally.

She felt a flare of anger—why was it his place to decide what she did or did not do? He was acting exactly like Pa, making all the decisions! And like Migizi's stepfather, making her change her name. But she remembered all the things Uncle Virgil had done for her: giving her the books, allowing her to attend high school, letting her throw the Halloween party. Guilt descended upon her—after all, perhaps he merely felt that he had to act like a proper father.

But on Norvia's fifteenth birthday, two things happened: she received the magnificent latest installment of the Patty series, *Patty's*

Suitors—and Uncle Virgil called her into the Study of Secrecy for a talk.

It had to be about Louis, she realized with mounting excitement. Uncle Virgil had finally decided to let her return Louis's handkerchief and ask him to the Valentine's Day Dance! Yes, that's what he would say....

Uncle Virgil smiled at her when she entered his study.

"I just wanted to let you know that I have given it a lot of thought," he said, running his fingers along the edge of his desk, "and I'll drive you out to the lumber company so we can drop off the handkerchief together. But I'd prefer that you didn't ask him to accompany you to the dance."

Norvia's heart dropped like a stone. "But..." But what? How could she tell him that Louis was her knight in shining armor, her prince, her hero? She would sound like a fool. But she had spent so long daydreaming of waltzing with Louis; of her dance card filled with brilliant names; of wearing a stunning gown and listening to the strains of the three-piece orchestra from East Jordan. This vision of the dance consumed her day and night, and Louis was the pillar of that vision.

"But—why not?" she asked, her voice louder than she had intended.

"I just think it would be better for you," said Uncle Virgil slowly. "I can't help but feel that you're too young for this sort of thing."

Norvia's words came out in a confused rush. "But it's only a dance—all the girls my age are going!" She could not fathom why he was behaving in such an odd fashion, unless he was afraid of gossip. And if that was the case, why make up an excuse?

Uncle Virgil started to say something, then stopped. His eyes flicked toward his many bookshelves, his leather-bound volumes, and back to his stepdaughter's face. "All right," he relented. "I will leave it up to you, whether or not you wish to ask him. I can take you tomorrow."

A balm of relief soothed Norvia instantly.

"Thank you!" she cried. "That would be wonderful!"

But what if Louis finds out that Uncle Virgil is your stepfather? The annoying little voice nagged at her. *No. He won't. He'll just assume he is my real father—I'll do all the talking. I have to do this!*

The Boyne City Lumber Company (Norvia liked the important sound of the name) was not far from home, just on the corner of Pleasant and Front. It was a small village of sheds, timber piles, and warehouses, and the *noise!*—wagons being loaded, voices, chaos, all intermixed with chimney smoke and the sweet smell of freshly cut wood.

Norvia felt shy among the tall, foreboding buildings and the throngs of workers milling about, but Uncle Virgil was unfazed by the bewildering environment. He led the way up a flight of narrow stairs to the lumber office, where a wave of calm washed over Norvia. The noises of the outdoors grew muted in here, and only the sounds of typewriters and pencils scratching on paper met her ears. She took a moment to straighten her new Mary Pickford hat—Ma and Uncle Virgil had given her the fashionable black velvet hat for Christmas.

It was a good-size office with several desks, where diligent workers bent over their tasks and barely noticed the arrival of two outsiders. Oh!—and there was Louis in the corner, keeping his books like a good bookkeeper. He appeared to be double-checking accounts, for he kept glancing between a ledger and a sheet, bouncing the tip of his pencil back and forth as he mouthed the numbers.

If only it were possible for her to perform such tasks someday!

Norvia forced a courageous smile, remembering that Pollyanna Whittier would doubtlessly smile if returning a handkerchief to Jimmy Bean. (Not that Jimmy Bean carried handkerchiefs, being a stray waif.)

"Excuse us," said Uncle Virgil, so suddenly that Norvia jumped.

A tall, sinewy man in an expensive suit came toward them. "What can I do for you?"

"We wanted to speak with a young man by the name of Behren. Is he here?" Uncle Virgil inquired.

"Yeah, sure," the man said, peering at them over his eyeglasses. "Lou, you got visitors. Take them out in the hall if you want to speak to them."

And *oh,* what a moment when Louis looked up, his brilliant eyes making contact with hers. A glimmer of welcome shone in those eyes—or was it a glimmer of *love?*—and he set aside his ledger and pencil.

"Good afternoon," Louis greeted them, rising from his seat—the sign of a true gentleman. Once he closed the door behind them and they were alone in the hallway, he asked, "Is there something I can do for you and your daughter, sir?"

Daughter! She had never thought of herself as Virgil Ward's daughter. For a second Norvia grappled with this new identity, but she shoved the thought aside. Louis didn't know any better, and that was exactly what she wanted.

"Yes. I—just wished to return this," Norvia said, producing the freshly laundered handkerchief from her purse. "I—I'm sorry I kept it so long. Thank you for giving it to me." When he hesitated, she added, "I washed it."

Louis blinked, then accepted it, stuffing the handkerchief in his pocket. "Oh, thank you. You know, I'd completely forgotten I lent it to you." He grinned, that world-saving half grin. "I appreciate it. My sister's always after me about forgetting where I've put things."

"I thought you had an excellent memory," teased Norvia, shocked at her own daring.

"Excellent with dates and numbers, maybe," allowed Louis with a laugh. "Forgive me, sir, I don't believe we've met. I'm Louis Behren; you're Mr. Nelson?" He extended his hand.

Oh—!

"Virgil Ward," he corrected with a gentle smile. "I'm Norvia's stepfather. It's a pleasure to meet you."

"Likewise," said Louis without missing a beat. "Norvia and I have met a few times—Elton and I are friends. I live on Cherry, just half a mile away from your place."

Norvia's mind raced. *He knew now. He knew she had a stepfather— and he would put two and two together—*

"Is that so? I was under the impression you lived on a farm out in Wilson," said Uncle Virgil.

"No, sir. I grew up there, but now I live with my sister and her family in town. It's a shorter trip to the office," explained Louis.

"So you attend high school with Norvia?"

Louis nodded, but he looked slightly guarded. "I'll be graduating this spring, Mr. Ward."

"Did you enjoy working on your parents' farm?"

"Yes...I did, but I like this better," said Louis.

Why does Uncle Virgil keep asking him all these pointed questions? Just leave him alone!

Now thoroughly flustered, Norvia found it hard to locate her courage. But she had to ask him....And yet, did he really want to be asked? Louis's expression was withdrawn now, almost a little bored. Did he really find her company so dull? Or was it all the questions from Uncle Virgil that had intimidated him?

Well, she couldn't ask him now. Whether he still viewed her as merely a "good kid" or whether he'd been put off by Uncle Virgil, Norvia wouldn't dream of asking him to be her escort. Anyway, now that he knew she had a stepfather, he would doubtlessly find out about the divorce, and then...

Norvia took charge of the conversation and ended it with a quick, "We don't want to keep you from your work. We'll leave now."

A spark of relief lit Louis's face. "Thank you for coming," he said.

Norvia was silent as they rode home in the carriage. Usually she liked watching Nuthatch—the bay mare—jog along the street ahead of them, her harness jingling, but today, she stared into space and thought and thought. She had never felt so deeply hurt. Why did Uncle Virgil want to ruin her one chance to have a beau? Why did he disapprove of Louis? Why was he suddenly so overbearing, just like...just like Pa? Norvia had no answers, and she didn't dare ask the questions aloud.

"What is it about young Behren that you like?" asked Uncle Virgil casually.

That surprised her.

"I know it's silly, but I—I just think he's nicer than anyone else I've ever met," said Norvia. She did not add how handsome he was, nor how kind and sensible and mature and well-spoken he was; nor did she expound on the enormity of her affection for him. "And—and I want him to think *I'm* nice, too."

And I don't want him to be interrogated!

"Oh, I'm sure he does think you're nice," said Uncle Virgil. "But the thing is, Norvia, you can't make other people *feel* certain ways about you. As I've mentioned before—you can't always control other people's actions and feelings. People are always changing, and young people—especially young men—aren't always very responsive, or observant, about the people around them. Take Louis Behren, for instance. He has his whole life and career ahead of him. He seems ambitious. He might not be too interested in girls, at this point. I just don't want you to be disappointed," he added gently.

There had to be another reason. Uncle Virgil hadn't even liked the idea of Aylmer walking her home from school. Could the reason be that he was as controlling as Pa? As controlling as Migizi's stepfather? It had to be.

But all Norvia said was, "Mm-hmm." How could she say anything else?

Boyne City High School could talk of nothing but the long-anticipated Valentine's Day Dance—especially as the scenario of the girls asking the boys provided a delicious amount of uncertainty. BCHS boys were accustomed to full authority where their dance partners were concerned, and giving the girls that power destroyed their complacency.

"Of course Ophelia Farris will invite me," boasted Ronald Filmore.

"No, she'll invite me," argued a thin, slouching freshman.

"Helen Haney asked me, but I turned her down cold," another boy reported, puffing up with importance.

The girls were all abuzz, too, tittering about this boy and that, their various strategies to approach them, and how to work up the nerve to ask boys from older classes.

Kittie had already asked Cal. "Of course he took it for granted that I would ask him," she told Norvia. "How silly. Why wouldn't I try for a junior? But then what junior would have me? I'm such a perfect ninny. Well, enough about me—*you've* got to ask Aylmer."

"Ask—Aylmer?" Norvia repeated.

Kittie slung her book bag over her shoulder. "Of course," she said, her eyes wider than ever. "Emrial Aylmer is crazy about you; can't you tell? He gets this sort of woebegone look on his face whenever you pass by, and—oh, remember that day you couldn't find your English book?"

"Ye-es," said Norvia, dragging out the word like stretched taffy.

"Well, *Aylmer* had it. He was just sitting and staring at your name on the flyleaf."

Was Aylmer really in love with her? The idea struck Norvia suddenly. Didn't that mean he might make a gallant hero for her story after all? And a suitable escort for the Valentine's Day Dance?

But what if he found out about the divorce from one of the girls who would doubtlessly be there? From Ernestine? Would she try to force Aylmer to take *her*?

She found she was determined to fight through it. *I won't care*, she decided, *what the other girls do. If I decide to ask him, I will simply do it, no matter what.*

You can't always control other people's actions and feelings, Uncle Virgil had said.

"You really think it's a good idea?" asked Norvia.

"Norvie, if you ask him to the Valentine's Dance, he would—well, I don't know! Lose his mind! Kiss your hand! A man in love says all kinds of gorgeous hogwash." Kittie giggled. "Not that I would know! I'm not the type men fawn over. I'm too tall, and I haven't a good figure. But you're small and slim and—well, perfect!"

Norvia blushed. "Oh, Kittie, *you're* the pretty one. Cal thinks you're everything. And you're funny and talkative—everybody likes that."

A shy smile appeared on Kittie's face. "You think so? My, I certainly hope so, but, well, I've got clouds for brains. Anyway, that wasn't the point. Aylmer *adores* you."

What if she did ask Aylmer to the dance?

He was no Louis Behren, of course—but she liked him well enough, and Aylmer liked her too, even if it was only because he didn't know about the divorce. Perhaps Aylmer *could* provide the happy ending to her storybook dance. In any case, she had to try it—she had no other alternative.

Norvia waited for Aylmer the next day after English class. She stood in the hallway, clutching her books, wishing she didn't feel such a swarm of butterflies in her middle.

He emerged from the classroom, his blond hair a bit untidy today. Usually he combed it immaculately. "Good day, queen of hearts," he said, bowing low to the floor in her presence.

"Aylmer," she said, taking in a deep breath, "you've heard about the Valentine's Day Dance, I suppose."

"It's been an unavoidable topic for the past two months."

Norvia sucked up a big breath of courage. "Will you please be my escort?"

Aylmer stared at her for a long moment. His eyes were unusual: deep pools of chocolate, a strange contrast to his fair hair. Now that chocolate seemed to melt. "Are you sure you really want me to?" he asked, lowering his voice to a hush.

"Oh—yes," said Norvia, disconcerted at his hesitation.

"*Ach*, I don't know, my girl," Aylmer continued, back to bantering. Yet something—joy, humor perhaps—was missing from his customary voice. "A boy has so many prospects for a Saturday night. Homework to do and life to live up. Besides, I don't feel like wearing a stiff suit all evening when I could be comfortable at home."

He doesn't want to dance with me. Was it because—it couldn't be because—of the divorce? Had he finally found out?

"I'm sorry," Norvia blurted. "I guess—"

"But for you, I'd do it in a heartbeat," finished Aylmer, and he grinned.

Joy surged back.

"Oh, I'm so glad! So *glad!*" Now she felt like a heroine. She felt like Emma Woodhouse in the book *Emma*—going to the ball that Frank Churchill so splendidly organized before he turned out to be such a cad. *A dance! With a beau!*

And then a thought occurred to Norvia. She wondered, for the first time, how she intended to waltz in a boy's arms if she had no idea how to waltz.

"Dance? Of course I know how to dance," said Marguerite, laughing. "I was the belle of the ball at BCHS in my day. Here, hold Olivia-dear and I'll demonstrate. Jim, can you turn on the Victrola?—that phonograph lying on the table. 'The Blue Danube' that we gave Vernie. Yes, thank you."

It was the night before the dance, and Ma and Uncle Virgil had gone to visit the Marys to enjoy a "nice quiet supper." Marguerite and Jim had been invited also, but they declined in favor of having a "rousing time with the children."

Jim settled the phonograph record neatly onto the needle, and a voluminous, rolling melody poured from the tinny Victrola. "Imagine the bluest of waters, the beautiful Blue Danube," instructed Vernon, closing his eyes and conducting to an invisible orchestra. "Think of Strauss. Of the majesty of the Austrian landscape. *Beispiellose pracht*."

"Ooh, Margie, is that a *waltz*?" Dicta cooed.

"Mm-hmm," said Marguerite, swaying softly in Jim's protective arms. "A very gentle waltz. Nothing flamboyant yet. Do you see, Norvia?"

Norvia did see. Sort of. It wasn't easy to pay close attention with baby Olivia gurgling and squirming in her lap. She saw Marguerite and Jim gliding along in perfect time, but there didn't seem to be an obvious technique to it. They just stepped and slid and stepped and slid in elegant harmony. She wished she had paid more attention to her parents' waltzing at parties on Beaver Island.

"Vern! Come show Norvia how it's done," urged Marguerite, taking the baby back into her arms.

"The waltz and I are not friends," wavered Vernon.

"Oh, he's just shy. Make him do it, Norvia," said Marguerite, giving her brother a little encouraging push. "He's got excellent rhythm."

Vernon cleared his throat and gingerly placed a hand on Norvia's waist. Then he placed his other hand in hers.

"We ought to be wearing gloves; it isn't proper otherwise," said Vernon, shaking his head in agitation.

"Stop stalling. Feel the music," Marguerite insisted.

"Yeah, don't be a fraidy-cat," said Casper.

Of course Vernon would not be called anything as dreadful as a fraidy-cat, so he began to waltz—one, two, three, to the uneven pace of the three beats, so flawlessly one would think he was a professional dancer. Norvia couldn't fathom it and only wished she could gain a semblance of such skill.

"So I only have to go along with Aylmer," said Norvia hopefully, "just following his lead."

"Yes, the lady always follows," said Vernon.

"Elton! Waltz me!" Dicta shrieked, jumping up and throwing herself into his arms.

"Hey, I don't know how it's done. Make Vernon Castle show you." Elton laughed.

"I would hardly class myself with the great Vernon Castle, but I am willing to try," Vernon allowed. But he went too fast for Dicta and her limp to keep up. "Go *slower*," she wailed as soon as the tempo increased in speed. "Go slow. So I can watch my feet—yes, that's the way. Look, Norvie, I'm waltzing!"

Norvia learned two other dances that night—the schottische and the two-step (her favorite, because it was the easiest). "We'll save the tango for another time," joked Jim. "Even Marg and I aren't proficient in that one."

"Do you think Aylmer will know all these dances?" Norvia asked, chewing on her lower lip.

"He's from New Orleans, isn't he? All the boys down there live and breathe music, according to the magazines. Don't worry," said Marguerite.

"Oh, good," said Norvia, the lines of worry on her forehead vanishing with relief. "I can't wait." Then they waltzed until Ma and Uncle Virgil got home.

Tomorrow, thought Norvia as she crawled into bed, *I shall become a real heroine.*

CHAPTER EIGHTEEN
THE VALENTINE'S DAY DANCE

On the morning of Valentine's Day, Norvia awoke to an anticipatory surge in her stomach. Her live-in herd of butterflies had remembered before she did: *The dance!* Norvia sat straight up in bed, a rapturous smile on her lips. Tonight she would waltz at her *very first dance!*

She got up early, although there was no reason to. The dance was not until seven o'clock in the evening. She pulled on her sailor suit dress, danced around for no reason, and raced to the sunny window. "Oh, thank You, God," she breathed.

And then she heard a smile—she could actually *hear* it. Or perhaps it was the low, musical laugh she heard—no, not even a laugh, but thoroughly happy words, coming from down the hall. Norvia cracked open her door and saw Uncle Virgil and Ma, sitting at the top of the stairs, talking—just chatting amiably. How *joyful* they looked—Uncle Virgil with a light in his eyes, Ma like a young girl, gazing eagerly at him.

This, thought Norvia, *is a valentine.*

"It's Valentine's birthday," piped up Dicta, who was already up and about. "He's nine years old now, just like me. I'm going to his birthday party, even though his mother is making coconut cake, which makes me gag. I'm going to wear my *blue* dress with the big buttons. What are you wearing to the dance, Norvie?"

Norvia had wondered about that. She had a white party dress, but it was a few years old and didn't completely fit anymore. Nothing else but a wide-skirted, flouncy dress would be *right* for waltzing and schottische-ing and two-stepping. The white dress would simply have to do.

"I'll wear the white one," Norvia told her.

"Come downstairs," said Dicta with a thrill in her voice. "I want to show you what I found!"

Norvia followed her to the parlor, where Dicta pointed to a sketch-book lying on the settee. With curious fingers, Norvia paged through the heavy, creamy book, charcoal images flying past her eyes. Birds, stands of trees, houses, all beautifully rendered and so lifelike. The shading, she noted, was particularly realistic.

Norvia was about to set it aside when she thumbed to a drawing of Ma: her dark hair encircling her rounded face; her deep, velvet eyes and delicate lips. She had never given a good deal of thought to her mother's looks before, but now Norvia realized that she was a truly lovely woman. This was how Uncle Virgil saw her—for there was his distinctive signature at the bottom of the page. He had accentuated her beauty and smoothed over her irregularities. Perhaps he had done the same with the portrait of Celestia?

"I loved drawing that," said Uncle Virgil.

Norvia jumped slightly. "Oh! It's—it's very pretty."

"She doesn't even look like a mother," declared Dicta. "She looks like—like *an actress*. I hope that *I'll* be an actress and make motion pictures and break people's hearts with my tragic performances."

Uncle Virgil smiled at Dicta's vision, then turned to Norvia. "And what would you like to do one day, Norvia?"

Norvia saw herself in an office, double-checking numbers just like Louis Behren. She pictured herself at a typewriter just like in typing class, fingers flying. But her face flushed. "I don't know," she murmured.

Uncle Virgil held out a small news clipping. "That reminds me, I found this in a paper recently," he said, a warmth in his voice. "I thought you might like to read it."

Norvia silently scanned the sheet of newsprint, heralded by the header INDIAN LAWYER.

THE COMMISSIONER OF INDIAN AFFAIRS... IS VERY PROUD OF THE INDIAN WOMAN LAWYER WHOSE NAME IS MRS. MARIE L. BOTTINEAU BALDWIN... REGARDED AS AN EFFICIENT EMPLOYEE OF THE INDIAN BUREAU... RECENTLY GRADUATED WITH HONORS FROM THE WASHINGTON COLLEGE OF LAW.

She drank in the fascinating words, especially these:

HER SUCCESS IS UNDOUBTED AND IS REGARDED AS AN INDICATION OF WHAT AN INDIAN WOMAN MAY DO FOR HERSELF IN PROFESSIONAL ACCOMPLISHMENT.

And she was from the Reindeer Clan! The very clan to which Migizi belonged, the clan of togetherness and grace and stories!

The discovery sent a little chill up Norvia's spine. These were such deeply encouraging words! It made being an Indian sound like—something *special*.

She reached the end of the clipping, where Uncle Virgil had torn it off. He had written in blue ink:

"For I know the thoughts that I think toward you, saith the Lord, thoughts of peace, and not of evil, to give you an expected end."—Jeremiah 29:11

It was a beautiful feeling to know that God had good plans for her. Perhaps if Marie Bottineau Baldwin could be a lawyer, Norvia Nelson could indeed be a bookkeeper.

Norvia could barely eat supper that night, with the infestation of butterflies coming to life. In a sort of dreamy haze, she placed each forkful of food into her mouth, not tasting anything but the sweet joy of anticipation.

"Norvie's thinking about *Aylmer*." Dicta giggled. "*Emrial Aylmer*, with the straight teeth and the creamy blond hair. I wonder if he's ever gotten a pimple?"

Just as Norvia was going to float upstairs to get ready, Elton halted her in the hallway. "A little something for you," he said, holding out a small, delicately wrapped package. "For the dance."

Norvia slowly undid the ribbons and tore off the paper to reveal a gleaming bottle of perfume. *Lily of the Valley,* it proclaimed on the sticker.

"Oh, Elton! It's so—*beautiful!* But it must have cost too much," she said instantly.

"I wanted you to have it," he said. "Mr. Redgrave is paying me a little now."

Norvia gave him an impromptu squeeze. "I love you," she whispered. "And I love the perfume." Unfastening the gilt seal and uncorking the top, she sniffed the heavenly fragrance. "It's *sumptuous.*"

"You deserve it," said Elton.

She flew away to her bedroom and placed the glowing bottle on her vanity table. Before she could race off to her luxurious bath, the Marys and Ma appeared in the doorway.

"There you are, sweet girl," said Old Mary. "We come bearing gifts. Well, one gift."

Young Mary presented her with a large, thin, white box. "A late birthday present."

"I hope you like it," said Ma.

"Oh—thank you," cried Norvia, even before she opened the lid of the box. "I can't imagine—"

Between the folds of the ivory tissue paper lay the loveliest, sweetest, *dancingest* dress Norvia had ever seen: silken; peach-colored; a full, billowing skirt, and ruffles on the edges.

"We all worked on it, in secret," said Ma.

"Your mother chose the pattern," said Young Mary.

"We sewed it together at our house," concluded Old Mary in a triumphant voice. "You like it?"

But Norvia could not answer, for her eyes filled with tears and her throat was too choked to reply. She hugged her mother, grandmother, and great-grandmother. "It's perfect!" she cried. "It's absolutely perfect! Thank you—thank you—*thank you!*"

It felt perfect, too. Norvia spent far too long twirling before the mirror, watching the skirt flounce around her legs forever and ever. She spritzed *Lily of the Valley* on her face and hands and breathed in its floral extravagance. She picked up the silver necklace Uncle Virgil had given her—but decided against it.

"Don't forget this," cried Dicta, trotting over with her treasured Japanese fan. "You can wave it at boys and be all coquettish and hide behind it when you blush."

"I shined your shoes," Casper announced, bursting into the room with her white dress-up shoes. "If you step on a guy's foot, then at least you won't get him dirty." He grinned.

Norvia's only trouble was her hair. It was so long and thick, it kept falling down when she tried to pin it up prettily. She wanted a style superior to the plain knot she'd taken to wearing ever since the Halloween party, but it was difficult to come up with anything else. She wanted a different look, something prominently coiffured—

"Let *me* try it," said Dicta, exasperated.

"No, it's all right—I've got it," Norvia struggled.

"Wait—perhaps I have something that would help," said Vernon. They hadn't even realized he was standing in the doorway, but evidently he had been watching long enough. Norvia followed him into the boys' room, where he made a beeline for the bureau. He yanked open the top drawer to reveal the bluish snapshot of his mother and the bicycle; yellowed sheet music for *Liebesträume* (which bore flowery handwriting with the words *For My Dearest Vernie with Love from Mama*), and the cards Dicta and Norvia made for his birthday. He withdrew a hair comb from the sacred drawer with great care—a many-jeweled comb that gleamed in the lamplight. "It belonged to my mother," said Vernon. "Would you like to wear it tonight?"

"I—I'm not sure I can," faltered Norvia.

"I want you to wear it," he said, closing his eyes. "You—you remind me of my mother. You have her—generosity. And her grace, and her kindness."

To Norvia's ears, those words were like the delicate music from Vernon's golden harp.

"Then I will wear it," said Norvia, "to honor her."

It felt funny saying it—it was such a regal, formal thing to say—but it made Vernon smile. And the comb *did* look beautiful in her upswept hair—a style she copied from the pages of *Hearst's* magazine—and kept every strand in place.

"Aylmer will be here any second!" Dicta shrieked. "Are you ready?"

Norvia adjusted her hair one last time. "Yes! I'm ready!"

She ran downstairs to wait—she watched out the window, looking into the dark night for her shining knight. In the distance, the town clock announced that it was six thirty on the dot. Norvia gave a little skip in her flouncy peach dress.

She waited. Six forty. Six forty five.

"I thought the dance started at seven," said Dicta.

"It does," said Norvia uncertainly.

Six fifty.

"Of course, it only takes a few minutes to walk to the school," Ma comforted her.

Six fifty-five.

At last the telephone rang—it jangled so loudly everyone jumped. Norvia ran to the kitchen and grabbed the tall candlestick phone, speaking loudly into the mouthpiece. "Hello?" she said, her voice full of hope.

Aylmer's rich voice—surprisingly low—said, "Hello, is this Norvia Nelson?"

"Yes." *Did he forget?* "It's—it's only a few minutes till the dance starts—"

"Yeah, that's why I called. I can't come."

He—is—not—coming. "Well, why not?"

Frustration seeped into his tone. "I just can't, that's all. I can't explain it. Look, I'm sorry—terribly sorry, and I don't know what else to say."

"But—"

"I have to go. That's all. Good night."

The click of finality on the other end of the line was too much for Norvia. After all the preparations and plans and hopes and anticipation—the dress and the comb and the shoes and the perfume and the fan and the joy—

This time her tears were not born of delight.

It was because her parents had divorced. What other reason could Aylmer possibly have for abandoning her at the last minute? He had been thoroughly unable to produce even a single excuse. *How had he found out?*

She stood in the kitchen, alone, for a moment. She would run upstairs, fling herself on the bed as always, cry until she fell sleep, and never ever speak of this again to anyone. First she had to get her hair out of this coiffed joke—

Norvia's fingers closed on the jeweled comb. *You remind me of my mother,* Vernon had said.

His mother? The great and illustrious Celestia Amanda Barnett Ward? She had traveled abroad. Perhaps that was the origin of this hair comb. Would *she* have gone to bed crying? Or would she have squared her shoulders and gone to the dance anyway?

A heroine would go to the dance. Perhaps—just maybe—she didn't even need a beau.

She stood still, undecided.

Marguerite's words from months earlier rolled back to her. *Mama was an angel.... Her face reflected so much light and joy. Life wasn't easy for her. She had a hard time of it when her own mother died. But nothing deterred her.*

It occurred to Norvia that the qualities that made up a heroine were inside them—*not* things that other people had control over. Jo March's noble desire to quench her temper and help her family; Anne Shirley's fervent quest to find friends and point others to loveliness; Sara Crewe's indomitable grace despite her poverty and loneliness—all these heroines were memorable because of their *spirit* and *heart* and *inward* beauty.

And there were real heroines, too. Hadn't Celestia forged a life of joy even though it had been marked by sadness? Hadn't Marie Bottineau Baldwin accomplished the impossible and graduated from law school? Hadn't Migizi held her head up high when the other children scorned her Dakota heritage?

That day on Beaver Island replayed in her mind once again, and her father's words of old echoed in the empty stillness. *There's nothing I can do about it. I know I'll never be able to do anything to change my life.*

But Norvia pushed the words away.

I am not going to make the same mistake that defeated Pa.

Norvia marched into the parlor, where Uncle Virgil and Ma sat. Above them, Celestia Ward stared down encouragingly, and at last Norvia felt she fully understood what Vernon and Uncle Virgil had been trying to tell her.

If God took the trouble to tell us eight hundred times to be glad and rejoice, He must want us to do it, Pollyanna had said.

And what had Uncle Virgil said?

There is Someone on whom you can always rely—completely. He will never fail you.

Well, she would be a true heroine. She would be an adventuress. She would be brave, and cultivate grace and fellowship and a life of stories. But most of all, she would choose joy, regardless of what happened to her. Norvia wiped her eyes on a dish towel. She stood erect; patted her hair.

"Aylmer can't take me to the dance," said Norvia, entering the parlor to address Uncle Virgil. "Would you please take me there instead?"

He stood up from his chair, where he had been reading Tolstoy. "It would be a privilege," said Uncle Virgil, extending his arm.

You will not be shy, she chided herself all the way to the dance. *You will talk! You will dance! You will be kind and not foolishly silly! And you will choose joy and rejoice!*

"What time will the dance be over, do you think?" asked Uncle Virgil, as they stood in the hall outside the Social Room.

"Nine," said Norvia, hoping that wasn't too late.

"I will be back at nine," he promised. "But if you need anything, telephone."

"Yes, I will."

And she pushed open the door—into the crowded gaiety of music and talk and laughter: wall-to-wall students, freshmen to seniors, enjoying the party and the swirl of light and commotion. Norvia smoothed her dress.

"Ooh, Norvie!" Kittie hurried to her side. "You look like a dream!" Her face fell as she realized Norvia was alone. "Wait, where's Aylmer?"

"He couldn't come." She plastered a smile on her face and immediately felt just a bit happier.

"That scoundrel!" Kittie exclaimed. "I bet the rat's coming with another girl—or, maybe he had the flu. Yes, the flu. Who else could he possibly want to bring?"

"It doesn't matter," said Norvia, smiling more naturally now. "I have my dance card."

Kittie grabbed her own card. "Mine's all full of Cal Evergreen. He wrote his name on three different dances—oh, but yours'll get full up in no time flat," she jabbered in excitement. "Cal will dance with you on the fourth—he's empty for the second schottische. And he's quite dazzling, really. Football gives you exquisite coordination." But her card had other names, too: *Stanley Collins. Joe Martin. Reginald Asheville.*

"You'll get names on your card. Don't worry," Kittie whispered. "Come on, I'll introduce you to Joe. He's a dream beyond description."

When she saw him—broad shoulders, trim suit, lock of dark hair falling over his eyes—Norvia felt a wave of bashfulness spreading over her. *No! Talk to him! Smile!*

"Hello," said Norvia, smiling as she held out a white-gloved hand. "I'm Norvia Nelson."

But Joe merely nodded and turned back to Ophelia Farris.

Norvia, however, maintained her smile. She clutched Kittie's arm. "I think he's crazy about me," she joked.

"Oh, yes! He's so much in love he can't even look at you!" said Kittie.

A strong voice spoke from behind them. "Excuse me. Norvia?"

Louis Behren stood behind her: dark-blue suit, white tie, neatly combed brown hair, poised and sophisticated. And that smile! He, too, wore white gloves, and he held out his hand. "May I have this dance?" he inquired.

All Norvia's composure vanished, and she clapped her hands over her mouth.

Louis laughed. "I received a telephone call from your stepfather, and I thought I'd pop on over and see if I could dance with my favorite freshman." He wrote his full name on her dance card three times in flawless cursive: *Louis August Behren.*

A call from her stepfather! But there was no time to wonder why.

Norvia placed her hand—with especial care!—in his, and Louis swept her breath away as he swung her into the first waltz. Oh, he could *dance*—but naturally he could. He could do everything! His movements were agile, graceful, and perfectly in time with the lilting music. She closed her eyes, relishing the bliss. Did this mean he didn't mind about her parents? And who cared if he viewed her as a child? *Children grow up!*

"You dance wonderfully," she said, opening her eyes so she wouldn't stumble on his well-shined shoes.

"Oh, I've had some experience," said Louis. "I've been to a dance or two in my time."

"As nice as this?" she teased, no longer having to force a cheery smile.

"Not quite," said Louis. Which was, of course, exactly what he was supposed to say.

It was a strange, strange feeling—dancing with a handsome young man. Magical and mystifying and marvelous all at once. But the strangest thing of all was the fact that *acting* upbeat had made her *feel* upbeat—even before Louis arrived. And when the orchestra began to play "Moonlight Bay," Norvia actually sang along.

As the dance dwindled at around nine o'clock, Norvia and Louis sipped punch at the refreshment table alongside Kittie and Cal. Louis and Cal got along famously; they laughed like old friends, and Louis complimented Kittie on her becoming appearance. Helen sidled up to them a few minutes later.

"Norvie! Aren't you going to let me dance with Louis?" hissed Helen, staring up at him with enormous eyes.

"I'm sorry," said Norvia politely, "but I promised my stepfather we'd be home at nine, so we can't waste any time." She smiled as Louis linked his arm through hers, and they walked out of the Social Room.

She was so triumphant that, once outside, she tripped on the school's front steps.

"*Vorsichtig!*" Louis exclaimed—and then stopped. "Are you all right?"

"Yes, I'm fine," said Norvia, too happy to mind that she'd nearly fallen down.

But Louis was ever-so-slightly flustered now. "I try not to do that. Speak German, I mean . . . My parents don't want anyone to think we're disloyal."

For the first time, Norvia felt a deep sympathy for Louis instead of mere admiration. She knew how he felt—trying to hide one's heritage was a burden she wouldn't wish on anyone. "I understand," she said softly, which made him smile.

Then—for the first time—Norvia got to ride in the gleaming green auto. Louis opened the passenger door for her—such gallantry!—and she slipped into the smooth seat. Sitting in his auto felt like perching atop the world. Louis cranked up the engine before sliding dexterously behind the steering wheel.

Norvia fiddled with her gloves.

"Do you . . . know about my parents' divorce?" she asked at length.

"Yes, I know," said Louis, leaning on the wheel.

She almost couldn't meet his eyes. "And . . . does it bother you?"

"Not in the slightest," said her prince charming, flashing his special smile once more.

MARCH 1908
Zaawzi | YELLOW

It was one of those days when Norvia could not decide if she was hot or cold. She felt as if she were vacillating between the two incongruous temperatures—sometimes, she took off her bulky winter coat and carried it under her arm. Other times, she bundled back up in its warm folds and shivered.

But the middle of March was often this way on Beaver Island—the nights freezing, the days thawing—which made conditions ideal for gathering sap from maple trees. And the Marys were ready.

"I want to come this year," Norvia announced as she watched her grandmothers gather up their supplies for tree-tapping. "I've never gone before. I want to see how you do it." She had never quite been able to fathom how something as delicious as maple syrup—and as tasty as maple candy—came out of an uninspiring tree trunk.

"I suppose you're old enough now," said Young Mary briskly.

"When a girl turns eight, she begins to understand things," Old Mary concurred.

"Do be careful," said Ma from the porch as the trio left on their mission. Her voice had an inordinately worried tinge, and she gave Norvia's scarf one last straightening tug. "Don't stay out too long."

Old Mary took up her walking stick. "Too much worrying," she said once they were out of Ma's earshot. "As if I don't know these woods better than almost anyone."

Once they were ensconced in the woods, the two Marys worked their magic. Norvia watched in wonder as they drilled tidy holes in several stoic maple trees. The sap, surprisingly clear and not at all the rich color Norvia envisioned, began to run down the bark.

"It's flowing," Old Mary confirmed.

Somehow Norvia had expected maple syrup, brown and tantalizing, to ooze out of the tree. "Why doesn't it look like syrup?" she demanded.

The Marys laughed. "Oh, it's not nearly done yet," said Young Mary.

"It is a long process," agreed Old Mary, placing a small metal tap on the tree. "First we must collect the sap."

"Then comes the boiling down," Young Mary added, moving on to the next tree, a tall maple but not so thick that Norvia couldn't wrap her arms around it (which of course, she did). "We make syrup out of the sap."

Old Mary nodded her head with satisfaction. "We gather, we evaporate, and we make something new. We boil out what we don't need—the water—and keep the good, the sweet," she explained. "It is an old Indian tradition—we were the first to collect sap. Ojibwe women have been tapping trees to feed their families for many, many years."

"They would set up sugar camps in the middle of the woods at the start of spring, just as we're going to," recounted Young Mary as she began to hook their silver buckets underneath the drilled holes. "And it would serve as a reunion after a long winter of isolation—really, it was a kind of party! Back then their buckets were made of birch bark, but the process is more or less the same as it's always been."

"And now you will know how," said Old Mary.

Those words gave Norvia such a sense of delight, and bestowed upon her a feeling of accomplishment, of togetherness, of continuing the old ways and making them new again. She couldn't wait for the time when they would boil the sap and sit around the fire, flames dancing, starred sky overhead, songs in their souls.

CHAPTER NINETEEN
SHINING LIGHT

Norvia carefully slipped through the large wooden door that served as the entryway into Uncle Virgil's blacksmith shop.

At first it was difficult for her eyes to adjust to the dark lighting in the shop, but gradually she saw the outlines of the interior: the heavy beams and posts; a long flight of narrow stairs leading to the upper floor; endless tools hanging on the walls. Shimmering morning light shone through slivers of cracks in the old wood. In the middle of the main room stood Casper, wearing overalls and standing over a strange contraption that was almost like a sink, but with an overhanging hood.

"Hey, Norv," said Casper, his face as bright as the morning sun. "Come to see where we work?" He said it so proudly, with emphasis on the *we*.

"Yes," said Norvia, smiling. "And—and I wanted to talk to Uncle Virgil."

"He's in the back, getting the real work done," Casper joked. "I'm just trying to fix this thing—can you hold this?" he asked, holding out a wrench.

"Uncle Virgil must be really pleased with the work you do for him," observed Norvia.

Casper shrugged, but his grin didn't disappear. "I do all right," he said modestly. "I think he appreciates my help. I sure appreciate him teaching me all this stuff." Casper hesitated, then resumed his work. "I acted like such a—you know. Like I knew everything, and didn't like him, and all that—but he's swell. He really is. You know what he did? That first night, when we came to his house—he came into our room to say good night, and he said, 'Don't forget to say your prayers.' Well, I told him I'd quit praying, because—well…"

Norvia could hardly take in his words for a moment. "You had?"

"Yeah…well, I thought it wasn't doing any good. And Uncle Virgil wasn't angry or anything! He just talked it out with me. Made me feel better—and you know, praying *does* help. He's *swell*," Casper repeated fervently.

"I know," said Norvia softly.

She tiptoed to the other side of the building, which was open to the outdoors, where Uncle Virgil was heating up a new horseshoe for a chestnut stallion waiting at the hitching post. Norvia watched him work in silence at first, mainly because it was fascinating, but also because it took time to gather her thoughts.

After Uncle Virgil finished fitting the shoe and nailing it onto the horse's hoof, he looked up and saw Norvia standing in the doorway.

"Well, this is a surprise," he said with a welcoming smile. "Come to watch us work? Rather interesting, isn't it? In the spring, I expect I'll be doing even more mechanic work, since there's getting to be more autos all the time. I've even found one that might be good for our family—" Uncle Virgil broke off, realizing that Norvia was too agitated to listen. "Is something wrong?"

"I just—" Norvia took a deep breath and lifted her face to him directly instead of looking away. "I just wanted to thank you for asking Louis to come to the dance with me. It was—so nice."

Spontaneous tears sprang to her eyes, and she didn't even know why.

Uncle Virgil dusted off two somewhat filthy chairs, one for him and one for Norvia. "Sit down," he invited. "I feel I owe you an explanation for something."

Norvia shook her head, but Uncle Virgil continued.

"You know I only want what is best for you." He stared at the ground, as if reading a script that would prompt his forthcoming lines. "My daughter Julia was always a very popular girl in school. She was pretty, and the boys liked her. And she grew distant from us—Marguerite and Vernon and I—after Celestia's passing." He hesitated before continuing. "The fall after her mother died was when she entered high school, and she began to see this young man, Walter Robertson—a few years older than her. And Julia wanted to marry him during her sophomore year."

Norvia recognized the ache in his voice, and the sadness.

"The law required my consent for her to marry so young, and I gave it to her, because I wanted her to be happy." Uncle Virgil paused and smiled a little. "Now, my daughter has been blessed with a good, steady husband and two beautiful children, but the first years of their marriage were rocky, to say the least. And now Julia feels—unfulfilled. Discontented. She told Marguerite once that she often wonders what might have happened if she'd finished her schooling—hadn't been so quick to marry—and I hate to think what her life would be if her very young husband hadn't been staid and responsible and loving."

Norvia couldn't think of anything to say during the silence that followed.

Uncle Virgil cleared his throat. "I never want you to look back on your life with regret, Norvia, or to rush into a relationship you're not prepared for. I wasn't overly concerned about Aylmer, but I suppose that when I realized that the boy you *especially* liked was—not really a boy, but a young man with a job already, I'm afraid I let my overprotectiveness get the better of me. I was afraid that things would progress too quickly, just as they did for Julia." He hesitated, still trying to compose his words with the utmost care. "I realized I was too quick to judge the boys who enjoy your company—that's why I asked Louis to go with you. But, Norvia, please understand that I will always try to do what I think is best where you and your siblings are concerned. I want to provide you with security and stability."

Now, Norvia was sobbing—deep, racking sobs that clutched her throat and wouldn't let go. Uncle Virgil had acted the way he did—questioning Louis, encouraging her schooling, encouraging her to read—*because* he cared.

He cared about his family and his children.

She put her arms around him, and he hugged her, a long, gentle hug that—for one wonderful second—made her feel perfectly safe and loved. She hadn't felt those feelings in so long, she was almost afraid to believe them. But they were real.

"I love you," she whispered.

"I love you, too," murmured Uncle Virgil.

Aylmer had stopped speaking to Norvia. After months of easygoing banter and offers to carry her books, he had ceased all efforts of friendship. When she did see him now, it was in class, where he no longer passed furtive notes or winked behind his algebra textbook. He had vanished from the Social Room—*to get away from me, no doubt*, Norvia thought.

Norvia kept thinking of how he had behaved in the lead-up to the Valentine's Day Dance. She couldn't quite recall the exact wording of their conversation, but she was sure her invitation had been pleasant and friendly. Aylmer was the one who had been reticent—distant, even. When she invited him, was he already wondering if he should escort the daughter of divorced parents to a public dance? Evidently, he had decided she was asking too much.

As the weeks passed, Norvia resolved to put the matter out of her mind. She had too many other things to do: going to the ice cream parlor with Kittie, helping Vernon memorize Italian verbs, and reading *What Katy Did at School*. She even managed to catch Louis in the hallway at BCHS one day.

"I'm taking a bookkeeping class, too," Norvia confided, finally able to summon the courage to tell him this all-important fact. "And I hope to take another year of it so that I can become a bookkeeper once I'm done with school."

"Good idea!" said Louis, grinning. "You'll really enjoy it. It's great training for someone who wants to go into that line of work. Plenty of girls work in offices these days, and I imagine you'd fit right in."

"That's exactly what I want to do," agreed Norvia. These days she felt as if she could do anything—as if she could fly as high as a loon, or a crane, or even a bald eagle.

When Norvia walked through the door of North Star that afternoon, still full of determined anticipation, she noticed a slight difference in the parlor. A few foreign trinkets of Celestia's had mysteriously returned to their former places around the room.

Norvia's eyes traveled upward, drawn to the stairs by the sounds of sweeping and banging coming from one of the bedrooms. Setting her books on the foyer table, she hurried up the steps. Ma was sorting through the storage in the master bedroom, surrounded by cartons and old letters and photograph albums. Peggy weaved through the debris, tail swishing; tiny dust particles floated in the sunshine filtering through the windows.

"I was just doing a little spring cleaning," Ma explained. "Look at this photograph."

Norvia smiled as Ma pointed to a particular page in an album. The photo featured Grand-père and Young Mary with Ma as a baby.

"Time goes on," said Ma, turning the page.

Norvia's gaze landed on a photo she knew very well. It had been taken when she was eight years old—there were Ma and Pa and all their children, all together.

She would ask. She would not be afraid.

"Ma," said Norvia, gathering courage, "why did Pa...do the things he did? Gamble and...sail in dangerous weather?"

Ma looked up at her, and for a moment Norvia did not think she would reply.

"Sit down," she said at last, patting a space on the floor between two cartons of old clothing. They sat among the stacks of odds and ends, mother and daughter, time standing still.

"I don't believe you children ever really understood what was going on with your father," said Ma slowly. "You see, he used to be a rather wealthy young man, back when he lived in Sweden. He was well-educated—he even spent a year studying at a university. And then his father lost everything. Anders would never talk much about it, but the family fortune disappeared almost overnight. He had to come to America to seek a new life—a life of hard work and little pay and no prestige."

Norvia listened in silence.

"He spent a good many years trying to reclaim his wealth—and what he thought was his happiness—at the expense of everything else." Ma chose her words with care as she began sifting through another box. "He was always trying to gain back what he'd lost—which might have served him well, if he hadn't gone about it the wrong way."

These words hit Norvia squarely. She thought of how often she still lived on Beaver Island in her head, instead of embracing her new life—or even giving it a proper chance, like Vernon had suggested. She knew that she wanted to keep Grand-père's stories alive in her heart—but she could not get stuck in the past like Pa.

"Then one day I told him that there was really no point in his struggling to get back to his old life. In a way, I was wrong to say what I did," said Ma finally. "Because it defeated him. He essentially gave up on life—and on his dreams. And what is life without dreams, Norvia?"

A heavy tear slipped out of Norvia's eye and rolled down her cheek. Ma reached out and gave her a hug.

"I have some dreams," said Norvia softly. "I want to graduate high school. I want to work in an office. I want to get married. And I want to pass down Grand-père's stories to my children. But mostly..." She hesitated. Sometimes it was still so hard to get the words out. "I want to choose to be happy, and I want to enjoy—our family."

And I want to live here at North Star, because there's nowhere else I'd rather be.

That evening when the Marys came for supper, Norvia approached them with an idea. "In my sewing class at high school, we're each supposed to choose a big project to finish before the school year ends," she explained. "I was wondering—could you teach me to make a story quilt? Like the one that has all the scraps Lisette saved?"

"A story quilt," repeated Old Mary thoughtfully. "That is a good name for it."

"Well, first we'd need a good amount of scraps," Young Mary reminded her.

"Ma has plenty," Norvia assured them. "We have little pieces from dresses she's made for me and Dicta, and—" She hesitated, then rushed on. "And a square from the dress she wore for her second wedding journey...."

Old Mary nodded approvingly. "And we have bits left over from making your new dancing dress."

Marguerite had come for supper, too, and now Norvia realized she had been listening to the conversation. She stepped forward, holding little Olivia in her arms. "I'd be happy to contribute a scrap or two," she ventured, offering a slightly bashful smile to the Marys. "I—I don't know if..."

It was so unlike Marguerite to be shy that Norvia tried to help. "That would be wonderful!" she assured her. "Ma probably still has some fabric from the green dress she made you."

"And—I have my mother's sewing basket," said Marguerite. "There are some lovely pieces in it."

For the first time, Norvia realized something. Marguerite was not simply the type who didn't care that her childhood home, the house that had once been her mother's domain, was now taken over by strangers. She did care. But she had pushed past it, she had tried and was still trying. And it also occurred to Norvia that any quilt that was telling her story now would have to include Celestia.

"Oh, yes! I'd love to include them," said Norvia enthusiastically. The time had to come to boil life down, like sap: let go of the useless, and make something sweet.

"Let me hold her," said Young Mary, reaching out for Olivia, who smiled obligingly.

The following Monday at school, Norvia could feel that something was different as she walked to her first class. People in the hallways were staring at her and whispering—not in an overly obnoxious manner, but noticeable nonetheless. What on earth could be going on? Surely most of them knew about the divorce by now.

Martha Gibbs halted her just as she was turning into English class. "Helen Haney was just telling us that you and your mother are of *Indian* blood," she said, eyes alight with fascination. "Is it really true?"

"Did you ever live in a wigwam?" asked Imogene.

"How ever did your mother end up marrying a man like Virgil Ward?" Violet demanded. "*He's* not an Indian, is he?"

Norvia felt so many things all at once—humiliation; indignation (*Who did Helen Haney think she was?*); hurt; stupefaction. But underneath it all, she felt—something very strange. Could it be humor? These girls and their reactions to her heritage felt almost comedic. But still: the emotion swimming to the surface most strongly was hurt, and Norvia's eyes stung with abrupt tears.

"Yes, we're of Indian descent," said Norvia, finding the words to explain. Perhaps because they were true, they were easier to say than trying to hide the facts. "We...my mother's family are Ojibwe and French." Suddenly remembering her grandparents' stories, she added boldly: "And Acadian."

"I once went to a summer camp where we learned Indian words," said Martha eagerly. "Can you speak any of the language? We could try to communicate."

"I don't know many of the words," Norvia admitted, "but I do know a little." She felt too self-conscious, however, to share any.

Ernestine moved her way through the small crowd of boys and girls clustered around Norvia. "I thought all Indian girls were supposed to be in boarding schools, not *public high schools*," she said loftily.

For a second Norvia was too stunned to speak. What could she possibly say? That of course she could attend a public school—

"You never even knew what her family was until today!" Aylmer scoffed, appearing from nowhere with a dark cloud on his face. "She's not supposed to be here? Don't make me laugh! She's at the head of the English class, and from what I hear she does pretty darn well in book-keeping, too—which I seem to recall you claimed was 'too difficult.'"

Ernestine set her mouth in a thin line. "I didn't ask for *your* input—"

"I agree with Aylmer," said Kittie, pushing past Martha and Imogene to stand beside Norvia. "I think Norvia is one of the smartest and prettiest girls in the whole entire school. But most importantly, she's one of the kindest—which is more than I can say for other people."

The tears in Norvia's eyes did not dissipate at the sound of these words of support. Instead, they trickled down her face as she realized all over again what a true friend Kittie was. And Aylmer! Could it be that he did not completely despise her after all?

She tried to talk with him later, as they were getting ready to leave for the afternoon—but he darted away as soon as she began to speak.

The next morning Norvia went to school wearing her old hairstyle: two long, thick braids of brown hair, tied with silky white ribbons.

"You know, that style *does* suit your hair better," Ophelia Farris remarked.

Norvia liked Easter best when it was not too early and not too late, and in 1915, the timing of Easter was perfect: the fourth of April, a brilliant balance between the end of winter and the beginning of spring. Green shoots were just starting to poke through the last bits of slushy snow, and a horde of birds had returned from the south, chirping their arrival songs in jubilant tune.

Easter Sunday at the Presbyterian church was a glorious occasion. The building was decorated with candles and flowers—like Christmas, only prettier, because the colors were brighter and cheerier. Before the service, Norvia slipped the silver bird necklace from Uncle Virgil around her neck.

Ma baked a torte for Easter luncheon—a wonderful and decadent cake full of eggs and chocolate. Norvia had asked the Marys to help her prepare fry bread, too. Even Vernon ate the two special foods, his delicate stomach notwithstanding.

But the best part of Easter was when Uncle Virgil read aloud from the Bible after supper. He didn't read any single part; instead, he chose select passages—all about life and hope and joy. And the most beautiful line was the last line in the book of Matthew—when Jesus said,

"I am with you always, even unto the end of the world. Amen."

Uncle Virgil closed the Bible and offered a smile to his family, who were gathered around in the parlor. "I have a little something I'd like to say," he announced. "Your mother and I are thinking of taking you children on a trip to Beaver Island this summer. What would you think of that?"

Norvia let out a gasp of joy. "Oh! Yes!" *Beaver Island*—gulls swooping overhead, the lake reflecting the sun, the sparkling skies at night . . . and she would be there with her family, filled to the brim with joy.

CHAPTER TWENTY
WORDS OF TRUTH

In early May, the world exploded with news of the *Lusitania*—a British ship torpedoed by Germans. Newspapers blasted the black headlines, and BCHS was abuzz with talk and worry. Even North Star was affected, for Uncle Virgil and Ma discussed it as they read the papers.

"Do you suppose it will mean war . . . here?" Ma murmured, without looking up from the newspaper.

"No way to tell," said Uncle Virgil grimly.

Norvia's chest tightened as she listened to them—she could barely look at Elton, whose face was drawn. But she thought of the verses Vernon had shared and she exhaled deeply. *God will take care of us.* She folded her hands, prayed, and then put a smile on her face.

Later that day, Aylmer came by. He came wearing the old jacket with the patched sleeves he wore so often. He arrived in the backyard, where Norvia was hanging laundry on the line, billowing sheets slapping her cheeks in the wind.

"Hello," said Norvia, unsure whether to look directly at him or keep her eyes focused on the laundry.

Aylmer leaned on the picket fence, apparently unwilling even to enter the backyard. "I suppose you think I'm quite the cad," he said—almost jokingly, but also ashamedly.

"Oh . . . No. You're not," said Norvia, blushing. "You—you stood up for me that day."

"Well, I am. I was a fool not to tell you why I didn't escort you to the Valentine's Day Dance. It was selfish," Aylmer admitted bitterly.

"It doesn't matter," she assured him.

Aylmer shook his head. "It does matter, because it's been lying on my chest. I feel guilty when I think of it. Norvia, the reason I couldn't go...didn't go...is because I—" He swallowed, then plunged ahead. "Well, I didn't have anything suitable to wear. And it—it was embarrassing to admit it. I'm sorry."

"But...," Norvia whispered. "You don't...?"

"I don't have a decent suit. And I thought that's what was expected." His southern drawl thickened. "Isn't that what every guy there was wearing?"

"Well...yes," said Norvia slowly. "But can't your parents—?"

"The family I live with," said Aylmer, "are Mr. and Mrs. Bell. And they..." His voice became rushed, as if the words had to escape his mouth before he shut it for good. "Anyway, I asked them if I could have some new clothes, but—they didn't feel like paying for them, so that was that."

She thought of the mouse. So Aylmer couldn't even have bought a Christmas present if he had wanted to....

And what of Aylmer's real family?

Norvia wished there was something she could say to make him feel better. After a pause, she said, "Thank you for telling me."

"Of course." Abject relief characterized Aylmer's face. "And I'm glad you understand." In an instant his demeanor changed, and he bowed once again in a courtly gesture. "My sentiments are of utmost gratefulness, m'lady. By-the-by, did you hear about the *Lusitania*?"

"Yes, I did." It was also the last thing Norvia wanted to discuss.

Aylmer shook his head theatrically. "What I can't understand is that the ship carried civilians. Not soldiers. Cowardly move, eh? Whatever became of the lost art of chivalry—the lost art of *common decency*? Can you imagine it? Two thousand people...people like you and me..."

Norvia didn't want to imagine it, although her quick brain painted a vivid picture. "What about it?" she asked stolidly.

"Maybe it'll be war. Maybe I'll join up."

"You won't," said Norvia.

"You don't want me to?"

She laughed. "Of course not!"

An odd, joyful light flashed into Aylmer's eyes. "I guess we'll see, eh?"

Norvia hesitated—but she knew she had to say it, no matter what the cost. "I have something to tell *you*, too," she said, straightening her shoulders. "My parents are divorced."

She waited for him to stare at her in amazement—in disgust—to say something rude or hurtful.

But Aylmer smiled. "Why, m'lady, you make it sound so black. I say, so what? The reason I live with the Bells is because my father left my mother not long after they were married, and she decided she couldn't raise me on her own. Does that make me some sort of circus sideshow?"

Norvia shook her head—the tears were coming again. Happy tears. She half smiled at him.

"Say, I have a question." Aylmer leaned on the fence again. "When I asked you to go to the football game, it didn't seem to matter so much to you. Why was that dance so all-important?"

Norvia closed her eyes momentarily. "I suppose I thought—" *Oh, it sounded so ridiculous now!* "I wanted to—to be like a heroine in a book," she concluded in a murmur.

Aylmer nodded, as if mulling over the idea. "Well, maybe I can be your hero," he said lightly. "I'll be heading on. Good day!"

And he took off. She smiled as she finished hanging the linens.

Norvia awoke the next morning to find Dicta scribbling away in a composition notebook. The spring sunshine poured through the windows, landing on Dicta's blonde hair and transforming it to gold in a most impressive display of alchemy.

"Norvie," said Dicta triumphantly, "I'm fixing my play—you know, *Love's Lovers Lost!*"

"Dicta!" Norvia had no desire to relive last fall's theatrical escapades. It was horrifying to even imagine that Dicta was considering the resurrection of this lost "masterpiece." "It didn't go well last time. Why don't you just make it a story and read it out loud to us?"

"It's a *play*," Dicta insisted, flashing Norvia a stubborn look. "I don't want it to be a story. Shakespeare is only remembered because his stories *lived*."

Norvia felt a sense of panic rising within her. She simply couldn't endure another failed performance of Dicta's ludicrous play. Norvia's previous edits had improved it, but not enough.

"What do you think of this line I've added? 'Do not trouble me with these fool's errands, Lieutenant Snowcap....'"

Even after Norvia had put on her sailor suit dress and they were ready to go down to breakfast, Dicta was still chattering about her play.

"It needs a new opening," Dicta declared as she stood in the hallway, staring at her notebook. "I don't think Arabella should faint at the beginning—that's not clever enough. She should recite the Gettysburg Address."

"I know," said Norvia, suddenly blessed with a happy influx of inspiration, "Vernon and I could help you fix the play again."

Dicta threw her *Love's Lovers Lost* notebook to the floor in a heap.

"Ooh, Norvie! Let's change the whole thing and make it about a poor girl named Mabel who has to leave a trail of breadcrumbs in the forest—"

"No, not *Little Red Riding Hood!*" Norvia protested.

Vernon emerged from his bedroom and closed the door. "You mean *Hansel and Gretel*," he corrected, suddenly an authority on fairy tales. "And I disagree. We ought to simply prop up the play we already have. Norvia made good changes to it last time, and now all it needs is a bit of . . ." He hesitated, debating what word to choose.

"Polish," said Norvia.

"Creativity," said Dicta.

"Genius," said Vernon. "What if we added a villain to the story?"

"There already is a villain," Dicta replied, tossing her hair. "The Evil Whiz-Bang. Remember how he goes into a monastery at the end? I wanted him to fall into the Grand Canyon, but Ma said no one could die."

Vernon was still dissatisfied. "But the Evil Whiz-Bang is too comical," he argued. "He ought to be a tax collector instead of a dog-catcher. And his name should be something dignified, like—"

"Colonel Corrigan," said Norvia, drumming up one of the names she'd considered in her Dashing Young Man daydreams—before deciding that Louis Behren was a far nicer name.

"Ooh!" Dicta squealed. "I want there to be a Lady Corrigan, too. She can stamp her foot whenever she doesn't get her own way—"

Vernon snapped his fingers. "Stamps! That's it. We'll have Arabella be a stamp collector—"

"Nobody collected stamps in medieval times," said Norvia.

"Sealing wax, then," Vernon mused. "We could do that instead. Arabella collects impressive waxes from envelopes and one day the courier brings a message from this colonel, the tax collector, and—"

"And they bond over their mutual love of collecting," teased Norvia, unable to resist.

"But she knows she oughtn't to marry him, for he is a rogue," Dicta continued bouncily, "and one day—"

Vernon plowed on ahead, leaning against the staircase banisters as he invented. "Anyway, this special seal is only used by this one particular prince that Arabella thought was dead—"

"Ma said no dying!" Dicta repeated.

"All right, he was lost at sea, then," allowed Vernon.

Norvia thought that sounded too much like real life. "He won't really be dead; she just thought he was."

Dicta debated. "We could say 'd-worded.'"

"This is supposed to be Art," said Vernon. "He was lost at sea, except he wasn't, and now here is his special royal seal on a letter from Colonel Corrigan, and she realizes it has come from Prince Dudley Paramount, who—"

"Porter," Dicta corrected.

"That's a commoner's surname—it won't do," Vernon objected. "Dudley Paramount, and he needs to be more important in the story. Right now he goes along with everything Arabella says—he needs a backbone of his own."

"Ooh!" Dicta breathed. "Should it be his idea to elope to Venice with Arabella?"

They had made their way to the parlor by now, and Vernon thrummed his fingers on the piano top. "I don't think eloping is proper."

"But Uncle Virgil eloped with Ma," Dicta pointed out.

"Shh!" Norvia exclaimed.

"Going to the Justice of the Peace in one's own town when one's family knows about it is not *eloping*," Vernon contradicted.

Dicta wasn't finished. "And Herman eloped with Bernice." But Vernon had stopped listening; he was already busily composing an overture for their performance.

Over the next three days, Norvia, Vernon, and Dicta worked exhaustively on the revision of *Love's Lovers Lost*. Many times Norvia wondered if their story would be comprehensible to anyone outside their circle, but she realized that it wasn't half as bad as she feared when it began to take real shape.

When the day of the performance finally arrived, they were ready.

Kittie, her mother, and her younger siblings came, smiling and eager. Aylmer graced the performance with his presence, as did Dr. and Mrs. Rayburn, who seemed a bit less regal on this visit and more ordinary. Marguerite and Jim came with baby Olivia, of course, along with Dicta's friend Valentine, and—by special request—Louis Behren, looking handsomer than ever in a lovely gray suit. All were seated in varied Adirondack and dining room chairs on the lawn of North Star.

Uncle Virgil played the role of Arabella's father (surprisingly well, Norvia thought—he never once forgot his lines), and Ma played her little role admirably before slipping back into the audience with flushed cheeks. Casper enjoyed his cameo as a page, and Elton was convincing enough as the tax collector colonel, even if he delivered his lines more humorously than Vernon would have preferred.

Norvia was also surprised by how easily she could play her own undemanding role. She started out shakily, but by avoiding the onlookers' eyes, she got into the part and did quite well.

Dicta did not run away crying or faint with fright as Norvia had worried she might. She spoke her lines boldly and bravely, even if her voice often squeaked with excitement.

Vernon, though, rather outdid himself, and Norvia was proud of him. He played Prince Dudley Paramount to perfection—even the lines where he confessed that he had "passionately loved Arabella from afar for years." He, too, avoided looking at the audience, but that didn't mar his believability—in fact, it increased it.

When the play came to a close, and Dicta urged the others to take their requisite bows, Norvia thought how sweet the sound of applause was—especially when the sound came from loving hands. As she looked at everyone in the audience afterward, during a celebratory garden luncheon—at Ma chatting amiably with Kittie's mother and Mrs. Rayburn; at Uncle Virgil holding his granddaughter with delight in his eyes; at Aylmer giving her an approving wink and Louis Behren smiling his brightest—she was so full of satisfaction, she felt as if she would burst.

"I think we make a very good collaborative team," said Norvia to her cowriters.

"We make a passable family, too," Vernon remarked.

Elton had worked at the Redgrave farm all spring long, and Norvia could tell he was eager for summer. He came home each day drenched in perspiration, covered in bits of grass, and thoroughly exhausted, but he had never looked happier.

One late afternoon right after spring planting, Norvia went to the farm with him. He took her out to the wheat field, a look of satisfaction on his sunburned face.

"Look, Nan." Elton cast his eyes on the fields of promise. "It's ours, it's yours, it's mine, it's God's." Spreading his arms wide, he stared heavenward. "What did we do to deserve this? Nothing. Yet it's ours." He turned back to her, smiling face bereft of the old sorrow. "It's the joy, Nan. The joy of the land and the animals and the fruit. This is why I want to be a farmer—*this*. You know, there's a psalm that goes something like—'Thou visitest the earth, and waterest it: thou greatly enrichest it with the river of God, which is full of water: thou preparest them corn...'"

He took a great breath. "That's all I remember of that one. I don't have anything else to think about when I'm working—so I try memorizing pieces of the Bible. In the book of Job there's a fine one—I've memorized the whole section. 'Who hath divided a watercourse for the overflowing of waters, or a way for the lightning of thunder; To cause it to rain on the earth, where no man is; on the wilderness, wherein there is no man; To satisfy the desolate and waste ground; and to cause the bud of the tender herb to spring forth?'"

Norvia listened, holding her breath as he spoke. She remembered, and what had been brewing in the back of her mind now surged forth: that gold-edged book of Pa's—the one that had caught the rays of the sun on its pages like blinding gold, or the flash of a polished sword—it must have been a Bible. The only book he had brought with him from Sweden. And he had shared it with her, but he'd considered the words to be mere poetry—not the Truth. That was why she'd felt so compelled to send him that verse Vernon gave her.

"Do you see what it means? God waters land where *no one lives*. And if He does that—why, do you see how much *hope and faith* there are in this world? When I heard of the *Lusitania* sinking, I felt horrible inside—like a part of me was dying right along with it. But then I remembered what you told me, and what Uncle Virgil said, and . . . I see—we've got to hold to faith, Nan—keep it! And praise Him!" He tossed his cap in the air and caught it. "When I read those verses, I felt like they were written for me. And do you know the truly wonderful thing? *They were!*"

And he swung her around and around, until all the world was joy and blue sky and grass and promise and love.

Ma was waiting for Norvia on the porch when she came home.

"I have something for you," said Ma, in a gentle voice. She held out an envelope with familiar handwriting, proclaiming: *To Norvia Nelson*.

She ripped it open with trembling fingers, her eyes scanning the staccato sentences in labored English:

My Norvia:

I am glad you enjoy school and you are learning many things. I have found that I have some things to learn myself. I am glad you are well and healthy and happy. I love you more than words can say.

Your Pa

P.S. I am glad you found your voice, min dotter. And I thank you for sharing those words with me. I believe you are right.

CHAPTER TWENTY-ONE
GATHERING

That night the family gathered on the porch. The stars were out, it was dusky, and a feeling of great relaxation spread over Norvia.

Ma and Uncle Virgil sat on the porch swing, speaking in low, happy voices.... Mr. Bingley rested his head on Ma's lap.... Elton whittled a piece of wood.... Casper read one of the books Uncle Virgil had given him.... Dicta enacted a wedding for her dolls, trying to keep Peggy from lying on top of them.... Vernon played a delicate tune on his harp.... Norvia listened to the spring peepers... and felt contented.

"A beautiful night," said Uncle Virgil.

"Majestic," murmured Ma.

Vernon glanced up from his harp. "In Latin, the word is *sublimis,* Ma."

"Let's catch fireflies," said Dicta.

Casper sprang up. "I'll get a jar."

"Oh, let's just admire them," said Elton.

Norvia happened to look up, then—and there was the North Star shining down on her and her home, the other North Star. "In Ojibwe tradition," remarked Norvia, turning to Uncle Virgil, "the Little Dipper is said to be a loon."

As she uttered these words, she thought of the verses—the way everything intersected together with such beauty.

"'As constant as the northern star,'" whispered Norvia. "'And the firmament sheweth His handiwork.'"

AUTHOR'S NOTE

Like many of my own favorite novels, the main characters in this story are inspired by real people: in this case, my ancestors. Although names have been changed, the heart of their story feels very true to me.

At the turn of the twentieth century, a girl named Norvia was born on historic Beaver Island in Lake Michigan and grew up in nearby Boyne City. Her family included her mother, who was of Ojibwe descent; her father, who had emigrated from Sweden; her four siblings; and numerous grandparents. In 1914, when she was fourteen years old, Norvia's parents divorced and her mother subsequently remarried. This marriage gave Norvia an instant stepfamily that included a new father and three more siblings. While the arrangement certainly couldn't have been easy at first, Norvia came to cherish her stepfamily and the beautiful house on McKinley Street, while also maintaining her appreciation for Beaver Island.

During my first foray into genealogy, I discovered my great-grandmother Norvia's story and quickly became fascinated. To me, the events of her childhood sounded like the ideal backdrop for a middle grade novel, so I spent the next several years writing various drafts of this book and delving into further research. The project involved requesting newspaper clippings and other documents from libraries across Michigan; getting in touch with other descendants of Norvia's extended family to learn their stories and memories; and going down the delightful rabbit holes of Michigan history, vintage fashion, constellations, and old automobiles.

I was excited to receive scans and boxes of old photographs from relatives—which I later used to carefully describe Norvia and her family, the North Star house, and more. I studied maps and photos to familiarize myself with the streets of Boyne City and the shorelines of Beaver Island. I even wrote to Norvia's high school, where the secretary was able to find all Norvia's elementary and high school grades—and those of her siblings, too!

One of the most enjoyable aspects of writing this book was paying homage to classic girls' literature. Norvia's admiration for these stories matches my own: I count *Little Women, Anne of Green Gables,* and *Pollyanna* among my all-time favorite novels. As I wrote this book, my desire was to mirror the flavor of these timeless stories in a new way.

I referred to many helpful books during the process of this writing. For invaluable information on Edwardian-era sailing on Lake Michigan, as well as the ship Norvia's father might have sailed on, I consulted *The Historic Christmas Tree Ship* by Rochelle Pennington. I also enjoyed Bob Miles's *Charlevoix II; I Remember* by Anna Tainter Dietze; *The Journal of Beaver Island History Vol. I* and *II*; and the historical tour brochures produced by Boyne City Main Street. Many thanks to Central Michigan University, too, for making Helen Collar's invaluable Beaver Island research collection available online.

The writing and research process of *The Star That Always Stays* has been an absolute joy for me. It's always so special when we can learn about the people who came before us, thus realizing new pieces of ourselves in the process. I discovered my love for family history—this family in particular—and realized that sharing Norvia's story was not only a fun challenge but an extraordinary privilege.

GLOSSARY AND PRONUNCIATION GUIDES

ANISHINAABEMOWIN (OJIBWE LANGUAGE) WORDS

In Anishinaabemowin (*ah-ni-shin-aa-beh-mo-win*), double i's are pronounced with an *ee* sound, and double a's are pronounced with an *ah* sound. A single *a* is pronounced like the *a* in the word *above*.

agwaa'amaazo (*ag-waa-a-<u>maaz</u>-o*): she comes ashore singing
biidaasamishkaa (*bii-daa-<u>sa</u>-mish-kaa*): she comes in a boat
giizhigaanzo/giizhigaande (*<u>gii</u>-zhi-gaanz-o*): sky blue
giniiwaanzo (*<u>gi</u>-nii-<u>waan</u>-zo*): pink
mkadewzi (*mah-ka-<u>deh</u>-wi-zi*): black
minis: (*mi-<u>nis</u>*): island
memengwaa (*meh-men-gwaa*): butterfly
miskozi/miskwaa (*mis-<u>koo</u>-zi; mis-<u>kwaa</u>*): red
Ojibwe (*o-<u>jib</u>-way*): a Native American tribe from Canada and the upper Midwestern United States, also called Chippewa (*<u>chip</u>-a-waa*)
waabshkizi (*waab-sh-<u>ki</u>-zi*): white
zhoominaanzo (*zho-min-<u>aanz</u>-o*): purple
zaawzi (*zaaw-zi*): yellow

OJIBWE STAR AND CONSTELLATION KEY

Ajijaak/Crane (*a-jii-<u>jaak</u>*): Cygnus
Biboonke-o-nini/Wintermaker (*bi-<u>boon</u>-ke-oo-ni-ni*): Orion
Giiwedin'anang (*gii-<u>way</u>-din a-<u>nang</u>*): North Star or Polaris
Ikwe'anang/Women's Star (*ik-we a-<u>nang</u>*): Venus

Jiibay miikana/Spirit Path (*jii-bay mii-kan-ah*): Milky Way

Maang/Loon (*maang*): Little Dipper or Ursa Minor

Mishi-Biizhiw/Great Lynx (*mi-shi bi-zhew*): Leo and Hydra

FRENCH WORDS

argent (*ar-jahn*): money

au revoir (*oh-ruh-vwahr*): good-bye

beaucoup (*boo-coo*): a lot

bienvenue dans notre humble demeure (*bee-yahn-veh-noo dahn note-er ahn-bleh de-mehr*): welcome to our humble home

cela semble si excitant (*suh-la sahm-bleh see ex-si-tahn*): it sounds so exciting

c'est une obsession (*set oon oob-say-see-on*): it's an obsession

chère (*share*): dear

d'une grande beauté (*doon grand boo-tee*): of a great beauty

grand-père (*grahn-pehr*): grandfather

J'aurais aimé que nous ne soyons jamais venus (*jau-ray ay-me kuh noo nuh sway-yun ja-may vuh-noo*): I wish you had never come

Je souhaite que cette journée soit finie (*je swate kuh set jour-nee swah fi-nee*): I wish this day was over

Je t'aime (*je-tem*): I love you

la grippe (*la grip*): influenza

maman (*mah-mahn*): mama

mon amie (*mon-ah-me*): my friend

nous ne sommes pas nécessaires: (*noo neh sum pa ne-seh-sare*): we are not needed

pauvre enfant (*poo-vreh ahn-fahn*): poor child

très chanceux (*tray shahn-soo*): very lucky

NAME PRONUNCIATION GUIDE

Angélique: *Ahn-zheh-leek*
Aylmer: *Ail-mer*
Dicta: <u>*Dick*</u>*-ta*
LeBlanc: *Luh-*<u>*blahn*</u>
Louis: <u>*Loo*</u>*-ee*
Migizi: *Mi-gi-zi*
Norvia: <u>*Nor*</u>*-vee-a*

Family Photographs

Norvia's sister Dicta, c. 1919

Norvia at age 16, 1916

Seated: Norvia's stepfather (Uncle Virgil) and her mother (Ma), c. 1920

Norvia and Dicta with their dog, c. 1921

The North Star home, c. 1920

Young Mary and Old Mary, c. 1920

ACKNOWLEDGMENTS

First and foremost, I am incredibly grateful to my family, for all your love, ideas, support, and joy; for reading this book in its earliest versions and encouraging me to keep going. To Mom and Dad, for always believing in my writing journey; to Sam, for all your wonderful edits; to Dan, for our fascinating star studies; to Josh, for your inspiring notes of encouragement; and to Emy, for all our delicious bookish talks—especially about this book!

To Granny, for your memories and reminiscences, and for making my nine-year-old self feel like a creative genius. To Cheri, for giving me the albums and the portrait, and to Hannah, for all the fun! Also to Greg and Jenni, for your support and excitement.

To my delightfully insightful editor, Mora Couch, for making this book a possibility and giving me so much lovely encouragement throughout the process. And to the entire team at Holiday House for your hard work: I'm so very grateful.

To Jessica Schmeidler and Molly Shaffer at Golden Wheat Literary, for all your enthusiasm, editorial vision, and support! This book could not have been a reality without you.

To Mike, for so generously sharing your boxes of old photographs, and to Faye, Janet, Brenda, Ruth Ann, Sheila, Cindy, Peter, Robert, Barbara, and Karen, for the memories and photographs you shared with me.

To all the helpful people at the Boyne City High School, the Library of Michigan, the Boyne City District Library, the Charlevoix Library, and the history-documenting Greenwood Cemetery, for research assistance and offering priceless resources for family historians. Also to Gayle and Ethan, for taking new photographs of the North Star house for me!

To Marcia Hoehne, for invaluable suggestions on the structure of my novel.

To Jennifer Trafton, for the warm words that kept me going on my publishing journey.

To Stephanie Son, for the gorgeous cover!

To Susan and Cecil at the Sault Tribe Language Department, for assisting me with the Anishinaabemowin words used in this book. *Miigwech!*

To Rébecca for helping me with the French words included in this book. *Merci!*

To Erin, Savanna, Kendra, and Louise, for your kindness in reading early drafts.

To Anna, for your sweet cheerleading!

To Sarah Mackenzie, for your encouragement and for championing the kind of books I love.

To Brett Harris and Kara Swanson at the Author Conservatory, for your amazing mentorship and guidance throughout this process! Also to Juliet, Cara, Charis, Alyssa, Amanda, Sequoyah, Coralie, James, Abi, Savanna, Alabama, Hannah, Kellyn, Bailey, Kaitlyn, Linnea, Ryan, Jenny, Olivia, Hope, and everyone else in our group: thank you for your prayers and ideas and excitement.

To the authors who inspired my writing every step of the way:

L. M. Montgomery, Maud Hart Lovelace, Noel Streatfeild, Elizabeth Enright, Louisa May Alcott, Jeanne Birdsall, and Eleanor Porter.

To Gigi, Sarah, Eloise, Gracie, Peaches, and Ruby, for being my mascots.

God answered my prayers for this story in unforgettable ways, and I am grateful for His blessings forever!